THE RETREAT

THE ATLANTIC SERIES: BOOK I

PHIL PRICE

First published in 2022 by SpellBound Books
Copyright © Phil Price

The moral right of the author to be identified as the owner of this Work has been asserted by them in accordance with the Copyright, Designs and Patents Act, 1988.

All rights reserved. No part of this publication may be reproduced, stored in a retrieval system, or transmitted, in any form or by any means, electronic, mechanical, photocopying, recording or otherwise, without the prior permission of the publisher.
This is a work of fiction. All names, characters, places, locations and events in this publication, other than those clearly in the public domain, are fictitious, and any resemblance to actual persons, living or dead, or any actual places, business establishments, locations or events is purely coincidental.

Cover © ArtEAST 2022

For Brooke and Carla.
Two amazing friends who kept me moving forward.
Thank you.

PROLOGUE
NORTH CORNWALL – 2000

The three boys stood staring at the chainsaw, the noise from its motor filling their ears. Above, a flock of seagulls flew across the sky, their calls barely noticeable as three pairs of eyes looked down at the fascinating lump of metal, its teeth glinting in the sunlight. "Go on, Tom," Tristan urged, nudging his younger brother forward.

"We'll get in trouble," the younger sibling warned, brushing his dark fringe away from his eyes as he focused on the machinery.

"We won't," Tristan assured him. "Old Antony's having his lunch. No one will know."

"It looks heavy," Thomas countered, unsure if his puny muscles could even lift the monstrous thing from the tree stump where it rested. The summer sun beat down on the three boys, cooling winds from the nearby Atlantic, taking the edge off the temperature.

"Do you think you can lift it?" his cousin Matthew asked, almost reading his mind.

He looked at the older boys. One blond, the other dark-haired as they towered over him. His legs began to tremble slightly, seeing the expectant expression on his brother's face. "Okay, I'll try. What do I do to start it?"

"Come on, Tom," Tristan urged. "You just squeeze the handle. I've watched Antony do it hundreds of times. Piece of piss."

The younger brother baulked at the swear word, seeing the confident look on Tristan's face. Thomas was younger by three years and would never even think to use such language, let alone blurt it out. "Fine," he said, trying to sound brave as he took a step forward. His slender fingers grasped the orange trigger, his other gripping a large handle close to the glinting teeth. As he held it close to his body, he looked for encouragement from his brother and cousin. "Are you sure about this?"

"C'mon, Tommy," Tristan teased, knowing his baby brother hated that name. "You need to grow a pair and become a man."

Thomas looked at Matthew, whose expression had grown wary, his eyes flitting from his cousin to the sharp teeth that adorned the chain. "Here goes," he trembled, depressing the trigger with his fingers. The saw sprang to life, the noise deafening the boys.

"Woohoo," Tristan hollered, Matthew not quite believing that his cousin had done it.

"See, I could do it," Thomas exclaimed proudly, taking a step backwards as his muscles began to protest. A small branch snapped under his foot, Thomas's ankle twisting before he fell sideways. Time seemed to slow down as the young boy let go of the handle next to the chain, his other still gripping the trigger. He landed heavily, banging his head off a stone on the ground as the saw fell towards him.

Tristan had stopped whooping, frozen in horror as he saw the piece of machinery falling ever downwards, the noise still deafening. Another noise filled the air. A high-pitched scream as his younger brother felt the metal teeth strike flesh and bone. "Thom..."

"Nooooooooooo," the seven-year-old screamed as he regained his senses after the bump on his head. His fingers released the trigger, the chain falling silent as the others looked on.

"What the bleedin hell do you think you're doing?" A voice boomed behind them.

As Tristan looked around, he vaguely heard a rustle of leaves, not seeing his cousin pass out at the scene below him. *Shit!* The older brother took off, weaving through trees and undergrowth.

Thomas lay on the floor, unable to move, his cries echoing across the open parkland that led to a dense forest beyond. "My l-leg," he stammered before passing out, oblivion taking him mercifully.

Old Antony approached the boy, his ruddy cheeks paling as he saw what had transpired. Thomas was out cold, beads of sweat breaking out on the groundsman's brow as he saw how the chainsaw had come to rest. He turned, seeing his son approaching from across the field. "Malcolm. Call an ambulance. Quickly! Tell them to hurry. Major trauma." He knelt next to the boy as his son took off across the grass. Nausea washed over him, his eyes trying not to see the splintered bone and churned flesh that was once the boy's lower leg. "There'll be hell to pay for this," he said to himself, knowing that he'd left the chainsaw unattended. He wasn't sure what scared him more - losing his job or facing the wrath of the boy's father and grandfather.

CHAPTER 1
2000

Thomas looked out of his window, the nearby Atlantic Ocean stretching out towards the horizon. Summer was nearing its end, the boy feeling a change in the weather as he pulled his blanket up to his neck. He looked down, a shiver running through his body as his eyes settled on the bandaged stump that was once his right leg. After the accident, he'd spent a month in Truro hospital, struggling to understand the adult conversations going on around him. His mother had told him what the doctors had done, amputating his leg below the knee and that he would have to wear a prosthetic leg which would aid his rehabilitation and get him back on his feet. Or foot, he'd thought. He remembered his father shouting at the doctors, who'd backed away from the man as he'd jabbed fingers at them and swore repeatedly. His mother had stood next to her husband, a forlorn expression on her face as she'd stared at the elevated stump, wrapped in bandages. Tom knew that his mother always looked sad. But seeing her staring down at him made the little boy feel empty and worthless. Even more than usual, such was his position in the family hierarchy. He moved across the bed, sliding his legs over the edge, his left leg landing on the thick carpet, his right dangling in the air. He reached down, scratching the skin under the bandage as an annoying itch reappeared like a constant tormentor.

"Stupid leg," he sighed, reaching down for his prosthetic. The artificial limb was black, with a human-type foot. The graphite effect on the leg shimmered as he gingerly placed his stump into the end, wincing as he stood up. Tom limped over to the window, feeling the cold seep into his body as he peered outside. His father's Range Rover was parked on the gravel driveway, the tall blond man issuing instructions to his men as Tristan stood a few feet away, peering up at him adoringly. A noise from behind made the boy turn awkwardly as the bedroom door opened.

A dark-haired girl stepped in, smiling over at him. Elizabeth was two years his senior, her wavy hair framing a pretty face, adorned with light freckles. "Hiya," she beamed, walking over to him.

"Hi," he replied, enjoying the embrace that followed. He loved his older sister. When she was around, Tom felt safer and more self-assured. Since the accident, the little boy had developed a stammer, finding it almost impossible to string a few words together when his father, mother and brother were around. However, Lizzy always put him at ease, helping him combat the new affliction that had settled over him.

"What ya doing today?" she asked.

"Don't know, sis. What are you doing?"

"Dunno, but we should do something. School starts next week, and you've been stuck in the house since you came home. You should get some fresh air."

He loved his sister, who always sounded older than her nine years. She was smart but never talked down to him like his older brother did. She was gentle and funny, unlike the rest of the family. He loved being with her, along with his cousins, who lived nearby. "Well, I can't go too far. My leg is still sore, and it hurts when I walk."

"Okay. Why don't we go for a short walk?"

"To the beach?"

"Why not. Then we could come back through the forest and be back by lunch."

"Okay. I need to get dressed and have a wash first, though. I'll be downstairs in a bit."

Lizzy kissed the top of his head before skipping out of the room happily, leaving him alone with his thoughts. Tom looked down at his fake foot, knowing that he'd have to get used to it. "Can't stay around here all day," he said to himself before heading off to the bathroom, wondering what adventures were on the horizon.

"Come in," Joseph Stuart commanded as he sat at his desk in his home office, away from the main house.

The groundsman stepped in, holding his flat cap in his hands. "You asked to see me, Mr Stuart."

Joe looked up from his computer screen, seeing the older man standing there. "Sit down, Antony."

The older man shuffled across the room, seating himself opposite the owner of Sandy Shores holiday park. His ruddy cheeks were flushed more than usual; such was the intimidating power that the younger man held over him. Despite being half the groundsman's age, Joe Stuart was an imposing character. Not a man to cross. "We've been paid a visit by the local HSE inspector."

Antony knew about the HSE. Life had been so different before all those rules and regulations had come into play during the '70s. "Oh. What did they say?"

"They wanted to know why my son managed to slice his leg off with a chainsaw," he replied sternly, locking eyes with the older man.

"Oh."

"We could have been looking at a prosecution. They're red hot on accidents involving machinery and work equipment. Fortunately, I know the inspector. We have an understanding, and the issue will resolve itself. However, someone needs to take the fall for it."

The older man bowed his head, knowing what was coming. "I understand, Mr Stuart. I'll accept whatever comes my way. 'Twas my fault that young Thomas lost his leg."

Joe's expression softened slightly, smiling over at the older man. "It was, Antony. And if it were anyone else, I'd have sacked them on the spot. However, you've worked for us for a long time, and we've always been pleased with your work." *I need to keep the old bastard sweet*, he thought. "So, what I'm going to do is offer you early retirement. You're sixty, and I think it's time you put your feet up and let Malcolm take over."

The older man nodded. "I suppose you're right. And Malcolm knows what he's doing, probably better than old Antony does."

"Well, I'll talk to Malcolm separately. He's down at The Retreat, getting things ready for tonight. Are you okay with working your notice? Shall we call it a month? That will give Susie time to sort out your pension and redundancy package?"

"Redundancy?"

"Yes. I'm not firing you. I'm giving you early retirement." He wrote a figure on a small post-it note, handing it to the older man. "Will that do?"

Tony's mouth dropped open, words failing him for a few moments as he tried to comprehend the events unfolding. "Mr Stuart. That's very generous of you. I really don't deserve this in light of my incompetence." Tears peppered the older man's eyes, Antony wiping them away with the back of his hand.

"Nonsense. That's just a small token of our appreciation for all your work over the years. Tom will be okay. It was just a freak accident. Wasn't it?"

The older man looked at Joe, seeing how the park owner's expression had changed from affable to serious in the blink of an eye. "Yessir. A terrible accident."

"Good. I'm glad we understand each other. That will be all," Joe said, rising from the chair. The tall man extended his hand, the older man taking it readily.

"Thank you, Mr Stuart."

"Thank you, Antony," he replied warmly before the older man left the room. Sitting back in his chair, Joe picked up his new mobile phone, dialling a number from memory. He tapped his finger on the desk as it rang out before a crackling sound filled his ear.

"Hello," a male voice said.

"Malcolm," Joe replied smoothly. "Are we all set for later?"

"We are, Mr Stuart. Just gotta get the kegs down into the cellar and prepare the grill."

"Good work. I'll be down in a few hours before our guests arrive. I'll come and find you. We need to have a chat about something."

"Oh. Am I in trouble?"

"Not at all. I'll see you in a bit." He ended the call, walking over to his drink's cabinet. Pouring two fingers of brandy, Joe knocked the drink back in one go, enjoying the burn at the back of his throat. He looked in the mirror, smiling at the bronzed reflection as he ran his fingers through his blond hair. "Time for some fun," he said, knowing who he needed to see before the gathering later. His new project, one that would hopefully bear fruit. An older woman, tired of her husband's lies. And Joe knew how he would breathe life back into her, like all the others under his grip.

CHAPTER TWO

"Son of a bitch!" the man swore, sitting back in his swivel chair. Outside, the sun was dropping quickly, the shadows lengthening outside his window. Across the lawn beyond the building, the lights on the Ferris Wheel lit up as holidaymakers made their way from attraction to attraction. Usually, the man would have walked to the window, gazing out at the empire he was quickly building, seeing the fruits of his labours take effect. Not today, though. He had other things on his mind. He picked up his phone, pressing a button on the plastic base. "Melanie," he started, "ask Bill to come and see me." There was a brief reply before he hung up, staring once again at his monitor. He looked at the website, re-reading the text on the screen before rolling his chair back to stand up. He ran a hand through his greying curls, stretching his back after being seated for the last hour. As he walked over to his drink's cabinet, a man walked through the door. "Bill. Come in. I was just fixing myself a drink. Fancy one?"

The other man nodded amiably. "I'll have whatever you're having."

"Sit down, and I'll bring them over," the older man replied

before placing a tumbler on the mahogany desk. He lowered himself into the chair once more, looking at the other man over the rim of his crystal cut glass. "I've just discovered something."

"Oh," the man replied, wiping his mouth with the back of his hand. "What?"

The grey-haired man turned the monitor on its stand, letting Bill see what he'd found. He let him scan the page, taking another sip of his Bourbon. "What do you think?"

Bill rubbed his chin. "Interesting. Same name as us. How long have they been in business?"

"Longer than us," Emerich noted. "Looks like we have a distant cousin across the Pond."

"So, what are you going to do about it, Jim?"

Jim Emerich sat back in his chair, his brain kicking into gear. The only child of a Californian winemaker, he'd spent his youth in the heart of the Napa Valley, where he'd attended his local high school, before heading to Yale to study business. Whilst over on the east coast in the late '80s, Jim had fallen in love with his new surroundings, meeting and quickly marrying a young waitress called Tammy. Settling into married life just outside Bangor, Maine, the young entrepreneur had come across a tired amusement park and motel, persuading his parents to invest some of their hard-earned fortunes. It had paid off, the amusement park's infrastructure increasing until they had over a hundred chalets lining the waterfront nearby. More additions to the park appeared over the coming years: a small movie theatre, a lido, and an entertainment centre; Jim chose the right restaurants and bars to entice the east coast holidaymakers to Sandy Shores. As the '90s moved closer to the millennium, Jim once again persuaded his ageing parents to acquire a similar venue on the west coast, a few miles south of Astoria, in Washington State. And so, Jim's empire had continued to grow, loyal customers returning year after year, the wine cellars well-stocked with every varietal of the family's award-winning wines. Now, as he looked at the screen, an idea began to form in his mind. "I don't know. This place is undergoing significant improvements. Looks like a goldmine."

"Whereabouts in the UK, is it?"

"Cornwall. Near a place called Bude. Tammy has family in Bristol, which is only about an hour away."

"What's going on in that big old head of yours, Jim?"

Emerich looked at the younger man, a wolfish smile spreading across his face. "I want it. Imagine it, three Sandy Shores, in the Emerich portfolio."

"Sounds like a good idea in principle. But where are you gonna find the funds?"

He smiled again, a playful wink over the rim of his glass directed at the other man. "It's Ma's seventieth in a few weeks. I'll broach the subject then. They'll agree to it."

"You sure?"

"I am. They just don't know it yet."

Steve Sullivan climbed out of the van, slamming the door behind him as he strode up the path towards his house. Positioned on the edge of the village, he'd always liked the peaceful setting. He wasn't overlooked, front or back, which helped bring a sense of solitude and privacy. Something the young man craved. Opening the front door, three sets of adoring eyes greeted him, his children bounding down the stairs towards him. "Hi," he said, his dark mood forgotten as they crashed into him.

"Daddy," they all replied happily, Steve hefting his daughter onto his hip.

"Hattie, you're getting too heavy for me," he smirked as her twin sister bounced up and down.

"Daddy, pick me up," his other daughter demanded.

He scooped the little girl onto his other hip, the twins whooping with delight. "Chloe, what have you been eating?"

"Crisps, Daddy," she announced proudly.

Steve walked them into the lounge, Matthew trailing behind. "Where's your mum?" he asked, his jubilant mood tapering off, knowing what was coming.

"Upstairs," his son replied as he dropped onto the sofa, the girls settling on the carpet to watch a cartoon.

"Okay, guys. Wait down here while I go and see mum." Walking up the creaking staircase, Steve could hear music coming from his bedroom. Here goes, he thought, opening the door.

Rosie saw him enter the room as she applied her make-up in the mirror. "There's pizza in the freezer."

Steve walked over to the window, leaning on the ledge as he regarded his wife. A year younger than him, Rosie's red hair cascaded down her back, a tight black top barely containing her cleavage. She wore tight black leggings to match, her painted toes tap-tapping on the carpet to the beat. "I tried to draw some money for Matthew's bike, but the card was declined. I went into the branch, and they told me that you'd withdrawn three-hundred quid yesterday."

"I needed some new clothes," she replied flippantly.

"Three-hundred quid's worth?" he exclaimed. "I've never spent that much on clothes in my life."

She turned to him, looking him up and down. "Well, it shows. You really need to get some new threads, babe. Your brother always looks so smart. Whereas you..." She paused, finding the right words. "Look like you've just come in from emptying the bins."

Steve looked up at the ceiling, blowing out a long breath. "I'm a van driver. How exactly should I dress for work? And don't bring my brother into it. I don't want his name mentioned in this house."

"For Christ's sake, Steve! Let it go, why don't you. It was your choice to leave the family and change your name. They gave us this house. Can you not leave it at that?"

"I can't. You know what they did."

"So you keep telling me. It's all nonsense. Why would they do that? You're losing your mind."

"Am I? Well, one day, it will all come out."

"Yeah-yeah. I've heard it a million times before," she huffed, turning back to the mirror to apply her lip gloss.

"I hate that you work for them," he hissed. "Can't you find another job?"

"No, I can't. It's an easy job, and the tips are good. I'll make that money back in two weeks, and we can still get the bike for Matt's birthday."

The fight went out of Steve as he slumped against the wall. "What time are you going out?"

"In about fifteen minutes. Steph's picking me up."

"Right. Well, I suppose I'd better get tea ready."

"Okay. Don't wait up," she replied. *Loser,* Rosie thought as she applied hairspray to her red locks, pouting in the mirror before unboxing her new black heels. *He'll be putty in my hand later,* she smirked, knowing that her husband's older brother would always be a part of their family. She would always welcome him into their house. And into her bed.

A few miles to the north, Joe's Range Rover pulled up outside the small cottage at the end of a narrow lane. He knew that no other traffic would spot his arrival as he climbed out of the car. Moving to the boot, Joe lifted a wicker basket from inside, letting it rest on his hip before making his way up the winding path towards the building. He knocked twice, seeing his dappled reflection in the glass of the door. The sound of muted footsteps filtered through the door, a silhouette moving along the hallway before the door opened. "Joe," the woman said, slightly flustered.

"Linda," he smiled. It had the effect he was hoping for as the woman reciprocated, her cheeks flushing. "I've brought the hamper for the charity raffle. Is John home?"

She shook her head, her eyes never leaving his as she leaned against the doorframe. "He won't be back for hours. Golf," she shrugged.

"Of course. Saturday golf. Okay, would you be able to give it to him later when he gets home?"

"He'll be three sheets in the wind when he gets in. Useless sod! I'll leave it in his study." She regarded him for a second, moving to one side. "The kettle's on if you fancy a cuppa?"

Joe smiled. "I should be getting back, but I suppose a cuppa won't do any harm. Thank you." He stepped inside, following the woman down the hall, his eyes drifting down to her bare calves, noticing how the muscle stood proud as she moved.

"Coffee or tea?"

"Coffee, no sugar, please."

"Sweet enough?"

He smiled. "Aye, something like that."

Linda busied herself with the drinks, her heart hammering as she felt his gaze from across the kitchen. A minute later, she handed him his mug, stepping back to lean against the worktop, her shoulders sagging. "I'm sorry about last week," she began, her cheeks colouring slightly.

"Last week?" he frowned, knowing where the conversation was heading.

"At the pub. I was a bit drunk y'see. I shouldn't have said what I did."

"Oh, that. Don't worry about it. We were all a bit merry."

"Shall we sit in the lounge? Been on my feet all morning, and I'm not as young as I once was."

"Don't be daft. You're in your prime," noticing the skin around the woman's neck start to flush once more.

She led him from the kitchen, turning left into a cosy rear sitting room, the horizontal blinds almost closed, giving the room a muted coolness. Linda seated herself, pulling the hem of her dress down as Joe got comfortable. She looked at him, seeing a friendly expression gazing back at her, putting the middle-aged woman at ease. "I shouldn't have said what I did."

"Why did you say it?"

She fiddled with the button on her dress, her fingers feeling clumsy and shaky. "Things aren't great here. Haven't been for years. The kids have fled the nest, and John is either working or at that bloody golf club."

Joe sat back, draping his arm across the back of the sofa, his fingers close to her shoulder. "It's okay," he assured her. "I know how you feel, Linda."

"Really?" she exclaimed, seeing his expression drop slightly. "I thought you guys were so in love?"

"It's all for show. Cara likes the world to know that all's well. The truth is, she suffers from depression and drinks too much."

"Poor lass," she replied. "I suppose young Tom's accident hasn't helped."

Joe looked towards the window, wiping invisible tears with the back of his hand. "It's been tough. But it has been for years."

"Oh, hun," she soothed, patting him on the knee. "Just goes to show. We all smile and act like everything's peachy."

"I'm really surprised about you and John, though," Joe added. "Why he wants to spend the weekends playing golf when he's got a gorgeous wife at home is beyond me."

She smiled again, relaxing more and more as the handsome man gave her another heart-stopping smile. "No one's called me that for many-a-year," she blushed. "I'll be fifty next week and feel far from gorgeous."

"Well, for the record, you are, Linda. I've always thought that."

"You're a nice guy, Joe Stuart. I hope your Cara can see that," she stated, wincing as she slipped her strappy wedges off. "Bloody hell."

"What?"

"Feet are killing me. Should have worn my flatties to the shops."

"A nice hot bath will sort you out. Or a foot rub."

"Pah," she laughed. "You've gotta be joking. The only thing John rubs is his belly after his supper. Or his golf balls."

"Cara used to love my foot rubs," he stated, shifting slightly on the sofa.

"Lucky woman. I'd give anything for one right now."

He looked at the woman, her hazel eyes boring into his. Linda's shoulder-length dark hair was neatly cut, framing a pretty face. He'd always liked her, like many women in the nearby villages. She was curvy, her summer dress hugging all the right places. Joe looked down, noticing painted toenails, a small silver ring adorning one of them. "Well, I'm sure it would do no harm," he whispered, lifting her legs onto the sofa. His hands worked slowly, deliberately, his strong thumbs pressing into the ball of her foot as Linda looked on, her vocal cords deserting her. "Is that okay?" he asked, his large blue eyes searching for positive feedback.

"Oh, God, Joe," she breathed, the man noticing the skin around her neck turning a deep crimson.

"Good. Just sit back and enjoy." His voice was low but firm, the woman offering no protest as she almost melted into the fabric of the sofa.

Linda watched as his large hands gently kneaded her feet, the man's gaze concentrating on the task at hand. *Oh my God! Is this really happening?*

After ten minutes, he placed her feet on his lap, smiling over at her. "How was that? Relaxing?"

"It was amazing, Joe. I hope my feet didn't smell," she blurted, regretting the words instantly. Linda gawped in amazement as the younger man lifted her foot to his face, inhaling deeply.

"Smells nice," Joe breathed before kissing her ankle slowly. He kissed her again, slightly higher. "You taste nice too. Do you want me to stop?"

"Don't stop," she breathed, watching in awe as the blond-haired man's lips began rising ever upwards as the world around her melted away.

CHAPTER THREE

CARA STUART STOOD IN THE KITCHEN, WATCHING THROUGH THE window as Tristan played football in the garden with his two friends. *Just like Joe,* she thought, the mop of blond hair on the boy's head buffeted by the Atlantic breeze. The woman moved away from the window, walking over to the fridge. Pulling out a bottle of white wine, she caught her reflection in the mirror. She ruffled her dark hair, a thin smile appearing on her lips. "We can get our shit together tomorrow," she said. At thirty-three, Cara looked more Mediterranean than Cornish. She'd grown up in nearby Rock, the only daughter of a local brewer. Her parents had died a few years before, swept away by the tsunamis that had engulfed much of South Asia. Her already turbulent life had been plunged into new depths, the young mother trying to juggle her guilt with raising three children, with little support from her once loving husband. A husband that was never around unless his dinner was about to be served. Even then, the conversation between them was stilted at best, Joe focusing on his eldest son, wanting to hear how his day had gone, while the other two children sat looking at their plates. She poured herself a glass of wine, walking across the open plan kitchen to the lounge area. As she sat down with a glossy magazine, the French doors opened, Tristan running across the tiled floor towards the fridge. "Where's Lizzy and Tom?" she asked.

"Dunno," he replied as he slammed the fridge. "Saw them heading off earlier."

"Heading off?" she flinched, dropping the magazine on the sofa. "Where?"

"I don't know, Mum. They were heading in the direction of the park."

Her glass slammed down on the table, the woman clambering out of the sofa. "He's not up to it," she stated, grabbing her pumps from the floor. "I'm going to look for them. Stay in the garden. Do you hear?"

"Yes," the ten-year-old huffed, reddening as he spied his friends at the kitchen door.

Stepping out, Cara was glad of the fresh Cornish air, happy to escape the walls that seemed to close in on her whenever she felt anxious. She set off at a brisk pace, the long pristine lawn giving way to an impenetrable fence with a wrought-iron gate set within it. On the other side, she saw holidaymakers walking back from the beach towards the newly built log cabins that were part of the second phase of Sandy Shore's expansion. Right now, the woman couldn't care less about the sixty cabins, with their ensuite bathrooms and decked areas. Right now, her son was unaccounted for. She quickened her pace, approaching a fork in the path. One led to the caravan park, complete with clubhouse, amusement arcades and other activities to keep their customers happy. She took the left fork towards Trevinney Cove. An array of cars were parked on either side as the path widened, the woman scanning ahead for any signs of her two children. *Shit. Where are they?* She forged on, passing employees who smiled over at her, Cara reciprocating, her mind elsewhere. As she came down onto the beach, her dark eyes scanned ahead. The beach was narrow yet deep, twin headlands protecting the calm waters from the Atlantic beyond. Her heart starting thumping harder, seeing the breaking surf a few hundred yards away, trying to push dreaded thoughts back into the recesses of her mind.

"Mummy," a voice called out.

Cara turned, seeing Lizzy and Thomas sat in the dunes to her left, next to an ice cream van. They were both smiling, her youngest son's usually pallid complexion appearing almost sun-kissed. She breathed out, her anxiety seeming to blow away on the sea breeze as she made her way over to them. "I was worried about you two." Her tough resolve began to splinter as they looked up at her.

"We went for a walk, Mummy," Thomas replied, his mouth a circle of white as he consumed his treat.

"And what have we got here?" she said, pointing at the twin ice cream cones.

"I brought my purse with me. Would you like an ice cream?"

Cara laughed; her dark mood seared away by the warm Cornish sun. "Why not," she smiled, sitting between them. She reached out, pulling them into her embrace as she kissed the tops of their heads. "Love you guys."

"We love you too," Lizzy beamed before walking off towards the ice cream van, holding her purse proudly.

"How's your leg," the woman asked, her light mood tempering slightly.

Tom shrugged. "Okay, I guess. It did get a bit sore, but I'll get used to it." He tapped the leg with his knuckles, a metallic sound ringing out.

A young couple walked past, the girl noticing the little boy with the false leg. She stared momentarily, nudging her boyfriend, who looked over brazenly. They giggled, walking away arm in arm. *Bastards,* Cara thought, looking down at her son, who was too wrapped up in his ice cream to have noticed. "Don't worry, Son. I know it all feels very strange at the moment, but it will get better."

"I know, M-mummy," he faltered, banging his fist against his head in frustration.

"Don't do that, Tom," she soothed. "Just take your time with your words."

"S-sorry. I don't know why I do it? Seems to have gotten worse since the accid-dent."

"Well, it will get better. You've had a terrible shock, and your body needs to heal. Don't fret; I'll make sure you're okay."

"Promise?" He looked up, his eyes pleading for assurance.

She wrapped him in her arms, nuzzling the top of his head. "I promise. Nothing bad will ever happen to you again." She felt her emotions rise, swallowing them back down. Cara needed to be strong for him.

"I love you, Mummy," he said, his voice perfect and lyrical.

She lost her resolve, her strength dissipating as she sobbed. "I love you too," Cara croaked as Lizzy came back with a double cone.

"What's wrong?" she inquired.

"Nothing," Cara croaked, wiping her eyes. "Oh, wow. Is that for me?"

Lizzy handed her the ice cream, beaming at her mother. "Yes. I used my own pocket money."

"Thank you. You're most kind," she smiled, enjoying the feeling as her two children huddled close to her. Her metaphorical dark clouds blew away as the woman watched Tom and Lizzy devour their ice creams. She took her first taste, letting the coolness seep into her mouth as Lizzy stood up, wiping her hands together. "Shall we go for a walk? We could go to the amusement arcade on our way back home?"

"Why not," the woman replied, levering herself up from the

sand. She extended a hand, her son pulling himself to his feet before they set off back towards Sandy Shores.

"Can we watch a movie tonight, Mummy?" Tom asked as he tried to keep pace with her.

"Of course. Your father will probably be out, and Tristan will probably be in his room. Sounds like a plan. We can have popcorn too." They made their way away from the beach, walking happily towards the centre of the holiday park. *Just the three of us,* as usual thought Clara. Her shoulders sagged slightly, not knowing if they would ever be a proper family again.

Joe stepped out of his car, smiling as he saw the feverish activity going on at the Retreat. His favourite place was the pavilion-looking building basking under the warm sun; its Mock-Tudor frontage and decked area gave it a regal appearance. Men were unloading a white-panel van, wheeling kegs of beer inside, while others were carrying food for the grill around the side of the building. *I'm starving;* he thought as a wry smile appeared on his face. *Although, I've only just eaten.* An image flashed through his mind. Linda sprawled on the sofa, a rapt expression on her face. He shook the memory aside as a young man approached.

"Mr Stuart," Malcolm said.

"How's it going? All set?"

"Aye," the younger man replied. "The kids' party finished about an hour ago, so it'll all be set up by about five. What time are our guests arriving?"

Joe shrugged. "Probably about six. Good work, Malcolm." He looked at the man, taking in his features. The man was a few inches shorter than Joe, with a tanned complexion. His dark hair and eyes reminded him of his wife. They could be brother and sister, he thought. "I need to talk to you about something," he started, taking Malcolm's arm as he led him away from the others.

"What's up?"

"I spoke to your father this morning. He's going to take early retirement."

Malcolm's eyes widened. "What? Why?"

"The HSE visited us. They are very concerned about the accident. We could've been looking at prosecution. However, I have sorted it out, but your father was to blame for Tom's accident."

The younger man leaned against the fence, shaking his head. "But he loves his work."

"I know," Joe agreed. "If it were anyone else, they'd have lost their job, but old Tony's been with us for years. So, I've offered him a nice package, along with his pension. I want you to take over his duties."

"Me?"

"Yes, Malcolm. You're a good worker, and I know I can trust you."

The words were loaded, the younger man knowing what Joe meant. "Yessir, you can."

"Good. Pop up to the house on Monday so we can go through the paperwork. Congratulations, Malcolm. I know you won't let me down." He clapped the younger man on the shoulder, walking towards the house as a minibus pulled up. The driver climbed out, his massive frame barely escaping the bus's cab. "Martin," Joe said, looking up at the man.

Martin had worked for the Stuart's for years, the hulking man performing a myriad of roles from driver to security and lots in between. Like so many others in the Stuart's service, Joe knew how to keep Martin onside, knowing that the giant had a penchant for certain delicacies. "Joe," he replied, his thick Scottish accent seeming out of place on the North Cornish coast.

"Looks like we've got enough entertainment to keep the punters happy. Which one have you got your eye on?" he winked.

The large man slid the bus's door open, several young ladies exiting gratefully. Some stood there stretching their legs, whilst others walked over to the fence, lighting up cigarettes as they took in their surroundings. The last person to exit the bus was a young black male, his eyes furtively scanning the area before joining the others for a smoke. "That one over there," Martin nodded. "In the red dress."

Joe appraised the young woman, her dress looking like it had been spray-painted on. She looked Eastern European, her Slavic features like many of the others. "Nice. Well, you've got about an hour or so before the others arrive. I suggest you get cracking. If you know what I mean."

"Aye," Martin grinned, signalling for the woman to follow him inside the Retreat.

Joe caught the young black man's eye, tilting his head as he walked towards his Range Rover. As he approached, the blond man smiled amiably. "Welcome to Cornwall. I'm Joe."

"Oswald," the man. "But people call me Oz."

Joe detected his accent, knowing that the man was far from home. "Nigeria?"

The young man smiled. "Close. Ghana."

"Well, you're far from home. But don't worry, we'll take good care of you." He placed an arm around Oz's shoulder, turning him towards the building. "See that man there," he said, pointing towards Malcolm, who was wheeling a keg of beer inside.

"Yes."

"I'd like you to get to know him later. If you know what I mean."

"He's pretty," the other man observed.

"He is. And I'm sure he'll like you too. Just be discreet. I don't care what you get up to, but make sure others don't see." He took two notes out of his wallet, slipping them into the man's palm. "Do we have an understanding?"

"We do."

"Good. Have fun and enjoy the party." He watched as the man walked away, joining the women for a cigarette. *Whatever floats your boat,* he thought before climbing into his car. A minute later, he was heading back home, wondering what fun and games would ensue later. He smiled as the car rolled along the dirt track. He'd also chosen his prize. A young black girl whose dark eyes had met his a few moments before. Joe knew that he'd have plenty in reserve for the evening despite his foray earlier in the afternoon. His good mood faltered as he made his way up the long driveway, seeing his wife and two children walking across the manicured lawns. *Just need to placate the bitch before I head out,* he thought. Wondering how he could manage that. He knew that he couldn't keep her sweet with gifts and trinkets. How could he, when she had more money than him. A fortune that Joe wanted all for himself.

CHAPTER
FOUR

"Get yourself cleaned up before they arrive," Martin said as he buckled up his trousers. The woman, Katarzyna, lay on the bed, the duvet barely covering her nakedness. He'd been gentle with her, not wanting to damage such a prize. He hoped the others would be as considerate.

"I need a drink," she said, drawing her knees up to her chest as the man in front of her buttoned up his shirt. Her eyes rested on the large scar that traversed his chest, an angry red line that made the man more intimidating.

"Go in there," he motioned towards the small bathroom. "There will be plenty of refreshments later. Just don't drink too much. You'll need a clear head." He left the room, walking into the main hallway. To his right, a large open-plan space, complete with a bar area, gave way to a decked patio, where staff were busy adding wood and coals to the grills. He stepped into the room, liking the dark floorboards and panelled walls. It reminded him of an old inn back in his native Scotland, where he'd spent many a happy evening with his family. A family he'd left behind. The floorboards creaked under his weight as he strode across the room, coming into the fresh air as the sun was slowly edging its way towards the horizon. Woodsmoke wafted all around him, Martin's tastebuds coming alive as two men began laying a variety of meats on the griddle. *Work first*, he thought, heading over to the minibus where he retrieved a camera from the glove box. Switching it on, he checked the battery, which he knew had enough power, along with the memory card he'd cleared earlier in the day. "Let's go hunting," he said, scanning the nearby area before setting off on foot. Twenty minutes later, the shadows had begun to lengthen, Martin feeling a change in the temperature as he crept through the forest. From his lofty vantage point, he could see the cabins nearby, hearing children happily playing before heading down to the clubhouse and restaurants that made up Sandy Shores. As he edged forward, two large sheds and a workshop came into view. Taking out his camera, he got into position, seeing two writhing bodies on the dusty floor. One was white; the other was black. He snapped as many pictures as he could, not wanting to be heard by Malcolm, who was otherwise engaged. The man placed the camera into his jacket pocket, backing away slowly, leaving the two men to their fun.

Ten minutes later, Martin took his jacket off, placing it inside the minibus as a taxi pulled up. He was sweating, wanting nothing more than a cold beer and a juicy burger. Joe climbed out of the car, handing the driver a note before strolling over to the larger man. "Boss."

"Everything under control?"

"Aye. The guests should be here any minute. Oh, and I think young Malcolm has a new friend."

The blond man's eyes widened before a smile played across his lips. "Really. Pictures?"

"Plenty. Mucky bastards."

"Oh well, whatever floats your boat. And believe me, I intend to have my dingy inflated tonight."

Martin sniggered as a larger minibus, complete with blacked-out windows crunched along the gravel behind them. "The punters are here."

"Good. I'll do the greetings. Why don't you get some food before they get stuck in."

"Why not," he agreed, leaving Joe to welcome their guests.

Seven men stood in front of him, Joe casting his eye over them. Some he knew, two of them were new to The Retreat. One man hung back from the others, the host knowing his identity. He also knew not to call him by his real name, an alias agreed beforehand. All the men were much older than Joe, the eldest touching sixty. They were all professional types and had much to lose, especially the man at the back. If word of this got out, a national scandal would erupt. "Welcome to The Retreat. I hope you all had a pleasant journey." A few local men nodded at him; the two men at the rear stood immobile, devoid of expression. "Well, the grill is already underway, and there's enough booze to keep you all happy. Why don't you all get settled, and I'll fetch the entertainment." He walked inside as the men strolled over to the side terrace. Within the cool confines of the building, Joe made his way to the makeshift rear bedrooms. Opening the door, he smiled warmly as eight women looked at him, a mix of tentative smiles and wary glances. "Ladies. I trust you are all settled in and ready for a fun-filled night."

"Are they ready?" A blonde woman asked, her Eastern European accent to his liking.

"They are. Are you all ready to mingle?" They all nodded, Joe, focusing on a young black woman who was leaning against the windowsill. His eyes took her in, appreciated the contrast between the tight ecru dress and her ebony skin. She smiled coyly, looking down at the floor as the others filed out, heels clattering on the floorboards. The dark-skinned woman hung back, adjusting the hem of her skirt as Joe closed the door, the noise from the lock echoing around the sparsely furnished room. He cast his eyes over the double bed, then back to the girl.

"What's your name?"

"Olivia," she replied softly, Joe trying to place an accent.

"Where are you from?"

"Bruges."

"Nice place," he said, watching as she moved towards the bed. The woman sat down, looking up at him, her dark eyes boring into his as she bit her bottom lip.

Joe took two steps forward, standing mere inches away from her. "I think tonight will be unforgettable," he breathed as dark fingers began unbuckling his trousers.

"Shh," Lizzy admonished as they peeked through the trees.

"S-sorry," Tom replied, his sister casting him a stern look.

"It's okay. Just keep quiet. We don't want any of them to see us. Look, Martin is there. And there's Mr Samuels from school." Samuels was their headmaster, Lizzy spotting his balding pate easily from their vantage point.

"Is that Mrs Samuels with him?" Tom asked innocently, seeing how the middle-aged man laughed and slapped the woman's bottom in the purple dress.

"No. I've never seen her before," Lizzy frowned.

The smell of grilled meat wafted across the grounds, the two children inhaling as they surveyed the scene. They watched in silence as Mr Samuels led the woman away from the others, walking together until they reached the treeline. Both children saw the woman drop to her knees from their limited view, Mr Samuels resting his head against the trunk. "What is she doing?" Tom asked curiously.

"Don't know. Maybe his laces are undone?"

After a few minutes, Tom piped up again. "She's taking a long time to do his laces. Mummy is much faster."

"I don't know what she's doing," she replied curtly, her gaze tracking back towards the main building.

"What are they all doing here? I've only been here once for Lawrence's birthday party."

Lizzy looked at her brother, shaking her head. "I dunno. I've seen people here before. Matthew and I came here last year during the school holidays. There were lots of people, but it was getting late, so we headed home." Her eyes rested on a man standing away from the others, talking to a tall woman with long red hair and a figure-hugging black dress. She squinted her eyes, the man seeming vaguely familiar to Lizzy. He had his hand around the woman's waist, her dazzling smile telling Lizzy that she was having fun.

"We should be heading back. M-mummy will be worried about us."

"Okay, let's," she paused as another figure emerged from the building. "Look, it's Daddy."

Tom looked across the expanse of grass; his blond-haired father clearly recognisable. "I thought he was at the golf club?"

"Hmm, me too. Maybe he's on his way there later?" She watched as her father accepted a drink from Martin, the two men laughing at some secret joke as the children looked on. "Come on then. Let's go." As they took a few paces, Lizzy turned, a realisation hitting her like a train.

"What?" her younger brother asked.

"That man. I knew he looked familiar."

"Who is he?"

"He's on the television. Mummy watches his game show."

CHAPTER
FIVE

MARTIN LAID THE WOMAN CAREFULLY ONTO THE BED, THE SPRINGS protesting as Joe looked on, a concerned expression etched on his face. The man with two names stood by the doorway, his expression neutral as the woman groaned. Both men looked down at her, Martin pulling the duvet over her nakedness as she looked up groggily. "Bastard," she spat, aiming her vitriol at the man by the door.

He took a step inside the room, closing the door behind him. "Heard it all before, love."

Joe looked at him, cautioning himself to tread carefully. "What happened?"

The other man shrugged, an impassive expression on his face. "What can I say? It just got a bit rough."

Joe looked at the man. He was a good fifteen years his senior. A bland face and slightly overweight physique, making him wonder how he'd made it to the lofty heights of the showbiz world. "I think you've broken her nose."

"I'm calling the police," the woman yelled, pulling the duvet up to her neck protectively.

"Go ahead," the man said. "Who do you think they will

believe? A dirty prostitute from the arse-end of nowhere, or someone the nation loves? Someone who does *Children in Need* and *Comic Relief* every year. No, I think we will come to some agreement. Better that way."

"What kind of agreement?" Martin asked.

The man reached into his back pocket, pulling a roll of banknotes out. He tossed it onto the bed, the woman's eyes widening. "I think that should sort things out. It would take you a while to earn that kind of money."

Joe looked at the woman, who leaned forward to retrieve the wad of cash. She quickly thumbed through the notes, nodding reluctantly. "You're still a bastard."

"Sticks and stones, love. You sell your arse for money, but who am I to judge."

Sensing the situation had been resolved, Joe was keen to remove the woman from the venue. "Look, I'll get the driver to take you wherever you need to go. I just don't want the party to end on a bad note."

Wincing as she touched the bridge of her reddening nose, the woman nodded. "I'm staying at a guest house in Bude. He can drop me off there."

"Okay," Joe said as the anonymous man left the room. "And for what it's worth, I'm sorry. This is supposed to be a bit of fun. I don't condone what happened."

"But you'll turn a blind eye, like me."

"I guess I'll have to," Joe replied, putting on his most sincere expression. "Martin, could you take over from here. I need to get back outside."

"Sure, boss," the larger man nodded.

Joe left the room, crossing the interior of the building as giggles filtered from underneath a nearby doorway. *Let's hope there's no more drama tonight,* he thought before stepping into the balmy evening. He spied his sister-in-law serving drinks.

She looked over at him, smiling warmly before focusing on the two men. Joe could see why they were staring at her intently, her skin-tight leggings and tight top drawing their eyes. *Looking good, Rosie*, Joe thought, hoping to catch up with her later. He walked over to John Samuels, who was tucking into food like it was going out of fashion. "Having a good time?"

The older man wiped his lips, a beaming smile on his face. "You could say that. I've already had a taste of what's to come later. You always put on a good show."

Joe looked around, noticing the mystery man sidle over to a couple of the women. Straight away, he could see that they both appeared on edge, the host hoping that no more trouble would ensue. "I do my best. Which one is yours?"

John pointed across the open area towards the fence. "Natalia," he replied as he munched on a steak sandwich. "Proper little goer. Just what I needed."

"Things not good at home?" It was a leading question, Joe noticing how the older man's expression soured.

"They're the same as ever. Linda hasn't let me stoke her fire for years. Her furnace went out a long time ago."

I wouldn't be so sure, Joe thought, smiling at the other man. *She was on fire earlier.*

"This will keep me going for a few weeks until the next one." He tucked into his food once more, a blob of relish running down his chin.

"Well, you enjoy yourself, and I'll catch up with you later." He walked away, heading towards the vehicles as Martin came through the front doors with the woman. Over at the fence, Natalia and her friend's expressions changed when they noticed the woman's state as she walked shakily towards the minibus. The driver climbed out, a concerned expression on his face. "Brian. This young lady had a bit of an accident. Could you take her back to her hotel?"

The older man knew what had happened, the colour draining from his face when he saw the split skin on the bridge of her nose. But he also knew who was in charge. "Aye, Mr Stuart." He looked at the woman, guessing that she was probably the same age as his daughter, the man's heart rate beginning to simmer. "Come on then, my lovely. Let's get you back to your hotel. I'd get that checked out by a doctor as soon as possible."

Martin walked over to the deck area, noticing the man immediately. He was trying to talk to a young woman, her expression telling the Scotsman that she wanted to be anywhere else but here. He took a beer from the ice bucket, removing the cap before walking over. "Everything okay?"

The woman, clearly glad of his presence, cleared her throat. "I just need to pop to the ladies."

The men watched as she walked away, the smaller man sighing. "I was making progress there."

Martin looked down at him, the man's smug expression making his blood run cold. "Let's have no more mishaps tonight."

"Meaning?"

"You know what I mean, Jim."

At the mention of his real name, the man bristled. "I thought I made it fucking clear that I was to remain anonymous."

"Yes, I was made aware of that. However, you've hardly helped yourself. Have you?"

"You mean the dumb tart. She's forgotten about."

"Maybe. But the others know what went down. Word of warning. Hurt another one, and there'll be trouble."

"Are you threatening me? You don't want to do that, sunshine."

Martin stepped forward, towering over the television

personality. "I don't give a fuck who you are. How much money you've got, or how powerful you think you are. Hurt another one, and I'll snap you in two. Understood."

Jim took a step back, seeing the steely expression in the younger man's eyes. "I understand. Perfect gentleman from now on." He bowed theatrically before the bigger man moved away, leaving him ruffled.

Martin found Joe next to the minibus, the blond man talking on his new mobile phone. He stood patiently as his boss ended the call. "I had a quiet word with our esteemed guest."

"Oh. What did you say?"

"I just told him to watch what he's up to. I don't think he liked it, though."

"Well, he's paid us a small fortune to be here tonight. But you're right; I'll not be inviting him back. We don't need the hassle."

Martin looked across the vast expanse, noticing the young black man heading towards them. "It's getting dark. I'd better get to work."

"Good idea," Joe agreed. "As many pictures as you can. Especially Samuels."

"Leverage?"

"Always," Joe grinned. "You never know when you might need it."

～

Lizzy and Tom walked in through the kitchen door, giggling as their mother walked from the kitchen. "Where've you two been?"

"Just outside playing," the girl responded. "We're hungry."

Cara smiled. "You're always hungry. We've already eaten, but yours is in the oven."

"What is it?" Tom asked as he fiddled with his trainer.

"Shepherd's pie."

"Oh," Lizzy sighed. "I thought we could have a pizza."

"You had that last night. You need some greens inside you. Anyway, I've got a surprise for you."

"W-what?" Tom asked, suddenly curious.

"Come with me." She led them through the kitchen into the lounge, where a large cardboard box sat next to the Inglenook fireplace. "Take a look."

The children stepped forward, peering over the lip of the box, a double intake of breath making Cara smile. "A puppy," Tom squealed.

"Shh," Cara admonished playfully. "Don't scare him."

"I didn't know we were getting a puppy?" Lizzy pointed out. "I thought Daddy didn't like dogs."

"Well, Daddy will have to get used to it. He's got a cat, so it's only fair. Tom, I brought him mainly for you."

"Why?" he looked up at his mother, his innocent expression making her heart constrict.

"Because you've had a bit of a rough time of it lately. I talked to Kate a few weeks ago, who said that a puppy might be good for you."

"Well, I love him, Mummy. Can I hold him?"

"Of course. But you have to be careful. He's only three months old." Cara bent down, gently lifting the dog off the fleecy blanket before handing it to Tom. "Hold him like you would a baby. Cross your arms."

Tom did as instructed, a broad smile appearing on his face as he looked at their new addition. The dog mewled lightly, making the boy giggle. He took in the dog's features, liking his brown and white coat. The puppy's face was white, framed by light brown marking around its eyes, giving it a perpetually sad expression. "What kind of dog is it?"

"It's a beagle. Mrs Hooper breeds them."

"He's lovely." The boy dropped his head, kissing the dog's black nose. "I love him."

"What shall we call him?" Lizzy asked as she stroked its soft head.

"I'll have a think. For now, we'll call him, puppy," Tom stated as he bent down to place the dog back in the box.

Cara's eyes welled up with tears, watching how her beloved son struggled to get back up, knowing that his life would never be quite the same again. She only hoped that the new addition would give her youngest some companionship, knowing that Tristan barely spoke to him and that Lizzy was growing up fast. "Well, I want you two showered and back downstairs in ten minutes. Okay."

"Okay, Mummy," they said in unison, leaving her alone in the lounge. She knelt, ruffling the dog's ears playfully, another pitiful mewl drifting towards her. "Welcome to the family, little man. I think you'll be happy here." She walked into the kitchen, her stomach tightening as thoughts of her husband's reaction washed over her. *Oh well. To hell with him. He's never here anyway*, she decided, wondering where her husband was. And what company he was keeping.

CHAPTER
SIX

STEVE LOOKED AT HIS PHONE, SEEING THAT IT WAS GETTING CLOSE TO midnight. As usual, his wife was still out. His mind whirred, wondering if she was up to no good. Things had declined over the recent years, his attractive wife becoming bored with family life. He knew she liked male attention. Craved it from everyone else except him, it seemed. He'd heard rumours, but what could he do? Yes, the house was theirs, but his meagre wages were barely enough to keep it heated with more and more food needed as the children grew older. Then there was Rosie, whose wages were all cash-in-hand, Steve never knowing how much she earned or where it went. He'd spoken to his friends, who'd said he should leave her, but he knew that was easier said than done. A blazing row from a few months previous flashed before him, Rosie screaming that she would take him to the cleaners if they ever split up. No, he was stuck. Trapped in a loveless marriage with a wife that found her kicks elsewhere. He pressed a button on the remote control; the lounge plunged into darkness as he sat pondering on the sofa. *How did we end up like this?* Another thought presented itself—his mother. A stray tear slid from his eye, the man wiping it away in the darkness. "I miss you, Mum," he whispered, his emotions building as memories of her flooded back. He rose from the sofa, walking into the kitchen to make a drink before he retired for the evening. His mother had passed away twenty years before, her memory still shining brightly. Steve had loved her fiercely, his brother and father forming their own bond. His mother was a constant in his early years; whether cooking for him, bathing him or playing with the young boy, Margaret Stuart had been a doting parent. That was until her disappearance when Steve had just celebrated his tenth birthday. Her body had never been found, despite the best efforts of local police, who surmised that his mother had been swept out to sea. But Steve knew different. He truly believed his father and brother had a hand in it. As the kettle began to boil, Steve sighed. "I can't live like this," he announced to the empty kitchen. *I want to be happy. I want to achieve something in my life, not just driving that sodding van around.* The man looked over at the fridge, smiling at the blue crayon drawing that had been stuck there by Hattie. He switched off the lights before making his way up the stairs to bed to ponder his life and everything that was wrong with it.

~

Joe walked back outside, buttoning up his shirt as a cool breeze assailed him. The party had moved inside, the staff departing for the evening as the bedrooms and leather sofas had become occupied. Rosie sauntered outside, lighting a cigarette as she carried two bottles of beer in the crook of her elbow. She blew out a breath, handing the man his drink. She knew he needed to quench his thirst after their time alone. "Thanks," he smiled, chinking glass with his sister-in-law.

"Anytime, lover," she replied, accentuating her Cornish accent.

"Looks like they'll be occupied for a while. Let them fuck themselves stupid."

"Like you just did to me."

"I suppose you could say that." He took another swig, the cold liquid hitting the spot. He looked at her. "How's Steve?"

"That loser. Same as ever. Broke, no prospects. Same old Steve."

"Hmm. Not seen him around much."

"I don't see much of him either. He's always working or writing stupid short stories on his computer. Always the dreamer."

"Do you think he suspects anything?"

"With us?"

Joe nodded.

"Don't know, don't care. I'm only with him because we've got a roof over our heads."

The man shook his head. "We were so close once. But then he became bitter and angry about Mum. Families, eh?"

"He's still angry. Keeps telling me that he's going to expose the truth."

Joe baulked, his eyes widening. "What truth is there to expose? Mum was swept out to sea. A tragic accident."

Rosie looked at him, noticing his defensive response. There was a flicker of uncertainty in the man's eyes that vanished as soon as she'd seen it. "Well, he won't tell me anything. It's probably just empty threats."

He regained his composure, taking another swig. "He needs to chill out. It was his choice to leave the family. Dad didn't have to give him the house, but he did because he's one of us and always will be."

"Well, I'm not sure how long we can keep the marriage

going. I can't live with him anymore, Joe. He gets really low, moping around the house like one of the kids."

"So leave him." The statement was out of his mouth before he had time to process it.

"And do what?"

"Start again. You're young enough and sexy enough to do it."

She smiled, sidling over to him. "If only I could start again with you."

He chuckled. "Nice dream, sweetheart. But that would never happen. Cara would take me to the cleaners."

"Stupid bitch," Rosie spat. "Got a gorgeous husband, a stately home and three kids, yet she's always depressed, like Steve. God, we should pair them up."

"Funnily enough, I think she's always had a bit of a soft spot for him. But no, I'm stuck with her."

"Well, you know where I am, should you change your mind. Remember that."

He looked down, a sad expression washing over his tanned face. "Thank you."

"What's wrong?" she slipped an arm around his waist, pulling herself closer.

"It's nothing."

"Come on, Joe. This is me, Rosie. You can tell me anything."

He took a deep breath, composing himself. "I think she may be seeing someone else."

"What? Cara. Never!"

"I think she is. She's suddenly gone all secretive. Going out a lot more often."

"Where?"

"No idea. But one of the guys from the golf club saw her in St Ives last week. Why would she go there? We don't know anyone there. If she wanted to go shopping, she's got Truro or Plymouth."

"Have you said anything?"

"What could I say? Are you having an affair like me? No, I will keep an eye on her. She's not that smart. Sooner or later, she'll slip up, and I'll nail her."

I hope she's fucking someone else, she thought. That will clear a path for me. "I'm sure it's nothing. Maybe she fancied a change of scenery?" The words were hollow, without substance.

Joe shrugged. "Who knows." He shook the thought as Martin appeared at the door, tilting his head. "Back in a minute." As he approached the bigger man, he could see his expression, his stomach tightening. "What's up?"

"Inside, boss."

Joe followed Martin as giggles and grunts echoed around the building, the two men ignoring the antics behind closed doors. Martin opened a door at the end of a panelled hallway, motioning for his boss to step inside. His eyes took in the scene, seeing the other elusive man standing by the window smoking a cigarette. On the bed, a young girl lay, the sheets covering her naked body. Joe looked at the girl's eyes, seeing a cloudy blank stare that made the hairs on the back of his neck stand proud. "What's happened?"

"Things got a little rough," the man answered indifferently. "She liked to be choked. I think I was a little overzealous."

"She's dead," Martin added, seeing the expression on Joe's face.

"Fuck!" He walked back over to the door, closing it before pacing the room. "What have you done?"

The man shrugged. "It just got out of hand, but don't worry. No one will miss her."

"Are you fucking kidding me? She's dead," he retorted. He took a step closer, lowering his voice. "You've killed her."

He took a deep draw on his cigarette, blowing smoke out through his nose. "It was an accident. Never mind, we'll sort it out."

"And how do we do that?"

The man took out a black wallet, showing his identification to the others. "Don't worry," he smiled. "I know how this works."

CHAPTER
SEVEN

Frank Stuart stood in the centre of The Retreat, his steely-grey eyes flicking between the two men. In his early seventies, he stood ramrod straight, matching height with his eldest son. He ran a hand through his mane of grey hair as his son finished updating him on the events of the previous night. "Where's the body?"

"In the basement," Joe replied evenly.

"Christ! I thought you were supposed to be discreet."

"We are, Dad."

"A dead body is not discreet, Son," he bellowed the two men bowing their heads.

"I know. But how was I supposed to know this would happen? Don't worry; we've got it all on camera."

Frank walked over to the bar area, measuring himself a glass of Scotch from the hanging optics. Outside, blackness pressed against the windows, the flickering bulbs doing their best at holding off the night. The older man knew that his son had installed hidden cameras throughout The Retreat. It gave him a modicum of reassurance to know that they had evidence.

Evidence that could be used if the need arose. "So, this copper told you to bury the body?"

"He did," Martin confirmed.

"Did he say where?"

"Not exactly, but we think over by the outbuildings. It's off the beaten track, and no one goes there except Malcolm."

"Hmm," Frank replied. "How are you going to bury a body with him around?"

"I'll think of something."

"You better had. And fast. The body's going to stink to high heaven pretty soon. And digging a hole deep enough to conceal your mistake will take time."

"I've asked him to come up to the house in the morning to go over the paperwork." He looked at the bigger man. "Martin, could you get this sorted while I'm with Malcolm? After we've done the necessary admin, I'll take a walk with him and give him an overview of my plans for the park. That will buy us some time."

"Okay, Joe," the Scot agreed. "What about his dad? He'll be knocking around the place."

Frank walked around the bar, seating himself at a high-backed stool as his mind whirred. "I've got a delivery of logs arriving in the morning. Tell the old bastard to come over and put them in the shed. Save me doing it."

"Okay. I'll phone him first thing. Martin, what time can you get here?"

"What time are you meeting Malcolm?"

"Eight."

"Fine. I'll get here for eight then. I'll call you when I'm done."

"Okay. That should work. Any problems, call me straight away." He walked around the bar, filling two glasses with Scotch before refilling his father's glass. "And no more outsiders. That's on me. I thought it would bring in some extra revenue, but let's stick to what we know."

"And who we know," Frank added sagely. "It's taken years to get to this point. I'll not see it destroyed because someone overstepped the mark. This is our empire, and we need to keep it that way."

~

Monday morning was a hive of activity in the Stuart household. The first day of the new school year had arrived, Cara ensuring she was up early. The uniforms had been ironed and hung up, the woman supervising her three children before serving their breakfasts. Joe had strolled into the kitchen, grabbing a piece of toast and a large coffee before leaving her to sort out the children, Cara lightly humming as Rhythm is a Dancer filtered across the large kitchen. Once the bowls and plates were safely in the dishwasher, she drove the few miles to their school, ensuring Tom was okay with his first day back. "You'll be fine, Son," she said as the boy clung to her, seeing his classmates looking over at him.

"W-will I?"

She knelt, enveloping him in her arms. "Of course you will. Look, your friends are waiting for you. It might seem a little strange at first, but you'll be back to normal before you know it."

"Promise," he said, the words forced out of his mouth.

"I promise, and I'll be here later to pick you up."

"Okay, Mummy," he said, putting on a brave smile that made her heart constrict.

"Love you, Tom," she croaked, swallowing down emotions before her youngest joined his classmates, his teacher, a young

Cornish woman with cascading red hair putting an arm around his shoulder before leading him inside.

"He'll be alright," a voice said to her left.

Cara turned her head, smiling at Liz, one of the school mums who put an arm around her. "I know," she replied. "It just feels... I don't know. Real?"

"It's bound to feel a little strange. After all, he's been at home for a while. Don't fret; he'll be running around before you know it," she confirmed in her broad Cornish accent.

She smiled thinly. "So, how was your summer?" changing the subject as her emotions threatened to boil over.

"Not bad. We managed to make it over to the timeshare for a few weeks. Jed even managed to take some time off."

"Wow, that's not like him," Cara replied. She knew that Liz's workaholic husband would have to be dragged away from his fishing boat, reluctantly letting others reap the rewards from the Atlantic without him.

"I know. But he enjoyed himself. We all did. How about you?"

Cara sighed. "Very quiet. Joe's always working, so there was no holiday for us, especially after what happened to Tom. Joe wanted to stay put in case the local inspectors started sniffing around."

"Oh well, there's always next year or even half-term."

She smiled at Liz, loving how she always had a positive spin on life. If only Cara could emulate her friend's sunny disposition. "Maybe. I'd kill for a week on a sun lounger."

"Well, you're a long time dead, love. Tell Joe you need a break." Liz looked at her watch. "Anyway, I'd better get back. You around later in the week for a coffee?"

"I think so. I'll call you."

"Okay, love. Catch you later."

Fifteen minutes later, she pulled up outside her home, walking across the gravel driveway to the kitchen door. The house was quiet as she stepped inside, knowing that Joe was talking to Malcolm. *T.V or walk?* She pondered for a moment, letting the sun radiate on her skin as it shone through the glass-panelled door. She paced over to the fridge, pulling a bottle of mineral water out before heading out to fill her lungs with sea air.

∼

Martin removed his shirt, hanging it on a nearby branch as the morning's exertions took their toll on his massive frame. He was soaked through, his arms and clothing smeared in mud. Working for a few hours, the giant Scot had dug a rectangular hole in the forest floor, the depth reaching up to his chin as he'd stood admiring his handiwork. After climbing out of the grave, he took a break, letting the sounds of the forest fill his ears. Birds chirped above him as a salty breeze blew through the trees, steadying his nerves. "I get all the good jobs," he sighed, walking across the bracken-strewn ground towards the van. He stood in the treeline, scanning the open ground for any sign of activity. *The coast is clear.* Satisfied that he was alone, the man dragged a large hessian-wrapped bundle out of the rear, hefting it over his shoulders before trudging back into the shaded forest. He could feel the coldness of death permeate through the rough material, the man wanting to get the job completed as soon as possible. He'd never seen a dead body before, let alone buried one. His senses were on edge, Martin knowing that if someone saw him, he'd be spending years behind bars. As he placed it on the ground, an arm fell out, a cold hand landing on his foot. "Jesus!" he exclaimed, stumbling backwards into a tree, his skull thudding against the trunk. He crouched, his breathing ragged as the Scot massaged the back of his head.

"Get a grip, man." He walked back over, tucking the offending hand back into the hessian. The man stood up, checking the forest for signs of life. "Right, let's get this done." He rolled the corpse over a few times before it dropped into the hole, a muted thud drifting up to his ears as he grabbed the shovel. He set to it, shovelling dirt into the hole, not wanting to stop until his clandestine activities had been concealed. After thirty minutes, he took a swig of coke from his bottle before heading back over to the grave with two large bags of mulch. *Sorted,* he confirmed, hardly noticing any difference in the forest floor. For good measure, the large man kicked some surrounding earth over the freshly dug grave before heading back to the van for the final time.

Two minutes later, the engine noise died away, the forest returning to normal. Birds chirped in the trees as a light wind blew in from the Atlantic. A squirrel scurried along the ground, standing to attention before scooting up a tree as footsteps approached. "What the hell's going on?" Cara whispered. Her foot lightly brushed the forest floor, a chill running through the woman as her mind raced. *Does Joe know about this?* She looked at the ground, taking her house keys out of her pocket before scoring the nearest tree with three jagged lines. The woman looked down at the grave as a stronger breeze whistled through the trees. Hugging herself, Cara looked over at the outbuildings at the edge of the forest. *I don't know who you were, but I swear I'll find out. And if Joe's involved, I'll bring this crashing down on top of him.*

CHAPTER
EIGHT

Joe smiled as the bigger man approached. "No problems?"

"Like I said on the phone, all sorted."

The blond man blew out a breath, sagging slightly. "Good work, Martin. I owe you one. Let's hope that's the end of it."

"Aye, Frank looked pretty pissed last night."

Joe nodded. "Like he said - no more mistakes. Local clientele only. Anyway, I want you to do something for me. Something discreet."

"Go on," Martin replied, his eyes narrowing.

"I want you to keep an eye on Cara."

"Cara?"

"Yes. Not sure what my wife's up to, but she's been going out a lot more often."

"You think she's playing away?"

Joe leant against his Range Rover. "Honestly, no, but she's up to something, and I want to know what it is."

"Fair enough. When do you want me to start?"

"What have you got on today?"

"Just the usual stuff," he shrugged. "It can wait, though."

"Okay. Try and stay out of sight."

"C'mon," Martin smiled. "This is me you're talking about."

∼

She hurried out of the house, shoving her mobile phone into her back before shaking fingers tried to unlock her car. "Shit," Cara cursed, tossing her handbag onto the passenger seat before firing up her Toyota SUV. The tyres sent gravel skittering across manicured lawns before she pulled out onto the road, heading south. Her eyes flitted to the clock as the car lurched forward. "Should be there by twelve," she reckoned, flicking on the radio as Take That filled the interior. Cara began humming along, dark thoughts of dead bodies blowing out of the open window as she merged onto the Atlantic Highway towards St Ives. As the song ended, she dropped the volume as more thoughts invaded her mind. *Surely not,* she tried to convince herself. *A body. Not even Joe's that stupid.* The blast of a horn cut through her thoughts, Cara edging back over the road markings as an oncoming van flashed its lights.

"Stupid cow!" a passing voice hollered as the yellow van whizzed.

"Shit! Focus on the road," she scolded herself, lifting her foot as the speed reduced slightly. Off to her right, the ocean buffeted the rugged coastline, Cara's jangling nerves beginning to subside as the sound of the sea permeated the car's interior. "He'll know what to do," she reassured herself. "He always does."

∼

Ninety minutes later, her RAV4 pulled up on a side street, close to the town's harbour. Seagulls flew overhead as she set off on foot, their familiar calls easing her tension. The tang of the sea air filled her lungs, Cara's breathing coming under control as she turned a corner onto the harbour. Weaving through locals and holiday-makers, she quickly found herself outside a familiar fisherman's cottage, its dark purple door complete with a brass knocker. She rapped twice, turning as a boat chugged its way back to the stone dock, the boat's crew hastily preparing to offload their catch.

"Hello, you," a male voice announced.

She turned, smiling up at the man, a tinge of sadness settling over her. "Uncle Harry," she replied, tiptoeing to plant a kiss on the middle-aged man's face.

"Come in," he ushered his niece inside. "I'll put a pot of coffee on. Should be ready in a few minutes. Go through."

She walked down the hallway, turning into the property's kitchen, sunlight streaming in through the windows. Seating herself, she watched as her uncle made a big fuss about preparing the drinks. Her gaze settled on him, more sadness gripping her chest. "You even make coffee like he used to."

Harry stopped, a fully-laden spoon balancing its contents as he smiled sadly. "Aye. I guess I do. Not a day goes by that I don't think of him. Your mother too. I miss them, Cara."

A tear slipped down her cheek, brushing it away she fought to steady her emotions. "I know you do, Uncle Harry. They'd be happy to know that we've become close."

"They would." He turned, finishing the drinks before placing a chunky mug on the breakfast bar before he pulled up a stool. "Now. Tell me what's gotten you so spooked."

Cara took a deep breath, shaking fingers gripping the mug as she began. "I couldn't say much over the phone, but I saw Martin digging a big hole in the ground close to The Retreat."

"Go on."

"Then, he carried a large bundle from the van, dropped it into the hole and covered it over. It looked like a body."

The grey-haired man rubbed his chin, the police detective inside him kicking into gear. "Okay. Let's say you're right. Let's say it was a body. Who was it, and how did Joe come to be in possession of it?"

She blew out a breath, her shoulders sagging. "I've no idea. He was out on Saturday night, at the golf club with his usual cronies."

"Cronies?"

"You know, the well-to-do men of the surrounding villages. It's their weekly escape."

"We all need an escape from time to time."

She smiled, loving her uncle's pragmatic mind. "Tell me about it."

"Okay, so he was there all night?"

"Yes."

"And what time did he get home?"

"Not sure. After midnight."

"And where was he yesterday?"

Her mind was racing. "Home for most of the day. He did pop out, though, to see his father."

"Ah, how is Frank?"

"Same as ever. Ruler of Cornwall."

The man smiled ruefully. "Some leopards never changed their spots. Okay, so you think that a body has been buried. Let's say you're correct. There are only a few credible scenarios. First, they killed this mystery person and buried them in the woods. Second, they found a dead body but didn't want to alert the police. Or third, it was an accident, and Joe wanted to conceal it."

"But why would he do that if it was an accident?" Cara questioned.

"That's the sixty-four-million-dollar question. Why indeed? You say that he was at the golf club?"

"Yes."

"Okay. The golf club is a few miles away. Let's say that something happened, and a person wound up dead – they'd have to have kept it quiet from everyone there. No mean feat."

Cara twirled her dark locks, trying to build a scenario in her mind. After a few seconds, something came to her. "The Retreat."

"Go on."

"Maybe he wasn't at the golf club? Maybe Joe was at The Retreat. It's only a few hundred yards from where I saw Martin."

"Why would he lie about where he was going?"

"This is Joe we're talking about. It comes naturally."

~

An hour later, Cara wound her way through St Ives, her mind a tumult of thoughts and possibilities. Ahead, a flower shop came into view, the woman spotting a small car park opposite as she indicated to pull in. She noticed one remaining space as she pulled in, the SUV swinging over to the tightly packed cars as an engine revved nearby. Engaging reverse, she carefully backed in, looking over her shoulder as a red car skidded to a halt next to her driver's door. "Jesus!" she exclaimed, seeing the angry face of a young woman as she gesticulated at her from behind the windscreen. Regaining her composure, Cara edged back the last few feet, the red car moving forward to block her exit.

"Oi, that's my space," a female voice hollered.

Cara turned, seeing a young woman inches from her window. She was a few years her junior, with pale skin and long brown hair scraped back into a ponytail. She noticed the homemade tattoos that adorned her hands and arms, her pulse quickening. "Sorry, looks like it's mine now."

"Don't get smart with me, bitch! I was about to pull in there."

"Look, you could see that I was reversing into it. I'll only be a few minutes, and then it's yours."

"I want it now. Move your car, or else."

The skin drained from Cara's olive complexion, her knuckles turning white as she gripped the steering wheel. "Or else, what?"

"Or else you'll be sorry."

"Look, I don't know who you are, but childish threats won't work on me. I was here first. You go and find another space."

The woman pulled a phone out of her jogging bottoms, pressing it to her ear. "Callum. I need you to come down to Bridge Street car park. Now. Some bitch has stolen my parking space, and she needs sorting out."

Shit! I don't need this.

"She's going nowhere, but I need you to sort her out." She ended the call, sneering at the older woman. "Not so cocky now, are ya? Me fella's on his way, bitch! You picked the wrong people to fuck with."

"Look, I'll move. I don't want any trouble," Cara replied, her voice shaky as a bead of sweat slithered down her back.

"You're going nowhere. Not until Callum's set the record straight." She moved away from the driver's window, slouching on her red Vauxhall.

Shit. I need to get out of here. She weighed up the options, wondering who could help her. *No, not Uncle Harry,* she thought. *I don't want to drag him into this.* She stopped thinking about a possible escape as a man jogged into the car park. He was panting, his tracksuit clinging to his bulky frame. Cara noticed the scar on the man's neck as he slowed down, his eyes settling on her.

"Problem?" he began, stepping closer to the car.

"I don't want any trouble," Cara replied evenly, her stomach tightening as her hands trembled in her lap.

"The snooty cow stole my parking space," the woman piped up, enjoying the moment.

Cara looked around the car park, hoping someone would spot the altercation and offer some help. No one was around, though, the car park and street beyond seemingly deserted. "I didn't. I was just here first. Your girlfriend nearly crashed into me as I reversed in."

"Bollocks," the woman spat. "I was about to drive in when she almost reversed into me."

Callum edged closer to the window, Cara smelling the stale aroma of alcohol and cigarettes. "Looks like you picked the wrong car park, love. Now, how do we sort this out?"

"Look, I don't want any trouble. If your girlfriend moves her car, I'll let her have it."

The man shook his head, his eyes dropping down as he smiled. "Sorry. It's gone beyond that. Tell you what, you give me your watch, and we'll call it quits."

She looked down, tears peppering her eyes as she stared at the timepiece on her wrist. "You're not having my watch. It was my mother's." An image flashed before Cara. Her mother's smile, warm and full of life. In the blink of an eye, the memory faded. "I have money," she offered, pulling her purse out hastily. A vice-like grip encircled her wrist, Cara flinching as she tried to pull away. The man was too strong, unclipping the Omega before slipping it off her wrist. "Give me that back!" she screamed, opening the car door as the Callum took a step back.

"I'll have your purse too," he sneered, snapping his fingers.

She lunged for the watch in his hand, barging into him as they bumped into the car in the next space. "Give it back."

She heard laughter, the man toying with her as he pinned her against the car. "Proper feisty, aren't ya. I bet you're a right goer between the sheets."

Something snapped inside her, Cara reacting before she could think about her actions. She spat in the man's face, seeing his expression turn from victorious to fury. *Shit.*

"Bitch," he swore, slapping her hard across the face as she slammed into the RAV4, her vision swimming. "You know who I am? No one fucks with me in this town. I'll..."

The words ended, Cara looking up as another figure filled her view. A large man spun Callum around, his fist connecting. She heard the skittering sound of teeth hit the tarmac as the man went down in a heap. "Wanker," the woman screamed, flailing her arms at the unknown man, a sharp back-handed slap sending her to the ground.

"You okay?" Martin asked, stooping to retrieve the watch from the unconscious man's hand.

"Martin? How - what are you doing here?"

"Never mind that. You're bleeding. Are you okay?"

Cara touched her lip, wincing slightly as a blood-smeared finger came into view. "I'm okay, I think. Where did you come from?"

"I said never mind that. Get back in the car. I'll move this piece of shit," he gestured behind him. "Head straight home. You understand?"

She nodded, her body trembling as the man stirred on the floor. "Okay."

"Cunt," Callum slurred. "You know who I am?" He rose to his feet groggily, banging into the car behind him.

"No. But you've messed with the wrong woman."

"I'll fuck you up, bro," he shouted, reaching into his joggers.

Martin looked down, seeing the glint of steel as a knife came into view. Before the man could make his move, a thunderous right hand smashed into his face, Cara hearing the sickening snap of bone. Moving quickly for a big man, Martin released the handbrake from the Vauxhall, moving it back a few feet before motioning for Cara to drive out. "Straight home. You understand?"

"Yes. Thank you."

"This stays between us. Okay?"

"Okay." She gunned the engine, turning quickly out of the car park as she struggled to change gear. *Jesus Christ!* She looked down at her wrist, the watch back where it belonged. *Where did he come from? He's miles from home.* A realisation washed over her, Cara shaking her head in disbelief. *Was he following me? Why would he do that?* Another thought struck home, Cara drawing in a breath. "The body."

CHAPTER NINE

Steve sat at his computer, leafing through the notepad on the desk. He read and re-read the notes, an idea of starting his first project forming in his mind. Chapter One appeared on the screen, his fingers flying over the keyboard for an hour, his coffee and the outside world ignored as his fledgeling story began to take shape. Eventually, he stopped, pleased with his progress as he clicked save on the document before looking at the cold dregs of coffee in the bottom of the mug. Knowing that he tended to focus on the task at hand, like with his paintings, Steve smiled. Stretching as he stood up, he walked from the dining room into the kitchen, flicking the kettle on as he looked out the window. The rear garden was immaculate, save for the odd scooter and football that littered his pristine lawn. The phone rang, tearing his gaze away from the garden, he walked over to the wall to retrieve it. "Hello," he began, the noisy kettle making him step into the hallway.

"It's me," Rosie stated flatly.

"Oh, hi. You okay?"

"I need you to pick me up."

He frowned as the kettle finally settled down. "Where are you?"

"Bude."

"What are you doing there?"

"That's not important. I need a lift back home. What are you doing?"

He shrugged. "I was just doing a spot of writing."

"Writing? Writing what?"

"A book. Got a few ideas, so I thought I'd give it a go."

"Jesus, Steve! Can't you think of anything more productive to do?"

He gripped the receiver, his pulse increasing. "It's my day off. The house is tidy, and the kids are at school. Can I not have a bit of enjoyment?"

"Whatever," she sighed. "Well, I need a lift, and that's more important than some silly hobby."

He slumped against the wall, asking where she'd be waiting. After relaying the information, the line went dead, the man staring at the plastic handset before placing it back in the cradle. "Fuck," he cursed, the coffee forgotten.

Twenty minutes later, he pulled up next to an ice cream parlour, his wife stomping over to the van before slamming the door. "You took your time."

"Nice to see you too. Anyway, what are you doing in Bude?"

"A job interview," was the stilted response.

Steve looked at his wife's attire, her tight blue dress more suitable for a beach party than a job interview. "Where?"

She huffed. "Jesus! What's with all the questions? At the vets. They want a receptionist, and I thought I'd apply."

"Just asking. No need to get all defensive."

"Whatever, Steve. Anyway, what are you doing for the rest of the day?"

"I thought I'd do a bit more writing before picking the kids up from school."

"Bloody hell. Why bother."

"Because I enjoy it – like my painting."

"Always got your head in the clouds. Your paintings aren't even that good."

"Thanks! Kick a man while he's down; why don't you."

"Just stating a fact," she shrugged. They drove on in silence, Steve's mind working overtime as he navigated the narrow country lanes of north Cornwall. As they neared their destination, Rosie turned to him. "I need to pick something up from Steph's. Can you make a quick detour?"

"Fine," he shrugged.

A few minutes later, the van pulled up outside a row of cottages nestled close to the road. "I won't be long," she said, leaving him to his thoughts.

Steve stared across the open fields to his right, the Atlantic shimmering in the autumn sunlight. He took a breath, letting the stresses ease until a noise to his left made him start. It was the sound of a text message, Steve looking down at his wife's bag on the bench seat. He looked at the cottage, seeing no signs of activity. Reaching inside the bag, Steve pulled out a black Nokia handset. He activated it, a text message appearing on the yellow screen.

Same time next week, sexy. Xxx

A knot formed in his stomach as he read the message over and over. The sender was a man called Mark. He knew no one called Mark, but Rosie did. Scrolling up, more sordid exchanges appeared that made beads of sweat break out across his forehead. "Bitch," he spat, noticing something poking out of his wife's bag. A packet of male contraceptives, which on inspection had two condoms missing. He slammed his head into the headrest, punching the steering wheel multiple times until he heard laughter nearby. Looking over, Steve could see Rosie and Steph giggling on the front doorstep, the man unable to listen to the conversation. "Giving her the gory details, you fucking bitch!" he hissed. As the women hugged their goodbyes, Steve placed the phone and condoms in the glovebox, starting the engine as Rosie climbed into the cab.

"Let's go," Rosie chirped, a broad smile on her face. The van pulled away from the cottages, winding its way down the lane until they joined another, hedgerows skimming past them as Steve increased the speed. Rosie looked over at him, her ebullient mood vanishing when she saw his tear-streaked face. "Steve? What's up?"

"Open the glove box," he replied flatly.

She did so, her eyes widening as she saw her phone and the condom box. Rosie looked over at him, her complexion darkening. "You've been through my bag?"

"You had a text message. From someone called Mark who wants to do the same again next week. Tell me, did you use both condoms with him, or has someone else been screwing you?"

Rosie stuffed the items back into her bag, rounding on her husband. "What gives you the right to go through my bag?"

"Err, hello, you're having it away with someone else," he exclaimed. "Do you not think I have the right to know that?"

"I want a divorce," she countered, her words slamming into him.

"Suits me. I can't live like this anymore."

"Good. And I'm having the house and the kids."

"What?" he exclaimed. "You're sleeping with other men, but I'm the one who has to move out and lose the kids? I don't think so, Rosie. I'll fight you every step of the way."

"Well, we'll see about that. I'm their mother, and that counts more than anything."

"Really? Well, you're a terrible mother. You don't give a shit about the kids; you never have. All you care about is yourself and the men that you screw. You fucking slag!" He didn't see the slap coming, a left-hander that slammed his head into the window. His vision filled with a million stars, Steve feeling his body lurch towards his wife as a thundering sound reverberated inside the cab. Time seemed to slow down as he felt the seatbelt lock around his waist, his skull crashing into something hard. Then, darkness.

∼

His eyes opened, blinking a few times before they closed again, the harsh lights above almost searing his eyelids. He heard his pulse beating loudly between his ears, Steve becoming aware of a constant beeping sound and far-off voices. After a few minutes, he opened his eyes again, his vision eventually coming into focus. "Ugh," he croaked, a shadow falling across him, blocking out the overhead lights.

"Steve?" a female voice said.

He felt a hand wrap around his, the skin cool, the grip firm. He looked up, seeing a dark-haired woman staring down at him. "Cara?"

"I'll get the nurse."

"Hang on. Where am I?"

"Truro hospital. Do you remember what happened?"

He frowned, trying to recollect his last memory. "I was in the van with Rosie. She wants a divorce."

"Oh, Steve," Cara replied, squeezing his hand.

"The kids. Where are the kids?"

"Don't worry. They're staying with us. Malcolm is looking after them. They don't know yet."

Shaking his head, he looked up at his sister-in-law. "They don't know what?"

He saw the tears in her eyes, knowing something terrible was coming. "I'm so sorry, Steve. Rosie didn't make it. She died."

The next few hours were a blur, doctors and nurses popping in to check him over, informing Steve that he'd been fortunate to have only sustained a broken collar bone and bruising. He wanted to escape, to wrap his arms around his beloved children and hear their laughter. Although a dreamer, he was also pragmatic – knowing that laughter would be in short supply over the coming days and weeks. After a long conversation with the local police, Steve sat up in bed, trying his best to eat an egg and watercress sandwich, washed down with a cup of tepid water. Cara had promised to visit him later with the children. He wanted to see them more than anything in the world. But he knew he'd have to tell them about Rosie. Shit! *What do I say to them?* After finishing off his lunch, he pushed the table away, a weariness settling over him. Despite the activity around him, Steve succumbed to the darkness once more.

∼

"Daddy," Hattie squealed, diving onto the bed.

"Careful, princess," Steve winced, pulling his daughter onto his lap with his free arm. He buried his face into her blonde hair, inhaling her smell as his eyes shut tightly.

"Daddy," another voice exclaimed, Steve, looking over at his other daughter.

"Hey, pumpkin," he replied, welcoming Chloe into his embrace, the pain forgotten as the two seven-year-olds wriggled. He looked up, seeing Matthew stood by the door with Cara, his expression guarded. "Hi, Son."

"Dad," he replied, tears falling freely.

"Hey, come here," Steve croaked, his resolve beginning to crumble as his son walked around the bed before snuggling into him.

"Do you want a drink?" Cara asked from the doorway.

As he stared over at her, Steve noticed a discolouration to his sister-in-law's cheek, the man frowning before replying. "I could murder a cup of tea," he said, regretting his words instantly.

"Okay. I'll be back in a minute."

The girls fussed over him, curious expressions on their faces as they inspected his bandages and bruises. "Daddy," Chloe began. "Where's Mummy?"

His stomach turned to lead, Steve knowing that this would be the hardest thing his children would ever hear. Taking a breath, he composed himself. "I'm so sorry, guys. Mummy was hurt really badly when I crashed the van. She died."

"What?" Chloe replied, a look of disbelief on her face.

"Come here," Steve croaked, his emotions boiling over as his daughter's bottom lip began to quiver.

"Mum's dead?" Matthew said.

Steve looked to his left as he gathered both girls into his embrace. "I'm so sorry, Son."

His eldest child backed away, turning to run as Cara entered the room. "Whoa," she exclaimed as the boy darted out of the room.

"Matt," Steve cried, gripping the girls tightly as they began sobbing.

"No, Daddy. No! She can't be dead," Hattie blurted.

"I'm so sorry, pumpkin. Really, I am." He looked up at his

sister-in-law as she placed two cups on the cupboard next to the bed, walking over to the girls.

"Come here, Hattie," she soothed, the girl flinging herself into her auntie's arms. "I'm so sorry, poppet."

"Auntie Cara, Mummy's dead."

"I know," she replied, tears streaming down her cheeks.

"Why didn't you die?" Chloe asked her father.

"I don't know," he started, remembering the look of fury on Rosie's face before the world had turned dark. "I'm so sorry." He began to cry again, his daughter clinging to him, the embrace offering some solace.

"What do we do now, Daddy?" Hattie asked from across the room.

"I don't know," the man said, shaking his head. "But don't worry, we'll get through this." He watched his daughter retreat into her auntie's arms, not knowing how he could keep that promise.

CHAPTER 10
AUTUMN 2000

Eight weeks after his wife's funeral, Steve pulled up outside the shop on the edge of the village. "Wait here, guys."

Hattie and Chloe nodded quietly, the toll from the past few months clearly showing.

"Do you want something from the shop?"

Chloe looked across at her father. "Crisps."

"Hattie?"

"The same, please."

He gave them his best smile, deflating as his twins tried their best to reciprocate, the smiles never reaching their eyes. *Shit*, he thought as he climbed out of the van. Walking inside, Steve turned left, taking a few moments to fill in a lottery ticket before weaving his way through the aisles, his arms loaded with provisions as he reached the counter. A woman smiled at him. One that he'd never seen before. "Hello," she chirped, Steve's dark mood lifting slightly.

"Hi. Just this, thanks," he replied, dropping the groceries onto the counter. He studied the woman as she retrieved a plastic bag from below the counter. She looked in his age bracket, with short dark hair that was shaved on one side. A nose stud with a blue gem set into it twinkled under the overhead lights. "Are you new?"

"Been here a few weeks. Name's Dee," she responded confidently as a rustling sound filled the small convenience store.

"I'm Steve. Pleased to meet you."

"Likewise," she smiled, the rustling sound dying off as she moved the bag across the counter.

He paid for his goods, nodding his thanks before heading out into the sullen Saturday afternoon. He slammed the van door, handing over two bags of beef Monster Munch and a bottle of cola each. "Here you go." He breathed out. "Right, let's go and pick up your brother."

A few minutes later, the van rolled along the gravel driveway, Steve's nerves increasing as the large house filled the windscreen. He pulled to a stop next to his brother's Range Rover, looking for activity inside. "Chloe, do you want to go and grab him?"

"Can I go too?" Hattie enquired; her lips dotted with remnants of her lunchtime treat

"Okay. But we're not stopping, guys. We need to get back."

The girls hurried out of the van, Hattie knocking loudly on the stout front door. Breathe, he told himself as the door opened, Cara smiling down at her nieces. They disappeared, the dark-haired woman braving the chilly breeze as she walked over to the van. He rolled down the window, smiling out at her. "Hi."

"Hey. You okay?"

"Getting there. How's Matthew been?"

"Okay. A bit quiet when Tristan's around. He's been upstairs with Lizzy and Tom for a few hours."

"Thanks for having him, Cara. I really do appreciate it."

"We're family. Think nothing of it."

The crunching of gravel signalled someone approaching, a familiar figure coming into view. "Steve," Joe said amiably. "You okay?"

"I'm good," was the clipped response, the younger brother gripping the steering wheel.

Joe smiled. "You can come in. No need to sit out here."

"I'm fine where I am," was the curt reply, Steve's eyes burning into his brother's.

"Oh well, the offer was there." He turned to Cara. "I'll go and get ready then." He walked off, the front door closing as Steve breathed out.

Cara placed a hand over his. "It's alright."

He sank back in his seat. "Sorry. I just don't like coming here."

"Because he's here."

"Yes."

"That's understandable. I don't like it when he's here either."

Steve laughed. An alien sound that brought him up short. "That's the first time I've done that since Rosie."

"It will get better, love. That might sound like a hollow promise right now. But it will."

"Honestly, I'm okay. It's the kids who are going through the mill. They loved their mother."

"I know they did. And being honest back, I never liked Rosie. I don't want to speak ill of the dead, but she treated you like shit. You deserve better."

If only you knew. I could tell her. Steve went to reply, biting his lip. "Maybe. I just can't think straight at the moment."

"Look, you've got my number. Call me anytime. I could pop over for a cuppa, and we can put the world to rights."

A noise erupted behind them, five sets of feet running

towards the van. Steve climbed out, walking over to his niece and nephew. "Hello, you two."

"Hello, Uncle Steve," Lizzy and Tom replied happily.

"How have you been?"

"Good. We've been playing the PlayStation. Matthew wants one for Christmas," Lizzy beamed.

Steve looked at his sister-in-law, smiling. "Well, we'd better hope he's a good boy over the next few weeks. Or Santa will fly straight past." He looked up, seeing his brother standing in his bedroom, peering down at them. "Come on then, guys. Let's head home. Thank your Auntie Cara for having you, Matt."

"Thanks," he said, letting the woman pull him into her arms.

"My pleasure." She kissed the top of his head, closing her eyes briefly as the young boy clung to her. Then, he was moving around the van, opening the door for his sisters.

Steve looked at Cara, his peripheral vision noticing his brother's gaze upon him. "Thanks again," he began, hugging her. "I'll take you up on the cuppa."

She kissed him on the cheek. "Stay strong. For the children."

"You too," he breathed into her ear, the brief contact broken as he pulled open the van door.

She waved them off, standing under darkening skies as a chill ran through her. *Poor guy,* she thought, turning to see her husband staring down at her, arms folded across his bare chest. *If only you were more like your brother.*

∽

The van trundled up the gravel driveway, Martin looking in awe at the lit-up residence in front of him. He loved the Stuart's house, dreaming that one day he'd own such a palatial residence instead of his tiny cottage where he constantly had to bend down to get through doorways. As he applied the handbrake, Joe strolled out of the front door, a sports jacket slung over his shoulder. "Alright, boss," he said as the blond-haired man shut the door.

"I am. Very good, in fact."

"Oh. Like that is it?" He shot his boss a knowing smile that had Joe chuckling.

"Fat chance of that at home. It's what's awaiting me at The Retreat that I'm looking forward to."

"Well, they arrived about half an hour ago."

"Six?"

"Aye. One for each of us."

"Well, let's get over there sharpish. And do we have the cameras set up?"

"We do. I'm sure our friend won't notice them while he's got his hands full."

"Then lead on, good man." The van pulled out onto the country lane, Martin taking it slowly. Joe looked over at him, the events from earlier still on his mind. "I saw my brother earlier."

"Oh. Where?"

"At the house. Matthew came over for a few hours, and Steve picked him up."

"Did you speak?"

"Barely," Joe replied nonchalantly.

"What's the beef with you two?"

Normally, Joe would not divulge such information. But he was in a good mood, the thought of what was to come, lowering the man's defences. He played it cautiously, though. "He thinks we killed Mum."

"I thought she drowned?"

"She did, but Steve has some crazy conspiracy that me and Dad bumped her off."

The bigger man shook his head. "I don't understand; why would you bump her off?"

Joe knew he could trust Martin. He knew the bigger man's secrets, like Martin knew his. They both had the power to send the other one down for a long time, albeit at their own expense. "Mum was having an affair."

"Jesus! With who?"

"I know I can trust you, Martin. This stays between us." A brief nod from across the cab was enough for Joe. "She was seeing Antony."

"Old Antony?"

"Yes. I love my father, but I knew that things were not right at home. I guess I take after him, never satisfied with one woman." He breathed out, his eyes scanning the Cornish countryside as the sun dipped below the horizon. "I guess they just grew apart, Mum finding love elsewhere."

"Jeez," the Scotsman said, not knowing what else to add.

"Dad knew about it but was happy to keep the status quo. Not long after he found out, Mum was washed out to sea."

"Was she with Antony at the time?"

"No. She'd been walking the dog along the coastal path. She must have fallen somehow."

"What happened to the dog?" It was a fair question, or so Martin thought.

"Benji was the one who alerted us. We found him whining at the door. That's when we knew something was wrong."

"Sorry, boss. A sad tale."

"Yes, but Steve thinks something else happened. Something more sinister."

"But why would he think that?"

"Why indeed," Joe countered as The Retreat came into view, glad that the conversation was at an end, and the evening was just beginning.

THE RETREAT

~

Cara slipped out of the kitchen door, her friend supervising the children as she sipped a large glass of wine. The dark-haired woman made her way across the lawns into the treeline beyond, her dark clothing quickly being consumed by the night. After a few minutes traversing the forest, she unzipped her tracksuit top, Cara feeling beads of sweat trickling down her back. She carried on, the forest growing darker with each step until she saw far off lights, music drifting through the trees to her advancing position. The Retreat sat under a clear sky, illuminated like a lone sentinel a few hundred yards ahead. She could see people out on the decking, an aroma wafting around her. *Grilled meat.* She caught a glimpse of something, focusing on an individual next to the lawned area. *Joe!* Her quiet footsteps ate up the forest floor until she had an optimal view. Close enough to see what was going on. *Bastard,* she cursed inwardly, seeing her husband's long arm around a young woman in a tight black dress. She was young, no more than a teenager, Joe's hand firmly resting on her rear. Cara couldn't see her face, the woman facing the building. Yet, she knew she was glamourous. Sexy and totally into her husband. The father of their children. She gripped the branch of a tree, her knuckles turning white as they kissed, the others around them seeming to take no notice. "You bastard," she whispered as two others walked past him, heading towards her hiding place. Mr Samuels, Cara's eyes widening as the local headmaster almost hurried across the grass with another young woman. She was dark-skinned, Asian looking, Cara surmised as they closed on her position. *Shit!* She couldn't move; the fear of alerting someone froze her to the spot as giggling filtered through the trees. Pressing herself against the trunk, her fingers curled around the digital camera in her pocket as a conversation begun.

"Do you like me?"

"You've no idea," Samuel's rasped, Cara hearing his ragged breath nearby.

"How much?" the woman inquired.

"This much to start with." She heard the rustling of banknotes, peering around the tree and catching a glimpse as the woman tucked the money into her bra.

"Do you like me?" Samuels asked, fishing for compliments.

"I like you a lot more now."

"How much more?"

The conversation died, Cara closing her eyes until she heard the man gasp. Curiosity overcame her fears as she peeked around the tree once more, seeing the woman knelt in front of the middle-aged man, his hand resting on her head. *Jesus!*

"Oh yes. That's good. That's really good."

Oh my God! She closed her eyes, covering her ears as the pillar of the community was pleasured a few feet from where she stood. A few minutes later, a muffled cry made its way past her palms, signalling things had come to a head. Carefully, she pulled the camera out of her pocket, switching it on as Samuels clumsily pulled his trousers up. Switching off the flash, Cara took several shots of the retreating couple, taking a few steps to her right to capture some valuable images of her cheating husband. "Got you banged-to-rights," she snarled as Joe fawned all over his prize.

"You're trespassing," a voice said behind her.

Cara spun around, stifling a scream. In front of her, a giant loomed, dressed in dark clothing. "Martin?"

"Mrs Stuart," he frowned. "What are you doing here?"

Regaining her composure, she bit back. "I could ask you the same question. I thought my husband was supposed to be at the golf club?"

"Shite!" He noticed the camera in her hand, a knot forming in his gut. "Tell me you've not been taking pictures?"

"What if I have? That's my husband over there with his tongue down some young woman's throat. And John Samuels, what would Linda say if I told her what he's been up to?"

"You can't do that, Cara."

"Give me one good reason why not?"

He leant against a tree, his shoulders slumping in defeat. "I'm sorry you've had to see this. Really, I am. But I work for Joe. I'm loyal to Joe."

"Well, Joe's not loyal to me," she shot back.

"No, but neither are you."

"W-what?" she faltered.

"Why were you in St Ives?"

Cara did a double take, an incredulous expression spreading across her face. "What's that got to do with you?" A realisation hit the woman, like a spark triggering in her brain. "That's why you were there. He's asked you to keep tabs on me." The lack of a response confirmed her assumption. "Well, if you must know, I was seeing my uncle. But thanks for the heads-up. My husband is carrying on behind my back yet sends his bloodhound to keep an eye on his wife. His faithful wife. You couldn't make this shit up."

"Cara, I'm sorry. Sorry that you've found out like this. But I'm going to need your camera. You can't use those pictures as leverage."

"Watch me," she replied, making to walk past him.

He took a step to his left, blocking her path. "Don't make me do this."

"Martin. I've got no quarrel with you. You saved my skin down in St Ives, but don't think you can intimidate me."

"Give me the camera?"

"And if I say no?"

"Then I'll take it from you."

"No, Martin. You won't." She paused, taking a deep breath. "Y'see, this camera is not the only evidence I have against my husband. Or you?"

He flinched in the darkness, Cara seeing his expression change. "What do you mean?"

"The body, Martin. I saw you burying a body in the forest. Now, get out of my way, or I'll scream blue murder."

He stood there as the woman hurried past him, Martin sliding down a tree trunk a few seconds later. *Oh, no. We're fucked!*

CHAPTER ELEVEN

Snow blanketed the land as Cara wound her way along the country lane, the bleak Atlantic filling her view. She pulled off the main road, weaving around parked cars until she reached the red brick house on the edge of the village. Pulling her coat around her neck to ward off the chill, she trudged up the garden path, knocking on the door as she kicked her snow-covered boots against the wall. "Hi," Steve smiled as he opened the front door, warm air spilling out of the hallway.

"Hi," she replied. "What's all this about?"

"No idea," he smirked, seeing his sister-in-law's expression as she spread her arms wide. "Come in out of the cold; the kettle's on."

"Perfect timing." She kicked off her boots, following the dark-haired man into the kitchen as Oasis played quietly in the background.

"Tea or coffee?"

"I'd love a coffee," Cara smiled, watching as the man pulled a cafetiere out of the cupboard before letting it brew.

"So, how're things?"

"Oh, you know, same as ever."

"And the kids?"

"Good. Tom's getting back into the swing of it. I think his confidence is slowly coming back. Although, there's a boy in his class who's giving him a hard time. I've spoken to the headmaster, who assures me that he'll sort it."

"Kids. They can be right little bastards sometimes."

"Tell me about it. I've got one living under my roof."

"Tristan?"

"Yes. He never talks to Tom. Doesn't even acknowledge him, and I caught him kicking Hooper."

"Hooper?"

"Tom's dog. They're inseparable at the moment."

"Maybe Tristan's a bit jealous," Steve offered.

"Perhaps. I just think that he's a carbon copy of Joe."

"Jeez. Let's hope not," he winked, placing the coffee on the table.

"I'm not holding out much hope. Anyway, what's new with you? You sounded a bit tense on the phone."

Steve placed the cups on the table, blowing out a long breath. "I have something to tell you. No one knows about it yet, not even the kids."

"Okay, you know I can keep a secret."

"I know. That's why you're the first one to know."

"Come on then; the suspense is killing me."

"Okay," he began, trying to find the words. "Well, I kinda won the lottery."

She frowned, not digesting his words until a lop-sided grin appeared on his face. "The lottery?"

"Yeah. Last weekend. I put my usual numbers on and never gave it another thought until Monday. I had to check the numbers on the Ceefax about a dozen times before it finally sank in."

"How much have you won?" Cara placed her elbows on the table, the world around them forgotten.

"Fifteen million."

"W-what?" she stammered. "You're kidding?"

"No. I still can't believe it. Things like this happen to other people. Not me."

Cara was out of her chair, rounding the table to embrace her brother-in-law. "Bloody hell, Steve! I don't know what to say. Oh my God!"

He hugged her back, the pair laughing as snowflakes fell outside. After a moment, they came apart, Steve grinning like a schoolboy. "It's been a rollercoaster few days, that's for sure. Someone from Camelot's coming here tomorrow to do the necessary paperwork before they hand over the cash. That's another reason why I wanted to talk to you."

"Oh, why?"

He grinned again, an infectious smirk that made the woman reciprocate. "Well, because you're loaded. I've had the same bank account since I was sixteen. What do I do?"

She considered the question, depressing the cafetiere's plunger before sitting down. "Pour the coffees," the woman grinned.

Thirty minutes later, Steve rocked back on his chair, lacing his fingers behind his head. "Jesus! It's so much to take in."

"It might seem that way right now. But you'll get used to it."

He drained his mug, refilling the coffee pot as the weather outside took a turn for the worse, the once gentle snowflakes now pelting the windowpanes. "You want another?"

She checked her watch, nodding over at him. "Why not. I've got time." She watched him as he began to make the drinks. *I wish Joe were more like him. He's kind. A gentleman.* "Have you had any thoughts about what you'll do?"

"A few," he replied, turning around as the kettle started to rumble. "I'm going to sell this place."

"I thought you would. Rosie?"

He sighed. "Yes. This was her house. The house is full of her memories. The kids are okay – truth be told, they're coping better than I thought they would. We weren't happy, Cara. This house is filled with the wrong kind of memories. So, I've contacted the local agent, who's coming over next week to value it."

"I think you're doing the right thing. Even with Rosie gone, the house is a bit small." She caught herself, wondering if she'd said the wrong thing. Dark eyes looked over at her brother-in-law, gauging his reaction.

He smiled. "None taken," he chuckled. "It is small, not that I want something as palatial as your manor house. Just something nice, where we can stretch our legs."

She looked at him, smiling. "You've already found something, haven't you?"

He held up his hands, trying to calm his sister-in-law. "Look, it's early days, but yes, I've seen something."

"Where?"

"Upton," he replied, giving in to her infectious enthusiasm.

"Nice. Handy for everything too."

"I thought so. It's only a few miles to the kid's school, and Bude is just up the road."

"And we're just a stone's throw away."

"Good point. I saw it in the paper. An old barn that's been converted."

"Lovely. Well, I'm crossing my fingers for you. Jeez, I never expected today to go like this."

"I never expected this year to go like this." His smile waned, turning to fill the coffee pot. "Am I a bad man for feeling so happy?"

She came off her chair, putting an arm around the man's broad shoulders. "Don't be daft. Rosie treated you like shit, Steve. Yes, it's terrible what happened to her, but you've got a chance at a new life. One where the kids can grow up without hearing their parents fighting all the time. I'd love a life like that."

He kissed the top of her head, breaking the embrace to concentrate on the drinks. "You deserve better too."

"Maybe. But what do I do?"

"Divorce him. The family is toxic." His words were more potent than he thought, seeing Cara flinch. "Sorry. Not you guys. I love you all to bits. But Frank and Joe, they're something else."

If only you knew, she thought, banishing images of buried corpses. "Like father like son."

"Something like that."

"Anyway, what else are you planning? You've already bought a house."

"Well, I do have another idea."

∼

"Where have you been?" Joe growled as Cara entered the kitchen.

She walked over, her eyes drifting towards the stove, a pan full of baked beans slowly simmering. "If you must know, I popped over to see your brother."

"Steve? Why?"

Shit, she cursed, trying to backtrack. "He's been thinking of writing a book and wanted to run it by me," she countered smoothly, the memory of her brother-in-law's new hobby a grateful intervention.

"So, why does he need to run that by you? You're hardly an expert."

She deflected the barb, walking over to the fridge to retrieve a carton of juice. "Maybe not, but I read all the time. Steve knows I do, so maybe he wanted to bounce a few ideas off me."

"What else has he been bouncing off you?" Joe replied as two rounds of toast popped up.

"We're not all like you, Joe."

"Meaning?"

She knew that she'd started something, seeing the look on her husband's face. "Never mind. I'm going to freshen up before I pick the kids up. Enjoy your lunch."

A few minutes later, Joe pushed his empty plate to one side, dialling a familiar number. "Martin," he began. "Where are you?"

"At the clubhouse. The Christmas tree has arrived."

Knowing that the team at Sandy Shores would be busy all afternoon decorating the clubhouse, Joe nodded, ready for Christmas revellers. "Okay. I'll be down in ten minutes."

Nine minutes later, Joe walked into the clubhouse's entrance, the place a hive of activity as staff were in the throes of unboxing decorations, while Malcolm and a few others were erecting the large fir tree next to the stage. "Looks good," he began, noticing a few new staff, one woman, in particular, catching his eye. "Newbies?"

"Yeah, seasonal workers."

Joe's eyes settled on the one woman, liking her short dark hair. He never saw the other man approach, a nudge on his shoulder snapping him back to reality. He looked down at the wiry man, dark rodent-like eyes staring up at him. "David. How's it going?"

Sandy Shores, Operations Manager, smiled. "We're on track, boss," he replied, his nasal voice grating on Joe. "All the cabins are made up, ready for our guests next weekend."

"That's good. It looks like they're pulling out all the stops to have it all ready."

"They are," the smaller man agreed.

"Who's that?" Joe motioned over towards the dark-haired woman he'd spotted earlier.

"Dee. Tara's gone off on maternity leave, so I needed extra hands."

"Hmm, not seen her before."

"No, she's recently moved to the area."

An idea formed in Joe's mind, knowing that he was at a loose end this weekend, with no activities planned. He needed an outlet. "Why don't you give all staff a treat tonight. Put some food and drinks on. It's the least we can do."

He looked at Martin, who was one step ahead of the blond man. "Good idea," he affirmed.

"Yes, they would appreciate that," David gushed. "Malcolm can organise the grub."

"Okay, listen up, everyone," Joe called, the staff turning round as the man waved them over. "We all know how hard you've worked to give our guests an unforgettable Christmas experience at Sandy Shores. I really appreciate your efforts and would like to give something back. So, tonight, we'll hold a low-key pre-Christmas get-together for all staff." He let the news sink in, men and women nodding their agreement as an excited murmur drifted across the clubhouse. "I know some of the staff are out and about, so please give them the heads-up." He looked at the dark-haired woman, taking a step towards her. "What time works for you?"

The woman looked around at her colleagues, shrugging her shoulders. "Eight?"

More nods and murmurings before Joe clapped his hands. "Great. See you at eight then." He turned towards the two men as the workers went back to their tasks. "I take it you'll be here?"

"Wouldn't miss it, boss," Martin smirked, knowing what the owner had in mind.

"I'll square it with Helen," David added cautiously. "She has book club on a Friday, but I'm sure I can change her mind."

"Okay. See you later. Martin, a word," Joe said, his voice becoming more business-like. "Any more news on my wife?"

The bigger man shrugged. "Not much. She's stayed close to home all week, except today."

"Where did she go?"

"To your brother's. She was there for about an hour or so."

"Notice anything unusual?"

"To be honest, no. I watched her go in, and then I headed around the back of the house. They were talking in the kitchen. They did hug. It looked like Steve had some good news because they both seemed excited about something."

"They hugged?"

"Yes. After a few minutes or so. That was all that went down."

"What good news could my brother possibly have? He's just buried his wife. Keep an eye on them."

"Will do."

"I'm gonna take a walk around the place. See you at eight."

As Joe walked through the kitchen door thirty minutes later, laughter filtered from the lounge. Dropping his keys on the windowsill, he walked into the large room at the rear of the property, seeing his wife and two children giggling as they hung decorations on their new Christmas tree. "Nice," he commented.

Cara turned, her happy expression tempering as he

approached. "It turned up just after you left. It's great, isn't it, kids."

"Yes, Mummy," Tom chirped as he pulled red plastic baubles out of a large cardboard box.

Joe looked down at his son, baulking slightly at the sight of his black metal foot that poked out from underneath his jogging bottoms. He looked at Cara, motioning towards the kitchen. Pulling a bottle of beer out of the fridge, he turned towards her. "I'm throwing the staff a thank you party at eight. So don't wait up."

She looked up at him, shrugging her shoulders. "Okay."

"So, what else did you and Steve talk about?"

"Why are you so interested?" She folded her arms, her defences coming up.

"I just find it strange that you want to spend time with my brother, especially as we no longer talk. He's not part of the family anymore, which was his decision."

"He's still my brother-in-law, and he loves the kids. Why would I cut him out of our lives just because you've fallen out?"

"Because he's fucking crazy," he retorted. "He came up with some half-baked conspiracy theory about Mum's death. And now, his own wife has bitten the dust. He's bad news."

"He's a nice guy, Joe. Yes, he's not cut from the same cloth as you and Frank, but he's a decent bloke."

"Stay away from him," he ordered. "I don't want you meeting up for cosy coffee mornings or anything else."

"You don't get to tell me who I can and can't speak to, Joe Stuart."

"Don't push me on this, Cara. He's bad news."

Something flashed into her memory - a comment from earlier in the day. *The family is toxic.* It was as if a lightbulb had exploded in her brain, Cara realising that her brother-in-law was right. She straightened her shoulders, levelling her gaze at him. "Don't push me either, Joe. You might think you're all high-and-mighty. But I'm not scared of you. Remember that." She turned away from him, walking back to the Christmas tree as Joe stood there, at a loss for once.

Bitch! I'll find out what you're up to. And when I do, you're fucking history.

CHAPTER
TWELVE

WITH THE CHILDREN ENTERTAINING THEMSELVES IN THEIR ROOMS, Cara sat down at her computer, ensuring the study door was closed. Logging into her email, she smiled when she saw a message from Harry. She gulped half a glass of Cabernet before her eyes settled on the first line of the email.

My dearest Cara,

    I trust you are well.

    I've been pretty tied up over the past few weeks with Mrs Thorne next door, but it looks like she's finally managed to secure a place at a care home closer to her daughter. At least I won't be called upon to change lightbulbs anymore, but I'll miss the old bugger.

    Anyway, I've also been digging into the information you'd given me. It's not good news. You may or may not know, thousands of people go missing in the UK every year. Some turn up, and others are never found. With the influx of migrants from Europe, tracking down missing persons has become much more difficult. Some people settle here, only to return home without letting work colleagues/friends know, so pinpointing a young woman who may or may not have been in Cornwall a few months ago is nigh on impossible. I wish I had more positive news, but old Harry doesn't have the connections he once did.

You could check local hotels to see if any guests had failed to check-in or return to their room to check-out, etc. If I'm making any assumptions about the kind of girls that may have been at The Retreat, I'm guessing that they'd be staying nearby in relatively modest accommodation. That may be an avenue that you could explore.

Let me know what you think, and it would be wonderful to see you and the rug rats before the Christmas holidays.

Take care of yourself, and I'm always here if you need me,

Uncle Harry

Cara took another sip of wine, trying to digest her uncle's email. *Shit*, she cursed. *Whoever she was, it'll be like trying to find a needle in a haystack. Unless.* Her thoughts trailed off as she gazed out of the window, an idea taking shape in her head. She walked over to the large map on the opposite wall, a large red pin denoting her location, just a few miles north of Bude. Stepping to her right, she looked at the calendar, leafing back through the months until she stood staring at a date. "The 1st or 2nd of September," she breathed, returning to the desk before circling the date with a red marker pen. She turned to the map, tapping her finger on the town a few miles south of her location. "Bude. That's where I need to look."

∼

Joe leaned against the bar, watching his workers enjoy the fruits of their labours. Being left alone for a few moments, he counted forty staff, twenty-one male, the rest female. Of the nineteen candidates, four of them appealed to the holiday park owner. He knew three of them, Karen, Samantha and Natalie, who were part of the entertainment and events team. They were all in their twenties, their shapely legs on display as the blond man appraised them from across the room. The other woman, Dee, was stood with Malcolm and a man that Joe didn't recognise. *I need to create an opening*, wondering how he could get the woman alone. The woman detached herself from the two men, walking over to the bar with an empty glass. She nodded at Joe before ordering a pint of lager from the lone barman. "A woman who drinks pints," he began.

She turned to him, her gaze level. "Saves on trips to the bar," she quipped, brushing a lock of dark hair behind her ear.

"I like your thinking. If only all women thought that way." He extended a hand. "I'm Joe."

She took it readily, matching his grip. "Dee. Thank you for doing this. Just what the doctor ordered."

He smiled. His killer smile that had worked so many times before. "Think nothing of it. You've all put a shift in. It's the least I could do. Not seen you around before. Have you recently moved here?"

She thanked the barman before taking a sip of her fresh pint as she considered the question. "Moved here a few months ago. I was living in Plymouth but wanted a fresh start. Man trouble."

He chuckled. "Yes, us men certainly are that. Do you live nearby?"

"I'm renting a flat in Bude, just until I get on my feet."

"Cool," he nodded, liking how the conversation was unfolding. "Well, if you're interested in a job after the Christmas holidays, speak to David."

"Really? Thank you."

"I'm always looking for good team members," he went on.

"We're a family business, and having loyal staff is what's kept us running this long."

"Well, I'll keep that in mind. I've got a few part-time jobs, but I am looking for something more permanent. Need a bit of stability after all the toing and froing."

Putty in my hand.

"Anyway, it was nice to meet you, Joe. I'd better get back before they wonder where I've got to."

"No problem," he smiled as Martin strolled over to them. "Enjoy your night, and I might speak to you in a bit."

His eyes followed her, focusing on her shapely calves and rear end. "Do you ever let up?" the bigger man huffed.

"Only when I'm asleep. She's fit as fuck, but not like the other women around here. If I'm going to get her between the sheets, I'll have to work for it."

"Tenner says you don't."

He took the outstretched hand. "You're on." He signalled the barman, who headed over. "Now, let's get well-oiled. This might not be The Retreat, but who knows what the night will bring."

∼

"Been chatting up the boss," the man said as Dee re-joined them.

"Leon, is that what you think of me?" Dee pouted.

The blond-haired man grinned. "You should keep away from him. He's a ladies' man. Isn't he, Malcolm?"

The head groundsman smiled. "You could say that." *If only you knew.*

"What makes you say that?" she inquired, suddenly interested.

"He's got a right reputation around here. I've only worked here for a few months, but Joe Stuart's extra-curricular shenanigans are well known."

"Is he married?" Dee continued.

"He is, to a right stunner. Have you seen the country house on the edge of the park?"

"Oh. Is that where he lives?"

"Yes, with his family, not that he ever sees them. He's either working or shagging."

The woman almost spat her pint over her drinking buddies, struggling to regain composure as the men laughed. "Jesus! What is it with married men?"

"His wife's lovely," Malcolm added. "Not that she's my type, but Cara is gorgeous. God knows why he would even look at another woman."

She looked over at him, watching as he shook hands with the bigger man she'd seen around the park. "He's good looking, but he knows it. Not my type. Plus, he's blond."

"And what's that supposed to mean?" Leon countered, his sails deflating.

"I've been with too many blond beach bums. Prefer my men a bit swarthy."

"Well, that won't stop Joe trying it on with you. Tenner says he'll be fawning all over you come closing time."

"Well, he'll get no joy. I'm not into married men."

"Good for you," Malcolm smiled. "They're nothing but trouble."

"Here, have you heard about the family mystery?"

She shook her head, intrigue surfacing once more. "Go on."

Happy to be centre-stage, Leon took a swig of his pint. "Rumour has it that his father, Frank Stuart killed his wife."

"What? You're pulling my leg."

"Straight up. She was having it away with someone else,

then vanished. That was years ago, but it split the family apart. Joe's got a younger brother, Steve, who left the family not long afterwards. There's bad blood on the Atlantic coast."

"Bloody hell! It's like an Agatha Christie novel," she replied, her eyes drifting across the dancefloor.

"They don't speak, even though he only lives a few miles away."

"And what's he like – the brother?"

Leon's face dropped slightly. "He's a really nice bloke. Lost his wife a few months ago. Car crash."

"Bloody hell! I came to Cornwall to escape the dramas of Devon. Out of the frying pan and all that."

"Oh, believe me, if you've come here for a quiet life, you'll be sadly disappointed."

They talked as the night wore on, colleagues coming and going until a bell sounded. "Last orders," Leon slurred, red-rimmed eyes looking over at the bar. "Fancy another?"

"I won't," Malcolm replied. "I'd better be heading back."

"I'll have one for the road," Dee agreed, picking up her spent pint glass. She hugged Malcolm before walking over to the bar, the two men perched on bar stools, watching her approach. "Hi," she said evenly as the barman approached.

"Had a good night?" Joe asked, smiling over to her.

"It's been great. Just what I needed after a long week."

"How are you getting home?"

"I'll call a cab."

"Good luck. They'll be in Newquay and Truro, so I'd order one now," Joe remarked before walking over to the barman, leaving Dee, Martin and Leon at the bar. "He came back thirty seconds later, his face neutral. "Tim's going to call you a cab. Well, he's going to try. If you're stuck, you can bed down in one of the chalets."

"I couldn't do that. They've just been made up for the guests."

"It's fine. I won't tell any of the others, but the offer is there."

Tim came back a few seconds later, a solemn expression on his face. "You're looking at least an hour."

"Bugger," Dee replied before looking at Joe, a neutral expression on his face. "Okay, why not. Thank you."

"Don't worry about it. I'd rather know that you're tucked up in bed than stood outside in the cold."

They chatted for the next fifteen minutes, Joe focusing on Dee as Martin and Leon made small talk. When the lights behind the bar dimmed, Joe stood up. "I think Tim wants us out," he said. He stepped behind the bar, picking up a bottle of Jack Daniels before nodding at Tim. "Right, let's get out of here."

They filed out into the crisp night, the four of them pulling their coats around them as a biting wind whistled through the holiday park. Leon and Martin said their respective goodnights, leaving Joe and Dee to walk the few hundred yards to her chalet. "That one's made up," he said, pointing to a thatched cabin nestled beneath the forest.

"That's so kind of you. Thank you."

"My pleasure." He held up the bottle, a smile spreading across his face. "Fancy a nightcap?"

She looked at him for a few seconds, wondering how to reply. "Err, I'm pretty wiped out. I'm just gonna crash."

"Are you sure? One drink won't hurt." He stepped forward, filling her view.

"I'm not sure your wife would approve of that."

"What makes you think I'm married?"

"Leon..."

"Was telling you all about me?"

"No," she replied, trying to backtrack. "He just said that you live in the big house with your family."

"Well, what my wife doesn't know won't hurt her." He moved in, trying to plant a kiss on her lips.

She turned her head, stepping back a few paces. "Well, I don't do married men, Joe. But thanks for the offer."

He smiled, shrugging his shoulders. "Not to worry. The key is under the mat. Get a good night's sleep, and I'll see you next week."

"Goodnight," She replied, backing away to retrieve the key before the door closed firmly a few seconds later.

He stared at the chalet as the lights came on inside. Cracking the seal on the bottle, Joe took a long swig before turning towards home. "Leon," he whispered, "you're fired."

CHAPTER
THIRTEEN

TWO DAYS BEFORE CHRISTMAS, A WHITE MINIBUS PULLED UP OUTSIDE The Retreat, eight women spilling out under a dark sky. Freezing rain was coating the north Cornish coast, the entertainment shivering in the downpour as Martin beckoned them over from the covered veranda. As they all entered, shaking themselves off, the giant Scotsman welcomed them. "Sorry about the weather," he began. "Make yourselves comfy and help yourselves to food and drink. Our host will be here soon, along with a few others."

"I need the bathroom," a dark-haired woman stated.

Martin smiled, pointing towards the rear of the open-plan area. "Knock yourself out," he winked before heading towards three panelled doors. Closing the middle door behind him, he made sure the CCTV was ready to roll, knowing who the star of the show would be a few hours later. He smiled, looking forward to the footage that would tighten Joe's grip on one of the prominent locals. He exited the room, checking over the final preparations and talking to the chef who would be preparing more food as the evening wore on. Standing underneath the veranda, he watched as a procession of taxis pulled up, middle-aged men hurrying into the building as Joe strode over.

"All set?"

"Yes, boss. All accounted for. They all look Polish or Eastern European."

"Okay. That's good."

"You okay?" the bigger man asked. "You don't look your normal happy self."

Joe blew out a breath, looking at the ground. "My brother turned up as I was leaving. His feral kids have been at ours today, and Cara invited him in as I was heading out. Something's not right."

"I wouldn't worry about it too much. I saw them alone together. Nothing went on. Just enjoy the night."

He smiled, the old Joe reappearing. "You're right, as ever."

Martin nodded. "I'll be back in shortly. Just want to check the grounds."

"What for?"

The bigger man hesitated before regaining his composure. "Always better to be safe than sorry," he quipped, the memory of his boss's wife clear in his mind as he trudged into the rain. It was fully dark, the low cloud seeming to press down on the surrounding grounds. Ten minutes later, out of breath and soaked-through, Martin closed the heavy wooden door as a figure appeared from the treeline across the expanse of lawn. The hooded man stayed close to the trees until he held a prominent position next to the decked area. He retrieved a digital camera out of his heavy coat, adjusting the settings to not draw attention to himself as the festivities began inside. He started to snap pictures, knowing that he would be there all night. Collecting the evidence needed to bring it all crashing down.

· · ·

Cara sat on the sofa a mile away, a glass of merlot perched on her knee as the children giggled and played upstairs. She looked across at the man, smiling at him.

Steve smiled back, legs stretched as he patted his stomach. "That was lovely. We normally have pizza on a Saturday night. Didn't expect such a banquet."

"It was only a lasagne. Nothing too exciting, but it's nice to know someone appreciates it."

"Golf club?"

Cara smiled thinly, knowing that before the evening was out, she would have opened up to her brother-in-law. But not just yet. "Something like that. Anyway, I didn't want to ask you with the kids around, but what news do you have?"

He placed his mug on the coffee table, running his fingers through his hair. "Well, the money's come through, and I've managed to get my head around how it all works. I viewed the house on Thursday and have put an offer in."

"Wow! You didn't hang around."

"I know. I've not told the kids yet. I was planning on doing that on Christmas morning. Quite apt, don't you think?"

"Very."

"Plus, I've been speaking to Martin Beardmore in Port Isaac. You know him, don't you?"

"Yes. The guy who owns the gallery?"

"That's him. Anyway, a few days ago, I saw that the shop was up for sale, so I popped in. It turns out he's looking to retire. I've been toying with the idea of a project, and the conversation with Martin was perfect timing."

"Go on; the suspense is killing me."

"I'm going to buy the place. I think it would be a perfect place to open a gallery-cum-tearoom. Plus, those huge windows bring in so much light. Perfect for getting my creative juices flowing."

"Wow! You're not letting the grass grow under your feet. First the house, now a gallery. I'm so chuffed for you, Steve. Remember, nice things happen to nice people. And you're nice people."

"So are you. I'm just waiting for something good to happen to you."

She placed the glass on the table, her shoulders sagging. "I wasn't going to do this tonight, but I have to talk to someone."

Steve's expression changed, the man shifting in his seat. "What's up?"

She rose from the sofa, closing the lounge door before folding her legs underneath her, a severe expression etched on her face. "You know how Joe spends his Saturday nights at the Golf club."

"Uh-huh," he nodded.

"Well, it turns out he's been telling lies. He and his male cronies have been throwing parties at The Retreat. For how long, I don't know."

He leaned forward. "What kind of parties?"

She picked at a piece of loose skin on her thumb, avoiding his stare. "The type where young women entertain older men."

"What?"

"I saw it all a few weeks ago. I'll get to why I was there in a minute, but I watched them all from the woods. It's like some high-class knocking shop."

"Jesus! Although nothing surprises me with him. Who else was there?"

"Mr Samuels and others from the surrounding area."

"Okay, so what are you going to do about it? Confront him?"

"Not yet. You know Joe. He'll wheedle his way out of it somehow. But let me tell you how I came to be there."

An hour later, they were standing in the kitchen, the kettle bubbling away as Steve peered into the inky blackness on the other side of the window. "I can believe it, Cara. I know that they killed Mum. I can't prove it yet, but she wasn't washed out to sea. Dad got rid of a problem that threatened to embarrass him. And Joe was in on it too. Hearing what you've just told me confirms that my family is..."

"Dangerous?" she added.

"Yes. And a whole lot more too. It's like a bloody Cornish Mafia."

A phone started vibrating nearby, Cara scooting across the lounge to retrieve her Nokia. "It's Harry," she said, holding a finger to her lips as she answered the call. "Hi."

"There has been a development."

Walking over to the kitchen, she could feel her heart begin to beat faster. "What kind of development?"

"About thirty minutes ago, one of the girls had to leave. Not sure what happened, but she looked in pretty bad shape. Anyway, I followed the minibus driver, who took her back to their hotel."

"In Bude?"

"You got it. They're staying at The Bellevue."

She scribbled the name down on a piece of paper. "You think they're all staying there?"

"Makes sense. It's a fairly modest guesthouse. Not exactly The Hilton."

"Uncle Harry, you're a star. I think you've seen enough tonight. Why don't you head back to St Ives?"

"I will in a bit. I've not had any tea, so I might park up and get a bite to eat."

"Okay. Well, send me a text when you get home and enjoy your fish and chips."

"You read my mind. I'll send you a text and give you a call on Christmas day. If you need anything, just let me know."

"I will. Drive safe. Love you."

"Love you too, my dear."

Cara ended the call, looking at Steve, who stood close by. "I know where the girls are staying."

"Okay. What are you thinking?"

"Not sure yet. I can't just march in there and ask if one of their guests failed to check out."

"No. And if that's the place, Joe might have them well-drilled about people asking questions."

"I never thought of that. Shit!"

"We need to think."

"We?"

"Sure. You don't think I'm going to let you handle this alone, do you?"

She walked over, planting a kiss on the man's cheek. "What would I do without you?"

Steve blushed, smiling awkwardly. "Well, let's hope you never have to worry about that."

∽

Harry sat in his car, the windows open slightly to let the steam escape into the frigid night. The guesthouse was three storeys high, all of the lights on the upper floors switched off, except for one. "Is that you," he said in between mouthfuls of cod. "Show yourself." A few minutes later, a woman appeared at the window, lifting the sash before leaning out. Harry saw the flash of a lighter before gentle plumes of smoke disappeared into the night sky. Placing his supper on the passenger seat, he took several pictures, checking the images before finishing his food. *Oh well, I've come all this way*, he thought before climbing out of his car. The former detective walked past the entrance to the guesthouse, seeing a heavily built man standing in the reception area next to a tacky Christmas tree, his bare arms adorned with tattoos. *Classy.* Walking past, he turned right a few hundred yards later, doubling back on himself away from the main street. Similar hotels lined the street, twinkling fairy lights reminding him that it was only two days before the big day. His eyes took in the surroundings, looking for an opportunity. A few moments later, one presented itself. He pulled his jacket around his neck, ducking out of sight as cars rumbled past. He kept to the shadows, pressing himself against brickwork until he came onto a service road. Second from the end, he deduced, strolling towards the rear of the Bellevue. A black BMW sat under a streetlight, Harry taking a picture of the registration plate before trying the stout wooden gate that led to the hotel's rear. *Take it steady*, he warned himself as the gate opened with a creak, the former police detective slipping into a courtyard. Plumes of steam seeped into the dark space from the kitchen's boiler, Harry looked for a way to get inside. A few yards to his right, a fire exit door came into view, a house brick propping it open. Without thinking, he ducked inside, taking the rear stairs two at a time until he came out on the second-floor landing. Light spilt out from under one of the hotel room's doors, Harry composing himself as he listened for signs of life within.

"Drań!"

He flinched, not understanding the word but knowing it was said with force. With anger. He rapped on the door, knowing that he would be winging it. The man was used to that, though, his improvisational skills serving him well over a long career. "You can do this," he whispered as footsteps filtered under the door.

"Who is it?" a female voice barked.

"Err, hello. Sorry. I'm staying in the room next door and heard you crying. I wanted to check that you're okay."

What am I doing? he thought as the door opened a few inches.

A woman peered out at him with suspicious eyes. Piercing blue eyes, one reddening around the cheek. "Who are you?"

"I'm staying at the hotel. I heard a commotion and wanted to check that you were okay."

"Mind your business, old man," she countered, making to close the door.

A weathered hand stopped it before it could close, Harry taking a step forward. "Has someone hurt you? I can help."

"I don't need help."

"You heard her," a voice said behind him.

Harry spun around, the fist connecting with his jaw before he had time to act. Then darkness.

CHAPTER
FOURTEEN

JOHN SAMUELS LOOKED AT THE FLOOR, THE HEADMASTER NOT USED TO the dressing he'd just received. Joe and Martin stood together on the other side of the room as snowflakes fell outside the Retreat. The older man looked up, his expression clear to see. "So, what happens now?"

"Hard to say," Joe countered smoothly. "She's got every right to go to the police."

"Shit. I didn't mean to hit her. It just got out of hand, and I'd had a few."

"We know that, John. But the police won't care. They'll be more interested in what we're doing here. We've managed to keep these parties off the radar so far. What you did last night may have thrown a spanner in the works."

"I c-can pay her," he faltered.

Joe shook his head, playing with the older man. He was in his element, toying with men of power, showing them just who held all the cards. "It might be too late for that."

"If Linda finds out. Or the board of governors, I'd be finished."

Joe was about to answer when his mobile phone started ringing. He pulled it out, the name Paul appearing on the screen. "Hi."

"Joe. We've got a problem here."

"What kind of a problem?" Joe kept his face deadpan, not wanting to give too much away.

"Better you come and see for yourself. Not over the phone."

"Okay. I'll come over now." The line went dead, the blond man looking at the others. "Some kind of problem at the guesthouse."

"Oh my God! She's not dead, is she?"

"I don't know, John. For your sake, you'd better hope not. I'll call you later. Have your phone on you."

Samuels nodded, the colour draining from his usually ruddy complexion. "Okay."

"Martin. Let's go."

The two men watched as the headteacher's car slipped and skidded towards the country lane a minute later. "He fell for that one."

"He did, stupid old fool. Let's get over to Bude to see what's gone wrong." They drove in silence, Martin staring out of the SUV's window until the friendly seaside resort appeared before them. To their right, the ocean looked turbulent, white caps slamming into the rocks on either side of the large beach. Pulling off the main street, Joe parked his Range Rover next to a black BMW, both men climbing out as seagulls cawed overhead. They made their way into the rear entrance, a large bald man appearing from a lounge area. They shook hands, Joe, eager to find out what the issue was. "Okay, what's up? Is it Katarzyna?"

"No. She's in the lounge with the others, waiting for their ride to the station. I've paid her what you gave me. Did it do the trick?"

"It did. Got the headmaster pissing his pants. Anyway, spill the beans."

"Follow me," he replied, leading them down a flight of stairs until they came out into a small hallway with a door at the end.

Paul unlocked it, pushing it open before they piled in. Across the room, a figure sat, bound to a wooden chair, a hessian sack covering his head. "Here's your problem. Found him snooping about upstairs last night, trying to get into Katarzyna's room."

Joe walked across the room, pulling the sack off the man's head. "Jesus! Harry," he exclaimed, pulling the gaffer tape from the old man's face.

"You know him?"

"Yes. He's my wife's uncle. What the hell are you doing here?"

Shit, Martin thought, a cold feeling seeping down his spine.

"I was in Bude, visiting friends when I saw a girl escorted from a minibus into this place. She looked like she'd been roughed up."

Joe shook his head, a confused look on his face. "I don't understand. Why would you do that?"

"Duty."

"Harry, you're not in the police anymore. You've been retired for years."

"What the fuck! This old-timer was a copper?" Paul exclaimed.

"A long time ago," Joe replied, trying to calm the hotel owner.

"I don't care if he's retired or not. Once a pig, always a pig."

"Harry, there's something you're not telling me. This is too much of a coincidence."

The older man looked at Joe, his gaze steady, despite his injuries and discomfort. "I'll say it again so that it sinks in. I'd been visiting friends in the town and thought I'd stop for fish and chips before driving back to St Ives. My car is parked outside, with half my dinner still in it. Unless it's been towed."

"Boss. I need to speak to you outside. Right now."

Joe saw the grave expression on the bigger man's face, nodding before they left Paul with the retired detective. "What is it?"

"Don't go mad. This isn't the place, but I need to tell you something."

Paul heard the blond man's expletives from the other side of the door, wondering just what the bigger man needed to get off his chest. After a few minutes, they filed back into the room, Joe's normally calm exterior nowhere to be seen. "Talk," he ordered.

"About what?" Harry replied, smiling up at him.

The blow landed just below the jawline, almost knocking the retired policeman off his chair as his head snapped back. The other's looked on as Joe towered over the pensioner. "I said talk. Don't make this harder than it already is."

"What the fuck's going on?" Paul urged, his blood pressure rising.

"It seems that Harry might have been tipped-off about our little arrangement."

"By who?"

"By my wife."

"You mean?"

"Yes, the girl a few months ago."

"Fuck! This can't be happening, Joe. You know what I stand to lose."

The holiday park owner knew that the hotelier had his fingers in many pasties, the guesthouse a front for murkier dealings across the Irish Sea. "So, what do we do? He knows enough to bring us all down."

"I don't know what you're referring to," Harry began, knowing that he'd stumbled across something bigger than he'd first thought. "But you can't keep me trussed up like this. People will know I'm missing."

"You're right," Paul agreed. We can't keep you here. "Where's your car?"

"Across from the entrance to the hotel. A blue Toyota."

Paul stepped forward, retrieving the man's car keys from his jacket pocket. He turned to Martin. "Bring it around the back." The bigger man nodded, leaving the room as the hotel owner walked over to a workbench. "Let's get you untied," he said.

Joe's eyes widened. "What the hell are you doing?"

"Thank you. And we'll say no more..."

His words were cut off as the bigger man wrapped a length of rope around his throat, applying pressure as the older man's face started changing colour. Joe looked on in horror, watching his wife's uncle, who he'd known for over half his life, struggle against his attacker. His eyes bulged as a gurgled choking sound filled the basement. After a few minutes, Paul released the rope, the retired policeman falling sidewards, landing on the floor, his lifeless eyes staring straight ahead. "Fuck," Joe exclaimed as Martin re-entered the room.

"Jesus Christ!" the Scotsman gasped. "What the fuck's going on?"

"He left me no choice," Paul panted, sweat pouring down his face. "We've all got lots to lose. If I go down, the Ryan's will come for my family."

Joe didn't want to know what the bigger man was mixed up in, but guessed it involved drugs. "We need to figure this out. He was right; people will know he's missing. My wife will know he's missing. Shit!"

"You need to find out exactly how much she knows," the

bald man instructed. "If she knows everything, you'll need to sort that out."

"What do you mean – sort it out?"

"Joe, two people are dead. There's no going back from this. If your wife knows about the body, she'll put two and two together. Now that he's out of the picture," he said, pointing at the body on the floor, "She may start digging further. She may go to the police, and if she does, we're all fucked."

"But she's my wife. Yes, she's a pain in the arse sometimes, but you really want me to kill her?"

"Whatever it takes. If you can't do it, I know people who will, for a price."

Joe looked at Martin, the bigger man avoiding his gaze. "How much are we talking about?"

Paul shrugged. "Ten grand. I'm sure you can come up with that kind of money."

"Leave it with me," the blond man replied. "First, I want to know what she knows."

"And if she knows everything?" The words hung in the air, the basement charged with tension.

"Then I'll be in touch."

∼

Cara put the phone down, the first tingling of concern washing over her. She'd tried her uncle's landline numerous times, along with his mobile phone. *Where is he?*

"Mummy," Tom said as he entered the kitchen. "Can we watch a movie?"

"Of course, you can. It's nearly lunchtime, so why don't you get comfy, and I'll bring you something to eat."

"Where's Daddy?"

She shrugged. "I don't know, Son. Probably sorting some last-minute Christmas stuff."

"Okay," the boy replied, heading back into the lounge.

Cara looked out of the window as her husband's Range Rover pulled up, her stomach tightening as he watched him walk towards the kitchen door. "Hi," she said as Joe kicked off his boots.

"Hi."

"Where have you been?"

"Just down at The Retreat with Martin."

"Oh. What's going on at The Retreat?"

He looked at her, knowing that he had to play it cool. If he reacted, she'd know. "Not much. The decked area could do with a spruce up, along with some of the interior. If we're going to have more events there next year, we need it to look the part."

"Events?"

Joe flicked the kettle on, smiling as his eldest son walked across the kitchen. "Hey champ," he called.

"Hey, Dad."

"You were saying?" Cara pushed.

"Well, it's a lovely venue but hardly gets used. Having a few kids' parties there isn't making full use of it, so I was thinking about incorporating it into Sandy Shores entertainment portfolio. Apparently, themed nights are all the rage these days?"

"What kind of themed nights?"

"Well, Martin was telling me that the big holiday parks have '80s weekends, where adults can let their hair down. We could do that at The Retreat. It would be a good money-spinner."

"Oh. I guess that makes sense." *What's he playing at?*

"Remember when we went to Torremolinos a few years ago and the hotel did foam parties one night?"

She nodded, a happy memory flashing before her.

"Well, we could do the same, but not foam parties. The place would probably fall down."

For a split second, he was transformed into the man she'd fallen in love with. He smiled like a teenager, making Cara reciprocate. "Oh well, I'm sure you know what you're doing. Do you have any more errands to run?"

"Nope. I'm home for Christmas. And to be honest, I'm looking forward to a few days downtime with you and the kids."

"Really?"

"Of course. Why wouldn't I look forward to that?"

She shrugged. "We hardly see you, Joe. If you're not at work, then you're out with your cronies."

"I know I'm not around much. But I'm doing it for us," he stated, embracing his wife. He squeezed her, feeling the tension in her body until she gradually succumbed, burying her face in his chest. *Keep her sweet.* "Why don't we order some pizza and settle down in front of the TV? I'm sure there must be something worth watching."

"That would be nice," she replied as the kettle began to boil. "Kids," she called. "You guys fancy a movie night with pizza?"

"Yes, Mummy," she heard Tom and Lizzy shout.

"Okay. I'll pick them up later."

"Great," her husband replied. "I just need to pop upstairs and make a quick phone call and sort some paperwork out." He walked out of the kitchen, taking the stairs two at a time until he came out on the vast galleried landing. Pulling his phone out of his pocket, he closed his bedroom door, walking over to the French doors leading to a decked terrace. "John," he said as the headmaster answered the call.

"Joe."

"Are you all set for the festivities?"

"I can't look forward to anything at the moment. All I can think about is what I did to that girl."

"Ah, yes. About that – I spoke to her about an hour ago. She's pissed, John. Really pissed. She wants to report it to the police."

"Fuck," the older man blurted. "I'm ruined."

"Calm down, old boy. I managed to talk her round. But it's going to cost you."

There was a pause on the line. "Go on."

"She wants ten thousand."

"Ten thousand!"

He smiled, enjoying the powerplay. "I know, mate. That's what I said, but she was adamant. Ten thousand or she'll sing like the proverbial canary."

"Jesus, Joe! I need to think about this."

"Come on, John. I'm sure you can get your hands on a measly ten grand."

Another pause, Joe almost hearing the older man's brain ticking. "Well, yes, I do have the money, but Linda doesn't know about my secret stash. It might take me a few days to sort it out."

"Look. I tell you what. I'll pay the girl off, and then you pay me when you can."

"Really? You'd do that for me?"

"Of course," Joe beamed, trying not to laugh. "That's what friends do – help each other out."

"Okay, leave it with me, and I'll give you a call on Boxing Day. I've got to go, Linda wants me. Thank you, Joe. I owe you one."

The line went dead, the man smiling as he looked out over his estate. "You owe me far more than you think, John." He turned, closing the door behind him as plans began forming in his mind.

∽

"Kids, can you come downstairs," Steve called from the kitchen. After a minute, they filed in, seating themselves at the table. "We need to have a bit of a talk."

"About what?" Matthew inquired as he stared out at the garden.

"What is it, Daddy? We're watching a movie upstairs," Hattie proclaimed.

He smiled, ruffling her blonde locks before sitting down with them. "Okay. I know it's been really hard on all of us since Mum died – but I promise things are about to change."

Matthew turned towards him. "What do you mean?"

He rose from his chair, flicking the kettle on. Steve pulled three cans from the fridge, handing them out, the girls giggling as they cracked the seals. "Okay, a few weeks ago, I won some money on the lottery."

"What's a lottery?" Chloe asked inquisitively.

"It's a game where you choose six numbers. Then, on a Saturday night, they draw them out on the TV. Daddy won."

"How much, Dad?" Matthew asked, suddenly curious.

"Fifteen million pounds."

"Is that a lot?" Hattie asked.

"It is, princess. Enough to make sure that we're all comfortable."

"But I'm already comfortable," Hattie replied, shuffling on her chair.

"You're funny. Not like that. I mean, we'll have enough money to have a good life."

"Can I have a PlayStation 2?"

"Just hold your horses, Matt," Steve replied, placing a hand onto his son's. "I'm sure you will get one if you've been good."

"Come on, Dad. He's not..."

"Shh," Steve admonished, giving Matthew a stern look. "But what it means is that we'll be moving house soon."

"Why?" Chloe asked as she ran her finger around the rim of her can.

"Because this house is quite small. So, I've bought a new home for us. It has four bedrooms. One for each of us. Would you like that?"

"Wow, really!" his eldest piped up.

"Really, Matt. We should be moving next month, but I wanted to let you know now, so we can all look forward to Christmas. It's going to feel a bit strange, because of Mum. But she'd want you all to be happy."

"I know," Matthew sighed. "I still really miss her."

"I know, we all do," *except me*. "You'll never forget your mum, but in time you'll learn to live with it."

"We miss her cuddles," Hattie stated, the seven-year old's smile fading.

"Well, you still have daddy cuddles. Come here, guys." They went to him, Steve wrapping his arms around them as a stray tear slid down his cheek. After a moment, he broke the embrace, wiping his eyes. "Now, I want you all upstairs for a bit. Daddy has some jobs to do."

"What kind of jobs?"

"Hattie Sullivan, you ask too many questions. Now scram."

They left the kitchen, the girls giggling as footsteps thudded above him. Matthew turned to him as he reached the door. "Dad."

"Yes, Son."

"I love you."

His eyes filled with tears, going to his eldest child. "I love you too, Matt. Always remember that."

A minute later, Steve slid the bolt on the shed door, smiling at the presents that greeted him. "Looks like Santa Claus might just bring you what you want," he whispered as the shiny PlayStation box sat on top of the pile. "I just need to wrap you all without the kids seeing me." He smiled, a feeling washing over him that he'd not felt in a long time. Hope.

CHAPTER
FIFTEEN

"I NEED TO POP OUT," CARA SAID AS JOE SAT ON THE SOFA WITH Tristan, watching as Bill Murray played a newer version of Scrooge.

"Oh. I thought we were having pizza?"

"We are, but Uncle Harry is not picking up his phone. I'm a bit worried about him."

There was the tiniest flicker on Joe's face. Enough for Cara to pick up on. "Oh. Maybe he's just switched his phone off?"

"I've tried the landline too. Several times. Something's not right."

"Maybe he's out with friends? It is Christmas Eve. Perhaps he's in the pub?"

She knew it was a plausible argument. However, Joe didn't know what Uncle Harry was doing the night before. Or did he? "Maybe. But I just want to be sure. It's four o'clock. If I leave now, I can be home by seven."

"That's a bit late, love. Just relax. It's Christmas. I'm sure he's fine."

What are you hiding? "Maybe, but I'm not going to risk it. I'll pick pizza up on the way home." She left the house, jumping into her RAV4 before gunning the engine. Above, dark clouds threatened snowfall. *Please hold off*, she thought as Cara pulled onto the country lane that led to the main highway. Taillights lit the road ahead, a large white van trundling along in front of her with a mini digger sat on the attached trailer. After a few minutes, she pulled out her Nokia, dialling her brother-in-law. "Steve."

"Hi, Cara. You okay?"

"Not sure. Uncle Harry never contacted me after I spoke to him. I've tried calling him several times, but no one's picking up."

"Are you driving?"

"Yes. I'm heading to St Ives, Steve. I'm worried about him. Something doesn't feel right."

"Where are you?"

"Just pulled onto the main highway."

"Head over to mine. We'll come with you."

"You can't do that, Steve. It's Christmas Eve."

"I insist. I've wrapped all the gifts, and everything is set for tomorrow. Please, Cara. You shouldn't do this on your own."

"Are you sure?"

"One hundred percent. I'll get the kids ready now. See you in a few minutes."

"Thank you, Steve. You're the best." She ended the call, indicating a few seconds later as she pulled onto a narrow road leading to her brother-in-law's house. *Please be okay*, she thought, banishing the dark thoughts that were invading her mind.

Just over an hour later, they pulled up outside Harry's cottage. "His car's not there," she stated, a knot forming in her stomach.

"Maybe he's out somewhere?"

"It's Christmas Eve. I doubt he'd venture far. You wait here with the kids. I'll try the front door, then try his neighbours."

"Try the pub too. If he's anywhere, he'll be there."

"Good shout," she replied, trying to be positive. The terraced cottage was in darkness, Cara peering through the letterbox after repeating raps on the door. *Shit*. She moved a few paces along the cobbled path, ringing the doorbell of his neighbour. After a few seconds, a light came on inside, the blurred silhouette of an older woman approaching. She smiled as the door opened. "Hi, Mabel," she began as a biting wind ruffled her coat. "Sorry to disturb you, but have you seen Uncle Harry today?"

The old lady's face turned serious, her tight curls also buffeted by the increasing winds. "I've not seen him since yesterday, love. He was supposed to go to The Sloop with George to play dominos."

Cara knew the pub well, situated a few hundred yards away. "I'm worried about him. Where's George?"

"He left about twenty minutes ago. But Harry's car's not here, so we didn't know what to think."

"I'll try the pub, and if he's not there, I think I need to contact the police."

"The police?" she replied, a weathered hand rising to her neck.

"Yes. Uncle Harry was with me last night, up in Bude. He said he'd let me know when he got home, but he never did. Leave it with me, Mabel. I'll pop down to the pub and see if anyone else knows anything."

"Okay, love. I really hope you find him. It's not like Harry. Never ventures too far from home."

The words hung in the air, the dark-haired woman's sense of dread increasing. "I'm sure he'll turn up. Merry Christmas to you and George." The words were hollow, without feeling as she turned away.

Steve watched her hurry towards the brightly lit pub, a dejected Cara trudging back to the car a few minutes later. He climbed out of the Rav4 as she neared. "I'll drive. Get in."

"No one's seen him."

"Okay. You spoke to him about twenty-four hours ago, and no one's seen or heard from him since. I think you need to contact the police."

"What's going on?" Hattie asked from the rear of the car.

"Don't worry, princess. Auntie Cara and Dad are just looking for someone. They may have gotten lost."

"Not how I thought I'd be spending my Christmas Eve," she said, dialling 999.

∼

"Are you sure about this?" Steve asked as they pulled up outside the Stuart residence, the aroma inside the car making his mouth water, despite the grave situation.

"I am. But I know Joe. He won't take this lying down."

"Let's do this. Come on, guys, pizza time," he said, the sleepy children rousing themselves.

Cara entered the kitchen, the three youngsters darting into the lounge. "Breathe," she whispered as Joe walked into the kitchen, his eyes widening at the sight of his brother.

"What's going on?" he asked.

"I'm going to give the kids the pizza. Then, we're going to talk."

"About what?" the man replied nonchalantly.

"Stay there and don't move."

He did so, looking at his younger brother as his wife disappeared into the lounge. The wall clock ticked loudly, both brothers avoiding each other's gaze until she returned. "In the hall. Now."

He strolled into the large space, seating himself on the stairs as the others joined him. "Okay, what's going on, and why is he here?"

"He's here to help. Harry's missing. He never came home last night."

"I don't understand. Where was he?"

"Bude. Checking something out for me."

Shit! "Checking out what?"

"Don't act all innocent, Joe. This is serious. I know about the body."

"Body?"

"Stop lying. I know it comes naturally, but the police are involved now."

He rose from the stairs, his face paling. "I'm not lying, woman. Tell me, what's going on?"

"I saw Martin burying something over by Malcolm's workshop a few months ago. It looked like a body. I know what goes on at The Retreat. I've seen it all."

"What have you seen?"

"You, with your hands all over a young girl. John Samuels being blown against a tree by some strumpet. I knew you were up to something. I just didn't think it involved murder."

"You bitch!" he spat, taking a step towards his wife.

"Back off," Steve warned, blocking his brother's path.

"GET THE FUCK OUT OF MY HOUSE," the older brother raged, shoving Steve aside. He rounded on Cara, his face reddening. "Who the fuck do you think you are, spying on me? You saw nothing."

She held her ground, folding her arms to hide the fear building inside. "Joe. I have photos. I also know the location where the body is buried. Tell me what happened to Uncle Harry?"

"I don't know what you're talking about."

The lounge door opened, Tom, sticking his head out. "Mummy, what's going on?"

"Shut the door and eat your dinner," Joe ordered, the boy backing away until the lounge door clicked shut.

"If something's happened to him, the police will find out. And I'll be sure to tell them about the body. I don't know why I've held off this long."

He caught her wrist, pulling his wife towards him. "If you try and bring me down, you're coming with me."

"Leave her alone," Steve cut in, a firm hand clamping onto his brother's arm.

The backhand came from nowhere, Steve staggering back before slamming into the wall. "I told you to get the fuck out of my house! And take your feral kids with you."

Steve launched himself across the hallway, the two men going down in a tangle of limbs. "Stop it!" Cara yelled as twin headlights shined through the windows. "That'll be the police. Please stop it," she cried as fists crashed into flesh. The woman turned, seeing a tall figure stood behind the door. "Thank God you're..."

The words died in her throat, Frank Stuart smiling down at her. "Aren't you going to invite me to the party?" he quipped, his eyes widening at the brawl in front of him. The older man stepped into the house, clearing his throat. "Joe. Stop it."

Joe looked up; his fist halted in mid-swing at the sight of his father. He rolled off his brother, the two men climbing to their feet. "Dad," he gasped as Lizzy opened the lounge door.

"Go back in the lounge, sweetie. And don't come back out here." The girl complied, the look on her face making her mother want to cry.

"So, what have I missed?" Frank asked as he closed the front door.

"They think I've done something to Harry?"

"Harry? Your Uncle Harry?" He looked at Cara, noticing how close she was standing to his younger son.

"He's missing," Cara countered. "I asked him to check out The Retreat. The last time I spoke to him, he was outside a hotel in Bude where one of the women was staying. I've not heard from him since."

Frank looked at his youngest son, his heart constricting. "Son. Long time, no see."

"I'm not your son," Steve spat back, his lip beginning to swell.

Ignoring the jibe, Frank took charge of the situation. "Look, I don't know what's going on, but you must be mistaken. I'm sure Harry will turn up. He can take care of himself."

"Well, the police are looking for him," his daughter-in-law replied defiantly. "And I'll be telling them about the body in the woods?"

Frank's expression clouded. "Body?"

"Crazy bitch thinks we've buried a body near The Retreat."

"Okay, Joe. There's no need for name-calling," his father soothed. "Is there a body?"

"Of course not, Dad."

"Well, if there is, the police will be all over it."

"Careful, Cara. Do you really want to go down this path?" Frank warned.

"Meaning?" she countered, folding her arms.

"Okay, let's say you're right. Let's say that Joe buried a body in the woods, and the police find out. Do you know what will happen next?"

"They'll arrest him."

"Yes. They'll cart him off to the local nick. But they'll also be all over the house. Social Services will be called in, and the children will be taken away. At least temporarily. Is that what you want, just because you think you saw something?"

Cara paused, suddenly unsure of her convictions. "I know what I saw, and Harry is missing."

"Look, it's Christmas Eve. Let's get the festivities out of the way, and then we'll all sit down and go through this."

"Don't listen to his lies," Steve urged.

"Okay. Call the police, see where it gets you."

The woman pondered for a few seconds, the gravity of the situation settling over her. "I'll wait for them to call me about Harry. I don't want the kids dragged into this, especially at Christmas. But I'm not letting this go."

"And nor should you," the older man added. "Joe, I can't stay long, and I've got a boot full of stuff for the kids. Be a sport and give me a hand."

Father and son left the house, leaving Cara and Steve in the hallway. She went to him. "Are you okay?"

"I've had worse. God, that felt good!"

She smiled, despite the situation. "So, what happens now?"

He leaned against the wall, shrugging his shoulders. "As much as I hate to admit it, Frank has a point. Call the police in now, and it'll be carnage. The body is going nowhere. That's the ace up your sleeve."

"And Uncle Harry?"

His face dropped slightly. "Let's just hope he turns up."

"And if he doesn't?"

He blew out a breath. "Then we bring in the police and let them take over."

"Jesus! How did it come to this?"

"Cara," he smiled thinly. "You married a Stuart. It's always been like this."

CHAPTER
SIXTEEN

"Come in," Paul said as Joe stood on the windswept front step of the hotel.

"Thanks," he replied, walking into the deserted lounge.

"Okay. What's gone down?"

"Cara is threatening to go the police. They've not found Harry, which I expected as he's in your basement."

"Was in my basement."

"Oh. What have you done with him?"

"It's best you don't know, Joe. They will find him eventually, but it won't come back on us."

"I've been thinking about that. Wouldn't the police check local CCTV?"

"Maybe, but there isn't much in Bude, except on the main drag. I know this."

He blew out a breath. "Well, that's something, I guess. But what do we do about my wife? It all kicked off on Christmas Eve. I ended up having a punch-up with my brother."

"I didn't know you had a brother."

"We don't talk. Long story."

"Fair enough," the bald man replied. "So, why was your brother there?"

Joe's shoulders slumped. "Because she's told him everything, and he feels the need to stick his nose in."

"So, that's two people who could bury us. Jesus Joe. This is fucked up!"

"I know, but don't worry. I can't say too much, but I have my end under control, even if the police start digging around. Are things here watertight?"

"They are."

"Okay. So, we sit tight and ride out any storm that comes our way. Whatever happens, my marriage is all but over. She saw me with my hands all over another woman. She wants a divorce."

"Sounds like you've had a great Christmas, Joe. A bit like that, *Eastenders*."

"Well, she can go to hell. I know it will get messy. I know my wife; she won't take this lying down. I'm in for a right scrap."

"Can't you just buy her out?"

"Cara's a very wealthy woman. Her parents died a few years ago, leaving her everything."

"Well, best of luck. Whatever happens, we keep our story straight. I know nothing about yours and vice-versa."

"Agreed. There is another option."

"And what's that?"

"She will go to the police. I know she'll do anything to take me down. And if she does, she'll get everything. The house, the kids."

"What are you saying?"

He pulled out a brown envelope, placing it on the table between them. "There's ten grand. How soon can you get it done?"

"Come in," Frank said, Cara, ushering the children into the country house.

"Frank," she smiled as wellies were discarded on the mat.

"Right, you lot. I need to speak to your mummy. So, I've prepared some food in the conservatory and the TV's on."

"Thanks, Granddad," Tristan beamed, hugging the grey-haired man.

"Hello, pops," Lizzy said, letting her grandfather lift her into his arms.

"My-my, Lizzy. You're getting bigger every day. You'll be picking me up soon." He placed her back on the floor, rustling Tom's dark hair. "You okay, sunshine?"

"Yes, Granddad," he muttered before they disappeared down the hallway.

"How is he?"

She smiled. "He's doing well. His confidence has taken a knock, but he'll get there."

"Good. Now, I've made some coffee." He walked from the hallway into a large kitchen, Cara following as an aroma greeted her. Coffee and croissants.

"I've not been here in a while. New kitchen?"

"Yes. I loved the old one, but I'm getting on and using the Aga was becoming tiresome. So, I thought I'd update a few things. You like it?"

"Very nice," she replied, the white shaker-style cupboards and dark granite worktops to her liking. She gazed out of the window, her eyes drifting over the manicured lawns that led down to the sea. She seated herself at a high stool, letting her father-in-law play mother with the drinks and pastries.

"So, what's the latest?" he said before taking a sip of black coffee.

"Still no sign of Harry. I've spoken to the police, who are carrying out a county-wide search. Traffic cameras picked up his car outside Kilkhampton, but there is nothing from Bude."

He digested the information, nodding slowly. "I know Joe is my son, and I know he's no angel, but do you really think he had anything to do with Harry's disappearance or what you saw in the forest?"

She sighed, suddenly feeling unsure. "I know what I saw. Martin was digging a big hole in the ground, and then he dumped a body-shaped bundle into it."

"But how do you know it was a dead body? It could have been something else?"

"Like what, Frank? Who goes to the trouble of hiding something like that if it's all above board?"

"I know it looks suspicious. It could be money or drugs?"

"Drugs? Joe wouldn't be mixed up in that kind of stuff."

"But you think he could be mixed up in burying dead people?"

"I don't know what to think at the moment. All I do know is that Harry's missing, and no one's seen him for several days." Her words hung in the air, Cara trying to quell her emotions.

"Look. There may be a rational explanation for Harry's disappearance."

"Like what?"

The man looked out of the window, suddenly feeling all of his seventy years. "He may have crashed. The weather was bad with strong winds and snow. I'm sorry to say this, Cara, but he may come off the road somewhere. You know what the roads are like between here and St Ives. There are some treacherous spots, even when the weather is good."

Her emotions boiled over, the woman letting out a sob. Frank handed her a handkerchief, which she took willingly, trying to compose herself. "I'm sorry."

"Don't be silly. Your uncle is missing, and it's only natural for you to be worried. When Margaret went missing, I was beside myself for days. I couldn't think straight, I couldn't eat, so I know how you're feeling."

She looked at the man, seeing the family resemblance. He was a few inches taller than her husband, with a mane of grey hair and strong features. He'd always been kind to her and the children, Cara sometimes questioning Steve's version of events about Margaret's death. "I know it must have been hard on all of you, especially Steve." She let the words hang in the air, the man shaking his head.

"I know he thinks we killed her. I'll never change his mind about that, but I would never have hurt Margaret, even though she wanted to leave me."

"Families eh," she smiled, not wanting to push the conversation.

"They're the most wonderful things and the hardest things in life. I miss Steve, but I know he'll never change his mind, so I have to focus on the family that I do have. It's a great shame. I've got three grandchildren that I've only seen once or twice. How are they getting on?"

"They've had a tough few months, what with Rosie dying, but they'll be okay. They're great kids. Since Tom's accident, they've all become closer, which is lovely to see, especially as Tristan hardly has time for Lizzy and Tom."

"He's a chip off the old block, that boy, just like his father. Don't worry too much. He probably blames himself for the accident, but kids have a funny way of dealing with stuff like that."

"Maybe. I wish that they were a bit closer. But things might get a little rocky soon."

"You mean..."

"Yes, Frank. I want a divorce."

Later in the evening, the boy walked into his sister's bedroom. "Are you okay?" Tom asked as he sat down next to Lizzy.

She looked up, placing her Christmas gifts on the carpet before leaning back against her bed. "I heard Mummy and Daddy rowing last night. She said she wants a divorce."

"What's a d-divorce," the boy asked.

"It's when two people don't love each other anymore and break up."

"Oh." He processed the information, not fully grasping what that meant. "So, what will happen to us?"

"I don't know. Charlotte's mummy and daddy broke up a few months ago. They had to sell the house, and she now lives with her mum and only sees her dad every other weekend."

"Will Mummy and Daddy sell the house? I don't want to leave. I l-like it here."

"I do too, Tom, but I know that Mummy and Daddy are not happy. They are always shouting at each other."

A high-pitched squeal made them both turn, Hooper running into the bedroom with a clothes peg attached to his tail. "Hooper," Tom exclaimed, holding the shaking puppy as Lizzy gently removed the peg. "What happened?"

Their elder brother walked into the room, a smile on his face. "I was just trying to hang out the washing," he giggled.

"That's so mean," Lizzy admonished. "Leave him alone."

"I can do what I like."

"L-leave my d-dog alone," Tom faltered, his face reddening.

"L-leave my d-dog alone," Tristan mimicked, advancing on the pair as Hooper trembled in his master's lap.

"Don't come into my room," Lizzy ordered.

"Or what?"

"Or I'll tell Mummy."

"Oh, you'll tell Mummy. Well, Mummy isn't here, just Dad, so I will go where I please." He advanced on Tom, kicking his prosthetic. "It's so freaky. You're like a robot."

"You're so horrible," Lizzy hissed, rising from the carpeted floor.

"And you're pathetic," he countered, pushing her onto the bed.

Before Tom could speak up, Tristan grabbed his foot, pulling the false leg away from the stump. "Nooo," he wailed as he bumped his head on the floor.

"Dad can put his umbrella in this," he laughed, tapping the boot with his knuckle.

"Give it back," Lizzy screamed, trying to prize the black artificial limb from her older brother.

He was too strong, shoving her across the room as Tom climbed onto the bed. "H-here T-tom. You w-want this back?" he mocked.

Something snapped inside the seven-year-old, his foot flicking upwards, catching his older brother between the legs. Tristan let go of the limb, dropping to his knees. "You little shit!" he spat as Tom retrieved his leg.

"Don't hurt my sister or my dog," he shouted, bringing the metal limb down onto his brother's head. Tristan screamed in pain, falling to the floor, Tom landing awkwardly on top of him. "I hate you," he said, bringing the boot down repeatedly into the older boy's face until a voice halted the attack.

"What the hell is going on!" Joe shouted, seeing the carnage in front of him.

Lizzy ran to Tom, who'd rolled off his brother. She wrapped her arms protectively around him, looking up at her father. "Daddy, Tristan started it. He hurt us both," she pleaded.

Joe looked down at his eldest child, baulking at the sight of his face. Blood streamed from a graze in his blond hairline, one of the boy's teeth hanging by a flap of skin. "Jesus," he uttered, lifting the dazed boy from the floor. "Look what you've done to him. LOOK AT YOUR BROTHER!" Joe hollered, Tom and Lizzy cowering on the floor.

"H-he started it," Tom replied, holding his father's stare. "And he hurt Hooper."

"Stay here, both of you. I need to call the doctor." Joe hustled out of the room, banging his son's head on the door jamb as he went.

Tom flopped to the floor, his breath erratic as Hooper appeared from under the wardrobe. The dog trotted over, settling himself in the boy's lap as Lizzy put an arm around him. "I'm in s-so much t-trouble," he stammered.

"Don't worry. He asked for it, and Mummy will understand."

"I hope so. It's not the first time that he's hurt Hooper. He's so cruel."

Lizzy nodded, knowing that her older brother would not forget the episode. He was vindictive and would bide his time until he got even. "Just promise me something."

"What?"

"Keep an eye on Hooper. You know what our brother is like. He may try and hurt him again."

Tom looked down at the beagle, large brown eyes peering up at him. A knot formed in his stomach, knowing that his sister was right. Battle lines had been drawn.

CHAPTER
SEVENTEEN

As the New Year drew near, the temperature inside the Stuart household was comparable to the weather outside. Joe and Cara stayed away from each other; Tristan kept to his bedroom, peering at his missing tooth in the mirror. Tom, Lizzy and Hooper were inseparable, walking around the garden and park, sometimes with their mother in tow. Three days before New Year's Eve, they sat on the beach. They huddled together on a blanket, the dog happy to be tucked inside Tom's thick coat. Lizzy looked at her mother, trying to form the words that would start the conversation. "Mummy, are you and Daddy getting a divorce?"

Cara looked away from the sea, a sad smile spreading across her face. "I think so, my lovely."

"Why?"

She sighed, not knowing how to answer the question. "It's complicated. Sometimes, mummies and daddies grow apart. It's not nice, but it happens a lot."

"What will happen to us?"

"Now, don't you start worrying—neither of you. Whatever happens, you'll be loved and looked after. I promise."

"Who will we live with?" Tom asked.

"Well, it will take a long time to sort out, but I'm hoping that you'll live with me."

"Will we ever see Daddy again?" the girl asked.

"Of course. You'll still see him. Is that worrying you?"

She looked away from her mother, seeing the whitecaps breaking on the rocks. "Promise you won't be cross?"

"I promise."

"I'd rather be with you. Daddy is never here, and when he is, he only spends time with Tristan."

"Well, your father is busy. Don't beat yourself up about that. They are like peas in a pod."

"What does that mean?" The boy asked as Hooper began snoring.

"It means they are both the same. You two are more like me."

"You mean beautiful," Lizzy beamed.

"Aww," Cara smiled, pulling her children close, almost waking Hooper from his nap. "I don't know about that. But you're calm, like me. Daddy and Tristan are all macho and like man stuff."

"Mummy. Promise you won't get cross if I tell you something?"

"I promise."

"We saw Daddy at The Retreat. It was in the summer, and he was with lots of other women. Is that why you're divorcing him?"

She was more surprised than cross, wondering how her two youngest children came to be at The Retreat. "Well, you shouldn't have gone there. Especially on your own. But yes, that's one of the reasons."

"I think Daddy's mad. Why would he want to speak to other women when he has you?"

She signed. "It sometimes happens, my love. But don't you worry. You'll be just fine." Rain started to fall, Cara pulling her collar around her neck. "I think we'd better go."

"What are we doing later, Mummy?" Tom asked as he lifted Hooper from his jacket.

"I don't know. What do you fancy doing?"

"I don't know. Maybe we could go and see Matthew, Hattie and Chloe?"

"Hmm, I don't know. They may have plans."

"Please, Mummy."

She smiled, resigned to defeat. "Okay. I'll give Uncle Steve a call in a bit."

"I like Uncle Steve," Lizzy stated. "If only Daddy were more like him."

You read my mind.

~

"We're popping over to Steve's," Cara said a few minutes after they'd returned home.

Joe never looked up from his newspaper, grunted something she couldn't quite hear. *Don't hurry back.*

Thirty minutes later, Joe rose from the sofa as his wife's car crunched along the driveway. He walked into the hallway, peering upstairs. "Tristan. You okay, Son?"

He heard the muted footsteps, his eldest son appearing on the landing a few seconds later. "I guess."

Joe smiled, masking the feelings inside when he saw the bruising on the blond boy's face. "They've gone over to see their cousins. Do you fancy a movie night? We could have some popcorn or pizza if you fancy?"

"Okay. I'll be down in a bit." He watched his father nod before heading into the kitchen, leaving the boy alone on the landing. Tristan walked back to his room, stopping outside his brother's door. Opening it, he stepped inside, looking around the space. Toys were arranged on the shelves; miniature soldiers lined up on the seven-year old's chest of drawers. He picked one up, weighing it in his hand before snapping the figure's head off. He did the same for the others before spotting his brother's elephant comforter on his pillow. A smile appeared on his face, an idea forming quickly as the ten-year-old snatched it from the bed, walking back to his room. Finding his Swiss Army knife, the boy sliced the elephant's ears off, slashing the soft blue material until it was almost unrecognisable. "That'll teach you to fuck with me," he whispered before returning the comforter to its rightful place. He walked over to Hooper's bed, unzipping his fly before urinating all over it. "That's just for starters," he giggled before leaving the bedroom. He trotted downstairs, the smell of microwavable popcorn drifting up towards him.

"Almost ready," Joe said happily as the boy joined him at the counter.

"Dad, are you and Mum getting divorced?"

Joe's shoulders sagged, reaching out towards his son. "Come here," he soothed, hugging his eldest. "It looks that way, Son."

"Why, though?"

"Because your mum doesn't love me anymore. I think she loves someone else."

"Uncle Steve?"

They were more alike than Joe realised. "I think so. She seems to be spending a lot of time with him."

"But why would she do that? He's a loser, and you're rich."

"If only it were that simple. Sometimes, money doesn't matter when you fall in love."

"Well, it does to me," he countered.

"I know, Son. But you're young. Believe me, the older you get, the more complicated life becomes." He emptied the popcorn into a large wooden bowl, sliding it over to the boy.

"Where will we live?"

"Don't worry too much about that. I'll do everything I can to make sure you kids are taken care of. Who would you rather live with?"

"You, Dad. I do love Mum, but if I had to choose, I'd pick you."

Joe smiled. "What about Lizzy and Tom?"

He shrugged. "Honestly, they can live with Mum for all I care. I want to be with you."

"Thanks, Son. That means a lot. But we'll have to see what happens. If we go to court, the judge will decide where you all live."

"But that's not fair," he replied, his face darkening. "I want to live with you."

"I know, Son. But it might be for the courts to decide. Don't worry, whatever happens, I'll always be your dad, and I'll always be in your life."

The boy's emotions boiled over, Joe taking him into his embrace as he wept. *You heartless bitch. You think you'll have it all your own way? Think again.*

~

Frank sat in his drawing-room, looking at old photographs as the sun's light began to fade. Shadows lengthened as the man leafed through leather-bound albums, stopping at a picture of his wedding day. He stood there, ramrod straight, his black hair slicked back as his late wife smiled at the camera. He looked at the date written below, realising that it would have been their fortieth wedding anniversary a few months before. "You looked so beautiful, my love," he said, a tinge of sadness washing over him. *Maybe I could have been a better husband? If I had, you'd not have looked twice at another man.* He leafed through more photographs, smiling when he saw a picture of himself with his wife and sons on a family holiday. Setting the album aside, he rose from his chair, walking from the room into the kitchen to make a coffee. As he stood there staring out at his expansive garden, he pondered his family. *How can I make amends? How do I get Steve back onside?* He'd always known his younger son was stubborn, like his mother. Once he'd got an idea in his head, he was unmoving. And now, it looked like his eldest son was about to go through a messy divorce. He shook his head as the kettle started to boil, trying to fathom how he could make everything right.

∼

Joe excused himself from the lounge as Tristan watched Armageddon, the blond man walking into the hallway to answer the call. "Hello."

"Joe Stuart?" a heavily accented voice answered back.

"Who's asking?" as a cold sensation settled over him.

"I'm acquaintance of Paul. He told me to contact you."

Joe opened the lounge door, satisfied that Tristan was otherwise engaged. "Okay. How do we do this?"

"I need your wife's registration plate and model of car. I also need a recent photograph and her movements for the next two weeks."

"Okay. Shall I email them over to you?"

"No email!" the man stated. "I need you to drop an envelope containing the information."

"Oh, okay. Where?"

"Meet me at Truro coach station tomorrow morning at ten. I will be in car park. I drive a red Saab station wagon."

"Ten o'clock. Okay. I'll see you then." The line went dead, the man seated himself on the stairs, his mind a tumult of thoughts and emotions. *Shit, this is real. There's no going back from this now.* He tried to think of another way. A way to get Cara to drop her interest in the body in the woods, but nothing came to him. *She'll never let it go. And I'll lose everything: the park, the money and the kids. There's no other way.* A tear landed on his hand, the man wiping it away quickly before rising from the stairs. *I just need to stall her for a few days. Make her think that I'm going to tell her what she needs to know. If I can do that, it might just work.* Settling down on the sofa a few seconds later, he pulled his son into his arms, inhaling his scent as Joe buried his face in Tristan's hair. "Love you, Son."

"Love you too, Dad," the boy replied before carrying on with the movie. Unaware of the tears falling down his father's face.

CHAPTER
EIGHTEEN

Cara stood in the empty lounge, tears smudging her make-up as she wept. The cottage felt devoid of life without her uncle. The woman had driven down once the phone call from the police had confirmed her worst fears. Her uncle was dead, his car discovered a few miles south of Boscastle. He'd come off the road, not uncommon on that stretch, visions of a burning vehicle rocked Cara to the core. She tried not to visualise it, her dear uncle choking for breath as the ever-increasing flames licked at his skin, singing his hair. Heavy rain had doused the fire, making it harder for the police to spot, but the brief conflagration had been enough. Before entering the cottage, Cara had filled in Harry's neighbours, barely holding it together as shocked residents wept openly. She needed sanctuary, grateful for the silence of the stone-built cottage. Something stirred within, words from her uncle coming to her.

If anything happens to me, there's a folder in the bureau with all the things you'll need.

As she took a step towards the piece of furniture, her phone began to chime. "Hi, Steve."

"Hi. Sorry I missed your call. You okay?"

She wilted into an armchair, sobbing loudly. "He's dead."

"Oh, no! I'm so sorry, Cara. Where are you?"

She brought her breathing under control, wiping her eyes. "At his house. The police rang me a few hours ago. It looks like he came off the road." Cara closed her eyes, her body shaking. "The car was burnt out, Steve. Uncle Harry was trapped inside."

"Look, try not to think about that too much. You've had a terrible shock. Focus on one thing at a time."

"I know. That's why I'm here. To collect some paperwork."

"Okay, that's good. Doing stuff is good. Are you staying down there for a bit?"

"No. I'll be heading back in a few minutes."

"Well, you could pop in for a coffee if you want? No pressure."

"Thanks, I'd like that."

"No worries. I need to pick Hattie and Chloe up in about an hour from Vikki's house, but I'll be back by the time you get here."

"Is that Vikki Thorn's house?"

There was a pause on the line. "Err, yeah, I think so. Why?"

"I need to drop something off to her mum. I can do that on the way to yours and bring the girls with me."

"Only if you're sure?"

"It's no trouble. I think seeing the girls is just what I need right now."

Sometime later, Cara came off the main highway, heading towards Steve's house. A white panelled van filled her rear-view mirror, the woman unable to see the driver's face. *Impatient sod*, she thought, indicating left before pulling off the narrow lane as the van sped past. "We're home."

"I'm hungry," Hattie proclaimed, drawing a smile from her aunt.

"Well, let's see what Daddy has for you. Come on, jump out."

A large man appeared from the country lane as they entered the house, seeing the door close. He kept walking; his heart rate elevated at what almost happened. The man had tailed the car from St Ives, not having the opportunity to run it off the road due to constant traffic. Eventually, the RAV4 had made a quick stop, the van edging into in a lay-by a few hundred yards further on. As he planned his assault a few minutes later, something had happened. A little girl's face appearing in the rear window, making him ease off the pedal. "Jesus! That was close," he said as the rain began to fall. *Don't worry, princess. Next time, you won't be so lucky.*

~

"How did it go?" Joe asked as Cara walked through the front door, a large folder in the crook of her arm.

"What do you care?" she replied, her emotions rising.

"I do care. I've known Harry for years. He was a good bloke," he said, trying to appease her.

"I'm going to make a coffee and sit and read through this. I want to be alone."

"Okay. Shall I get a takeaway?"

"Do what you want. I'm not hungry."

Joe stayed in the hallway, remembering that he'd received a text a few minutes before. He looked at the screen.

No good today. She had kids with her. Tomorrow.

Kids? What kids? His mind began working overtime, quickly realising that it must have been Steve's children. *So, she's been seeing him again.* Joe shook his head, an unusual feeling nestling in his gut. He wouldn't say it out loud, but he knew what it was. Jealousy. He picked up his keys from the table, heading towards his Land Rover. Ten minutes later, he pulled up outside his local pub, his knuckles whitening as they gripped the leather steering wheel. *Cheating bitch*! He snapped back to the present as four women walked towards the New Inn, Joe recognising Linda, a smile appearing on his face. "Why not," he thought, watching them enter the whitewashed building before climbing out of his car. He approached the bar a minute later, appraising the females. The Friday before New Year, the pub filled up with local revellers, keen to keep the festive celebrations going. "Evening, ladies," he announced, the women turning around to see the tall, handsome man.

"Hello, Joe," Linda replied, the flesh around her neck reddening.

"Not with John tonight?" It was a loaded question, smiling inwardly at the sight of her darkening flesh.

"He's lying on the sofa, polishing off the Quality Street," she huffed. "He's not been himself over Christmas. Not sure what's up with the old bugger?"

I do. I know ten thousand reasons why he's not been himself. Joe smiled, turning to the three others. "You girls out on the tiles?"

"Too right," the tall brunette giggled, Joe not being able to fathom her name. "How about you? Where's your other half?"

Joe's face dropped slightly. "She's at home. And it looks like she'll not be my other half for much longer. She wants a divorce."

Three mouths dropped open, the women clearly shocked, except Linda. "Oh, no! I'm so sorry, Joe."

"It's okay," he replied, nodding at the barmaid as she approached. "Whatever they want, and I'll have a Heineken, please" The women nodded their thanks, ordering a bottle of white before aiming their eyes at their new drinking partner.

"Come and sit down. We're good listeners."

Good gossips, you mean, he thought, almost smiling. "I'll pay for these and come right over."

"Poor bloke," Valerie said, her eyes lingering on the man at the bar.

The two others, Helen and Louise, followed suit, their gazes drifting up and down the man. Helen leaned forward. "He won't be single for long. He's proper tasty. Just look at that rear end."

Louise giggled. "I know. I wouldn't mind seeing that uncovered."

"Really!" Linda admonished, suppressing a giggle. An image flashed before her - the man at the bar in her home, his lips on her body. She clamped her legs together, the others unaware of the racy thoughts the wife of the local headmaster was entertaining. For years she'd been the dutiful wife, her husband falling asleep before she'd even climbed into bed. She never imagined that a handsome man like Joe would have looked twice at her. And not just looked, her mind remembering his muscled arms and washboard stomach as he'd taken her to new places. Places the middle-aged woman had never been before. Places she'd tried to revisit over the past few months when she was alone in the house.

"Come on, Linda," Valerie winked. "I bet you wouldn't kick him out of bed. I know I wouldn't."

He seated himself a few seconds later, feeling four sets of eyes on him. He smiled, the action not quite reaching his eyes. "Cheers, ladies. Happy New Year."

They raised their glasses, trying to look cheerful, wanting to know what had gone down in the Stuart household. "Cheers," they echoed.

"Do you want to talk about it?" Linda asked, placing a warm hand on his forearm.

"I don't want to bore you with my hardships. You're out having fun."

"Nonsense," Valerie interjected. *I'd love to have some real fun with you.*

He sighed before taking a sip of his lager. "Okay. I'd better start at the beginning."

Twenty minutes later, Linda gulped her tepid wine, the woman hanging on the man's every word. "Oh, Joe. We had no idea."

He shrugged, spinning them a tale of a cheating wife, happy to spend her husband's hard-earned money while he was trying to provide for his family. He never mentioned names, wanting a bit of mystery. But he knew the women would be talking about it for days, weeks even, trying to unpick the truth. "I guess you don't know what goes on behind closed doors," he replied, his knee touching Linda's under the table.

"True," Valerie added. "I thought my Gordon was the model husband. I had no idea that he liked dressing up in my clothes when I went out. It just goes to show you."

Joe nodded sadly, trying to look empathetic to the woman sat next to him. He looked down, his eyes taking in a nylon-clad thigh that was almost touching his. He took a sip of his pint, his leg nudging the woman's before he shifted his position. He saw it instantly, the woman blushing before looking away: *I bet she's up for it*, wondering where the night would take him.

They sat drinking until Helen and Louise announced that they both had early starts and said their goodbyes. Hugs and kisses were exchanged, Joe seating himself as Valerie and Linda headed for the ladies. As they came out of their cubicles a few minutes later, Valerie turned to her lifelong friend. "Shall I invite him back to mine?"

"What, just the two of you?"

"Duh!" the taller woman replied. "I mean all of us."

"I don't know, Val. It's a bit forward."

"Is it? Come on; it's just a nightcap."

"Is it? What's on your mind?"

"Nothing," she assured, not wanting to tell her friend that the handsome blond man had been openly flirting with her for the past few hours. Her two recently departed friends had picked up on it, deciding to call it a night.

"Okay, well, let's see what he says. He might say no – after all, he's a bit messed up right now."

"Leave it with me," Valerie winked as she freshened up.

A few minutes later, they seated themselves, Linda handing the man another pint, the women switching to Bacardi and Cokes. "Cheers," he smiled, wondering what the topic of conversation had been in the ladies.

"So, where do you go from here?" Valerie began, the subject turning back to Joe's failing marriage.

"Not sure. I don't really know how all this works, to be honest."

"Well, if you need any advice, just say the word. It was all fairly amicable with Gordon and me. I was expecting a battle, but he was great about it all."

"Where does he live now?" the man inquired, suddenly curious.

"Torquay. Moved there a few years ago. We keep in contact, and the kids see him regularly."

"Have you met anyone else since?"

The woman shook her head. "It gets harder to meet new people at my age."

"Nonsense," Joe countered. "You're not old."

"Well, I'm nearly fifty. Not many decent men out there at our time of life, eh, Linda?"

"She's right. If John and I divorced, I'd probably just become a crazy cat lady."

They're fishing. "Well, for the record, I think you're both gorgeous."

"Steady on," Valerie gushed. "You'll give us hot flushes."

I hope so.

The bar door swung open, a group of young men entering the pub, the decibel levels increasing as they all joked and jostled at the bar. "Here comes the riff-raff," Valerie huffed. "Probably gonna get tanked up before heading to a club."

"Shall we go with them?" Joe joked, nudging the brunette.

"My days of clubbing are long gone. Give me a decent pub and a nightcap afterwards." She let the words hang in the air, seeing if the man would take the bait.

"Sounds like the perfect evening."

More laughter from the bar erupted across the cosy pub, Linda tutting. "Bloody yobs. I know most of them too. Good job, John isn't here. He'd be straight over."

"They're just having fun, but you're right, kinda spoilt the atmosphere."

"Why don't we drink up and have that nightcap. You fancy it, Linda?"

The headmaster's wife nodded, trying to look casual despite her flushed cheeks. "Why not. Joe. You up for it?"

You've no idea. "Sure. Why not?" He shifted his hand under the table, placing it on the woman's knee. Joe looked at her and smiled, his fingers gripping the dark nylon, wondering what the next few hours would bring.

"What can I get you?" Valerie asked as they entered the hallway of her cottage.

"What have you got?"

"Scotch, brandy, rum. Oh, and I've got some Advocaat left over from Christmas day."

"I'll have a Scotch, please."

"Linda?"

"I'll have a brandy, please, hun."

Joe slipped off his leather boots, watching as they removed their high heels, both women slightly unsteady on their feet. "Do you need a hand?"

"Nah. You two sit yourselves down, and I'll bring them in."

They did as instructed, Linda flicking on a few lamps as the man seated himself on the large L-shaped sofa. His eyes took in the lounge. Despite being used to the lap of luxury, Joe liked the cosy room, a coffee table its centrepiece. He turned to Linda, who was watching him. "You okay?"

She smiled. "I am. How are you holding up? Sorry that we've badgered you all night about your marriage."

"That's okay," he smiled as Valerie came in with the drinks, placing them on cork coasters on the table. "It's been nice to talk about it. I think it's helped to get it off my chest."

"Well, for what it's worth, I think your wife's mad. Why would she want to warm the bed of another man when she's got a gorgeous husband at home?"

"You're too kind," Joe replied, reaching for his glass, the two women exchanging smiles.

"She's right, Joe. Cara's bonkers to let you go," Linda affirmed. "If I were twenty years younger, I'd snap you up myself."

"Get in the queue, love," Valerie laughed.

"Thank you," he said. "You two have really helped. You've helped me forget the pain, if only for a while."

Valerie placed a hand on his knee, patting it gently. "Well, we're always here if you want to talk. Aren't we, Linda?"

"Anytime," her friend confirmed.

"Thanks, ladies. That's very kind of you. I just feel a bit empty. Have done since she dropped the bombshell. I just want to block it out at the moment and forget what's heading my way."

Valerie smiled. "Well, you do what you need to do. And our doors are always open."

"Thank you," he replied, placing a kiss on the woman's cheek.

"Careful, you'll make Linda jealous," Valerie breathed, a warm sensation stirring within.

"Sorry, Linda," he replied as he pulled the headmaster's wife towards him, their lips meeting as Valerie looked on.

Linda moaned softly as the man's tongue snaked into her mouth. *Oh my God!*

As the contact was broken, the man sighed. "Well, I didn't expect this kind of nightcap?"

"Is that a bad thing?" the brunette replied huskily, edging closer.

He sat back on the sofa. "No, but I'm sure my wife would hit the roof if she could see this."

"Well, what goes on in his house, stays in this house." She pulled the man towards her, their lips coming together as Valerie began to unbutton his shirt.

"Happy New Year," Linda whispered, her trembling fingers tugging at the man's belt buckle as the year came to a close.

CHAPTER NINETEEN

THE FOLLOWING DAY, VALERIE OPENED THE DOOR, A FLURRY OF SNOW blowing into the hallway. She half-smiled at her friend. "Hi."

"Hi," Linda replied awkwardly.

"Come in. I think we need a cuppa."

Linda stood in the kitchen a moment later, removing her coat as her friend boiled the kettle. "How are you feeling?"

Valerie's shoulders sagged, the woman shaking her head. "In truth, a bit guilty."

"Me too. I slept like a log, but when I woke up, it's all I've thought about."

"Well, it certainly wasn't how I thought I'd be ending my night?" The words hung in the air as the woman's thoughts rewound a few hours, a naked man pleasuring both of them on the sofa. Her cheeks began to flush. "I can't stop thinking about it."

Don't tell her what happened before. You can't tell her. "I know he's getting divorced, but I still feel bad, even though it was incredible."

She let out a laugh. "God! Wasn't it, though? I've never had a threesome before."

"Nor me. I struggle to have a twosome, most of the time," Linda smirked, relieving the tension some more.

"One minute we were sat there, the next we were romping on the sofa. Bloody hell, Linda! I'm a middle-aged woman. Naked on a sofa with my best friend and a sexy younger man. You couldn't make it up."

"So, what do we do?"

The taller woman shrugged. "Dunno. What can we do? Obviously, it stays between the three of us. It doesn't matter to me, but you're married, and Joe's wife would use it as ammunition."

"Okay." They sat chatting, enjoying the coffee as the rear garden slowly turned white.

"So, how's John?"

Linda rolled her eyes. "Something's definitely up with him. Been very distant all Christmas."

"You think he's got another woman?"

"He gets tired taking his socks off. I don't think he's got the energy for an affair."

The brunette chuckled. "So, what is it then?"

"No idea, but I'll find out. John's terrible at keeping secrets." She suppressed a smile. *I have a few secrets of my own now—all concerning a sexy younger man.*

"Maybe he's having a midlife crisis?"

"He had one of those about five years ago. Wanted to go travelling and buy a motorbike. Can you imagine John on a Harley Davidson?"

"Err, not really." Val reached over, placing a hand over her friend's. "I'm glad you popped over. And I'm glad we're both okay with what happened last night."

"I'm glad too."

"Would you change it?"

"God, no! That'll keep a smile on my face until next Christmas. And you?"

Valerie winked at her friend over the rim of her mug. "Change it. I want a second helping."

～

"Are you okay?" Steve asked as they stood outside his new project.

"So-so," Cara replied, trying in vain to ward off the cold.

"Does Joe know you're here?"

"No. He thinks I'm shopping, which I am, I suppose. When do you get the keys?"

"In about a week. Martin has cleared all his stuff out and has kindly let me have his keys. I want to put up a sign in the window. Under new management, vacancies, etcetera."

"This is amazing, Steve," she replied, meaning every word. "Funny how life turns out, eh?"

"You could say that. This time last year, I was broke. I was always fretting about where Rosie was. I was a mess. And now look at me. I'm still a mess, but a rich one."

"Steve Sullivan. You're far from a mess." She smiled at him, the man grinning back as their eyes met.

"Stop it, you'll make me blush, which isn't a good look. Do you want to see what plans I have for the place?"

"Lead on; it's bloody freezing out here."

He ushered her inside, his boots loud on the wooden floor as he pointed towards the closest wall. "Well, that's where the counter will go. I know a local guy who is coming over in a few weeks to give me a quote. It looks like the electrics will need stripping out. And there are a few walls that I want taking down to open it up a bit."

"Look at you, Mr Grand Designs." Her smile was infectious, making her brother-in-law grin like a naughty schoolboy.

"Sorry. I'm like a kid in a sweet shop. Well, coffee shop."

"So, where are the art and books going to go?"

"Follow me, young lady," he beamed, walking towards the rear of the property, where two large rooms lay empty. "I want to knock through here and display local art in this corner," he said, pointing at the wall. "And the books will go over there." He looked up at the floor-to-ceiling bay window. "The light is amazing, and there's another window directly above it just like this one. That's where I'll paint and write."

Cara looked back at the main shop, visualising how it would look. "You'll easily fit thirty or so people in here. And when the weather is nice, you can have tables and chairs outside."

"I thought so too. There are only two cafés in Port Isaac, and they're nothing to write home about."

"Been checking out the competition?" she grinned.

"Something like that."

Cara went to answer, her phone starting to ring in her coat pocket. "Shit! It's Joe."

"Okay. I'll leave you to it while I sort out the sign."

"Hello," she began, watching as the man walked towards the front of the property.

"Where are you?"

"About to go into Tesco's. Why?"

"Lizzy's been sick."

"Oh! She did feel a little warm this morning. Okay, well, I won't be long," she said, rolling her eyes at her brother-in-law.

"If you could. I need to check on a few things at the park. Something's come up."

"What?"

"It's nothing. One of the residents set fire to the kitchen in our new cabins. The fire brigade is there now."

"Oh no! Look, I'll head back now. The shopping can wait."

"Thanks, see you in a bit." The line went dead before she could reply.

"Everything okay?" the man asked, noticing her sombre expression.

"Lizzy's sick, and there's been a fire at the park."

"Oh shit! You'd better head home."

"You sure? I hate to leave you in the lurch, especially as you were so excited to tell me your plans."

"Lizzy comes first. I'm sure she only wants her mummy. Don't worry about all this. You'll be here for the grand opening."

She walked over, hugging the man. "I'm so pleased for you. You're a wonderful man, and, like I've told you before, nice things happen to nice people."

He smiled, planting a kiss on her forehead. "Thank you. It means so much hearing you say that. Now scram and take care of Lizzy. Send her my love."

She placed her hands on his shoulders, planting a kiss on his cheek. "I'll give you a call tomorrow. New Year's Eve and all that. Have fun, and don't forget to lock up."

"I won't. See you later." He waved her off, watching her walk down the cobbled street until she disappeared around a corner. A few minutes later, Steve was sticking a large sign in the window, heading towards the shop's rear to get another piece of card. He heard the bell chime as the shop door opened. "Hang on a sec," he called before heading back. A woman stood there, her dark hair covered in snowflakes. "Hi," he said. "I've met you before somewhere."

"The convenience shop, up by Bude."

He smiled. "That's it. Hi, I'm Steve."

"Dee," she said, extending a hand, which he took readily.

"So, what can I do for you?"

She looked around the empty shell, liking the feel of the place. "I saw your sign in the window. I'm looking for a job."

~

Cara's RAV4 weaved its way along the windy lanes, approaching the main highway. Brake lights could be seen ahead, the woman slowing as a line of traffic came into view. "Shit," she mouthed, seeing a left turn just ahead of the traffic jam. She pulled onto a narrower lane, a white van following suit. The woman knew this stretch of road well, hoping that no cars would be travelling the other way. Her speed increased to fifty, Cara deftly steering the 4x4 around turns before increasing her speed once more. She glanced in the rear-view mirror, seeing that the van had fallen back and was almost out of sight as she pressed on towards the next junction. The woman did the maths, knowing that she'd be home in fifteen minutes if the gods favoured her. A T-junction came into view, Cara letting the car coast along until she looked left and right to check the coast was clear. She was in luck, turning right as rain started to fall. Switching on her wipers, the pitter-patter of raindrops suddenly increased, the woman activating the wipers in the hope of keeping a clear windscreen. To her right, the ground rose, a steep ravine darkening the interior of the car as she splashed through puddles. To her left, the ground dropped away, a metal barrier the only thing between her and fresh air. *Slow down,* she cautioned, taking her foot off the pedal, the RAV4 dropping to forty as a tight right hairpin quickly approached. She felt the car understeer, Cara leaning to her right as she steered. Something in the wing mirror caught her eye. However, she couldn't react in time as the white van slammed into the back of her car. Time seemed to slow down; Cara slamming into the door as the vehicle struck the safety barrier. The driver's airbag deployed, coating the interior of the car in white mist. Then, she was tumbling. Over and over until the world around her went dark.

The man came to the lip of the ravine, an angry welt on his forehead. A hundred feet below him, the RAV4 had come to a rest. The underside of the car and tyres were barely visible amongst the trees and undergrowth. He looked over to the Transit van, the engine ticking over. *Need to get to Mariusz's. Quickly.* He took one more look into the void, his stern expression hiding the emotions inside. It is done, he thought before jogging back to the van, hoping it would take him to where he needed to be. To make sure there was no trace of him, or his weapon of choice.

CHAPTER
TWENTY

"How are you feeling?" Joe asked as he touched his daughter's forehead.

"My tummy still hurts, Daddy." She looked towards the window, seeing the dark clouds that seemed to press down onto the trees nearby. "Where's Mummy?"

"She's on her way. Just lie there, and I'll go and ring her. The sicky bucket is there if you need it."

"Okay," Lizzy replied as Joe left the room.

Where the hell are you? I need to be somewhere. Joe pulled out his phone, dialling his wife's number as he descended the stairs. It went straight to voicemail, a press of a button ending the call as a message appeared on his screen from an unknown number—the hairs on the back of his neck springing to attention as he read the short text.

It is done.

"Jesus!" he whispered, knowing what the message implied. He reread the message, sweat breaking out on his brow. *Shit!* Joe walked through to the lounge, spotting Tristan sat in front of the television, unaware of his presence. "You okay, Son?" he said, his voice shaky.

"Hi, Dad. Where's Mum?"

"She should be here by now," he lied. "I've tried to ring her, but she's not picking up."

"Okay. I'm hungry."

"Help yourself to something. I need to pop outside." Joe opened the front door, standing under the canopy as heavy rain blanketed North Cornwall. In the distance, he heard sirens, wondering if they were racing to attend to his wife, a shudder running through the man as they faded, only the sounds of falling rain and nearby birdsong drifting towards him. *Is she really gone? What do I do now,* never thinking past the actual act itself. *Think, man, think. They may be knocking on my door soon. I need to keep my shit together and act like the grieving husband. I can do that;* Joe assured himself as he walked back inside.

∼

Police Constable Jess Fairfax looked down into the darkening forest as the downpour intensified. Ten minutes before, they'd received a call from a passing motorist that a section of the crash barrier had been damaged just south of their position. Ditching their makeshift dinner, the police officers had traversed the country lanes until they spotted the smashed barrier. She looked along the road, seeing her partner, Josie, waving through a fire engine. A few seconds later, a large man in full uniform approached her, his eyes flicking towards the smashed barrier. "What's the latest?"

She walked with him towards the lip, peering down at the carnage below. "No update," she replied, unsure of what else to say.

He looked behind him as three firefighters approached. "We need two lines, the cutter and the RTC," he stated, two of the men jogging back to the vehicle as flashing blue lights strobed across the forested area. "We'll need the road blocked off."

"Right. I'm on it," she replied, trying to hide her inexperience. The young woman wouldn't admit it to the towering fire officer, but this was her first road traffic accident since she'd joined the force a few months before.

Five minutes later, Chief Fire Officer Mark Draper unhooked the line and moved towards the car. "Shit! What a mess," he said as his colleague landed next to him clumsily.

"Chief."

"Need to get around this," he said, pointing at a tree that was holding the car in place. "And quickly. It won't hold it for long."

"Righto," the younger man replied, scooting around the rear of the up-turned SUV. "We're in luck, Chief," he called. "The driver door is wedged open."

"Well, that's something," he huffed, moving around the car until he knelt next to the opening. "Stu, pass me the neck brace and the Stanley." The younger man did as was asked as the Chief checked the unknown woman's condition. "We've got a pulse. It's faint, but she's still with us." His radio crackled to life, the older man listening for an update.

"Chief, the ambulance is here. What's the status?"

"Woman. Looks to be early thirties. She's alive but in pretty bad shape. The paramedics won't get down here, Daz." He looked through the forest. "Back up the road; there's a track that leads towards the river. I've used it before. Might struggle to get down there but tell them to give it a shot."

"Okay. Stand by."

"Need to get her out of here," he barked, the smell of fumes beginning to overpower them. "Hang on, sweetheart," the man said as he began cutting the seatbelt, hoping that the whole thing wasn't about to go up in flames.

Joe heard the knock at the door, his heart rate quickening as he spied the police car on his gravel driveway. *Breathe*, he assured himself as he walked through into the hallway. Two female officers looked up at him as the door opened, Joe's expression uncertain. "Err, hi."

"Mr Stuart?"

"Yes."

"I'm Sergeant Haines, and this is PC Fairfax. Could we come in, please?"

"Err, sure," he replied, letting the officers into the hallway.

"Dad, what's going on?" Lizzy asked from the top of the stairs.

"Nothing to worry about. Go and lie down, princess."

"Where's Mummy?"

"Lizzy, back to bed. I'll be up in a minute," he replied as Tom peered over the balustrade.

He turned to the officers, liking the look of the younger one. "What's happened?"

"Your wife's been involved in an accident, Mr Stuart."

"W-what?" Joe replied, his eyes widening.

"Let's go through to the kitchen," Haines replied, her voice softening. "Jess, put the kettle on."

He motioned towards the door, the officers walking into the vast kitchen. *Keep it together.*

Jesus! This is gorgeous, Fairfax thought as her boots squeaked across the flagstone floor. She filled the kettle as Haines seated the blond man at the breakfast bar.

"Where's my wife?"

"On her way to Truro hospital, Mr Stuart."

"What happened? Is she okay?"

"We're not entirely sure. Where had your wife been this afternoon?"

He shook his head, unable to retrieve the information. "Err, she'd gone shopping. I called her earlier as Lizzy's unwell, and we've had a fire at the park."

"The park?" Constable Fairfax inquired as the kettle began boiling.

"Sandy Shores."

"Oh, that park. Do you own it?"

"I do," he replied as the women looked at him. "The fire brigade was there."

"Yes, we heard about that, Mr Stuart."

"Call me Joe," he replied.

"Okay, Joe. So, your wife had been shopping. Where was that?"

"I don't know. Probably Barnstable, I guess. Yes, at Tesco's."

The officers looked at each other, both knowing what the other was thinking. "Okay. So, you spoke to her a few hours ago. Did you speak to her after that?"

"No. Lizzy's sick, so I've been upstairs with her. I did wonder why she was so late, but Cara can sometimes get sidetracked."

The officers nodded before writing notes in their respective pads. "Okay. Well, she was in pretty bad shape when they pulled her from the wreckage, but she was alive. Do you need us to call someone for you?"

"Call someone?" he replied dumbly.

"Yes, a family member or friend who could come and look after the children."

"How many do you have?" Fairfax replied, trying not to stare too much.

"Three. Tristan, Lizzy and Tom."

"Okay. So, is there someone we can call?"

"Err, no, it's okay. I'll call my father. He only lives a few miles away."

"We'll hang on while you do that, Joe," Haines replied.

"Sure." He pulled his phone out to make the call.

"Joe," a puzzled voice said.

"Dad. I need you to come here. Cara's been involved in an accident."

"Accident? What kind of accident?"

"A car accident. They're taking her to Truro hospital. Dad, I need to be with her. How soon can you get here?"

"On my way, Son. Is she okay?"

Tears brimmed in his eyes, Joe's emotions simmering. "I don't know. The police are here now. They said she's in a bad way."

"Okay. I'll be there shortly." The line went dead.

Joe turned towards them, blowing out a breath. "He'll be here in a few minutes. Shit, what do I tell the kids?"

"Don't worry about that, Joe," Haines replied. "We'll call a family liaison. They'll support. You get yourself off, and we'll wait here until your father arrives."

"Okay. Right, keys," he said to himself, heading towards the back door.

"What's your father's name?" Fairfax asked as Joe slipped on his trainers.

"It's Frank. Frank Stuart. Sorry, I'd better get going."

"I hope she's okay," Haines said as the man ducked out of the kitchen door. They looked at each other, the sergeant speaking first. "If she was shopping in Barnstable, what's she doing on the road from Port Isaac?"

"My thoughts exactly," the younger woman replied.

"Did you notice anything unusual about him?"

"Apart from being fit?"

"You seriously need a man! No, I mean, how he reacted?"

The PC pondered the question for a moment before speaking. "Well, he didn't seem too shocked or upset, but that might just be shock kicking in."

"Shock doesn't kick in that quickly. Call it intuition, but something doesn't feel right about all this. I think we need to do a bit of digging."

CHAPTER
TWENTY-ONE

HE STOOD THERE WHILE THE DOCTOR EXPLAINED THE SITUATION. JOE heard the words, but they were not registering as the man stared at the wall. "Sorry, what was that?"

The doctor, a young Asian man, nodded in understanding. "It's okay, Mr Stuart. They've taken your wife into theatre. We won't know much more for a few hours, possibly longer, as your wife has suffered multiple injuries."

"Multiple injuries? What does that mean?"

"Well, I don't know for sure as they rushed her straight in. Her car rolled down an embankment, Mr Stuart, so I'm surmising broken bones and possibly some internal injuries," the younger man said evenly.

"Jesus!" Joe replied, shaking his head. "Is there somewhere I can sit?"

"Of course. I'll take you down and show you where the refreshments are. Come with me."

He walked behind the doctor, his footsteps echoing loudly along the stark corridor, a tumult of thoughts running through his mind. *She may pull through. And if she does, she'll think I had something to do with this. Shit!*

In the Stuart household, Frank sat on the sofa, his grandchildren clinging to him. After speaking to the female officers, he'd told the children what had happened, being as frank as Frank could be. Despite their obvious upset, the older man enjoyed the closeness, especially from his eldest grandchild, who had broken down as soon as he dropped the bombshell. "When will we know anything," Tristan demanded, his face slick with tears.

"I don't know, sunshine," his granddad replied softly. "She may be in the operating theatre for a few hours. Probably best that we wait for news from your dad."

"Will Mummy die?" Lizzy asked as she sat up.

"Look, let's not think about all the whys and wherefores," he soothed. "I'm sure she's in good hands."

"D-daddy did this," Tom uttered.

Frank's eyes widened, seeing the mask of hate on the boy's face. "Of course he didn't, Tom. It was an accident. Your dad was here with you."

"They're getting divorced," the boy countered. "He hates Mummy." Tom shuffled off the sofa, hobbling out of the room as his sister followed.

"He's just upset," Frank said to Tristan. "Are you okay?"

The boy wiped the tears from his eyes, looking up at the old man. "I don't know. I don't want Mum to die."

"Come here," Frank soothed as he pulled the boy into his embrace. "She'll be just fine. A bit battered and bruised for a while, but your mum's strong." *Two car accidents. Jesus, Joe. I hope you're not behind this.*

Joe's eyes flickered open as he felt contact on his shoulder. He looked up, seeing a surgeon stood over him. "How is she?"

"Mr Stuart, I'm Doctor Rutherford," the older man said evenly, taking a step back as the blond man rose from his seat. "We've had to put your wife into an induced coma."

"Coma! What for?"

"Well, she had some swelling on the brain, which was a concern. The surgery went well, except for the pressure on her skull."

"Can I see her?"

"I'll take you down in a minute. She's in the ICU."

"How bad was the swelling?" Joe asked, not fully understanding the implications.

"We'll know more over the coming days. It's not uncommon in car accidents for the injured party to receive head injuries. Also, your wife lost a lot of blood due to a nick on her aorta from a broken femur. Another thirty minutes, and she may not have made it."

The younger man leaned against the wall, his insides churning. "So, what happens now?"

"We wait, Mr Stuart. I'll take you down to see your wife, and we'll monitor her condition closely."

Joe followed the man, his gait ponderous as he struggled to keep up with the surgeon. After a few left and right turns, Joe was ushered through a set of doors, a beeping sound drifting towards him. *Oh God!* Cara lay motionless, tubes and wires running from her body to an array of machines next to the bed. He took a step forward, seeing how tiny she looked. Fragile, like a broken bird. A sob escaped his lips, the surgeon taking a few steps back to let the man's emotions come out.

"I'll give you some space, Mr Stuart," he affirmed. "The nurse will be along shortly."

Joe nodded, hearing the door close before he moved closer

to his wife. "I'm so sorry, Cara," he breathed. "But I didn't know what else to do." He looked behind him, making sure that the coast was clear before leaning over his wife. "Just slip away. There'll be no pain. I'll make sure the kids are looked after." He checked his watch, seeing that it was the early hours of the morning. *I'm starving,* he thought before walking out of the room, plans forming in his mind.

∽

Martin winced as the slap echoed around the room. *Shit!*

Frank stood there, his hand stinging from the contact with his son's face. "You've gone too far this time."

Joe's vision cleared, taking a step forward, his fists bunched. *Bastard!*

It's gonna kick off, Martin thought, not knowing what to do. He looked at the older man, seeing the steel in his eyes. *I bet the old dog could still show the pup a thing or two.*

"Just try it, Son," Frank warned. "You're in no position to be angry. Do you know what you've done?"

"What else could I do?" Joe retorted as the pain radiated across his cheek. "Cara and Harry could have dropped us all in the shit. All of us, Dad, including you."

"Me, how could I be implicated in your sordid dealings?"

Joe was in full flow, his inhibitions melting away. "Mum."

The grey-haired man's face darkened as he took a step forward. "Leave her out of this. That was years ago. It has nothing to do with this."

"Maybe, but the police might start digging. And there's Steve to consider. He's adamant that you bumped her off."

Frank looked at Martin, making a snap decision. "Can either incident be linked back to you?"

"No. Paul made sure of that."

"How, Joe? Have you heard of forensics? If they think he's involved, they'll turn his hotel upside-down to find evidence."

"Well, he was killed in the basement. Paul assured me that everything is clean. Even when they moved the car, they'd have worn gloves and made sure nothing would come back on them."

The head of the Stuart family slumped against the sideboard, feeling weary. "And Cara?"

"All taken care of. The guy was a pro. I dropped the information needed at a random location and kept the phone calls to an absolute minimum."

"But there are still phone records, Joe. The police know how to access that kind of information."

"I know, Dad. But they'd have to suspect me first."

"Do you not think they will? If Cara wakes up, she might sing like a canary. Then, you've had it."

"What am I supposed to do?" Joe countered.

"Well, you should have come clean at the start, boy. You didn't kill that woman. The copper did. You should have reported it straight away."

"And risk losing the park? Not to mention all the shit that would have come out about The Retreat. It could have ruined us."

"And the body?"

"They'll never find it," Martin cut in.

"Well, I don't know what else we can do. Just wait to see what happens with Cara and hope to hell the police aren't already on the scent following Harry's death."

"We'll get through this," Joe offered, his words hollow.

"Maybe," Frank replied. "But it's not all about saving your hide. If Cara dies, think what it will do to the kids."

Joe looked at the floor, his children's feelings and futures only coming to bear after his father's words. "Whatever happens, they'll be okay."

"I hope so, Son. For your sake."

"For our sake, Dad. Just remember, You have secrets too."

∽

Steve burst through the ward doors, the nurses calming him down before he followed them to Cara's private room. He walked inside, tears rolling down his face at the sight of his sister-in-law's battered body. "Oh, Cara!" he cried as he took her hand. "What have they done to you?" After a minute, Steve pulled up a chair, his eyes flicking over the array of monitors against the wall, the cloying aroma of the hospital coating the back of his throat. He stroked her hand, the familiar feeling of dread settling upon him. "You need to wake up. Please, wake up." Steve sat there for a while, the sun's rays brightening the room as the early morning cloud blew out to sea. "I get the keys to the café tomorrow," he began. "I've even taken someone on to help me run the place. Her name's Dee. You'd like her, Cara. In truth, she'll probably run the place for me once we get going. I really want to concentrate on my painting and writing. Oh, and we'll be moving into the new house next week. You've gotta bring the kids over. There's a lovely garden with hidden nooks and crannies that they can get up to all kinds of mischief in. Just get better. I think the world of you, and so do the kids. I know he was behind this, and I'm pretty sure he was behind Harry's death too. Jesus! What a fucked-up family this is. You can see why I wanted out. As much as I hate Frank for what he did, I don't think he's involved in this. This is all Joe, trying to cover his tracks and keep his little secret hidden from the world. Well, he'll not keep it hidden for long. As soon as you're better, we'll bring him down, Frank too." He sat back, wiping the tears from his cheeks as the woman lay motionless, the rise and fall of her chest the only indication that she was still alive. After a few minutes, he stood up, walking into the small bathroom, leaving the light off as he pulled the door almost shut. Unzipping his trousers, Steve stood there, trying to be as quick as possible in case a nurse or doctor walked in. He heard the door open as he was about to flush; his hand, a few inches from the handle as a male voice, drifted through the crack in the door.

"Hi," Joe said as he walked over towards his wife.

Shit! Steve cursed, moving silently in the darkness to get a better view.

"You're a fighter; I'll give you that. Just slip away, Cara. It's for the best. The kids will be devastated, but I'll look after them. I promise." He paused, looking back at the entrance door. "You would have ruined me. I couldn't let that happen. I know you'd never understand, but I did what I had to do."

"What did you have to do?" Steve said as he walked into the room, colour draining from the blond man's face.

"Steve? What are you doing here?" the older brother asked, his voice unusually shaky.

"I came to see Cara. She's my sister-in-law," the younger brother stated as he stood his ground. "And I'm glad I did because you've just filled in the pieces of the puzzle. What did you do?"

Joe straightened, trying to look imposing. "I don't know what you're talking about?"

"Fuck off, Joe! I just heard you. You said she'd have ruined you and that you did what you had to do. Tell me, did Uncle Harry meet the same fate as your wife?"

"Steve, you're delusional. You heard nothing."

"Oh, but I did, and don't worry, because when Cara wakes up, I'll tell her everything."

Joe growled, his fists bunching. "It's your word against mine. Who will the police believe, a successful pillar of the community, or some down-and-out loser whose just lost his wife?"

"Let's find out. And leave Rosie out of this. She's gone."

"And that's a shame. Because her death was your fault. You're a loser, Steve Sullivan. That's why Rosie warmed the beds of many other men, including mine. That's why she wasn't happy, because she was married to you."

Steve took a step back, shaking his head. "You're lying."

"No, Steve, I'm not. She came to me many times because she needed a real man. If you think I'm lying, she had a small tattoo just below her waistline. A blue dolphin. Many a time I ran my fingers and lips over it, making her feel like the woman she deserved to be. So, think on that while you're driving home to your little grief hole."

Steve leaned over the bed, kissing the woman on the cheek before facing his brother. "Rosie's dead. I know she never loved me. But thanks for bringing your little secret out into the open. It'll make me more determined to bring you down. Frank too. Mark my words - your days are numbered." He walked past his brother, striding out of the room with his head high. *Please wake up, Cara. There's so much I need to tell you.*

CHAPTER
TWENTY-TWO

"Why can't w-we visit Mummy?" Tom asked as he sat on the bed with Hooper.

"I don't know," Lizzy replied. "I asked Dad this morning, but he doesn't want us to see her in the hospital. He said she was getting better though, and that Mummy would be home soon."

"I miss her."

Lizzy hugged her younger brother, feeling his body relax. "I miss her too. I want her to come home as much as you do, Tom. Plus, Daddy's cooking is horrible."

The boy smiled as Tristan entered the bedroom, his bruises barely noticeable. "What do you want?" Tom asked confidently.

"Where's Dad?"

"At the hospital. Malcolm's in the kitchen. Babysitting."

"Whatever," the older brother shrugged, walking out of the room as a voice rang out.

"Kids, dinner."

They entered the kitchen a minute later, the aroma making Tom's mouth come to life. "What's for dinner?"

Malcolm smiled, the dark-haired man grabbing the oven

glove from the countertop. "Well, I thought I'd go all out and treat you. Chicken goujons, chips and beans."

"Sounds great," Lizzy replied, trying to sound cheerful.

"Well, there wasn't much left in the freezer. I'll have a word with your dad when he gets home. He's probably not noticed that you're running low on stuff."

The man busied himself before laying three places at the breakfast bar. "Where's Tristan?"

"Gone out," Tom stated.

"Out, where? Joe told me to look after you."

"It's okay," Lizzy reassured. "His friend Toby lives through the hedge. That's where he'll be."

"Are you sure?" Malcolm asked, his pulse beginning to increase.

"I am. He goes there a lot. Probably to get away from us."

The dark-haired man smiled, shaking his head. "Why would anyone want to get away from you two? You're totally cool."

Lizzy beamed, nudging her brother. "Did you hear that? We're totally cool."

Tom grinned, liking the new title that had been bestowed upon his small shoulders. "Thank you."

"Malcolm, why aren't you married?"

The man was taken aback; his composure lost as two sets of eyes peered up at him. "Erm, well, I don't know."

"Do you have a girlfriend?" Tom inquired, suddenly interested.

"Not at the moment," he replied cautiously, his decreasing blood pressure beginning to rise once more.

"Well, you're nice. I think you should get married and have lots of babies," Lizzy proclaimed before she got stuck into her beans.

"Leave it with me, and I'll keep you posted."

"How's old Antony?" Tom asked in between mouthfuls of goujons.

Thankful for the change of direction, the man seated himself next to the children. "He's doing okay. I think he's a bit bored, though."

"Why?" Lizzy asked.

"Because his job was all he ever knew. When he left school in the '50s, he started work straight away. Now, he's just knocking about the house like a bear with a sore head."

"What does that mean?" Tom said.

"It means..." Malcolm's words halted as a set of headlights swung past the kitchen window. "Never mind, kids. It looks like your granddad's here."

"Granddad," Lizzy chirped, jumping off her stool before running towards the front door, Tom hobbling after her.

Malcolm stayed where he was, washing up the pots and pans until Frank walked into the kitchen, the children at his heels. "Thanks for looking after them," he smiled. "Joe's on his way back from the hospital, so I'll take over."

"How's Mrs Stuart?" the head groundsman asked.

The older man's face dropped slightly. "No change."

"Such a shame. These roads are treacherous at the best of times," the younger man added.

"That they are." He looked around the kitchen, peering into the lounge area. "Where's Tristan?"

"At his friend's house next door," Malcolm replied as he pulled his jacket off the stool. "I really hope she wakes up soon."

"We all do. Thanks, Malcolm. Give your dad my regards."

The younger man nodded before leaving by the kitchen door as another set of headlights pulled up outside the house. "What's going on, Son," Frank whispered as he watched Joe hurry into the kitchen.

"Hi, kids."

"Hi, Dad. How's Mummy?"

"Still the same, Lizzy. But don't worry. I'm sure she's going to wake up soon. Look, I need to speak to granddad. You finish your tea, then put the tele on." He motioned for Frank to follow him. They headed out into the oncoming darkness, Joe leading his father around the side of the house until they were stood underneath a thatched carport.

"What's up, Son?"

Joe turned around, his emotions boiling over as he fell into the older man's arms, "Oh, Dad," he blurted, sobbing and shaking as Frank held him tightly. "I've really fucked up."

"Joe, calm yourself down. Take a deep breath and tell me what's happened."

The younger broke the embrace, seating himself against a brick pillar. "I went to the hospital. Cara was the same, but I said something I shouldn't have. Jesus! Why am I so fucking stupid?"

"What did you tell her?"

"That she'd ruin me if she found out. That it's for the best if she just slipped away."

"Why would you say that?"

"Because it would, Dad. If she recovers, Cara will go straight to the police."

"But you said it's all taken care of?"

"It was. It is, but there's something else I need to tell you."

Frank looked at the younger man, seeing the fear in his eyes. "I've got a feeling I'm going to need to sit down too."

∾

Steve had sat there for an hour, updating Cara on his new developments. With bubbling enthusiasm, he updated her on the café and the house move. "It's going to be a busy week. We get the keys on Wednesday, so it's going to be pretty full-on. I'm moving the stuff myself. My neighbour's giving me a hand, so by the time the kids come out of school, they'll have a new house." He stopped, the excitement tempered by the beeping machines. "Please wake up. I really miss you, Cara." He stood up, leaving the room for refreshment, unaware that his sister-in-law's eyelids had begun to flutter. A few minutes later, Steve shouldered his way through the door, placing his coffee next to the bed.

"Hi," Cara croaked, Steve almost falling backwards over the chair.

"Jesus!" the man exclaimed. "You're back."

"What happened?"

He went to her, tears flowing freely. After a few seconds, he seated himself on the bed, taking her hand. "You were in a car crash. What do you remember?"

She frowned, turning her head towards him. After a few seconds, something came to her, Cara's eyes widening. "There was a van. I think it hit me from behind. Then all I can remember is going over the edge."

He kissed the top of her head. "You've had us so worried. I thought I'd lost you." More tears started to fall, Cara squeezing his hand weakly.

"Well, I'm still here. Just about." She looked down at the trailing tubes and plaster cast on her left arm. "I can wiggle my toes," she smiled. "That's a good thing, right?"

"That's a good thing. Shall I call for the nurse?"

"In a minute. Could I have some water, please?"

He carefully held the plastic cup to her lips, trickling a few drops over her dry lips, Cara nodding her head in thanks. "How long have I been out?"

"A few days. I'm so relieved"

"Well, it'll take more than that to get rid of me." She smiled, her face transforming for the briefest of moments.

"Good. You need to stick around. We'd all be lost without you."

She smiled briefly, something coming to her as she stared out of the window. "The white van."

"White van?"

"Yes," she began. "The one that hit me. I'm sure it was following me earlier in the day. I remember now. I was on my way to your place, and a white van was right up my backside."

He sighed, shaking his head. *I can't tell her. Not now. She's just woken up.*

"Steve, what is it?"

"Nothing. I'm fine."

She squeezed his hand. "I love you to bits, but you're a hopeless liar. What's wrong?"

"I wanted to tell you later, once the doctor has checked you over."

"Tell me now, Steve. Whatever it is, I can take it."

"Okay. Here goes. It was Joe."

"Joe? I don't understand."

"He was behind your crash. Not personally, as he was at home with the kids. He must have paid someone to run you off the road."

"What? How do you know?"

He relayed the conversation with his brother, Cara's already pale complexion seeming to whiten even more. "I'm so sorry."

"The bastard! He did the same to Harry too. He wants to silence us. Fucking hell, Steve! My own husband wants me dead."

"Well, he knows that I know. And now you know too."

"I can't get my head around this. First the body, then Harry, and now he's tried to have me bumped off. What the hell did I marry?"

"I'm so sorry. This is the last thing that I wanted to tell you. But now you know."

"And I know what I have to do?"

"You mean..."

"Yes. I'm calling the police. I'm going to make him pay."

CHAPTER
TWENTY-THREE

Joe replaced the receiver, staring out across the garden as the news sunk in. His wife had come around. *Shit! What do I do now?*

"You okay, Dad?" Tristan asked as he walked into the lounge.

"What? Oh, yes, I'm fine, Son. You okay?"

"I guess. Any news on Mum?"

Joe nodded. "Can you keep a secret?"

The boy's eyes widened, nodding his head. "Sure."

"She's going to be okay. Mum woke up a few minutes ago."

Tristan ran to his father, burying his face in Joe's midriff. "Oh, Dad. I'm..."

"Shh," Joe warned the boy. "I don't want Lizzy and Tom to know just yet. I want to visit Mum to see how she is before I let them know. Can I trust you?"

"With anything."

Joe knelt, hugging the ten-year-old. "You're a good boy, Tristan. And I love you more than anything in the world. Always remember that, whatever happens."

"I love you too. To the moon and back."

He kissed his son, rising from his knees as his mobile phone began to chime. "I need to take this outside. Mum's the word on Mum," he winked, ruffling the boy's hair before heading through the kitchen. "Dad."

"Any news?" Frank asked.

"She's awake."

There was a pause. "Okay. That's good news and worrying news."

"I know. Look, I hate to put on you again, but could you watch the kids for a few hours?"

"Lucky for you, I'm at a loose end. Give me twenty minutes, and I'll be over."

"Cheers, Dad. I'll see you in a bit." He ended the call, noticing his shaking hands before he re-entered the house, wondering what the next few hours would bring.

∼

"When he gets here, please don't tell him that my brother-in-law was here. Sorry, Mandy, it's a long story."

The dark-skinned nurse nodded, winking at the younger woman. "My lips are sealed, hun."

She sat there, playing out scenarios in her head as the minutes ticked away. Lunch came and went before the door finally opened, her husband stepping into the room. "Hi," she said, trying her best to smile. *I hate you. Bastard!*

"Oh, Cara," Joe gushed as he strode over towards the bed. "I'm so glad you're back. I've been beside myself with worry."

Like hell you have! "Are the kids okay?"

Always the kids, never me. "They are worried sick. But I'll give them the good news when I get home. I didn't want to tell them just yet, but I will as soon as I get back."

More secrets. "That's fine. I can't wait to see them." She shifted across the bed as her husband sat down, trying to put space between them.

"So, what happened?"

"It's all coming back to me now," she began. *You know what happened.* "I was coming along the road from Port Isaac. There was a white Transit van behind me. I tried to put some distance between us, but then it rammed me. I don't remember anything after that."

"Jesus! Why would someone do that?"

She looked at him, her dark eyes boring into his. "Who knows? Maybe it was road rage? Maybe it was planned?"

"Planned. What do you mean, babe?" *Shit!*

"I don't know. Yet. But Harry died a few days before in similar circumstances. You have to admit; it can't be a coincidence."

"Harry's car came off the road," he countered.

Cara's eyelids drooped, the woman lying back on her pillow. "Joe. I'm tired. I think I need to rest. Could you bring the kids with you next time?"

"Sure. Whatever you want, babe. Get some rest and try not to overthink this. It's probably just road rage or something."

"Well, I have an idea about who was behind it. And as soon as I can, I'll be contacting the police. Close the door on your way out."

He went to reply, seeing his wife's eyes close as the room darkened slightly. *Oh God! She knows I did this.*

∼

Frank sat on the sofa, ignoring the television as his mind raced. *This is the only way,* he thought, rising from the sofa as his son's car pulled up outside. Rain pattered against the windows as the old man made his way across the kitchen, leaning against the counter as Joe entered. "How is she?"

The younger man sighed. "Awake."

"What has she said?"

"Not much. She remembers the van, and before she dozed off, Cara said she knew who was responsible."

"And?"

"And then she fell asleep, Dad. Although, I think she's playing with me."

"What do you mean?"

"She knows it's me. As soon as she wakes up, she's going to call the police."

"Bloody hell!"

"I'm screwed, Dad. I've really fucked this up."

"Yes, you have. But let's not cry over spilt milk. What's done is done. We need to keep you away from the law."

"How? They'll find me."

"Do you trust me?"

"Of course. With my life."

Frank took an envelope out of his pocket, handing it to the younger man. "Read through this. Everything is in place, Joe."

"I don't understand?"

"I know, but that will explain everything." Frank took a step forward, embracing his eldest son. "I'll be back later. You need to get things in order while I'm gone. Can you do that for me?"

Breaking the hold, Joe looked up at his father. The man who'd been a constant in his life. The man who now stood before him with tears in his eyes. "What's in this letter?"

"Read it. I'll be back later."

He stood there, watching his father walk out of the kitchen, wondering when or if he'd ever see him again. After making himself a coffee, Joe sat at the breakfast bar, reading and re-reading the letter. After five minutes, he refolded the paper, tucking it into his back pocket as the gravity of the instructions hit home. "Fucking hell!" he whispered as Tristan walked into the kitchen.

"Hey, Dad. You okay?"

"Come here, Son." He placed a steady hand on Tristan's shoulder, lowering his voice. "I need you to do me a favour."

"Sure," the blond-haired boy replied.

He talked quickly and quietly, holding up his hand to silence the protests from the ten-year-old. After a few minutes, Joe took his son in his arms. "It's the only way."

"I'm scared."

"I'm scared too. But if I don't do this, the police will lock me up and throw away the key. Now go, and once you're done, ask Lizzy and Tom to come downstairs."

Joe's heart constricted as he watched the dejected boy walk out of the kitchen. *I'm sorry, Son.* Then he was off the stool, running up to his bedroom, closing the door behind him.

Five minutes later, they walked into the kitchen, Lizzy smiling as Joe walked in from outside. "How's Mummy?"

He smiled. "She's awake, princess. Mum's going to be okay."

She went to her father, crying as he held him. Joe looked down, tears spilling from his eyes as his youngest son walked over. "Come here, Tom," he soothed, taking the seven-year-old into his arms.

"When's Mummy coming home?" Tom asked.

"No idea, champ, but I'm sure she'll be home in a few days or so. Are you all happy?"

"Yes, Daddy," Lizzy beamed. "I love you, but your dinners are not good."

Joe laughed, more tears shed as he looked down at his daughter. "Well, Mummy's better at that sort of stuff. But Daddy will have to help out when she's home because Mummy will need to take it easy."

"As long as she's home, I don't care what I eat," she giggled.

Joe ruffled her dark hair, clapping his hands together. "Well, I think we should celebrate. Who wants a pizza?"

"Yes, please," Lizzy replied happily, Tristan and Tom nodding their heads in agreement.

"Okay. Granddad will be back in a bit. I'll call the pizza place and pop and get them. Can you guys go and play in your rooms for a bit?"

They filed out of the kitchen, Joe placing a hand on his eldest son's arm as he went to walk past. "Always remember that I love you. Whatever happens and whatever you hear about me, I'll always be your dad."

"I don't want you to…"

"Trust me, Son. There's no other way." He knelt, embracing his eldest child, tears flowing freely as the boy wept in his arms. The man's heart was breaking, knowing that he'd brought all this on. He only hoped that in time, fresh wounds would heal over. After a moment, Joe stood up. "This is not the end. Trust me. Be good for your mother and never forget me."

Lizzy and Tom sat on the floor, playing with Hooper. Unaware that their father had left the house, their brother sitting forlornly on the sofa above them. Scared and alone.

CHAPTER
TWENTY-FOUR

Cara felt drained. She sat opposite two plain-clothed detectives, taking a sip of water. "What happens now?"

The woman placed her pad on the side table, a serious expression etched on her face. "We bring your husband in for questioning. If what you say is true, Mrs Stuart, your husband has a lot to discuss with us."

The younger detective, a man in his early thirties, cleared his throat. "Is there anyone who can take the children?"

"Yes. Either my father-in-law or my brother-in-law can help out. Hopefully, I should be able to return home in a few days. The kids will be distraught, but I couldn't keep this inside any longer."

"Is your father-in-law Frank Stuart?" the middle-aged woman inquired.

"Yes. Do you know him?"

"Only by reputation. My late father was also a copper. I remember what happened to your father-in-law's wife."

"Yes. A terrible tragedy."

"Hmm," the woman replied. "Well, we'll leave you to rest,

Mrs Stuart. When you're ready, we'd like you to make a formal statement."

"Of course. I'll pop along to the station as soon as possible. Will you keep me updated?"

"We will. DS Pearce will pop by tomorrow and let you know the latest."

"Thank you," she replied, her emotions simmering. "I never thought I'd be in this position. Yes, my husband has never been an angel. But if he's involved in two murders, along with trying to bump me off, well, he's got to answer for that."

"Would you be able to show us where you think the body is buried? It would be helpful, as we don't want to dig up half the forest."

"Of course. What will happen to Martin?"

"We'll be bringing in Mr Murray for questioning. I'm sure he can help us with our enquiries."

"I know what I saw, but Martin was probably just doing what Joe told him to do."

The detective nodded. "We'll speak to you tomorrow, Mrs Stuart."

"Thank you." Cara sat there as the door swung closed, wondering what chain of events she'd set in motion. Her husband would be rounded up within the next few hours, along with Martin. She only hoped that her father-in-law was not part of this. For all the stories and resentment from Steve, Cara had always liked the local business magnate. And she knew that the children idolised him, probably more than their father. *Except for Tristan,* she thought ruefully. *Lizzy and Tom will be okay, but I don't know how Tristan will take this. Shit, he may hate me for all this.* She picked up her phone, dialling a familiar number. It rang out for a few seconds until a male voice answered. "Hi."

"Hey," Steve replied. "How are you feeling? Sorry I've not been to see you today. Been bogged down with stuff."

"That's okay, Steve. I know you've got a lot on. I'm okay. Still feel a bit fuzzy, and it's not nice having a catheter."

"I'm sure it's not. Have they said when you'd be allowed home?"

"Not officially. One nurse said a few days or so. There's something else I need to tell you."

"Okay. I'm listening."

"The police have just left. I called them after Joe came to see me. I know he was behind this. I could see it in his eyes." She heard an intake of breath down the line, then a pause.

"What have the police said?"

"Well, they want to speak to Joe. And Martin. Not sure when that will be, though."

"Probably soon. If they think he's involved in all this, they'll want to bring him in sharpish. Did you say anything about Frank?"

"No, although his name did come up, but not related to what's happened. I know you've got history. I get it, but I really don't think Frank had anything to do with this. It was all Joe."

"As much as I hate to admit it, I think you're right. I think my brother has dug a massive hole for himself."

"Well, it's out of our hands now. I've pressed the big red button; let's see what happens."

∼

Frank heard the crunch of tyres from the sofa, levering himself upright before heading for the front door. "Where the..."

"Mr Stuart?" A middle-aged woman asked. "I'm DI Harris, and this is DS Pearce," she said as they both presented their warrant cards.

"I'm Frank Stuart. I thought you were my son. He went out for pizza earlier, and he's not returned."

The woman looked at her colleague, a young man in a dark suit. "What time was this?"

"Six-ish. I've tried calling him, but his phone's off."

"May we come in, Mr Stuart?"

"Call me Frank. Please." He gestured for them to enter, closing the door quietly. "The kids are all in bed. Come through to the kitchen. Would you like something to drink?"

"We're fine, thanks," the woman replied curtly.

"So, what's all this about? He's only been gone a few hours; the police don't normally turn up this quickly."

"We've reason to believe that your son was involved in the attempted murder of his wife, along with the death of Harry Phipps and the disappearance of an unidentified woman."

Frank's eyes widened, the old man shaking his head. "What? Joe? My Joe? There must be some kind of mistake."

"Well, we need to speak to him urgently. Do you know where he was going when he went out for pizza?"

Frank shook his head. "Not sure. Probably Bude. It's not far away."

"What car does your son drive?"

"A black Range Rover."

"Registration?"

Frank gave them the details, reaching for a bottle of whisky on the countertop. He poured two fingers into a tumbler, downing the fiery liquid in one go as the younger detective excused himself to make a phone call. "I don't understand what's going on?"

"Well, we need to speak to Joe urgently."

"Yes, it sounds like you do. I suppose I'd better stay the night here. There's no one else to look after the children."

"We can arrange for a family liaison officer to attend."

"No. Their mother is in hospital, and their father is missing. They need family around them."

"Okay. Thank you for that." She regarded the old man. *Not in bad shape for a pensioner.* "Frank. It would be really helpful if you knew anything about your son's whereabouts. Anything at all."

"I'm as in the dark as you are. Although…"

"Although what?"

Frank seated himself. "He wasn't himself earlier. When he came back from the hospital."

"Well, his wife's just come out of a coma. How would you expect him to be?"

"True, but it's something else. Joe seemed preoccupied. Like he wasn't really here. Then, he asked the kids if they wanted pizza and was out the door like a shot."

"Is that normal?"

"No. Joe's not easily rattled. He'd probably order one over the phone if I know my son. More money than sense."

DS Pearce re-entered the kitchen, his face tense. "Guv, they've found Mr Stuart's car."

"Where?" Harris urged as Frank looked on.

"On the beach at Port Isaac. Local police are on the scene. They've also found a pair of boots next to the car."

The female detective looked at Frank, seeing the colour drain from his face. "We need to get down there. Frank, I know that sounds worrying, but there could be a rational explanation. Is there a number we can reach you on?"

Frank gave them his mobile phone number, along with the Stuart's landline. "Oh my God! I can't believe I'm hearing this. Please, find my boy."

~

DI Harris looked out to sea, pulling her coat around her neck. He'd not last long out there. Four minutes maximum. She looked at her approaching colleague. "What have you got?"

"The local publican saw Mr Stuart's car drive onto the beach about half six."

"Did he not think that was a bit strange?"

"Not really. You get a lot of vehicles on the beach."

"Sorry. Us city folk are a bit out of touch."

"You weren't to know. Anyway, the publican, a Mr Bean, said that he came out about seven for a smoke and noticed the car's interior lights on, but no one was around. That's when he took a walk down to the car and spotted the boots."

"Okay, what's your hunch?"

"Not sure. One possibility is that Stuart knew the net was tightening around him, so he walked out to sea."

"That was my first thought too."

"Or he left the car here as a smokescreen."

"I thought that as well. See, us city folk catch on quick," she grinned. "Let's say option two is right; where would he go?"

"No idea. There's little to no CCTV around here, so it will be a stretch to capture him making off somewhere. Also, it's low tide, so if someone were picking him up, he'd have to swim a fair distance. I wouldn't try it."

"But you're not being chased by the police. Give a man motivation, and he'll do whatever it takes."

"Okay, say a boat picked him up; where would he go?"

"No idea. Ireland?"

"That's a stretch, but we can notify the Garda when we get back to the station. We'll need to do some digging to see if Stuart has connections across the water. What's your gut telling you?"

"That I'm hungry, and I should have eaten hours ago. Honestly, I think this isn't what it seems. I don't know the man, but he's very wealthy. And if he's like his father, he'll be confident too. I'm sure he'd get the best lawyer money could buy. If Stuart has topped himself, he's just given up before the storm."

"Well, it looks like the search team have arrived," Pearce replied as two Land Rover's rolled down the stone slope onto the sand. "Let's see what they can find."

Harris walked up the steep gradient, heading into the pub while Pearce spoke to the dive team. They leaned against the Land Rovers, sipping coffee as the search team headed out across the frigid waters. After an hour, the small inflatable grounded itself on the shore, a large man in a wetsuit hopping deftly into the lapping waves before heading towards them, a clear plastic bag in his hands. "What's that?" Harris asked expectantly.

"A jacket. A man's jacket. Nothing in the pockets." He placed it on the bonnet. "All yours."

"Thanks. Anything else to report?"

The man shook his head. "Nothing. The current would probably have pulled him under and carried him along the coast if he did go into the water. We can't do any more tonight, but we'll continue the search at first light. Normally, bodies are found to the south, on the rocks around Pentire Point or around the Camel."

Harris nodded, knowing the Camel estuary next to the pretty town of Padstow. "Thank you. We'll get that checked over and be in touch tomorrow."

They watched the man walk away, Harris blowing out a breath. "So, what do we do now?"

"We eat. It's gonna be a long night, and my belly thinks my throat's been cut."

"You always did have a way with words, guv," Pearce quipped as they made their way up the stone ramp, away from the dark waters and the mysteries it held.

CHAPTER
TWENTY-FIVE

"Oh my God!" Cara cried as the two officers stood at the end of the bed. "Joe wouldn't do that. Whatever shit he was in, my husband wouldn't commit suicide."

Harris and Pearce looked solemn, the woman pulling up a chair. "And yet, you didn't think he'd do the things you told us last night, Cara. Maybe you didn't know him as well as you thought?"

"But kill himself?" She reached for the tissues, dabbing her eyes as the woman's emotions began to boil over.

"We've had the coastguard out for the past few hours. There's no sign of your husband. In water like that, he'd have succumbed to hyperthermia within minutes. We'll keep looking, but the longer it goes, the less chance we have of finding him."

"The kids are going to be heartbroken. Especially Tristan. He idolised Joe."

"Your father-in-law is with them, Mrs Stuart," Pearce added. "We'll head there next and update him."

"Shit! The kids are supposed to be at school today. Frank

won't know what to put them in. Their packed lunches won't be made."

"Take it easy, Cara," Harris replied, placing a hand on the younger woman's arm. "I'm sure the kids are fine, even if they aren't dressed properly."

"I need to get out of here. They need me."

"Well, that's a decision for the doctors. You've just come out of a coma. They may want to keep an eye on you for a while longer."

"My husband is missing, probably dead. I can't sit here doing nothing!"

"We understand. Oh, quick question," the female detective said. "Does your husband have any connections in Ireland?"

"Ireland? No, why?"

"It's just a lead we're following up with. Not to worry, and we'll keep you updated, Cara. We're very sorry."

She sat there, unable to think, her chest tightening. *It can't be true. Not Joe. He wouldn't do this to the kids.* Cara sat there, her mind working overtime, trying to unlock the latest mystery that had settled over the Cornish coast.

∼

A few hours later, Harris and Pearce sat in an interview room at Truro police station, a hulking man seated opposite. "Interview started at twelve-thirty hours on Monday 8th January, 2001. Present in the room are DI Harris, DS Pearce, Martin Murray and duty solicitor Karen Maddocks." Harris looked at Martin, who stared back at her through red-rimmed eyes.

"So, Mr Murray, how long have you worked for Mr Stuart?"

Martin stared straight ahead, the man shrugging his shoulders. "A few years."

"And what do you do for Mr Stuart?"

"I'm his right-hand man."

"Meaning?" Pearce pressed.

Martin looked at the ceiling. "I help out at Sandy Shores. Handle the entertainment. General stuff."

"By entertainment, are you referring to the activities at The Retreat?"

Shit! He looked down, picking at a piece of loose skin on his thumb.

Harris noticed the man's demeanour change, taking the advantage. "Yes, Mr Murray. We know all about the goings-on at The Retreat. It would save us all a lot of hardship if you cooperated with us. Mr Stuart is missing, presumed dead. There are a lot of loose ends to tie up. Let's focus on the first one. Mrs Stuart claims that she saw you burying a body in the forest close to The Retreat."

Martin looked at his last-minute solicitor, the young woman glancing at him, offering nothing else. *Fuck!* "I don't know what you're talking about?"

"Come now, Mr Murray. Mrs Stuart was very specific about what she saw. Help us."

"I can't. I don't know what you're talking about."

Harris took a sip of her lukewarm coffee. *He's going to be a tough nut to crack.* "What goes on at The Retreat. In your own words."

He sighed, his brain working overtime. *Keep it together.* "We hold parties there. For some of the locals."

"Okay, we'll take their names after the interview and follow up with them. What kind of parties?"

"The kind where young women entertain older men. Do you want me to draw you a picture?"

"Thanks, Mr Murray. I think we get the idea. So, was there ever an incident during these parties? Maybe someone got hurt. Maybe drugs were involved. Paint a picture for us."

Sarky bitch! "There were no incidents. Women arrived, men arrived, they had some fun, and they all went home happy."

"You mean the men went home to their wives, and the women went back to the hotel in Bude?"

"Probably. I wouldn't know."

"Do you know all of the men who attend the parties?" Pearce inquired.

"Some of them. They live in the local area. Others come from further afield."

"Like whom?" Harris shot back.

Shit! "Not sure," the Scotsman replied. "Many use false names. You can probably understand why."

The detectives glanced at each other before the woman continued to probe. "Tell me, are there any men who look familiar? I know they may use false names, but has there been anyone that you've recognised?"

"How do you mean?"

"Famous people," the DS elaborated.

"Not that I can think of," Martin replied, his pulse beginning to quicken.

"Look, Martin," Harris softened. "Help me out here. We've got a local man who's missing, accounts of a body in the woods, and we've not even touched on Harry Phipps."

"Harry? What's he got to do with this?"

"You tell me? Mrs Stuart claims that she'd asked him to check out The Retreat. The last time she spoke to him, Harry was parked outside The Bellevue in Bude. We'll be paying them a visit in due course. After that, there was no sign of him until his car was discovered a few days later. So, that's two dead people, three if you count Mr Stuart. It's not looking good, is it?"

"I guess not. But I don't know about a body in the woods or about what happened to the old-timer."

Harris leaned back in her chair, ruffling her brown hair. "I know you're loyal to Mr Stuart. I get that. You probably feel that you owe him. However, protecting Joe isn't going to do him any good, or you."

"As I said, I don't know about a body. I don't know about what happened to Cara's uncle, except what I heard about on the news. Are you going to charge me or let me go?"

"You're just helping us with our enquiries, Mr Murray," Pearce replied smoothly. "Once the interview is over, you're free to go."

"Do you know where the women arrive from?" Harris continued.

Give them something. Don't play too dumb. "London, I think."

She made a note in her pad. "Okay. Tell me, are they mainly British girls?"

"Most are. Although, there's been a few European ones too."

"Polish?"

"I couldn't tell you. I don't get to socialise with them."

"Thank you, Mr Murray."

Pearce leaned forward. "So, where are you from?"

"Scotland. The accent kinda gives it away."

The young detective smiled thinly. "What made you move to the bright lights of Cornwall?"

"I fancied a change. Not much going on up there."

"Whereabouts in Scotland did you live?"

"Aviemore."

"Family?"

"None to speak of. Okay. So, are we done?"

"For now, but please don't go too far. We may want to speak to you again. Interview terminated at twelve thirty-four."

An hour later, Martin watched as the police car pulled away from the kerb, two old ladies peering at him from across the street. "Joe, where the fuck are you?" He unlocked his front door, walking into his ground floor flat, dropping his keys on the hall table before heading into the kitchen. The kettle started to boil, the man hunched over the sink, his mind working overtime. *Is he dead? Did Joe top himself rather than face the old bill?* Martin walked into his bedroom, ducking under the doorframe before kneeling next to the skirting board. Meaty fingers dug into the side of the wood, prizing it from the others before he reached into the void. Sweat peppered his brow as he pulled a box through the aperture, dusting it off before opening it. *It looks like I might need this sooner than I thought*, as the man looked at several wads of banknotes and a passport. *Where can I go?* He had no family to speak of and no contacts, except for a cousin who lived in Greece. *That's an option, but I'd need to find Luke's number. Shit, the police might be watching me. They might be tapping my phone or email. Fuck!* A few minutes later, Martin sank onto the sofa, blowing on his coffee before taking a sip. *I haven't done anything wrong. I didn't kill that girl. Yes, I buried her body, but the bent copper killed her. And I had nothing to do with Harry's death*. He knew that they were false hopes. Even though he wasn't directly involved, he'd been an accomplice in the murder of the girl and had witnessed the old man's demise. The Scotsman knew that the police would nail him for that, a custodial sentence the likely outcome. *Unless*, he thought as a slither of hope presented itself. *I come clean and ask for a deal.*

CHAPTER
TWENTY-SIX

"I'M SO SORRY, MRS STUART."

Cara looked at the two detectives as her nurse left the room, silence hanging in the air for a few moments. "I can't believe it."

"There was no sign of his body, but as I'd previously mentioned, the divers recovered his jacket from the water."

"So now what happens?"

Harris moved around the bed, leaning against the window ledge. "You'll have to apply to the courts so they can deal with your husband's estate. If they're satisfied with the information provided, then they will issue a declaration of death. We will provide information to the courts on your behalf if that will help?"

"I guess so. Jesus! What a year it's been. First Tom's accident, then all this."

"What happened to your son?" Pearce inquired.

She sagged against the pillows, her eyes moistening. "Tom and his brother were messing around with a chainsaw. He fell over whilst holding it and lost his leg below the knee."

Both detectives looked shocked, Harris moving over the

bed. "Sounds like you've been through hell over the past few months, Cara."

The door opened, Steve halting mid-step as he saw that his sister-in-law had company. "Oh, sorry. I'll wait in the corridor."

Tears formed in Cara's eyes as she stared over at him. "Come in. This is my brother-in-law, Steve."

He let the door close, walking over to the window. "Are you okay?"

Her walls crumbled, the woman sobbing as he went over to her. "He's dead. Joe's dead."

"Jesus!" Steve breathed as he held her. He looked over at the officers, who stood there immobile. After a minute, Steve gently laid her back against the pillow. "I'm so sorry. I can't believe it. My brother's dead."

"We're very sorry, Mr Stuart."

He looked at them, sighing. "My surname's not Stuart. It's Sullivan."

Harris frowned, taking out her pad as the man on the bed took his sister-in-law's hand. "Oh, was Mr Stuart your half-brother?"

Steve looked at Cara, who nodded. "No, we had a falling out many years ago, so I cut myself off from the family and took my mother's maiden name."

"Forgive me for asking at such a sensitive moment, but what was the falling out over?"

"Shit!"

"Tell them," Cara reassured.

"When my mother died, it turns out that she was in love with another man. Frank knew this. Then suddenly, she went missing, the police concluding that she was swept out to sea whilst walking the dog. I didn't believe them. I thought that my father was responsible."

"Do you still think that?" Pearce asked.

"Yes. It was many years ago, but I still don't believe she was swept out to sea. Mum knew the coastal paths like the back of her hand. Bad weather or not, she was too wily to have come a cropper out there."

"Do you have any evidence, Mr Sullivan?"

"That's the thing; I don't. All I have is my gut instinct."

Harris closed her pad, her attention turning towards Cara. "We'll be in touch over the next few days. Once again, we're very sorry for your loss."

They left the room, silence descending for a few moments until Steve turned around on the bed. "I'm sorry."

"Don't be," she sniffed, wrapping her arms around him. "I'm shocked and upset, but part of me still believes that this is all a smokescreen. Joe knew the net was tightening. It wouldn't surprise me if he's done a runner."

"Nor me, but Joe had so much to lose. The park is worth millions. Surely, he'd not just fold his cards and run? Whatever his flaws, Joe's a survivor."

"Jesus! What am I going to tell the kids? They're coming later with Frank."

"You'll just have to tell them. It will be hard, but they need to know."

"How did yours take it when Rosie died?"

He shrugged. "They were upset for sure. But then I won the money, which changed things. They all miss her, but they're taking it well. Kids are resilient; remember that."

"Honestly, I think Tom and Lizzy will be fine. It's Tristan I worry about."

"I know. He'll take it the hardest. The boy idolised Joe."

"What a total mess. If someone had told us a year ago that both Rosie and Joe would have died."

"We'd have thought they were crazy," Steve cut in.

"I am sad. I know you fell out, but when I first met Joe, he was a lovely guy. Cocky and brash, but lovely. But then, we were getting divorced. He went with other women and had a hand in Harry's death. So yes, I'm upset, but I have to focus on the kids."

"That's all a good parent can do. And you're an amazing mum. Remember that."

She hugged him, not wanting the man she'd grown so fond of to let her go. Ever.

∼

"Mummy," Lizzy chirped, diving onto the bed as Tristan, Tom and Frank followed the little girl into the room.

Hugs and kisses were handed out, all three children embracing their mother as carefully as they could. She noticed a coldness from her eldest child, who gave her a brief squeeze before standing next to his grandfather. "Oh, guys. I've missed you so much."

"What happened?" Tom asked from the other side of the bed.

"Mummy was in a nasty car accident. But I'll be okay. I'm hoping to come home in a few days. Has Granddad been taking good care of you?"

"He has," the boy replied. "Granddad's a good cook. We've had sausage and b-bacon sandwiches every day."

She smiled at her father-in-law. "Well, that won't do you any harm. I'd kill for one of those." The words hung in the air.

"Where's Daddy," Lizzy asked as she hopped on one foot next to her mother.

Cara looked at Frank, who nodded grimly. "Guys. Come and sit down. All of you," she replied, looking over at Tristan. As they sat down, the woman felt her emotions rise. "I don't know how to say this."

"Just say it," Frank replied from the far side of the room. "We're all together."

She composed herself, trying to locate the right words. "I've got some bad news," she began, her voice shaking. "Daddy died."

She felt Lizzy and Tom flinch, the mattress shifting. "What?" the little girl exclaimed.

"Daddy wasn't well. Sometimes, when people are unwell, well, they do bad things to themselves."

"What do you m-mean?" Tom countered, his dark eyes staring up at her.

"He went for a swim and never came back. I'm so sorry."

Silence hung over them like a dark blanket until Lizzy began to whimper. "Daddy's gone to heaven?"

She hugged her daughter, letting the emotions spill out. "He has, sweetheart. He's up there now with Nanny Margaret." She saw Frank stiffen, looking away as she pulled Tom towards her.

"Why would he do that?" the little boy asked.

Before she could reply, Tristan shot off the bed, tears in his eyes. "You're lying! You did this to him!"

"Tristan," the woman replied. "Come here, love."

"He told me. Dad told me that you were going to the police and that his life was over. You killed my dad. I hate you. I fucking hate you!"

Before Cara could answer, her eldest child ran across the room, flinging the door open before disappearing down the corridor. Frank looked at her, his face drawn. "I'll go after him." The old man jogged down the stark hallway, seeing his eldest grandson ahead. *Slow down,* he thought as he struggled to keep pace. After a minute, Frank strode out of the hospital's entrance, seeing the blond-haired boy sat on a low wall next to a smoking shelter. He walked over, his breathing ragged. "Tristan."

The boy looked up, his face streaked with tears. "I hate her. She killed Dad."

Frank sat down heavily, placing an arm around the boy's shoulders. "No, Son. She didn't."

"Dad told me what was going on. He said that Mum was going to report him to the police and that his life was over."

"Tristan, look at me." The boy did so, looking for answers. "I know you're not a kid like Lizzy and Tom. You're mature for your age, but there are things that you don't yet know or understand."

"Like what?" the boy demanded.

"Life's complicated. It's so much simpler when you're a child. Your mother and father were getting a divorce." He held the boy's hand. "Can I trust you?"

"Yes."

"Cara thinks that your dad had something to do with her uncle Harry's death."

"Why?"

"I don't know. I know Joe wouldn't do that," he lied. "But he thought the police would come for him and lock him up."

"I want to come and live with you, Granddad. I hate Mum. I hate Tom too."

"What about Lizzy?"

"She's okay, I guess, but she's very close to them. I don't want to live with them. Tell me I can live with you?"

"It's not that simple, Tristan. I'd love that, but your mother would never allow it."

"But I don't care. I hate her."

"You're upset. And you're in shock. That will pass in time. Your mother has rights, and she would never let you come and live with me."

"It's so unfair!" he shouted, as two smokers looked over.

Frank looked deep into the boy's blue eyes. A memory came

to him, a young Joe's pleading eyes staring up at him after his mother had gone missing. *History is repeating itself,* he thought. "Look. Your mother would never let you live with me. But I tell you what, why don't we spend as much time together as possible? I'll talk to her when she gets home, to see if you could spend some weekends with me. Would you like that?"

The boy nodded. "I miss him, Granddad."

Frank began to cry as he drew the boy onto his lap, his heart constricting. "So do I, Son. So do I." *One day, you'll know the truth. Even if it's with my last breath, you'll know what happened to your dad.*

CHAPTER
TWENTY-SEVEN

STEVE SMILED AS THE TWO OLD LADIES BID HIM FAREWELL, THE MAN placing the tip into a glass jar on the counter. "I think they may return," he said to the woman across the café.

Dee smiled back as she collected empty cups and plates, weaving her way through the tables where new customers enjoyed warm drinks to fend off the Cornish winter. "I think you have two new admirers," she chuckled, placing the tray at the end of the counter.

"Well, they may have to fight amongst themselves." He glanced to his right, smiling once more as customers looked through the packed books shelves at the back of the property. "Anyway, how're things at your end? When are you moving?"

Dee smiled, brushing her dark hair away from her eyes. "All good. I get the keys in a few weeks. Dead handy for work too."

"I'm really pleased for you."

She moved around the counter as two more customers bid their farewells. "And thank you for helping me out with the deposit. That was so kind of you, and I will pay you back."

"No, you won't. That's my treat. Having you here is great, and it allows me the flexibility to do the school runs."

"I think it was written in the stars," she quipped before her face dropped slightly. "I'm really sorry about your brother."

Steve nodded, his face dropping too. "Thanks. We weren't close, but he was still my brother. It gets you thinking. Life being too short and all that."

She surveyed the room, all the customers happily chatting. "I wanted to tell you something but didn't know the right time."

"Go on."

"Your brother tried it on with me."

"What? When?"

"Just before Christmas. I was doing some casual work there, and Joe held a bit of a shindig for the staff. He seemed nice. Cocky but nice, until the end of the evening when he invited me for a nightcap."

Steve rolled his eyes. "That was my brother all over." He sighed, looking at the floor. "He told me something. A few days before he died."

"You don't have to tell me, Steve. No pressure."

"He'd been sleeping with my wife."

Her eyes widened. "Oh, God! Really?"

"Really. I knew Rosie was a flighty so-and-so, but I never thought she was warming my brother's bed. Life eh. It's a bitch."

She placed her hand over his, stepping closer. "Well, for what it's worth, your wife must have been mad. I don't like to talk ill of the dead, but it's true. You're a good guy, Steve. And your brother should have known better. Why would someone do that?"

"One day, I'll fill you in on my family, and my past. You may need a lie down afterwards. It's not a pretty tale."

"It's a date," she replied, blushing slightly. "You know what I mean. I'll give you the gory details about my family and abusive ex-boyfriend. You'll probably need a lie down too."

He smiled, not noticing a woman enter the café and approach the counter. "Hi," she said, the two looking around at her.

"Hi," Steve smiled. "What can I get you?"

"Are you Steve Sullivan?"

He was taken off guard for a split second. "Err, yeah. Why?"

"Sorry to drop in like this, but could I have a word?" She looked at Dee. "In private."

"Okay. Dee, can you watch the café for a few minutes?"

"No problem," she replied, slightly deflated that their conversation had come to an abrupt end.

"Follow me," he said, leading the woman to the rear of the property. He held the door open, letting her enter the rear kitchen. "So, what can I do for you?"

"My name's Sarah. I don't really know how to say this, so I'll just say it. Your wife is having an affair with my husband. I found out a few days ago, and it looks like she may have taken some items of jewellery from my bedroom."

"Oh. I'm so sorry to hear that. What items of jewellery?"

"Well, there was my mother's engagement and wedding ring, along with two diamond necklaces."

"Forgive me for asking, and I'll explain why in a minute, but how have you only discovered them missing now?" He looked at her as she leaned against the counter. She looked a good ten years his senior with shoulder-length dark hair and an attractive face.

"I've been working away for the past six months in Germany. My husband, Mark, stayed in the UK. It looks like he kept himself entertained in my absence."

"I'm really sorry to hear that. How can I help?"

She was taken off guard by the man's cool demeanour,

expecting tears and raised voices. "Well, I'd like the items back. We're getting divorced, as it looks like your wife was one of many, but he swears that Rosie was the only one whom he entertained in our bed."

"I'm really sorry to hear that, Sarah. Truly, I am. I still have some of Rosie's belongings. If I sort through them and find any jewellery, I'll let you know. Or I can keep them here, and the next time you're in the area, you can pop in and take a look."

"That's very kind of you. When you say belongings, what do you mean?"

"She died a few months ago. Car accident."

The woman's hand went to her mouth. "Oh no! I'm sorry."

"It's okay. I knew about my wife's extra-curricular activities. I just don't know how many other wives are going to come knocking on my door."

"I'm so sorry. I was expecting this to be quite awkward. I had no idea."

"It's okay, Sarah. As you're here, can I get you a coffee and a slice of something nice?"

"Well, it would be a shame not to, if you're sure" she smiled, the tension seeping out of her.

"By the way, how did you find me?"

She blushed slightly, her composure rattled. "The article in the paper. I saw a picture of you a few days after I found out about what had been going on."

He smiled, shaking his head. "Oh, that. Yes, some reporter came in to ask me a few questions. Before you know it, I was being interviewed and supplying him with cake."

"Oh, well, perks of the job, I suppose."

He chuckled before walking her back into the café, placing a menu on the table. Here you go."

As he walked back a few minutes later she smiled up at him. "Could I have an Earl Grey and a slice of carrot cake, please?"

"Coming right up," Steve smiled.

"What was all that about?" Dee whispered as the man prepared the refreshments.

He looked over at the woman, satisfied that she was out of earshot. "Her husband was having it away with Rosie. She's just found out. Also, it looks like my late wife may have lifted some jewellery from the lady's bedroom."

"Bloody hell! And here's us talking about it a few moments before. Spooky, eh. What are you going to do?"

"I've told her that I'd take a look through Rosie's stuff. I threw most of it out but kept the photo albums and her nicknacks. She said she'd pop past again to see if any of it's hers."

"Nice looking woman. Great legs. I'd kill for calves like that."

Steve looked over, silently agreeing. "I guess so." He placed the items on a silver tray, walking over towards the unexpected distraction.

He's a lovely guy. Good looking, kind. A gentleman. She wondered when they would have that coffee. When she could tell him about her past. A past she hoped would never catch up with her.

∼

"Welcome home," Frank said as Lizzy and Tom ran down the hallway, whooping and crying as they tried to embrace their mother.

"Hello, my darlings. Mummy's home," she croaked as tears slid down her cheeks.

"Careful, guys," Frank chided. "You'll have your mum out of her chair."

"Sorry, Granddad," Lizzy replied, climbing off her mother's lap, letting Cara wheel herself into the hallway.

"That's okay, princess. You're just happy to see me. Where's Tristan?"

"In his room," Tom answered. "He's been there all day. Malcolm's been playing with Lizzy and me."

"Well, that's kind of him," she replied, the wind taken out of her sails. "I'd go up and say hello, but I'm not sure how I'll manage that."

"Don't worry," Frank interjected. "I've made you a makeshift bedroom in the lounge, and you can use the downstairs bathroom until you're out of those casts."

"Thank you," she smiled, feeling slightly pathetic. She'd always been so active, suddenly faced with the prospect of weeks of rolling around the house followed by trips to the hospital. Cara suddenly felt old. Old and tired as she tried to mask her thoughts with a wide smile.

"Hi," Malcolm said as he walked into the hallway. "Good to see you home, Mrs Stuart. I've just brewed some coffee if you'd like one?"

"That sounds wonderful. You've no idea how bad hospital coffee is. And thank you for helping out in my absence, Malcolm. It's very kind of you."

"Think nothing of it. You and Joe have always been good to me." The words hung in the air, the young man realising he'd put his foot in it.

"Let's not tread on eggshells," she smiled. "I know what you meant." Cara wheeled herself into the kitchen, the smell of fresh coffee assaulting her tastebuds. "God, I've missed that aroma."

Frank looked down at Lizzy, placing a hand on her shoulder. "Go and tell your brother to come downstairs."

"Okay, Granddad."

Cara overheard the exchange, her pulse quickening at the thought of seeing her eldest son, who she'd not seen since his outburst at the hospital a few weeks before. It'll be okay, she told herself. He was upset. Hopefully, he's calmed down a bit. "Thanks, Malcolm," she said as the head groundsman placed a coffee next to her. Footsteps approached, Cara turning her head. "Hi."

"Mum," the blond-haired boy replied.

"Are you not going to give your mother a welcome home hug?" Frank asked.

"What for? This isn't home anymore. Not since she did what she did to dad."

"Err, I'd better be heading back," Malcolm said hastily, heading out of the kitchen door as the standoff began.

"Tristan, love. I didn't do anything to your father. He did what he did by his own choosing."

"Only because you were going to get the police involved. I hate you, Mum. I wish I'd never been born."

Tears brimmed at the corners of her eyes, Cara shaking her head. "Son, it's more complicated than that. You're just a child. One day, you may understand."

"I'm not a kid. I know that you wanted Dad to get in trouble. You're evil!"

Hooper bounded into the kitchen, japing at Tom's heels as the boy glared at his brother. "Don't be nasty to Mummy. This isn't her fault. It's Daddy's fault."

"Shut up, you little prick," the older boy shouted as the dog stood between them. "And keep your mutt on a lead," Tristan spat, aiming a kick at Hooper's head.

The dog yelped in pain before the older boy ran out of the kitchen. "Hooper," Tom cried, gathering the dog into his arms as the others looked on.

"Is he okay?" Lizzy asked as she peered down at him.

"I think so. You okay, boy?" The dog looked up at his master, his brown and white body trembling.

"He'll come around," Frank said to Cara. "Kids can be nasty sometimes. This wasn't your fault. Joe made all this happen."

"Come here, you two," she croaked, her children flanking her as she looked up at her father-in-law. "I know it's not my fault. But I don't think Tristan will ever understand." *Will he ever come around? Or will he turn nasty, like his father did?*

CHAPTER
TWENTY-EIGHT

Martin's fingers trembled as he opened the front door. "Come in," he said, ushering DI Harris into his flat.

"Thank you," she replied, following the man into a cramped lounge, taking a seat opposite him. "You wanted to speak to me?"

"I did. Where's the other guy?"

"We're a bit short-staffed today, so you've got the pleasure of me and me alone."

"Fair enough," he replied, the detective noticing his knee bobbing up and down. "Before I begin, I want a deal."

"Deal?"

"You know. Anonymity."

"Okay. From whom?" She leaned forward, taking her pad out.

"From a few people."

"Why don't you start at the beginning, Martin." She used his first name, trying to gain the man's trust.

"Mrs Stuart was right. I did bury a body near The Retreat."

"You've got my attention." She looked at the windows, then

the door. She was alone in a flat with a man who was about to come clean. *Keep your cool*, she told herself, knowing that things could turn ugly very quickly. Knowing that the man across the room could snap her in two with little effort.

"I don't want to go to prison."

"Martin, tell me what you know."

"You need to promise me that I won't go to prison."

"Look, that's not my call. That's down to the CPS, and it depends on what you're about to tell me. Work with us, and I'll do everything I can to keep you safe."

"There was a party at The Retreat—last autumn. The usual men turned up, but there were two new ones. One we knew of, the other we didn't."

"Who were they?"

He blew out a long breath. "Jim Walsh."

She frowned. "The Jim Walsh? The game show host."

"Yes."

"Jesus," she whispered. "And the other one?"

"I'll get to him in a minute. Anyway, everything was going okay until Walsh gave one of the girls a smack."

"Do you know her name?"

"Katarzyna. I don't know her surname. Sorry."

"That's okay. We can check that out. So, what happened after that?"

"Well, I told the guy that if he touched anyone else, I'd snap him in half."

Like he could snap me in half. "Why did you say that?" She pulled her jacket around her, the room suddenly feeling cold.

"Because I don't approve of men hitting women. It's not right."

She nodded, her pulse still elevated. "So, what happened after this episode?"

"The other man called me into his room a while later. There was a girl on the bed. She was dead. He'd choked her."

"Did you check for a pulse?"

"She was dead. You could just tell. Anyway, I ran to get Joe, who was outside. We didn't know what to do. This kinda stuff only happens in the movies."

"Do you know the girl's name?"

"Only her first name. Mandy."

"What did this Mandy look like?"

"Young. Probably early-twenties. Blonde hair and a pretty face."

"How tall?"

"I dunno. A lot shorter than me."

She nodded. "Okay. Do you know who the man was?"

"At first, no. He didn't seem to care that she was dead, even though we were freaking out. It was then that he pulled out his identification."

A cold shiver ran down Harris' spine, dreading what was about to be revealed. "Who was he?"

"A copper."

"Do you have a name?"

"Graham Jenkins."

She did a double take, the cold shiver turning into an icy blanket that settled over her. "Graham Jenkins. Chief Constable, Graham Jenkins?"

"Do you know him?"

"Know him; he's my boss."

∽

"Hooper," Tom called out as he walked around the house.

"Tom," Cara called from the lounge. "You okay?"

"I c-can't find H-hooper," he replied.

"He's probably asleep somewhere."

"Where's Tristan?"

"Hmm, I don't know. He was kicking his football about earlier. Why?"

She heard the awkward gait of her son as he headed through the kitchen door, more footsteps coming down the stairs. Lizzy walked into the lounge, her school uniform all untucked at the waist. "Where's Tom?"

"He's gone outside, looking for Hooper."

"Where's Tristan?"

"I don't know, love. He was outside…" Cara looked out of the lounge window, the sky ever darkening. "You don't think that?"

"Tom!" Lizzy called before slipping on her wellies and heading off in pursuit of her younger brother.

"Shit," she cursed as the woman levered herself into the wheelchair. Moving as fast as she could, Cara reached the front door, clumsily bouncing over the step before struggling to maintain momentum on the gravel. "Lizzy. Tom. Where are you?" She heard a girl's voice to her right, Cara setting off across the grass, thankful that the cold conditions made going relatively easy. A flash of white in the treeline made the wheelchair change course, the woman's arms and lungs beginning to protest at an intense pace. "Where are you?" An icy dread settled over her as she approached the trees, knowing that a deep well was a hundred yards ahead underneath a clearing in the forest. "Lizzy. Tom! Where are you?"

"Mummy. Help!" Lizzy screamed from the darkness.

"Oh my God!" the woman cried as her daughter burst from the undergrowth.

"It's Hooper. He's fallen down the well. Hurry, Mummy."

"I can't get there. My wheelchair won't get through that lot. Shit!" An idea came to her. "Lizzy. Run inside and fetch my mobile phone. It's on the sofa. Hurry." The girl sprinted away as her mother tried to creep forward over the uneven ground. "Tom. Where are you?"

"Mummy," a boy's voice called. "I think he's dead."

No. Please no. Not Hooper. Please, not his dog.

Sobbing drifted through the trees. "Mummy," the boy wailed, Cara's heart constricting.

"Hang on, Lizzy's getting..." The wheelchair lurched to the side, the woman spilling out of her seat, landing heavily on the forest floor. She cried out, a white-hot pain shooting from her fingertips to the shoulder. From her prone position, a pair of red wellies came into view. "Lizzy."

"Mummy," the girl exclaimed, trying the pull her mother into a sitting position.

"Ugh," Cara grunted, trying not to swear in her daughter's face as she lurched into a sitting position. "The phone." Quickly, she dialled a number, hoping it would pick up. "Malcolm."

"Mrs Stuart?" the man replied.

"Oh, thank God you answered. We need your help." She quickly filled the groundsman in, the horrendous pain in her shoulder abating as the adrenaline kicked in. "Bring some rope and a bucket. Please hurry." She ended the call, looking into the forest. "Tom. Come here, Son. Malcolm's on his way."

The boy headed through the trees, his face streaked with moss and tears. "He's not moving," Tom cried. "Tristan killed my dog!"

"Come here," she soothed, awkwardly reaching out with her good arm. After a hug, she looked up at them. "Do you think you can help me into the wheelchair?"

"Okay," they replied in unison, a series of grunts, winces, and one muted swear word before Cara sat crumpled within her steel protective cage. "Lizzy, can you push me over to the well?" A minute later, she peered over the mossy lip, a cold feeling of dread seeping into her already frozen bones. "Hooper," she called, barely seeing the white patches on the dog's coat.

A whimper drifted up towards them, Tom's tears returning. "He's alive," the boy cried. "Did you hear him?"

"I did," she cried back, a swell of emotions washing over her. "Malcolm will be here in a minute." Cara peered back into the well. "It's okay, Hooper. Helps on its way." As her echoed words died off, a set of headlights cut through the trees, followed by the slam of a van door.

"Mrs Stuart," Malcolm called.

"In here. By the well."

A few seconds later, the dark-haired man skidded to a halt. "Lizzy, take this," he said, handing her a thick rope and a black bucket. He peered into the well, shining a torch down into the depths. "He's breathing," the man confirmed. "But he's in no condition to climb into the bucket." He looked at Tom, an idea forming in his mind. "Okay, this is what we're going to do. I'll make a rope seat, then lower you down into the well. Once you've got him, I'll pull you back up."

"That's too dangerous," Cara countered as rain started to fall through the trees.

"Mrs Stuart, if we don't get him out soon, he'll die. I've done this before. I won't hurt either of them."

"Okay, just be careful."

Malcolm busied himself with the rope, issuing instructions to the boy as he paced around the edge of the well. The man climbed onto the rim, dropping the makeshift seat into Tom's outstretched hand. "Okay, step into it, then sit on the wall."

Tom did as instructed, peering down into the abyss until the tightening rope made him look up. "Ready."

Malcolm draped the rope over his shoulders, his one arm

gripping the rope tightly. "Okay, push yourself off. Don't worry; I've got you."

Here goes. The boy closed his eyes, a momentary feeling of weightlessness overcoming him before his feet bumped into the opposite side of the well.

"You okay?" Malcolm asked.

"Yeah," Tom replied before he started to drop slowly, his back grating the wet bricks.

"Tell me when to stop."

The boy looked down as the dog peered up at him. "Almost there. Hang on, boy." His one foot touched the dank floor, Tom bending down to lift the puppy into his arms. Hooper whined, Tom, feeling his small body flinch before he lay trembling in the crook of his elbow. "Okay. I've got him."

Cara and Lizzy looked on in silence as the man began to pull on the rope, his hands working steadily until a mass of dark hair appeared over the lip. "Lizzy, can you take him," her brother asked, the girl happily receiving the shivering bundle.

Malcolm landed next to them, patting Tom on the head. "Well done, Captain Tom. You did great." The man's gentle hands played over the dog's coat and limbs. "Okay, Hooper. I know it hurts." He looked at Cara. "I think he's got a broken front leg. I know a vet in Bude. I can have him there in twenty minutes."

"I'm coming with you," Tom stated.

Malcolm looked down, noticing the steel in the boy's eyes. He looked at Cara, who nodded. "Come on then. But first, we need to get your mummy into the house."

"Just get me inside. Lizzy can help me with the rest. Thank you, Malcolm. You've saved the day."

The man smiled awkwardly. "I just brought the rope. Tom's the hero."

"How did he manage to fall down there?" Lizzy asked as she walked over to the well. "He can barely climb onto my bed."

"I don't know," Cara began. "But I intend to find out." Her stomach tightened, knowing that her eldest son was to blame. *If he can do this to a dog, what else is he capable of?* She shuddered as Malcolm pushed her through the forest, trying not to think about what was coming next.

CHAPTER
TWENTY-NINE

Jackie Harris welcomed Pearce into her house, showing him into the kitchen as her family watched television in the lounge. She flicked the kettle on, turning towards the young man. "So, how's fatherhood going?"

"I'm knackered, but it's been great so far. Ask me again in a week. I might be screaming to come back to work. Anyway, you didn't ask me here for that. What's up?"

"Martin Murray called me earlier. Said he had some information for me but wanted to talk at his place."

"And you went?"

"I did, but part of me wishes I didn't."

"Why?"

"He came clean. About everything. He did bury a body in the forest."

"Shit! I knew he was holding something back. Who was it?"

"A young girl called Mandy. It sounds like the girls travel from all over. This bunch came from London, so I'll need to follow up on that. But there's something else."

"Go on," he replied as the kettle started to boil.

She poured two cups of tea, letting them brew as Harris

turned to her partner. "Murray identified who killed her. Graham Jenkins."

His eyes widened, Pearce's mouth not catching up with his brain for a few seconds. "Jesus Christ!"

"I know. Look, we've heard the rumours about him. The links to organised crime and his extra marital activities. But this is murder, David. Our own Chief Constable killed that girl and told Stuart and Murray to bury the evidence."

"I can't believe I'm hearing this!"

"There's more. Another girl was assaulted at the same party. By Jim Walsh."

He frowned as Harris placed a mug next to him. "Jim Walsh. Where have I heard that name?" Harris looked at him as recognition shone in his dark eyes. "The game show host?"

"The very same. It looks like Stuart had some VIP guests that came along for some action."

"Jesus Christ! What a mess."

"My thoughts exactly. Plus, Murray confirmed that Harry Phipps was murdered in the basement of The Bellevue by the owner. The place was clean when we visited them, but we'll need forensics down there soon."

"I thought you'd have jumped on that, guv?"

She leaned against the counter; her eyes lowered to the floor. "Murray wants protection. And I don't think it's from the Chief Constable."

"The hotel owner?"

"Right. Paul Douglas. I spoke to Vice, who gave me the lowdown on the hotel owner. Nothing jumps out at you. But the guy I spoke to thinks he's connected to an Irish family called Ryan."

"I've heard of them."

"Well, I've not been down here as long as you. It looks like they're involved in drugs, guns and extortion. I think that's who Murray wants protection from."

"If Douglas goes down, the Ryans will lose out."

"Exactly."

"Where's Murray now?"

"At home. Under normal circumstances, we'd have brought him in. But what could I do? If we make this official now, the Chief will find out. We need this to be watertight."

"What if he does a bunk?"

"I've two uniforms watching the house. He won't go far, even if he wanted to. But I think he'll play ball in exchange for a deal."

"Okay, so what's your play?"

"I need to speak to the Garda. I've got a contact over there who can give me some more info. Then, I need to figure out who this Jane Doe, or Mandy, is. Martin will show us where the body is buried. If the Chief had some fun with her, we've got enough to nail the bastard."

"I've got ten days paternity leave left. Do you want me to cut it short?"

"No. Enjoy this time with your family. Because we're going to be knee-deep in shit very soon."

Pearce looked at his boss, wondering just what the next few weeks would bring. A high-profile arrest would be good for both their careers. However, they were going up against the Chief. A cold shiver ran down the detective's spine, knowing that one wrong move could spell disaster—both professionally and personally.

∽

"Answer me," Cara ordered as her eldest son stared defiantly at her.

"It wasn't me," Tristan countered.

He's just like his father. Slippery. "Tristan, there's no way that Hooper could have climbed up onto the well. He's only a puppy."

He shrugged. "It wasn't me."

"I don't believe you. You did this because you're angry about your father."

"Yes, I am angry," he spat. "Dad's dead because of you. I hate this family. All of you. I want to live with Granddad."

"Well, that's not going to happen, sunshine. You live here."

"I fucking hate you!"

She was about to explode, the woman not able to tolerate language like that from anyone, let alone her own child. Cara took a breath, calming herself. "Well, I can't change that. But while you're living under my roof, you'll live by my rules. You're grounded."

"What? For how long?"

"For as long as I say. Unless you want to come clean about Hooper. If you admit to it, then we can talk."

"I'm going upstairs."

"Fine. Brush your teeth and get ready for bed. And no messing around."

"Whatever," he huffed before leaving the room.

Cara sat there, the wall clock telling her it was just after nine. *I hope they're back soon. It's getting late.* On cue, twin headlights shone through the kitchen window, the woman walking to the front door. Malcolm and Tom hurried towards the house as icy rain fell from the skies as she pulled it open. "I was about to send out a search party."

"Sorry, Mrs Stuart. It took longer than expected."

"How is he?"

"He's fine. The vet will call you in the morning, but it looks like Hooper will be home in a few days. They'll sort out his leg and were a bit concerned about hypothermia, so they're going to keep an eye on him."

"Thank you, Malcolm. I don't know what I would have done without you?"

"No problem, Mrs Stuart."

"Please, call me Cara. Mrs Stuart makes me sound old."

"Righto."

"Would you like a cup of coffee? It's freezing out there," she offered as she struggled to close the front door from her seated position.

"Go on then."

She pulled Tom into her arms. "Are you okay?"

"Yes, Mummy. Did Tristan do this?"

"He said not, but I've sent him to bed. I want you to go upstairs, have a shower, and I'll give you a call in a bit. It's late."

"Okay."

She rolled into the kitchen, Malcolm following as she put the kettle on and busied herself. "How's old Antony?"

The man shrugged. "Okay, I guess. Dad's a bit bored to tell you the truth. He loved his job and doesn't really know what to do with himself. Here, let me help you with that," he offered.

"It's okay. I'm getting used to making things sat down." She looked up at the man, her face softening. "It must be difficult for him. But Joe's not in charge anymore. I am. Do you think he'd come back?"

"In a heartbeat," Malcolm replied, a broad smile appearing on his face.

"Tell him to pop by. I'm not suggesting he takes over your role, but there must be something that can keep him busy."

"Mrs...Cara, that's so kind of you. He'll be over the moon."

"Think nothing of it. I have a lot of time for your dad. I know that Joe did what he did, but it was just an accident." The kettle clicked, Cara filling the two mugs.

"Well, Joe was very good to Dad and very generous too."

"Can I ask you something?"

"Sure?" the man nodded.

"Has your dad ever mentioned my late mother-in-law?"

His face dropped, the man's shoulders sagging. "He has, but not for a long time."

"I don't mean to pry, but I've heard snippets from Joe, but it was years ago, and he didn't give much away."

"That's okay. Dad said it was all very hush-hush and not to talk about it."

"If you'd rather not tell me, it's fine."

"He was in love with Frank's wife, Margaret. And she was in love with Dad. Mum died when I was a boy, and Dad raised me on his own. I'm not sure how it all started, but he said that Margaret was unhappy. Frank didn't love her and just wanted a wife to wait on him hand-and-foot."

"Well, that sounds like the Stuart's."

"She wanted to leave him and move away with us. But then she died."

"Be honest with me, Malcolm. Do you really think that she was washed out to sea?" she asked as she slid the mug over to him.

"Honestly, I don't know. It does seem like a massive coincidence. She was about to walk out on one of Cornwall's richest men to set up home with a groundsman, then she disappeared."

"Well, I suppose when you put it like that, yes, it does. How did your mother die?"

He looked down, Cara wondering if she'd overstepped the mark. "She was an alcoholic. Dad said she pretty much drank herself to death. I barely knew her, but I can still picture a dark-haired woman smiling at me."

"Sorry to hear that."

"Dad told me that they'd been unhappy for years. They

were going to break up, but then I came along, and they stayed together. Maybe that's why Dad fell in love with someone else."

Cara digested the information, something not making sense. "Hang on; I thought they fell in love after your mother had died?"

He sighed, placing his mug on the counter. "No. Dad told me that they fell for each other years before I was born."

"How old are you, Malcolm?"

"Twenty-six."

A face flashed before her. A handsome man with wavy dark hair. *Oh Jesus!*

CHAPTER

THIRTY

S<small>TEVE WALKED INTO THE CAFÉ FROM HIS STUDIO AS</small> D<small>EE WAS CLOSING</small> up for the day. Outside, locals went about their business, walking home from work or heading to the bars and restaurants that dotted the popular village. "Fancy a coffee before we head off?"

She turned, smiling over at him. "Why not."

He busied himself with the coffee machine as tables and chairs were put in place, ready for the next day. Matt walked up to the counter, the man sliding three flapjack bars over to him. "I won't be long, Son."

"Okay, Dad," the boy replied, scooting off to give his sisters a pre-dinner treat.

Once the coffees were ready, Dee pulled up a high stool, savouring the heady aroma that seemed to ward off the outside conditions. "Thanks," she smiled, taking a sip which left a creamy line on her top lip. She giggled and quickly licked it away, the man smiling.

"Been pretty busy today."

"It has. They're shooting a new TV drama in the village, and most of the crew were in here throughout the day."

"Oh, I didn't know that," he replied.

"Your finger's not on the pulse of Port Isaac. That's what I'm here for."

"True. How long are they here for?"

She shrugged. "Not sure. Probably a few weeks, I suppose."

"Well, I'm not complaining. Takings are good, and we're getting a nice little reputation."

"You are. It's all working out."

"Thanks to you. I come and go; it's you that's bringing in the punters. Thank you."

She smiled, trying not to blush as the man's gaze settled on her. Dee changed tack, wanting to broach a new development. "I might need to take Friday and Saturday off."

"Okay. I can fill in."

"Sorry it's short notice, but something has happened in Plymouth."

"Oh, do you want to talk about it?"

"Where do I start?"

"The beginning is usually a good place," he smirked.

The tension went out of Dee's shoulders, knowing that she could trust the man in front of her. "I mentioned before about my ex."

"Briefly."

"Well, I didn't want to say too much as the timing wasn't right. He's called Jason. We were together for a while, but then he started to knock me about. In the end, it got so bad that I went to the police. He was sent down for six months, and I decided that I needed a fresh start."

"Sorry to hear that."

She smiled, swallowing back her emotions. "Thing is, he's out of prison now and is trying to find me."

"Isn't there some kind of restraining order on him?"

"There is, but Jason won't abide by that. Plus, I took some money from his flat just after he was arrested."

"Oh," Steve replied, his eyebrows raising. "How much?"

"Five grand. It's not like I stole it. Well, I kinda did, but it's dirty money."

"Drugs?"

"You guessed it. He's a small-time dealer in Plymouth and keeps his money in various places. Most of it's with his mum, but he kept a stash in his flat that he thought I didn't know about. He wants it back."

"Do you still have it?"

"Most of it. Well, about three grand or so. I used the money to pay my initial rental but didn't want to just blow the lot. I feel bad because you gave me the deposit for my new place, even though I could have stumped up the cash myself."

He sighed, placing a hand over hers. "Don't feel bad. I'd have probably done the same thing."

Tears began flowing, the woman's resolve splintering as the man handed her a napkin. "I'm sorry. I didn't want to bring my problems to you. You've been so kind to me since we met, and I love working here. I just need to sort Jason out and get on with my life."

"Do you think it's wise going down there?"

"Probably not, but he's been hassling my parents, trying to find out where I live."

"Did they tell him?"

"No. My folks can't stand Jason and told him to do one. It turned a bit ugly, and he gave my dad a smack."

"Jesus. Could you not go back to the police? I'm sure they'd round him up pretty quickly."

"I could, but when he was dealing, I turned a blind eye to it all, even had some of his gear in my flat. He'd use that against me, and I may end up in trouble."

"So, what's your plan?"

"Go down there on Friday and give him what I've got and promise to make up the money."

Steve shook his head. "Dee, you can't do that. Even if you had all the money, he might still turn on you. After all, he went down because you'd reported him to the police. Money or not, he's not going to let that go."

"So, what do I do? My parents are worried that things will get worse."

"Give me the money. I'll take it down to him on Saturday, providing you know where he lives?"

"I don't, but I know where his mum lives. But Steve, I can't involve you in this," she said. "You've had enough to deal with over the past few months. I don't want you getting hurt."

He looked down as she placed her hand over his, smiling as she squeezed it gently. "I can take care of myself."

"No, Steve. I can't let you do that. You've got three children to think about. Three children who've just lost their mummy."

"Well, If I'm not going down there, nor are you. What can this guy do, apart from harassing your parents? All they need to do is phone the police, and he'll be back in prison."

She wrung her hands, the man noticing her agitation. "Well, a few days ago, I saw one of his mates in Port Isaac. He didn't see me, but it freaked me out. Turns out one of my cousins told Jason's sister that I was living here."

"Okay. It could just be a coincidence?"

Dee shook her head. "Not a chance. I followed him and could see that he was snooping around the place. Fortunately, I ducked into the chemist when he headed back towards the car park."

"Okay, that changes things. You think he's trying to find you so your ex can pay you a visit and take back the money?"

"Yes. But it won't end at that. I sent him down. He'll want revenge."

Steve rubbed his chin, his mind working overtime. "You need to go to the police. Even if it all comes out in the wash about the drugs."

Tears brimmed at the corners of her eyes. "I can't, Steve. It would destroy my parents if I got caught up in all this."

"I'm sure they'd understand. And you wouldn't be the first person in that situation."

"Maybe not, but I can't do it."

"So, what are you going to do? Hope that it was a coincidence and be on edge for the rest of your life?"

"I could move again. I've done it before."

"But then you'll always be running. You've made a life for yourself here, Dee, and I love having you around."

Her eyes widened, as did her smile as she looked up at the man opposite. "I love being here too. But what else can I do?"

"Let me think about it. I'm sure there's a way out of this. You're safe here. You have my number, and please call me if anything happens. Day or night."

"You're a good man, Steve. One of the nicest I've ever met."

"Oh, I don't know about that. I'm just a guy."

"Nonsense. You're very kind and a great father too."

"Well, I'll take that. I guess that's what I need to focus on for a while. The kids are growing fast and are increasingly demanding. Especially the girls."

"All girls are demanding, even when we grow up. Just make sure you leave enough time for yourself."

"I will when they all leave home." He laughed, the noise echoing around the café.

"Jesus! You're too laid back. How old are you?"

"Thirty-one in a couple of weeks."

"Really, you never mentioned you had a birthday coming up?"

He shrugged. "Been focusing on other things. And anyway, it's not a special birthday. I'm just a year older."

"God, listen to you. You're still young. You need to have some fun, Steve. You're a long time dead." The words hung in the air, the woman's face dropping. "Sorry, that came out wrong."

He smiled. "Don't worry about it. One thing you need to know about me, don't walk on eggshells. I can take it."

"Phew!" she giggled before taking a swig of coffee. "Seriously, you need to get back out there one day. You're young, good looking too. They'll be queuing up."

"Well, I don't know about that. And after Rosie, I kinda want to find myself again. We had a tough few years, and finding out all the shit that went on has knocked my confidence. But one day, I'll be ready."

"Good, because you need the old Steve back. Not that I knew the old Steve, the new one seems fine to me. All the women moon over you when they're in here. Even the old dears."

"Don't be soft," he countered playfully.

"It's true. Even your sister-in-law has a soft spot for you."

His eyes widened. "Cara. No chance!"

"I'm telling you. A woman knows these things, and I've seen the way she looks at you."

"But she's my sister-in-law."

"What does that mean these days? And anyway, she's your ex-sister-in-law now."

"Daddy, when are we going home?" Hattie demanded from the rear of the café.

He looked at Dee, smiling. "I guess we'd better get you lot home. Don't want you starving. Tell the others that we're off."

He turned to the woman, his lopsided grin returning. "Thank you."

"What for?"

"For making me realise that life does go on." Steve stood up, embracing the woman before straightening his stool.

It was a fleeting contact, Dee hoping it had lasted longer. She looked at the man as he placed the two empty cups in the dishwasher, a sinking feeling washing over her. *Shit! Have I just planted a seed?*

~

Paul Douglas ended the call, his shoulders wilting. His wife had just given him the lowdown. The police had swarmed over the hotel, a warrant issued for his arrest. Paul was one step ahead, having been tipped off about the impending visit. His wife Tracey was as streetwise as they came, telling the police detectives that he was out at the cash-and-carry and had no idea what time he would be home. She knew his dealings, standing by her man no matter what. He knew his wife was cut from the same cloth and that she would be well looked after if the shit hit the fan. As he looked across the moorland, a large man entered the low-slung lounge. "Beer?"

He looked over at his brother, nodding his head before a can of Carling flew across the room, the smaller man catching it one-handed. "Cheers."

"So, what's the plan?"

"Not sure yet. Tracey will just play dumb, but they'll be combing the area for me."

"Good job they don't know I exist," his brother added. "Don't worry, bro. You're safe here."

"Cheers," Paul replied as he cracked open the beer. He took a long pull, wiping his lips. "It was the Scot that dropped me in it."

"Or Stuart's wife?"

He shook his head. "I thought that, but no. I reckon it was Martin. He was there when I did for the old-timer. Joe's wife wouldn't have known about that. And Joe's dead, so I'm guessing that the Old Bill brought Martin in, and he sang like a canary."

"So, what are you going to do?"

"I need to contact Gerard."

"The Ryans?"

He sighed. "He won't be happy. We had a nice little arrangement, and it's all gone to shit."

"Because of Martin."

"Because of Martin," he echoed.

"I'll ask again. What are you going to do?"

"Find him, and sort him, before he vanishes into thin air."

"Well, I can help with that. And don't worry about the Irish contingent. I can help out."

"Rob, you've got enough on your plate."

The older brother smiled. "I can handle it. Things are ticking along nicely here. I'm off the grid and don't mind some extra work."

"Fair enough. I'll let them know that you'll be taking over for a bit."

"And then we find the Jock."

"Yes. A seven-foot giant won't be hard to find."

"He won't be easy to take down either," Rob warned. "We need to be careful."

"I'm past careful. If the police find me, they'll throw away the key."

"All the more reason to be careful then. I know people down on the Costa who could use a reliable guy."

"How can I go to Spain? If I turn up at any airport, they'll nab me."

"There are other ways. I know a guy in Dartmouth who sails to Bilbao every few weeks. He'll take you, no questions asked."

"Okay. That may be an option. But I still need to settle the score."

"Do you know where this guy lives?"

"No, but as you said, he should be easy to find." Paul looked over the pine bookshelf, seeing the shotgun and the box of shells. "And it doesn't matter how big he is; he'll be no match for that."

CHAPTER
THIRTY-ONE

Martin looked out of the window; a thick fog blanketed the village he called home. The road was clear, the man watching as an elderly lady walked out of the convenience store a few doors down. *Why haven't I heard anything?* His usual logical reasoning was fast being replaced by uncertainty and anxiety. *Fuck it, he* thought as he walked into the hallway, donning his jacket and trainers before squeezing himself through the front doorway onto the street. A few minutes later, he exited the store, putting two pieces of gum into his mouth before he set off for a mid-morning stroll. The village was deathly quiet, the Scotsman barely hearing the sound of the nearby Atlantic. It seemed to add to his emotions, Martin quickening his pace as a dark saloon car rolled past. A man peered up at him before the car sped up, vanishing into the thick grey mist. *Get a grip*, he admonished, crossing the road before entering a bridleway that skirted the Sandy Shores estate. "Where are you, Joe?" he said, his eyes scanning the surrounding forest. "You're not dead. I know you're not." Movement in his peripheral vision made the man freeze, Martin checking the trees for signs of danger.

"Mr Murray?" a male voice called out.

"Who's there?" Martin countered, bunching his fists together as he scanned the forest floor for potential weapons.

Two uniformed officers appeared from the mist, the larger man relaxing somewhat. "I'm PC Dixon, and this is PC Braithwaite."

"Why are you following me?"

"We've been asked to keep an eye on you. I'm sure you know by whom?"

"DI Harris." It was a statement.

"Yes. We've just spoken to her, and she'll be paying you a visit sometime today."

"You came out here just to tell me that?"

"Mr Murray, we don't want you to do anything rash."

"You mean do a runner?"

"Well, yes," Dixon replied calmly.

Martin emptied his pockets, showing the officers the contents. "I'm not going to get far with a set of house keys and some chewing gum. I just fancied some fresh air. Clear my head."

"Okay, well, we'll leave you to it. Don't go too far; DI Harris could be knocking on your door soon."

"Okay," he replied as the officers turned to walk away. He set off again, skirting the holiday park, and hugging the tree-line. *I miss that place. I miss Joe.* Through the trees, he could make out several vans, Martin knowing that out-of-season maintenance and repairs would be taking place. The sound of a rotary saw pierced the forest, sending small animals and birds fleeing. He considered his options, wondering if Cara would ever allow him back into the park. *She'd never go for that. She knew that me and Joe were thick as thieves.* The man sighed before resuming his journey back to his cottage. Thirty minutes later, he unzipped his jacket, his upper body clammy despite the cool temperature. Vaulting a farmer's gate, Martin walked the final stretch back to his home; the same dark saloon parked a few yards from his front door. He looked down as he walked past, the police officer nodding before Martin took his keys out to unlock the front door. *I'll put the kettle on and wait,* he thought, busying himself in the kitchen before walking into the lounge. The mug landed on the carpet, the coffee burning his foot as Martin froze on the spot.

"Martin," Paul Douglas said, a wolfish smile spreading across his face.

Before he could speak, he felt something hard pressed into his lower back, a similar-looking man ushering him into the cramped lounge. "Sit," he ordered.

The Scotsman looked at them, not recognising the second man. What he did recognise was the sawn-off shotgun that rested in the crook of his elbow. "What do you want?"

"A chat," Paul started, his voice firm. "Mainly about why you grassed me up to the Old Bill."

∼

PC Braithwaite stretched his legs, buzzing down the window to let the sea air permeate the car. "I'm bored shitless," he sighed.

Dixon smiled thinly, following suit as his window slid down smoothly. "Only a few more hours to go until..."

A loud bang sounded nearby, both officers flinching as another boom echoed across the quiet street. "Fuck!" Braithwaite gasped, activating his police radio. "Shots fired at two Pennamoor Lane. Request back-up immediately."

The cottage window exploded outwards, the men staring in horror as a shaven-headed figure landed heavily on the ground. "Jesus," Dixon shouted, reaching for the handle. Another shot rang out, the smell of cordite blowing in through open windows. "Move."

They came around the rear of the car as silence descended over the street. Next to the cottage, a front door opened, an older man peering out. "Back inside," Braithwaite called. "Police." The man did as instructed, the door slamming shut as a car approached from their rear.

It skidded to a stop, DI Harris climbing out before heading to her boot to retrieve her body armour. "Stay there," she ordered as she slipped the black vest over her head, fastening it hastily as she made her way over to them. "Update."

"Three shots fired, guv. About two minutes ago. There's someone in the front garden. He came out through the window."

"Shit," Harris cursed, seeing the upturned feet of an unknown person. "I heard the request for back-up. They'll be here any minute." Seconds later, two unmarked police cars screeched to a stop a few yards from their position. *Please don't be dead,* Harris thought, knowing that it was a forlorn hope.

∼

She stood in the small lounge, looking over the carnage as her paper suit crinkled with every movement. Outside, the street had been cordoned off by Dixon and Braithwaite, officers telling residents and the local shopkeeper to stay indoors. A cool breeze blew in from the shattered window, Harris grateful for the fresh air as prickly heat tickled her skin. She looked down as two ambulances slowed to a stop outside. Paul Douglas' body lay prone on the blood-stained carpet, a large depression clearly visible at his left temple. His skin had already started to pale as the detective turned towards the far wall. *How am I going to explain this one?* She knew that it would all come out, the Chief wanting answers. Answers that may implicate him. She needed to move quickly. A feeling of sadness washed over her as she looked down at Martin. The giant Scotsman lay on his back, a large open wound in his chest. Blood was everywhere, a large puddle on the floor that had already started to congeal. She was in for a long day, the detective fully aware that the coming weeks and months could either define her career – or ruin it. She turned around, walking out of the house as forensics went to work. "I need a coffee," she whispered under her paper mask, wondering just how she was going to navigate the dark waters that threatened to engulf her.

CHAPTER 32
MARCH 2001

Cornwall was bathed in warm sunlight as the child walked through the holiday park. It was the weekend, Tom enjoying a stroll with Hooper, the dog showing no signs of his recent injuries. The boy smiled as holidaymakers milled around, Sandy Shores opening its gates earlier than previous years. He didn't know why, but it felt nice to hear the arcade machines and carousel rides as fellow children whooped and laughed. As he walked past the main entertainment complex, Tom's leg started to feel sore, his limp becoming more pronounced as Hooper began to strain against his lead. "Let's sit down," he said, seeing a wooden bench with a grey-haired man seated upon it. The boy sat down heavily, s Hooper got comfortable under the bench. "Stupid leg," he huffed.

The man turned to him, noticing the boy's actions. "Hi," he said.

Tom looked up, his throat constricting. "H-hello," he croaked.

"What's up with your leg?"

"It's just hurting today. I h-have a prosthetic l-leg."

"Okay. How did that happen?" The man shifted on the bench, focusing on his new companion.

"I had an accid-dent," he stammered.

"Sorry to hear that."

"It's okay. I'm g-getting used to it." He looked at the man. "Your voice sounds different."

"I'm not from around here."

"Oh, where are you from?"

The man pointed towards the beach. "From over that way."

"Oh," the boy replied, wondering why the stranger lived out at sea

"Can I ask you a question?"

"Yes."

"How long have you had a stammer?"

Tom looked down, his throat closing. "I..."

"Just breath. Take your time and pretend I'm not here."

He composed himself, taking a deep breath. "For a while, but it seems worse since I hurt my leg."

"It will do. You've suffered severe trauma."

"What's a trauma?"

"A trauma can be lots of things. In your case, the loss of your leg."

"Oh," he shrugged as Hooper whined under the bench.

"Can I let you into a secret?"

"Sure?"

"I used to stammer when I was a boy. I had it for years. High School was not much fun, I can tell you."

"But you don't do it n-now?"

"No. Someone helped me with it. I still do it occasionally, I but manage to live with it."

"How?"

The man smiled. "Do you ever think about the words you're about to say, then struggle to say them?"

"Yes."

"So did I. About two seconds before I spoke, I knew that a certain word would trip me up."

"Trip you up?"

"Make me stammer. So, you know what I did?"

"No?" Tom replied, focusing all his attention on the grey-haired stranger.

"I chose to use different words. I always used to struggle with words beginning with N or B. So, I learned how to use another word instead. Or put another word before the one that would make me stammer. Does that make sense?"

Tom thought about it for a moment, nodding his head as something sparked in his mind. "I get stuck on mummy. So maybe I could say, hi, Mummy?"

"Why not. You should give it a try."

"I will. Thank you."

"No need to thank me. One day, you may have a similar conversation with someone else. Just remember, there's no reason why you should stammer, but sometimes we get nervous or unsure of ourselves. Have some confidence in yourself. You seem like a very clever young man. Remember that."

"Thanks, mister. I will." He looked to his left, the sound of the waves catching his attention for a moment. He looked back at the man, suddenly curious. "Are you on holiday here?"

He smiled. "Kinda. Call it pleasure, with a bit of business."

"What does that mean?"

"You ask a lot of questions. That's good. Questioning things is a good quality to have. It means that I'm on holiday, but I'm also looking at investment."

"Does that mean buying something?"

"It does. You're very astute for such a young man."

"My dad used to use that word a lot."

"Well, it's a good word to use. Tell me, are you on holiday too?"

"No. I live here."

"Well, it was good to meet you, and I wish you every success." He held out his hand. "I'm Jim, by the way."

The boy took the proffered hand, shaking it. "I'm Tom."

"Take care, Tom. And remember what we talked about."

The boy stood up, flexing his leg before carrying on towards the beach with his dog, a renewed sense of purpose flowing through him.

∾

"I'm sorry to drag you out here again, Cara," Harris said as she leaned against a tree.

"Not a problem," she replied. "I need to get some strength back, so taking a daily walk helps. I'm hoping to throw this thing in the bin soon," she smiled, waving her walking stick in the air.

Harris smiled back; the exchange lost on Pearce, who was walking around the outbuildings a few yards away. "We've hit a dead-end since Mr Murray died. Forensics have examined the ground here, and you were right; there was something buried here. However, Martin was astute enough to dig up the body and move it. And there lies the problem. Where?"

"I've no idea. You've been over The Retreat, along with every square inch of Sandy Shores. Wherever it is, it's not around here."

"Try and think back a few months. Can you remember anything out of the ordinary? Anything at all that may help us."

Cara stood there, leaning against a tree as she transported herself back to the winter months. "You asked me this before. I can't think of anything."

"What about the night of your accident. You said that things were coming to a head at home. Did Mr Stuart or Mr Murray say or do anything that felt unusual?"

An image appeared in her mind, the white van ramming into her car. "Hang on. The white van."

"You mean the one that rammed you?"

"No. There was another white van."

Harris took a step forward. "Go on."

"When I left to check on Harry, there was a white van towing a mini digger. I never really thought about it at the time. But looking back, why would someone be using something like that on Christmas Eve? Especially at the time I saw it."

Harris had her pen and notepad out, a tingle of anticipation settling over her. "What time was that?"

Cara frowned, looking down at the forest floor. "Five-ish, maybe? And it would have come from the park, but the park was closed. Maybe that was Martin, moving the body because Joe knew I was going to speak to the police."

"What kind of van was it?"

She sighed. "No idea, apart from the fact it was white. Big too. Like a Transit. It could have come from The Retreat."

"Pearce," Harris called, the younger detective walking over.

"Guv."

"Check out all mini-digger hire places in the vicinity. We're looking for someone who hired one on Christmas Eve or thereabouts."

He made a note, nodding towards the senior officer. "I'll make a start when we get back to the station."

Harris turned to Cara. "Thank you. It might not come to anything, but as you say, who would be using a digger on Christmas Eve?"

"I hope you find out."

Harris put her notepad away, her face softening. "How's everything else?"

She shrugged. "Not great. My eldest won't talk to me. He blames me for what happened to Joe. Plus, I'm trying to run a holiday park. Well, in truth, I'm just letting the team run it. I haven't got a clue. For all Joe's faults, he ran the place like clockwork."

"It must be very hard, raising three kids after what's happened to you."

"I'll be okay. Things have been tough, but at least I have some closure over Uncle Harry."

"Yes, although I'd hoped that Paul Douglas could have stood trial for that, along with the murder of Martin Murray. Cornwall eh. I escaped the city for a quiet life. No such luck."

Cara smiled. "Well, it was quiet until recently. It just goes to show how life can throw you a curveball." Silence descended over the forest for a few seconds, each lost to their thoughts. "Is that the end of it?"

"Not just yet, Cara. We're following up on two more lines of enquiry."

"Oh, related to my husband?"

"Yes, I can't say anymore currently, but hopefully, we'll be tying up all loose ends soon."

"Good. I want our lives to return to normal again. We've had enough drama to last us a lifetime."

Harris nodded, a sinking feeling settling in her stomach. *If only it were that simple,* she thought as they made their way towards The Retreat.

CHAPTER
THIRTY-THREE

"But why not, Granddad?" Tristan argued as he stood facing Frank outside the country house.

"Tristan, I'd love to spend more time with you. You're my favourite, even though grandparents are supposed to say that." He sighed, looking up at his home, the building where he'd lived alone for the past twenty years since his wife's disappearance. It was his sanctuary, a place where he could lock himself away from prying eyes and idle gossip. "Truth is, your mother would never allow it. We've been over this, Son. It's not fair, but that's how it is."

"But I hate living there. I just wanna burn the place to the ground."

Frank looked down at the blond-haired boy, seeing the changes that had taken place over the past few months. Gone was the cocky, self-assured ten-year-old – replaced with a bitter, resentful child. A child that was soon to become a young man. The boy reminded Frank of his eldest son - how he looked and carried himself. The confident streak that Joe had carried twenty years before was plain to see. He hoped that history was not repeating itself. "Look. You've had a tough few months. You all have. First, there was Tom's accident, then your father and all the goings-on around that. It's natural to feel this way, Tristan. But I've got to set the record straight. This was not your mother's fault."

"I don't agree," he countered.

"I loved Joe. He was my firstborn, but I knew that he was doing things that he shouldn't have been doing."

"Like what?"

"You're not old enough to understand."

"I'm nearly eleven," he pointed out.

"Yes, and eleven-year-old boys don't need to know such things. One day, when you're old enough, we'll sit down and talk about it. I promise."

Tristan wilted, resting against his grandfather's car as he looked across the manicured lawns towards the treeline. His eyes took in the sprawling building; his interest piqued when the boy stared at the triple garage next to the forest. "Why have I never been above the garage? None of us has."

The reaction in the man's face only lasted a split-second, the boy not picking up on it. "That's my study."

"Study? What are you studying, Granddad? You're old."

He relaxed slightly. "That's what people call it. Yes, I don't study. I'm too old for that, but that's where I keep all my books and paperwork."

"Sounds boring."

"To you, it might be, Son. But all my life's work is stored in that room. That's why I keep it private."

Tristan peered at the building, a shiver running through him. "Looks a bit creepy. It's not haunted, is it?"

Frank laughed, ruffling the boy's hair. "No, Son. There are no ghosts in there. I promise. Come on; I'll make you some lunch." As he led the boy into the house, Frank looked across the lawn towards the garage. His buoyant mood seemed to taper off as he peered at the locked windows, knowing what lay beyond them.

~

"Hi David," Cara said as she looked out of her kitchen window, smiling at the sight of Lizzy, Tom and Hooper as they played happily.

"Mrs Stuart," the man replied, his nasal reply grating on the woman. "One of the guests has asked to speak with you."

"Oh, is there a problem?"

"Not sure. I don't think there's anything wrong with his accommodation. He doesn't look the complaining type but asked to speak to you directly."

"Well, I can't come down at the moment as I've got the kids with me."

"Well, I could come up and keep an eye on them for a while. Or I could find Malcolm." There was a pause on the line, the static filling her ears. "Yes, Malcolm will do it."

She sighed. "Okay. Well, I suppose I'd better get some shoes on. Where is he?"

"He's in the coffee shop. Grey-haired chap."

"What's his name?"

"Sorry, Mrs Stuart. Someone's just set one of the fire extinguishers off in the arcade. You'll find him easy enough." The line went dead.

"Shit," she huffed, her coffee forgotten as she slipped her pumps and jacket on. Walking outside, she ducked as a tennis ball narrowly missed her head. "Woah, careful," she exclaimed, her children staring over at her guiltily as Hooper retrieved the ball before trotting over to his master.

"Sorry, Mummy," Tom blushed. "Didn't see you."

She smiled, the sun's warmth a welcomed change to the

dreary weather she'd been used to lately. "That's okay, just watch the windows."

"Where are you going?" Lizzy asked, her rosy complexion making the woman smile.

"I've got to go down to the park for a bit. Malcolm's on his way up to play catch with you."

"What's happening at the park?" Tom inquired.

"I don't know, Son. Someone wants to talk to me. It's probably nothing. You guys carry on, and there's juice and snacks in the fridge."

"When's Tristan coming home?" the boy asked.

Her sunny mood dipped behind a cloud, her last exchange with her eldest child fresh in her memory. "Not until later. I'm sure he's having fun, though." She saw Malcolm walk onto the lawn, relieved to change the subject. "Here he is." She kissed both children, ruffling Hooper's ears before thanking the young man.

"No problem, Cara," he smiled. "I'd rather be playing catch than taking orders from David."

She smiled back before setting off towards the park. A salty breeze filled her lungs as she walked under dappled sunlight, smiling at holidaymakers before crossing into the entertainment area. A familiar aroma assailed her as she opened the door of Beany Business, the park's popular daytime eatery. A woman walked over, a beaming smile on her face. "Ello, Mrs Stuart," she said. "Not seen you in ere for a while."

Cara grinned, liking the woman's thick Cornish accent and friendly demeanour. "Hi, Caroline. I'm here to see one of the guests." She looked around the interior, seeing a grey-haired man looking over at her from one of the booths at the far end. "Could you pop over in a minute and take a drinks order?"

"No problem," she replied before heading back behind the counter.

Cara walked over, the man rising from his seat. "Hello," she offered.

"Mrs Stuart?" His accent caught her off-guard.

"Yes. You're not from around these parts?"

He smiled as he extended his hand. "No, ma'am. I'm from across the Pond. Jim Emerich."

Cara took his proffered hand, matching his grip. "Please, call me Cara."

"Nice to meet you, Cara."

She slid onto the opposite bench, waiting for the man to follow suit. "So, what can I do for you, Jim?"

"Straight to business. I like that. As you Brits say, I won't beat around the bush. I want to buy your park."

Her eyes narrowed as Caroline walked over with a pen and pad. Cara looked up at the waitress, ordering two coffees, her mind in overdrive. As Caroline headed back to prepare the drinks, Cara cleared her dry throat. "Okay. Why don't we start at the beginning? Why do you want to buy Sandy Shores?"

Jim sat back on his seat, running a hand through his steely hair. "Well, I own two holiday parks similar to yours. One on the east coast, the other on the west. They're both called Sandy Shores. Coincidence, eh? I stumbled across your place by accident and had to come over to see it for myself."

"You came all this way just to see the park?"

"Yes. Well, yes and no. I've got family about an hour away. My wife's there now, so I thought I'd take the opportunity to get some sea air and sample your fine cuisine."

"Fine cuisine?"

"Your fish and chips are to die for. We Americans are very fond of British food. And don't get me started on Cadbury's chocolate and pork pies."

She grinned, the tension ebbing out of her body as she

looked across at him. "Okay, so you own two parks and want to bring ours under your umbrella?"

"In a nutshell, yes."

The drinks arrived, both of them thanking the waitress, Cara taking her time with the sugar, feeling the man's gaze upon her. "What makes you think the place is up for sale?"

"I'm sure it's not, but that's why I'm here. To hopefully convince you and your husband to sell it to me."

Her face dropped slightly. "Well, my husband died a few months ago, so if you're going to convince anyone, you're looking at them."

"I'm so sorry, Mrs Stuart."

She could see the man wasn't shocked. *He's done his research.* "It's fine, Jim, but thank you."

"So, I'm talking to the organ grinder?" He grinned over the rim of his mug.

"You could say that. The park has been part of the Stuart family for many years, Jim. What makes you think I'd sell it? Especially to someone from across the Pond."

"You make a good point. Why sell it to some random American guy. Truth is, I can really see the potential."

"Potential? Do we need to up our game?"

He gave her a lopsided grin, knowing he'd put his foot in it. "I didn't mean it like that. It's a great place, and even if I didn't buy it, I've got some great ideas to take home with me. But if I did own the place, I'd want to put my stamp on it."

"Okay, Mr Random American. Let's say I was willing to discuss, what about all the staff? Some of them have worked here for years."

"We can get to the ins and outs of all that if you were willing. But for now, I give you my word. All staff would be kept on. What you Brits might call TUPE'd over."

Cara knew the expression from her younger days when her

parents owned one of Cornwall's most successful breweries that had to transfer staff another company "Okay. That's good to know. But it's not just the park that we own. Our family home is within the boundaries, along with The Retreat."

"What's The Retreat?"

She placed her mug on the table. "It's a pavilion on the far side of the park, where functions and children's parties are held. And a lot more besides. So, it's a bit more complex than you might have thought."

"Business is never straightforward, but I'm sure that can be taken care of. So, what do you think? Have I overloaded your brain?"

She giggled, liking the man's humour. "Well, I'm a mother of three children. My brain is constantly overloaded. Or what's left of it."

He slid a business card across the table. "Look, there's no rush. As you say, I'm a random American who just dropped a hot potato in your lap. I'm not expecting you to make a decision straight away. These things take time."

"Do you have any children?" she asked, changing tack.

"No. We've tried for years but haven't struck gold yet. You say you have three. How old are they?"

"Tristan is ten, Lizzy's eight and Tom's seven."

"I bet they keep you on your toes."

"Always, especially after Joe's passing. And your wife, what does she do for a living?"

Jim shrugged. "Not too much. Sorry, that's a bit unfair. Angela doesn't really need to work. She used to work in law but gave all that up when the family business grew."

"A lady of leisure. I'm totally jealous."

He smiled before draining his mug. "Look, I've taken up way too much of your time already. I'll be here for the next few days, and you have my card. It was a pleasure meeting you, Cara."

She rose from the bench, shaking his hand. "Likewise, Jim. If you're here for a few more days, I could give you a guided tour. Show you what you might be letting yourself in for."

His face lit up. "It's a date."

After he'd left the café, Cara stood there, her mind a tumult of thoughts and possibilities. "Jesus! I never saw that coming," she said to herself. The woman looked around the café, then out into the park, wondering, just wondering if the time was right to start a new chapter.

CHAPTER
THIRTY-FOUR

"Really!" Steve exclaimed a few hours after Cara's unexpected business proposal.

"Straight up," she replied, a smile spreading across her face.

"Wow! So, what are you thinking?"

Cara placed her feet on the coffee table, flexing her calves. The woman felt tired, knowing that it would take many more months until she'd recovered. "Honestly, I'm thinking about selling."

"Has he given a figure?"

"No. It was just the initial chat. I'd have to contact Joe's solicitor in Truro to get the place valued."

"But you're thinking about it?"

"What do you think I should do?"

"Sell the place."

Her eyes widened. "Really?"

"Cara, I love you to bits, but what do you know about running a holiday park?"

"Well, when you put it like that."

"You know what I mean. This was Joe's empire and Frank's

before that. Joe's gone, and Frank isn't that far behind him. Why don't you make a fresh start?"

"I was thinking along the same lines. But I would want to keep the house. And The Retreat."

"The Retreat? Why?"

"Because for all the shit that's taken place there, it's a lovely building, and the setting is gorgeous. If I sell Sandy Shores, I'll probably pocket a few million, which will top up what I've already got. I may even have as much money as you one day," she smirked, feigning to her left as he went to jab her in the ribs. "But seriously, I'd want some kind of outlet, and The Retreat may just be the place to set that up."

"Then I think you should go for it."

"Hmm. I might just do that."

"What's the guy like?"

She pondered the question for a moment, her face impassive. "He's probably a few years older than me. Grey hair. Handsome, in an American kind-of-way."

"Married?"

"Steve Sullivan!" she admonished. "Are you trying to pair me off with the first man that talks to me?"

"No. Just curious," he replied, holding up his hands.

"Well, for your information, he is married. And I'm guessing his wife looks like Cindy Crawford."

"Still got nothing on you, though."

"Oh, stop it!" she pouted, enjoying the compliment before her face turned sombre. "Look, there was another reason that I asked you over."

"Oh? What is it?"

"Okay, you need to promise me that you'll not freak out. And please, keep an open mind."

"I'm all ears. Do I need popcorn?"

She punched him on the arm playfully, the tension lessening slightly. "What do you remember about your mother?"

He frowned, his face matching hers. "It's a bit blurry. She was beautiful and kind, with lovely long dark hair. Why?"

"I'm getting to that. Tell me, do you remember her being happy?"

He thought about the question for a moment before shrugging. "Only with me. Frank was never around. I remember arguments, but Joe and I were only young. Okay, where is this going?"

"Okay, here goes."

Ten minutes later, Steve took a swig of lukewarm coffee before slumping back on the sofa. "Jesus!"

"That's what I thought," she agreed. "It might be nothing, but Antony was having an affair with your mum around the time that you were born. Then there's your appearance. You don't look like Frank or Joe, but Malcolm looks like your younger brother. And Antony has a similar look about him."

He rocked forward, his face in his palms, his body tense. "I can't believe this."

She placed a hand on his shoulder. "Whatever happens, I'll be with you every step of the way. But I think you should at least try and find out the truth."

"How?"

"Take a paternity test. I've looked into it. They're pretty quick and incredibly accurate. Steve, it might give you peace of mind. Your relationship with Frank has been dead for years. What if he wasn't even your father. How would you feel then?"

His face reddened, dark eyes staring straight at her. "Then I'd hate him even more."

Linda's eyes fluttered open, the sun's rays making her turn away from the window. Her mouth felt dry, the woman's head gently throbbing after last night's bottle of wine. Glancing over at the clock radio, Linda flinched. "Shit," she cursed, knowing that she'd slept in again. *Why didn't he wake me? Useless bugger!* The woman lay there for a few minutes, the sounds of seagulls outside calming her before she sat up and slid her feet out of bed. Locating her slippers, Linda walked into the bathroom, chugging a glass of water to quench her growing thirst. She peered at herself in the mirror, not liking the reflection that stared back at her. *Snap out of it.* As she walked to the top of the stairs, the woman listened for sounds of activity downstairs. The house was still, no frying bacon or kettle boiling. *He must have gone out.* Her slippers skimmed the thick carpet as she descended, Linda walking into the lounge as the postman walked past the bay window. She froze at the sight in front of her. "John?" she croaked. Her husband of twenty-seven years didn't reply, his head lolling to one side. His skin had paled, the process of death already well underway. There was a loud rap at the door, Linda flinching before she saw Cyril, the postman, outside.

"Morning," the man replied. "I almost forgot you," he beamed, handing her a large envelope.

"Oh, thank you," she replied robotically, her face expressionless.

"You okay, Linda. You look like you've seen a ghost."

"What? No, I'm okay. I overslept, is all."

His smile returned once more. "Lucky devil. I've been up since five. Anyway, be seeing you."

"Bye," she replied before closing the door. Walking past the lounge, Linda shuffled into the kitchen, filling the kettle before staring out at the rear garden. The sound of the kettle ebbed away, a realisation that her life was about to change, washed over her like the Atlantic surf. Linda hurried back into the lounge, nudging her husband's shoulder. "John. Wake up, love. I'm making a cuppa." She knew he was dead. Linda had known that since she'd first set foot in the lounge. However, feeling the coldness that seeped through the man's cardigan confirmed it. She was a widow. "Oh, John," she whispered before she returned to tea-making duties. A few minutes later, the woman stood in the kitchen, sipping hot tea as a sense of anticipation covered her like a welcoming blanket. "Maybe now I can start living my own life. On my own terms, without having to worry about that useless sod." Her face dropped, a vision of a blond-haired man appearing before her. *Poor Joe. What I wouldn't give to have you back here once more. But thank you. You made me realise I'm not some old biddy. There's a life to be had out there, and I'm going to live it.*

∼

Steve paced the lounge as Cara walked towards the kitchen door, a vehicle trundling to a stop outside. He chewed his thumbnail before seating himself on the sofa as two men entered. *Shit! This is happening.*

Antony came up short when he saw the man on the sofa, a frown appearing on his weathered face. "Steve?" The man's shoulders slumped, a look of resignation on his face.

"Sorry to ask you both over like this. I've made a pot of coffee, so why don't you all sit down and get comfy," Cara said before walking back towards the kitchen.

Father and son did so, seating themselves across the lounge from the lone man. "How're things?" the older man asked.

"We're doing okay," Steve replied.

"I hear you came into some money. Good for you," Antony replied, his face sincere.

"Oh, that. Yes, I suppose I was in the right place at the right time. You okay, Malcolm?"

"Can't complain," the younger man shrugged as Cara placed a silver drinks tray on the coffee table before fussing over how they all took their coffee. The seconds played out in silence as they all took a sip of their drinks, the tension almost palpable before the woman broke the spell. "Look, there's no easy way to say this, so I'm just going to say it."

"Are you firing us?" Malcolm countered as he gripped his mug.

She scoffed. "God no! It's a bit more delicate than that. Antony, I'm going to ask you a few questions. You don't have to answer them, but it would really help us if you were honest with us."

He placed his mug on the table, tears forming at the corners of his eyes. "Yes, I am your father, Steve."

The man's eyes widened, his mug clattering onto the silver tray. "W-hat?"

"I'm sorry, Son. I always knew this day would come. I'm so sorry that I've not told you sooner. I wanted to, but I couldn't."

Steve came off the sofa, embracing the older man as tears fell and they cried together. "Dad," he faltered, the older man embracing him as Malcolm wrapped his arms around his family.

"Son," he replied, his vocal cords constricting as thirty years of emotions boiled over.

Cara sat there in silence, tears rolling down her cheeks as she looked up at them. *I knew it.*

After a minute, the three men seated themselves; Steve flanked by his new family, a dazed expression on his face. He went to speak, doubling over as fresh sobs wracked his body. "It's okay, Son," Antony soothed, rubbing the man's back. "Take your time. It must be quite a shock."

Cara cleared her throat. "I never expected it to be this easy. How do you know for sure that you're his father?"

Antony blew out a breath, dabbing his watery eyes with a handkerchief. "I loved Margaret. I fell for her the first time I saw her. But she was betrothed to Frank. Anyway, I got married, and so did she, so I would never have said anything. It was different back then. It's not like today with all the goings-on. Anyway, I spent a lot of time up at the house, and we got talking. Margaret was unhappy with Frank, and my marriage wasn't great." He turned to his youngest son. "Sorry, Malcolm. I know we've talked about this but saying it to someone else makes me feel ashamed."

"Don't be silly, Dad. There's nothing to be ashamed of. You can't help who you fall in love with."

"I know. Life, eh. Wasn't supposed to be this complicated. Anyway, we got friendly, and one thing led to another, as they say."

"When was this?" Steve asked, his eyes never leaving his father's.

"Sixty-Nine," he replied. "Joe had just been born, and Margaret knew then that she wanted to leave him."

"So why didn't she?" Steve asked.

"This is Frank Stuart we're talking about. People don't walk out on him. He made threats, telling Margaret that he'd take Joe away from her."

"Did he know about your affair? Sorry, that came out wrong," Cara blushed.

"Not at that point. But he soon found out when Margaret became pregnant."

"Did she tell him about you?" Steve urged.

"She didn't have to. Frank knew that she was in love with another man."

"How?" she responded.

"Because he'd had the snip but never told her." He looked at Steve, his expression grave. "He always knew that he wasn't your father but played along with it rather than face the shame of it all."

Steve slumped back on the sofa. "Jesus Christ!"

"I'm sorry, Son. Believe me, I am. And that's not all of it."

"Go on," Cara urged.

"She wasn't washed out to sea. I know that more than I know myself. Frank did for her."

CHAPTER
THIRTY-FIVE

DEE LOCKED THE FRONT DOOR, STEPPING AWAY FROM THE CAFÉ AS streetlights came to life, bathing Port Isaac in a mellow hue. She looked up and down the thoroughfare, the road devoid of life except for two fishermen who were climbing stiffly into a battered pick-up truck. *I'm starving,* she thought, forgetting to have a proper lunch after the early afternoon rush. *Go on, why not?,* she told herself, heading towards the harbour as the smell of fish and chips wafted towards her. Her heels echoed off the road as she pulled her jacket closed, the early afternoon warmth being quickly replaced by a chilly evening, despite the dawn of spring.

A few yards down the hill, a man sat slumped in a doorway, his dog peering up at her. The hooded man looked up, his face hidden behind a thick beard. "Any spare change," he asked.

She came to a stop, fishing around her handbag before pulling her purse out. Dee dropped a few pounds into his cardboard cup, catching a whiff of him. "There you go. Get yourself something to eat."

"Very generous of you, Dee," he replied, lifting his face towards her.

She heard the words, but they didn't register. What did register was the collar around the dog's neck. She knew that collar, and she knew who owned the dog. Her luck had run out.

"I knew I'd find you, babe. Let's go and have a chat."

She went to move, two hands spinning her around as the dog began to bark. She caught a glimpse of another face. A face she also recognised before her lights went out.

Water splashed across her face, Dee coming around slowly. Above, the sky was almost dark, the woman quickly noticing the rocking motion underneath. "Where am I?"

"Don't worry," Jason smirked. "We're going on a pleasure cruise."

"What?" she sat up, seeing the twinkling lights of Port Isaac moving further away. "Jason, stop! Please, take me back. This isn't funny."

"I'll tell you what's not funny, bitch! Sending me down and stealing my money."

Her head snapped to the side, a stinging slap almost knocking her overboard. "No," she cried, scrambling back towards the rear of the boat, the man at the wheel laughing as they made their way out into the Atlantic. Water splashed her sleeve as the boat cut through the sea, Dee pulling her coat tightly around her neck to ward off the elements.

"That'll do, mate," Jason shouted, the boat's engine dying down to a gentle putter. "Now, where's my money?"

"It's in my flat," she cried, the skin of her cheek still tingling from the blow.

"Keys," he barked.

"In my bag," Dee offered, watching as her ex-boyfriend quickly found them, along with her purse.

He fished out a few notes, slipping them into his back pocket. "What's your address?"

She relayed it, her voice quivering as she instructed him how to find it amongst Port Isaac's winding streets. "Please don't hurt me."

"I'm not going to hurt you. You're coming with us. I want my money back."

"Okay, yes, I'll come with you."

"Good girl," he replied, walking over to the man at the wheel to issue instructions. The engine picked up, the boat beginning to turn back towards the coastal town. Jason lifted Dee to her feet, placing his hands gently on her shoulders. "I bet you never thought you'd see me again?"

She shook her head. "No. I'm sorry for what I did, Jason. Really, I am."

"Don't worry. Very soon, you won't have to worry about that or anything else."

"What do you..." her words were cut off as the man shoved her forcefully. Dee felt her legs thump against the rear of the boat. Then, she was falling, the icy Atlantic engulfing her a second later. The sea drove the wind from her lungs as it assaulted every inch of her, Dee breaking the surface a few seconds later, gasping for breath. "Jason," she screamed, panic rising in her chest as she saw the boat moving away from her. Her limbs felt heavy, Dee trying to pull the heavy coat from her body as the sea rolled over her head. Finally, she discarded it, the woman treading water, feeling an impenetrable coldness seep through her skin. *Got to make it back.* She focused on the lights of the nearby town, the woman kicking her legs as she started a steady breaststroke back to Port Isaac. *Breathe,* she told herself; the twinkling lights her goal. After a minute, her movements became laboured, Dee swallowing a mouthful of water, her body spasming as she fought for breath. Rolling onto her back, she used her arms and legs to carry on her journey, panic starting to resurface as the woman's teeth began chattering. *Please let me make it.* A swell engulfed her, Dee flailing underwater as more seawater invaded her mouth. Surfacing again, she felt weighed down, as if every movement sapped more and more of her reserves. "Nooo," she cried as the lights of Port Isaac were lost once more as she went under the waves. After rolling onto her back once more, Dee floated, her vision darkening as thoughts of friends and loved ones came to her. She thought of her grandmother, who'd passed away the year before. A smiling image seared itself into her mind before the darkness of night consumed her.

∽

Frank walked from the garden with the dinner tray, stepping into the kitchen as headlights lit his driveway. He placed the tray on the counter, dropping the remains of the dinner into the bin as his driveway sank back into darkness. Frank didn't recognise the car, the man reacting to the loud double knock on his front door as he made his way into the hallway. "Okay, I'm coming," he said before pulling the front door open. His eyes widened. "Steve?"

The younger man strode into the hallway. "We need to talk."

"Come in, why don't you. I'll put the kettle on."

"I don't want anything from you. I just want to say my piece."

"I'm listening," Frank replied, an uncertainty settling over him.

"I know you're not my father. Antony told me."

"He's lying to you, Son. Probably after your millions."

"Bollocks! He's not after my money, Frank. He didn't come to me. It was Cara who figured it all out."

"Figured it out?"

"Yes, but you don't need to know about that. Anyway, Antony told me all about Mum. How she wasn't happy and that she fell in love with Antony back in 1969. He also told me that you had a vasectomy after Joe was born. How could you do that? You heartless bastard!"

"Now, look here. You may be angry, but don't come into my house and start shouting the odds. It was thirty years ago. You know nothing about what was going on back then, apart from the ramblings of some old fool."

"That's my father you're talking about. At least he's owned up to the truth, even though he'd been told to keep his mouth shut. How could you do that? How could you raise me as your son when you knew I was someone else's?"

"But I didn't raise you."

"What?"

"Margaret raised you. I wanted nothing to do with you, I just played along. Joe was my son, and I loved him dearly. You were just a mistake. The result of some fumbling's in the potting shed."

"Bastard!" Steve swore, taking a step towards the taller man, his fists bunched.

"Go ahead. Take it out on me. Maybe I deserve it. I never wanted any of this to happen, Steve. It was your mother's doing, not mine. She had an affair while I was working all hours to provide for my family."

"You mean Joe," he hissed.

"Yes. He was my son. Margaret wanted to leave me. And eventually, that would have come to pass. I did all I could to make sure that Joe had the best start in life. I didn't really care about anything else."

"Is that why you killed Mum? To stop her taking half your empire."

"Oh, we're back to this again, are we? You're like a broken record."

"But I'm not, and I have proof that it was you. Enough proof to involve the police."

Frank's eyes narrowed, the older man taking a step forward. "Go on then. Enlighten me as to how I killed my wife."

"You said that she was swept out to sea."

"Yes."

"Well, Antony said that's not possible. He remembers the day vividly. It was warm and sunny. There were no storms that could have washed her off the coastal path."

Frank sighed. "No, on the day she disappeared, it was stormy. You can check with the police. They'll have it on record. September 15th, 1980."

Steve smiled thinly. "That's what Antony said. That's the date she was confirmed missing."

"See. Like I told you."

The younger man shook his head. "Thing is, Antony knows for a fact that she went missing the day before. On a sunny September afternoon. He knows this because he was waiting for her on the coastal path, but she never turned up. He came here, hiding in the treeline to see if he could spot her. He stood there for hours, but there was no sign of Mum. Explain that one."

"I think it's time you left. I have nothing more to say to you. Get out of my house and don't come back."

Steve saw something. Something he'd never seen before. Fear. He could see that the great Frank Stuart was rattled. He knew that his alibi had holes in it—big ones. "Don't worry. I'll go. Back to my family. But mark my words, Frank. I will be back.

269

And the police will be with me. I'm going to make you pay for what you've done."

He walked away from the house, his words hanging in the air. Frank stood there, his legs trembling as sweat beaded his grey hairline. *Oh, God!* He walked into the kitchen, pouring himself a sizeable whisky, which he downed in one go. Placing his hands on the draining board, the man looked out at his garden. His empire. *There's no going back now.*

CHAPTER
THIRTY-SIX

Steve walked from his car, the sun gently warming Port Isaac as people milled about its streets. He turned a corner, his mind turning over the conversation from the previous night with the man who he once called father. He was so consumed that the man didn't see the four people stood outside his café. "Hi," he began. "Has Dee not opened up?"

An elderly woman that he'd seen in his café numerous times before shook her head. "No. We've been stood here for five minutes. It should have been open over an hour ago."

He was about to pull out his keys to open up when he saw the police cars down by the beach. "What's all that about?" he asked the woman.

"No idea. Probably drugs."

"They pulled a woman out of the sea last night," another woman said. "My son told me this morning. She was found floating about a mile out."

"Jesus!" Steve exclaimed. "How did she get all the way out there?"

"My son reckons someone threw her off a boat. After all, all the fishermen would have been home by then and there's not many boats out at that time of night, except for the Coastguard."

"Oh, God! I hope she's okay, whoever she is."

"Don't know about that. All I know is what my son told me."

Something occurred to Steve, the man pulling out his phone, dialling a number. It went straight to voicemail, the man hanging up as a feeling of dread seeped through his bones. "Dee!" He turned to the woman who'd given him the news. "Do you know where they would have taken her?"

She shrugged. "Probably Truro hospital. Why?"

Steve took off towards the beach, flagging down a police officer. "The woman that was pulled from the sea. Do you know where she is?"

"Who are you?"

"My name's Steve. Steve Sullivan. I own the café up the street."

"Oh, that one. Well, it's not open yet," he countered. "Wanted something to warm my cockles."

"Well, the woman that runs it with me didn't turn up for work. Her name's Dee Wilson. She thinks an ex-boyfriend might have been stalking her."

"Ex-boyfriend?"

"Yes. From Plymouth. Can you give me any details?"

"Well, the woman pulled from the sea had no identification. So she's a *Jane Doe*, as they say." He smiled, pleased with his turn-of-phrase.

"Do you know what she looked like?"

"Only what I was told. Probably in her thirties. Short dark hair." The police officer was about to continue as the man took off up the stone ramp towards the town. "Bugger. Doesn't look like I'll be getting that coffee any time soon."

After arriving at the hospital thirty minutes later, and after many heated conversations, Steve was shown into a small room. *Oh no!* Across the room, a woman lay there, the rhythmic beep of the monitors telling him that she was still with him, for now. "Oh, Dee," he faltered, slumping in a chair next to the bed. "What have they done to you?" He held her hand, the warmth of her skin comforting. After an hour, he walked into the private bathroom, drinking a cup of cold water before resuming his seat next to the bed. The nurse walked in, checking her over before smiling at Steve as she left the room. A few minutes later, he felt her fingers move. He looked at her face, relief washing over him as her eyes fluttered open. "It's okay. I'm here."

It took a few seconds for her to come around, her blurred vision sharpening as a dark-haired man came into focus. "Steve?"

"Hello, you." Tears streamed down his face as the woman squeezed his hand.

"Where am I?"

"Truro hospital. The nurses told me that the RNLI pulled you out of the water. What happened?"

"Jason," she replied, her eyes widening. "Steve, he found me."

"He did this?"

She nodded, her hands beginning to tremble. "He took me out to sea, then pushed me overboard."

His heart constricted as tears ran down the woman's face into her hairline. "The bastard."

"I knew it was him. I recognised his dog, but it was too late."

"Well, don't worry," he soothed. "I'll let the nurse know that you're awake. I'm sure the police will want to speak to you." He went to stand up, a hand stopping him.

"Please don't leave me. Not yet."

"I'm not going anywhere." He sat back down on the bed, brushing her hair away from her face. "You had me so worried. When I saw the café wasn't open, I knew something was wrong."

"I'm so sorry. I'm nothing but trouble. I brought this to your door."

"Hey," he replied. "This is not your fault. He did this, not you. And don't worry. The police will soon catch up with him. He can't hurt you anymore."

"Promise?" Her eyes pleaded with him, the woman trembling under the sheet.

"I promise. Don't worry; I'll keep you safe."

"You're a wonderful man, Steve. Always remember that."

"I'm just a guy. A guy who really cares about you."

She sat up slowly, embracing him, not wanting to let him go. "Thank you. I won't let you down again."

"Good," he smiled. "I'm terrible at making coffee. I need you back on your feet."

She looked into his eyes, smiling back at him. *I love you.*

∼

"Hi," Cara smiled as the man noticed her approach.

"Good afternoon. Nice weather," he grinned.

"This is Cornwall. It can be lovely one minute, then blowing a hooley thirty seconds later."

"Huh?"

"It's a British thing. I guess you'll get used to it."

Jim's eyes widened, his pulse quickening when he saw the woman's expression. "Did that mean what I think it meant?"

"I think it did. Let's take a walk. I want to show you a few things."

"Lead on," he agreed as they fell in alongside each other.

A few minutes later, Cara spread her arms wide. "This is the beach."

"I've walked along it every morning," he replied. "Love this stretch of coastline."

"Me too. The coastal paths take you to Bude and Sandymouth Bay."

"Noted," he smiled.

"We get lots of surfers in the summer. Most flock to Newquay, but it's much quieter here, and the waves are good." They walked away from the shoreline, heading back through the park until Cara motioned towards a stile. She climbed in slowly, trying not to wince as she landed on the other side.

"Are you okay?" Jim asked from the other side.

"I'm good. I was involved in a car crash a few months ago. I thought I'd be back to normal by now, but it's slow going."

"Jeez! How did that happen?" He vaulted the stile, landing lightly as the woman rested against the wooden fence.

"Okay, if you're interested in the place, I suppose I'd better fill you in on a few things."

A few minutes later, Jim shook his head. "Wow! And here's me thinking that the UK was a quiet place. It sounds like you've been through the mill."

She smiled. "Something like that. Anyway, that's why I'm thinking of selling. Well, I wasn't until you came along," Cara grinned.

"Well, I'm glad I came along when I did." His face dropped slightly. "I can't believe your husband would try and do something like that?"

"Well, Joe was one of a kind. But we're trying to get on with our lives. It's been tough, but maybe a change in direction will do us all good." They walked in silence for a few minutes, weaving around the trees until they came out on a large meadow. "That's The Retreat."

"Impressive."

"It is. This is where my late husband entertained certain ladies, if you know what I mean," she winked. "If I am to sell the place, I would want to keep The Retreat, along with our family home. Does that sound unreasonable?"

He considered the question, shaking his head. "I don't think so. It's a mighty fine building. What are your plans for it?"

"Not sure yet," she replied as they walked across the grass towards the building. "I used to paint in my younger days. There's great natural light inside, so it could be used for that. Plus, my brother-in-law has just come into some money and has opened a book café in Port Isaac. This could be a similar kind of place. What do you think?"

He walked up the wooden steps in front of the entrance, running his palms along the wooden handrail. "I think it's a great idea. Although, I have an idea that I think you might like to hear."

"I'm all ears."

"One of my friends from high school has been writing books for many years now. Her name's Sonia Haffner. Have you heard of her?"

Cara shook her head. "No, does that make me a Philistine?"

He grinned. "No. She's not on Stephen King's level, but she's doing very well for herself over in the States. We've kept in touch over the years, and I've read all her books. They're excellent. Family sagas, y'know. Anyway, there's a place in Aspen that she goes to every year. It's a writer's retreat."

"What's a writer's retreat?"

"It's where a bunch of authors go to get creative. In truth, a lot of alcohol is involved, but you get my point. They get ideas from each other and take notes. Stuff like that. This could be that kind of place," he said, spreading his arms.

She smiled, turning around to look at the place. "I like that idea. No, I love that idea. I will see what Steve thinks."

"Steve?"

"My brother-in-law. He's a lovely guy, unlike his late brother," she replied, walking across the wooden boards towards the side of the building. "What do you think? Could it work?"

"I don't see why not. I don't really know Cornwall that well, but I'm sure you could make a success of it. Plus, the UK isn't that big, so authors could get here fairly easily. Not like Aspen."

They continued their tour, walking back through the forest, the conversation flowing freely. Cara's stiff gait lessened, a sense of purpose and excitement taking hold of her. After twenty minutes, she led him through a natural archway in a thick hedgerow. "Welcome."

"Wow!" Jim exclaimed. "What a place." His eyes scanned the manicured lawns that gave way to an imposing 19th Century house. "It's amazing."

"I love it, so do the kids." As if hearing her words, Lizzy appeared around the corner of the house, trotting over to her mother.

"Hi, Mummy. Who's this?"

"Hello, love. This is Jim. Jim, this is my daughter, Lizzy."

"Pleased to meet you, Jim," the girl stated, holding out her hand.

Jim took it, smiling down at the girl. "The pleasure is all mine, young lady."

Lizzy beamed up at him. "I'm a young lady, Mummy."

"You certainly are," Cara replied. "Where's Tom?"

"Malcolm's showing him how to whittle something."

"Whittle?" the woman replied.

"I don't know what it means," she shrugged.

"It means you make something out of wood," Jim cut in. "Like a knife handle or figurine. I used to do it as a kid."

"Oh. Well, you learn something new every day," Cara replied as her youngest son walked around the side of the house.

"Mummy," he called, spotting the man standing next to her. A smile spread across his face as he walked over. "Hi, Jim," he said confidently.

Cara looked at both of them. "You know each other?"

Jim smiled, shaking the boy's outstretched hand. "We had a very nice conversation a few days ago. How's it going, sport?"

"Good, thank you," the boy replied. "Malcolm's been showing me how to make a knife handle."

Cara looked at her son, noticing something different. *He said that perfectly*, she realised, ruffling his hair. "You want some lunch, guys?"

"Yes, please, Mummy," Lizzy replied, Tom nodding his agreement.

"Okay, go and find Malcolm and ask him if he wants something too."

They ran off across the grass, Cara turning to Jim. "What did you speak about the other day?"

"Well, he was telling me about his leg, and I picked up that he had a stammer, so I gave him a few tips to help."

She smiled. "Well, it's early days, but it looks like there's already an improvement. That was so kind of you, Jim."

"Think nothing of it. I was in the same boat as Tom when I was his age."

Cara extended her hand. "We have a deal. Sandy Shores is yours."

Jim's eyes widened. "Really?"

"Yes," she replied happily. "I know that you'll look after the place and continue to improve it. Let's get the ball rolling soon, but for now, we have an agreement in principle."

He took her hand, tears welling at the corners of his eyes. "You won't regret it. I promise."

She stepped forward and hugged him, the contact feeling strange at first until she felt strong arms wrap around her. After a few seconds, she let go, blushing. "Sorry, my emotions got the better of me."

"No need to apologise. It was the perfect way to seal the deal," he laughed.

"Right, now that's sorted, would you like to stay for lunch? I cook a mean toasted ham and cheese sandwich."

"I couldn't think of anything better," he winked as they walked towards the house, a new chapter unfolding for both of them.

CHAPTER
THIRTY-SEVEN

Antony waved Malcolm off before walking back into The Retreat. Walking across the creaky polished boards, he made his way to the kitchen area, needing another cup of coffee before carrying out a stock take in the cellar below. As steam began to cloud the window, the man looked out at the grassy expanse before him, pleased that he was working once more, albeit part-time. He felt younger, the previous months of inactivity seeming to fall from the man's shoulders when he got the call to report for duty. Antony walked around the expansive interior, taking his mug, looking in each room as he sipped his coffee. *I dread to think what's been going on in there;* he thought as he stared at a double bed with matching table lamps on either side. Other rooms were similar in appearance, Antony needing fresh air after a few minutes as the walls seemed to close around him. He stepped out onto the decked area, the spring sunshine a welcome relief. The man breathed deeply, smiling as rabbits darted around the lawns next to the treeline, a lone buzzard circling above. "Run, you fools, before you end up in his belly," he laughed before heading back to the kitchen to rinse out his mug.

"Right, let's get cracking." He picked up his clipboard, walking to the rear of the building where a door led down into the basement. "Bloody hell!" he swore, his weathered hands eventually turning the key in the lock before the door creaked open. His fingers found the light switch, Antony carefully navigating the stout wooden staircase before coming out in a dusty room filled with old furniture, beer kegs and large storage chests. He set to work, counting the barrels, bottles of wine and spirits and boxes of crisps. He worked methodically, grouping everything together until he sat down on the bottom step an hour later. After a few minutes, his breathing had settled, Antony's eyes settling on three large chests next to the far wall. A few remaining beer kegs sat beside them, partially obscured from view. Come on, old 'un, let's finish this off. He walked over, lifting the first keg before depositing it with the others. He did the same with the second before pressing his fingers into the small of his back, kneading the muscles for a few seconds as he psyched himself up for the last one. His eyes didn't notice the uneven floor as he stumbled forward, his shoulder crashing into the middle chest. "Argh," he cried out, falling backwards as the top chest landed on top of him. His head bumped off the floor, a million stars appearing before him as he lay on the floor, dazed and winded. The man sat up, shoving the chest away from him, its contents spilling out onto the floor. *Bugger!* He looked over at the empty chest and old clothing that lay scattered on the floor. He set to work, refilling the chest and snapping the locks closed on the lid before turning back to the far wall. He stared at the brick wall, his eyes narrowing when he saw a hole in the brickwork. He moved towards it, his finger gingerly probing the two-inch hole where the chest had damaged the wall. "What the hell?" Antony hooked his finger against the hole, exerting pressure as the façade shifted slightly. "It's a false wall." After a few minutes inspecting the borders, he noticed countersunk screws in various places, most of them disguised with a mortar-like substance. He quickly left The Retreat, heading for the outbuildings in the nearby forest. Fifteen minutes later, he was back in the cellar, a lump hammer, crowbar and bolster chisel in his hands. He started in the top left-hand corner, the fake wall coming away from its fastenings. After ten minutes of sweating and cursing, the fake wall lay propped against the adjacent wall, the man staring at a solitary door with a stout padlock barring the way forward. "I never knew that was there," he said to himself, staring at a wooden door. Curiosity took over, the man shifting the crates until he stood staring down at the padlock that kept it secure. The old man starting to wonder what lay beyond. "Why would they hide it like that?" He reached down, twisting the padlock against its hasp, feeling the steel start to give way until on screw snapped off. *To hell with it.* He grabbed the crowbar, sliding the tip behind the hasp until he knew that pure force and leverage would do the trick. He applied pressure, the lock falling to the ground with a muted clunk a few seconds later. The crowbar landed on the floor, Antony's fingers curling around the door before he pulled it open. It grated against the stone floor; more exertion required until it stood open. He peered inside, his eyes growing accustomed to the gloomy interior after a few seconds. The room was sparse, with a few objects lying on the floor. *What's that?* At the far side of the room, a large object lay against the stone wall. It was stained with dirt, about six feet long, tied with orange rope. As he moved closer, his heartbeat increased, noticing the shape that lay inside. "No, it can't be," he gasped, his boot nudging it. It was heavy, Antony kneeling on the floor as he loosened some of the rope at one end. After a minute of cursing and sweating, the knot came away, his hands unravelling the coarse material. "Oh Jesus!" he cried out, falling back onto the floor, his eyes locking onto the last thing he'd expected. Matted human hair.

∼

"I've called DI Harris," Cara said as she walked into The Retreat. "She's on her way." She looked at the man, placing a reassuring hand on his shoulder as Malcolm handed him a coffee. "Are you okay?"

Antony exhaled. "I'll be okay, Mrs Stuart. I've never seen a dead body before."

"I bet it gave you quite a shock. But don't worry, the police will take care of it all." She turned towards the younger man. "Malcolm, could you come with me?"

"Sure," he replied. "Stay here, Dad. We'll be back in a minute."

They walked towards the rear of the building, down the stairs into the cellar. The light cast shadows across the floor, Cara noticing the cool temperature as she stood facing the door. "I just want to see for myself before the police arrive."

"Are you sure?"

"I need to see it. Don't worry; I'll not touch anything. Are you coming?"

"Aye," he agreed, following her into the smaller room.

Once inside, Cara felt her breath catch, the air seeming to coat the back of her throat as she walked towards the bundle on the ground. She looked down, seeing an emaciated face, frozen in time as it stared at the ceiling. The skin had darkened, stretched tight over the woman's cheekbones, giving the face a ghoulish appearance. "Poor girl," she whispered. "I'm so sorry you ended up like this."

"It's not your fault, Cara," Malcolm added.

"Maybe not, but Joe had a hand in this. Even if someone else did it, my husband knew about it and ensured no one would find out. Until now."

"I wonder who she was?"

"No idea." She looked down at the matted blonde hair. "But she didn't deserve this. And I hope whoever did this pays for what they've done." Something occurred to her. "What if Martin was driving the van away from the park with a mini digger attached to the back? He could have used that to exhume the body, hiding it down here in the hope it was never found. I can't believe the police never spotted this when they were here."

"Cara, I've got a confession to make," the man said.

"Oh. What?" she replied, turning towards him.

"I knew what went on here."

She sighed. "That doesn't surprise me, Malcolm. And let me guess, Joe made you keep quiet or face the consequences."

"He did at first. But then he used to offer me things to buy my silence."

"Oh? Like what?"

Malcolm leaned against the wall, unable to look at her. "Young men."

Her eyes widened. "What?"

"I'm gay, Cara. Have been for years. Joe knew this and used to make sure I had a bit of fun when the girls arrived. Never in here, though. Away from The Retreat."

She walked across to the man, embracing him. She felt his body stiffen, then gradually relax as she held onto him. "It's okay, Malcolm. I always wondered why you never got married or had a girlfriend. Now I know."

He eased himself out of her arms, wiping tears from his face. "Only Dad knows about it. Joe and Martin knew, but they're not around anymore. I feel ashamed because I used to turn a blind eye to all this. So did Dad."

"Look, we both know the hold that Joe and Frank had over people. So don't feel bad about this. I've known that Joe was playing away for years, but I chose to ignore it because of the kids. So in a way, I should feel ashamed. Ashamed that I never confronted him sooner."

"Jesus, what a mess!"

"It is, but it will get sorted out. And don't worry, I won't breathe a word of what you've said to anyone."

He smiled, blushing slightly. "That's okay. I think it's time that I came out, so to speak. Times are changing, and being gay isn't quite the scandal that it used to be."

"Of course it's not. You're a good-looking bloke, Malcolm. And I'm sure Mr Right is out there somewhere. You need to start living a little."

"Dad says the same thing. Maybe now I can."

They heard cars pull up outside the building, Cara walking towards the door. "Come on, let's get this done. I have a feeling it's going to be a long day."

CHAPTER
THIRTY-EIGHT

"I CAN'T BELIEVE THIS WAS MISSED," HARRIS GRUMBLED, SHAKING HER head at her department's less-than-thorough work ethic.

"Oh well, better late than never. We've got Antony Shaw to thank for this. I was down here, guv. I never noticed the fake wall."

"Hmm, well, it does look pretty convincing," she agreed, her voice softening slightly. "We need forensics down here, pronto. And they only go through me. I don't want a word of this to get out until we know who she is and if she was involved with the Chief before her death."

"I'll make the call," Pearce nodded, heading through the secret door and up the wooden stairs.

Harris stood there, looking down at the mummy-like appearance of her Jane Doe. "Mandy, I will catch the bastard that did this to you. I promise." She bent down, using a pen to shift the clothing from around the woman's neck. After a few seconds, the Inspector stood up, knowing that the experts were needed to unfold the events that led up to the young woman's death. All she could do was keep her head down and wait. She walked out of the rear cellar, thankful for the fresh air a few seconds later. Two uniformed officers had pulled up, making a cordon around the pavilion-type building. Harris walked across the decking, seating herself next to Cara and the two men. She exhaled, feeling a numbing tiredness wash over her. "I'll need you all to come to the station today to make formal statements and give a sample of DNA."

"DNA?" Antony asked.

"It's standard procedure, Mr Shaw. And as you found the body, your prints and possible DNA may have contaminated the scene. Taking a swab will eliminate you from our enquiries." She turned to Cara, who was chewing her thumbnail. "Have you ever been in that cellar before?"

"Yes. A few times, but I never noticed the fake wall. I'm no Sherlock Holmes, but I'm guessing that Martin installed that after he moved the body from the forest."

"We'll make a detective of you yet," Harris smiled. "Pearce will follow up with the Bellevue. Most girls use false names when carrying out this kind of activity, but it's worth a shot. Plus, if the girl's DNA is on the system, we'll get a match pretty quickly."

"Does anyone want a cup of tea?" Antony asked.

"Not for me, Mr Shaw. But thank you."

Cara shook her head, Malcolm nodding as the two men walked back inside. "Stay close to the kitchen area. Don't go anywhere near the cellar," she called after them, both men nodding before disappearing inside.

"Can I say something?" Cara asked.

"Sure."

"You look exhausted."

Harris smiled, swallowing her emotions. "I am. Between you and me, my home life isn't great at the moment. Plus, there's lots going on at work, and this case is weighing heavy on me."

"But you've found the body. I'm sure that's a start."

"Walk with me," she replied, the two women heading onto the grass, away from The Retreat. "What I'm about to tell you is strictly off the record. I know I can trust you, Cara, but my career is on the line."

"Of course, just between us."

"I told you about the leads that I was following up on regarding your late husband."

"Yes. To be honest, I'd forgotten about it."

"Lucky you." She tried to smile, it not quite reaching her eyes. "Martin Murray spoke to me a few days before he died. He opened up about the body in the forest."

"Really?" Cara's pulse began to quicken, wondering where this was heading.

"Yes. The girl's name was Mandy. Whether that's her real name or an alias remains unclear. He also told me how she died and who killed her."

"Joe?"

Harris shook her head. "No. My boss."

Cara's mouth dropped open. "A policeman?"

"Not just any policeman. The Chief Constable of Devon and Cornwall. That's why I look so strung-out. If I get this wrong, that's my career over. If I get this right, the fallout will be biblical. A national scandal. And that's not all. Another man was there that night. He assaulted one of the girls. Jim Walsh, the television personality."

"Bloody hell! I can see where this is heading."

"Look, I'm only telling you this now because your family may get caught up in it. You could have press outside your door or taking pictures of The Retreat from the forest. I know you and your family have done nothing wrong, but that won't stop them."

"So, what should I do?"

"Carry on as normal. Although, I'd probably look at beefing up the security around the park for a while. Those reporters can sneak in anywhere and cause trouble. That's the last thing you need when trying to run a holiday park."

Cara smiled, biting her bottom lip, the detective noticing her expression. "Well, that's the thing. It looks like I'm selling the place."

"Oh," she replied. "I had no idea you were looking to sell."

"Nor did I until a few days ago. There's a guy staying at the park from the US. He asked to meet me, then explained how he owns two Sandy Shores holiday parks in America. We got chatting and have agreed in principle to a deal."

"Wow! Is that what you want to do?"

"God yes! I have no idea how to run the place. That was Joe's world. I have a few ideas about what I'd like to do next, The Retreat being my focus. Well, it was, until we found a body in the basement."

"Don't worry too much about that. Yes, there will be police swarming all over the place for a while, but the body had nothing to do with you. Joe and Martin are gone, and hopefully, the Chief will take the fall for all of this. The focus and outrage will be squarely directed towards him. Or me, if I screw this up."

~

"Come on in," Steve said, ushering Dee into his home.

"Wow! Steve, this is gorgeous," she gushed, her eyes taking in the main living area. To her left, there were large chocolate brown sofas arranged around a large television. There was an oak dining table and chairs away from the lounge, with brass retro lighting above. Her eyes scanned to the right, admiring the modern kitchen, complete with a Range Master and island unit.

"You like it?"

"Like it. Jesus, it's amazing!"

"Come on, I'll give you a quick guided tour before I put the kettle on." He led her away from the living area into a long hallway with doors on either side. "This is where the kids sleep. They've got a nice bedroom each, and Matthew even has an ensuite. Although the girls spend more time in there than he does."

"That's girls for you," she smiled.

They came out of the hallway into another large living area. Next to the folding French doors, an imposing wooden desk complete with computer was set up overlooking a manicured lawn and forest beyond. She could see the Atlantic in the distance, the ocean completing the impressive vista. "Oh my God! I thought the rest of the house was stunning. Steve, this room is amazing. Look at all the natural light."

He grinned like a schoolboy. "I know. I love this room and spend a lot of my time in here, especially when I want to escape for a while."

She noticed a wooden staircase leading towards a mezzanine floor. "What's up there?"

"The master bedroom. My sanctuary. I'll show you." They walked up the staircase, which came out onto a large landing area. Through double doors, a huge double bed sat under an apex roof, complete with roof lights. "I did splash out a bit on this room."

"Oh, Steve," she exclaimed, noticing the canvas paintings that adorned the three walls. "I love the artwork." Looking to her left, she noticed the bathroom, taking a quick peek inside. "What a lovely home you have. And you deserve it."

He blushed. "Thanks. The kids are so happy here. It's safe and secure, the garden is perfect, and the beach is only a ten-minute walk away."

Dee walked across to a large window, seeing the swings and

trampoline sat next to a row of tall conifers. Then, she spotted something else, a large wooden structure nestled into the treeline. "What's that?"

A smile spread across his face. "Come on, let me show you." Steve led her back through the house, through the French doors into the garden.

The sun warmed her skin, the sound of nearby seagulls filtering through the trees. Ahead of them, a large log cabin sat waiting for them, its Hansel and Gretel appearance looking like something from a fairy tale. "Bloody hell! Did you buy this?"

"No. It came with the place. Cool, huh."

"Cool doesn't do it justice," she countered as Steve led her into the main living area. Two small sofas, complete with tartan throws, sat a few feet inside the doors, an open fireplace with a log burner taking up a large part of the stone feature wall. Behind the living area, a compact kitchen with shiny granite work surfaces and modern appliances gleamed as the sun's rays caught them.

"And there's a double bedroom through there, complete with ensuite," he said, smiling at the expression on the woman's face.

"What a lovely place. You could rent this out as a holiday let."

"The previous owners did that. From what the estate agent told me, the place was occupied for about eight months of the year."

"And are you going to do the same?"

"No. I have other plans for it."

"Oh, like what?"

He took a step forward, taking her hands. "I've grown very fond of you, Dee. And after what's just happened, I don't want anything else to happen to you. Think it over, but I would really love it if you lived here, just while things are a bit all over the place."

"W-what?" Her throat seemed to dry up, her words failing her as she stared up at the man she'd grown to love.

"Just think it over. I don't want you to agree to something for the sake of it. Give it a few days and let me know."

She looked around the place, the sound of the Atlantic drifting in through the open doors. "What about your kids? They might think it strange if I'm living at the bottom of the garden."

"The kids think you're cool. Even Matthew does. They miss Rosie, but I don't think having you here will be awkward. If anything, the girls would love it."

She hugged him as tears fell from her eyes. "You're such a lovely man, Steve. I don't know what to say."

"Say yes," he replied, his breath warm on her neck.

She pulled back, her face and neck flushed. "Okay, if it's alright with you guys, I'd love to stay for a bit." Her heart constricted as he smiled at her, his eyes narrowing. *I love your smile.*

"That's the best news I've had all year," he beamed, leaning forward and planting a peck on her cheek. "Welcome to your new home."

She twirled around slowly with her arms outstretched. "I hope I'm not dreaming. Please, tell me I'm not about to wake up."

"It's no dream. However, I do have a few house rules."

"I'm listening," she replied, wondering what was about to come out.

"You can come and go as you please. But if you're passing the kitchen, I'll have a latte."

"Is that it?"

"That's all I could think of at short notice."

"Steve, you've no idea how happy you've made me. Words don't do it justice."

"Come on. Let's celebrate."

"What did you have in mind?"

"Oh, I don't know. A nice pot of tea and some cucumber sandwiches."

She smiled, the weight of the past few days blowing away on the sea breeze. "I could get used to this kind of treatment. Lead on, kind sir."

CHAPTER
THIRTY-NINE

HARRIS LOOKED OUT OF HER WINDOW, WISHING SHE HAD A BETTER view. Dull grey buildings seemed to press against the glass, the woman turning around as her phone began to chime. "Harris," she said officially.

"Jackie, it's Sarah."

The female detective came forward, her eyes scanning the open-plan area beyond her office. "What have you got?"

"I've got news. Can we meet?"

"Sure. When?"

"Thirty minutes. Usual place."

"Okay, see you there." She replaced the receiver, rubbing her clammy hands together as Pearce poked his head around the door. "You okay, guv?"

"Fine. Just popping out for a bit."

"Oh, you want me to tag along?"

"It's okay. I just need to pop to the chemist and run a few errands."

"Did you know the Chief's here?"

She came forward in her chair. "No. When did he arrive?"

"About thirty minutes ago. Went straight in with the Chief Super."

"Shit," she whispered. "Hold the fort. If anyone asks where I am, just think of something."

He could see his boss' agitation, the young detective knowing something wasn't right. "Oh, okay. See you in a bit."

Jackie grabbed her keys from the desk, walking out of the police station as quickly and calmly as possible. She sat in her car, her fingers trembling on the steering wheel before she gunned the engine and pulled out of the enclosed courtyard, heading for a roadside snack bar a few miles away. A short time later, she pulled off the main road, thankful for the cover of trees that hid vehicles from view. The car dipped and bounced over the uneven road before she pulled in next to a picnic area, a woman seated there with two Styrofoam cups.

"Hi," Sarah said, placing a cup of tea in front of the approaching detective.

"I had a lucky escape. Jenkins is in town."

"Oh, was that announced?"

"Not to me. He showed up about forty-five minutes ago." Harris could see the concern on the pathologist's face.

"Okay. Well, I suppose I'd better give you an update. DNA samples taken from the body confirm her identity as Mandy Higgins. Twenty-four years old, from Hackney in East London. We got lucky. She's got previous and was easy to find."

"Well, that's something. At least we know who she was."

The younger woman took a sip of her tea, the hot liquid preparing her for the next piece of news. "She died from strangulation, which you thought would be the cause. Also, we've extracted traces of semen from inside her."

"Any matches?"

"Nothing. Come on, Jackie, tell me what your hunch is."

"I think it's the Chief."

The younger woman stared at the detective. "Jenkins?"

"Yes. One of the witnesses confirmed his identity at the scene. But that's the only proof I have."

"Could they testify against him?"

"They're dead."

"Fuck! So, what are you going to do?"

"I have no idea. I can't exactly walk into Jenkin's office and ask for a DNA swab."

"No, but you can obtain DNA by other means."

"I know," she smiled, shaking her head. "But unless I sneak into his house in the middle of the night and pull his hair out, I've got limited options."

"How about his mug or toothbrush?"

"Hmm, that might work, but I'd need a reason to be in Exeter and how to I steal a mug from his desk?"

"Well, that's why you're the detective, and I'm the pathologist."

Something came to Harris, a smile appearing on her face. "I've got an idea. It's a long shot, but it's all I've got."

"Do you need any help?"

Harris placed a hand on Sarah's. "I don't want to put you at risk."

"He murdered a young woman," she replied, her face set. "It's worth the risk."

∽

The threesome sat around the garden table, enjoying the warm spring sunshine as the children played happily in the garden. Cara looked inside the house; her happy mood tempered as she stared at her eldest child. Tristan lay sprawled on the sofa, headphones on as he played a hand-held game. *What am I going to do with you?*

"Mummy, we're hungry," Lizzy stated.

Cara turned around, focusing on her daughter. Tristan could wait. "You've just had some crisps. Uncle Steve is cooking some pizzas in a bit. Can you manage until then?"

Steve and Dee looked on and smiled as Lizzy pondered the question. "Okay, but I'm really hungry, Uncle Steve."

"Okay, Lizzy. I promise they won't be long. Go and play, and I'll give you a shout in a bit."

The girl ran back towards the trampoline, laughter filling the air as the three adults enjoyed the scene in front of them. "Bless them," Dee remarked. "I wish I was that age again. Not a care in the world."

"I'll second that," Cara added. "Although, I'm not so sure about that one," she said, cocking her head towards the lounge.

"Still no better?" Steve asked. He looked at his nephew. God, he's a carbon copy of his dad.

"No. He's hardly speaking, except when he's with Frank. Never speaks to Lizzy or Tom and just grunts most of the time."

"Don't worry; he'll come round eventually. By the way, any news on you know what?"

Cara smiled over the rim of her mug. "I guess so."

Five minutes later, Steve embraced his sister-in-law, Dee following suit before they all regained their seats. "That's great news," Steve said. "A new chapter for all of you."

"Congratulations," Dee echoed. "You must be thrilled."

"I am, although I've not told the kids yet. Or Frank."

Steve's face dropped slightly. "Why would you need to tell him?"

She shrugged. "Just out of courtesy, I guess. I know Joe owned the park, but Frank laid the foundations."

"I suppose. Just don't let him talk you out of it."

"I won't. And what's new with you? Have you seen Antony and Malcolm?"

"They're coming over later. The kids don't know yet. With everything that they've been through, telling them that they have a new granddad might be a bit much."

She turned to Dee. "And how're things with you?"

She sighed, smiling at Steve. "Okay, I guess."

Cara sensed something was up. "Oh, well, that's good."

"You can tell her, Dee. I trust Cara with my life."

"Did you read about the woman pulled from the sea last week?"

"Yes, I saw it in the local paper. How aww…" a hand went to her mouth. "Oh my God! Was that you?"

The dark-haired woman blushed. "Err, yeah. That was me."

"Jesus! What happened? Sorry if I'm being nosey."

"That's okay. If Steve trusts you, that's good enough for me. "I sent my ex-boyfriend down a few months ago after he set about me. I also took some of his drug money. He caught up with me and thought I needed a swim."

"Bloody hell! I read about it all. I bet you were terrified."

"I was until I blacked out. The next thing I knew, Steve was smiling down at me in the hospital. The police have arrested Jason and have asked me to head down to Plymouth to give a statement."

"I'm so sorry, Dee. How awful for you." A thought occurred to Cara, a wry smile spreading across her face. "Looks like we've got quite a lot in common."

"I suppose we have. Steve kind of told me what you've been going through. It must have been horrendous."

"Something like that. But hey, we've both lived to tell the tale, and things are looking up for us all."

Steve rose from his chair, draining his mug. "I suppose I'd better put the pizzas in. And I'll see if Tristan would like to have a play on my computer."

"I'm sure he would," Cara agreed. "Thanks, Steve. That's very thoughtful of you."

He walked inside the house, leaving the two women alone, silence descending over them. Finally, Cara broke the ice. "He's such a lovely guy. Has he spoken much about Rosie?"

"Not really, except a little bit when we first started working together. She sounded like a real piece of work."

"Oh, she was. A real handful. It was terrible what happened to her, but he's a changed bloke."

"I'm glad about that," Dee replied evenly, wondering where the conversation was heading.

"Dee, can I ask you something?"

Here we go. "Sure."

"Do you like Steve? I mean, like that? Sorry if that came out a bit direct."

Is this where she warns me off? I bloody knew it. Play it cool. "He's a lovely bloke, but I've not really thought about him like that."

Cara smiled. "Dee, I'm a woman. I can see the way you look at him."

"Okay, yes, I do really like him," she confessed. "But I think he has eyes for someone else."

"Really? Who?"

"You, Cara."

She was taken aback, turning to look at the dark-haired man as he put the pizzas in the oven. "Don't be daft; he's my brother-in-law."

"What does that matter these days?"

"Look. Steve's the most caring guy I have ever known. And he is very handsome, but I see him as a part of the family, not a potential partner."

"Really? I thought you two would get it together at some point."

"Never going to happen. Plus, I think he's in love with you?"

It was Dee's turn to be shocked. "Pah! There's more chance of finding hen's teeth."

"Dee, I'm a woman, like you. But I'm on the outside looking in. I can see how he looks at you. Trust me; Steve has feelings for you."

She looked inside the house, seeing her boss ruffle the head of his nephew as they made their way across the house. "I think it's too soon for him to be thinking like that. You must be mistaken."

"I'll bet my house on it. I'm not saying it's going to happen today, but mark my words; it will happen."

"But I'm trouble. Look at the shit I've already caused." Tears formed at the corners of her eyes, the woman dabbing her eyes with a serviette.

"We're all trouble to some degree. I can see that you care about him. After the shit he's been through over the years, it's about time he found some happiness. And not just the money. I mean love. Real love."

"So, what shall I do?"

"Just go with the flow. And enjoy the life you're living." She placed a hand on Dee's. "Be happy, and look after my brother-in-law."

They hugged as Steve walked out of the house, the man stopping mid-step. "Is everything okay?"

They both laughed, Cara wiping tears from her eyes. "We're just talking about our friend, Nunya?"

"Nunya?" he replied, slightly confused.

"Yeah, nunya business," she smirked. "Now get back in the kitchen; we're in need of refreshments."

Steve walked back inside, giggles following him towards the kitchen. *What was that all about?* He filled the kettle, unaware that his life was about to take another twist.

CHAPTER
FORTY

FRANK GAZED OUT AT HIS GARDEN; HIS MIND OVERLOADED WITH thoughts. With rage. He'd worked hard his entire life, trying to be the best man he could be. Yes, he'd made some hard decisions along the way, but it was Frank's way, and he wouldn't have changed anything. Well, nearly anything, aware that the one thing he'd strived hard for, now, lay in tatters—his family. Minutes before, he'd replaced the receiver of the house telephone into the cradle, a wave of acceptance washing over the man. He drank in the sight of his garden once more. The place where he'd spent nearly fifty years, hoping it would have been his forever home. And it had been just that, until now. He finished his coffee, limbs feeling stiffer than usual as he rose from the kitchen table. He had things to do, plans to be set in motion before he could move on. Frank walked from the kitchen, taking the stairs as he headed towards his bedroom. After a few minutes of sorting through various things, the greyhaired man looked down at the bed, mentally going over what he'd done an hour before. Being meticulous had propelled him to what he was today. There was no room for error. But deep down, he knew that mistakes had been made. And not just by him, but also by his son. The local entrepreneur had turned a blind eye over the years, knowing that his eldest son was engaging in activities that would land him in trouble. For all Joe's brilliance, Frank knew that Joe had one weakness. Women. Something that he'd not inherited from his father. Frank was not the same animal, only being married to one woman, knowing the love of one woman. His wife, Margaret. Leaving the bedroom, Frank made his way downstairs to his home office, his fingers playing along the lip of his mahogany desk before he stood at the window. He knew the world was changing, computers and machines taking over. But not for Frank, the room contained hundreds of lever-arch files and a telephone on the desk. That's how he'd operated. He was old school, and it had worked, the bricks and mortar around him proof of what hard work and the odd slice of luck can bring. A single tear slid down his cheek, a weathered hand wiping it away quickly. Tears were for the weak; his own God-fearing father had taught him that when the world was recovering from the war. He looked to his left, smiling at the picture on the wall. His father's eyes caught him, Frank moving closer to study the black-and-white image. He smiled at his younger self, trying to remember what it had been like nearly seventy years ago. His mother's eyes also found his, Frank remembering her as a lump formed in his throat. The polar opposite to Henry Stuart, Nancy, was the epitome of a caring mother. She'd never raised her voice to his younger self, Frank feeling pain in his chest as the last memory of her came to him. A frail old lady with paper-thin skin, smiling up through rheumy eyes. He removed the picture from the wall, placing it on the desk. He couldn't leave it there. Snapping back to the present day, the man headed outside, spending the next thirty minutes loading up his boot. As he leant against his car, a weariness crept over him, a feeling that was all too familiar lately. But now was not the time for lethargy. Things needed to be done. Things he never thought possible. But such is life, as the saying went.

∼

Dee looked up from her book as Steve knocked on the door. She placed the novel on the coffee table, motioning for the man to come in. "How did it go?" she asked expectantly.

"Really well," the man replied as he pulled a bottle of wine from around his back.

"Good thinking, Batman," she smiled. "I'll get the glasses out."

"I'll do it. You stay where you are."

"I'm loving the service around here." The woman watched him open the bottle, unsure of what to say next. "So, what did you guys talk about? Sorry, that's probably a dumb question."

"It's a good question," he replied as he handed her the wine glass. They chinked them together, both enjoying the crisp taste of the Sauvignon Blanc. "We waited until the kids were in their rooms before we talked about that kind of stuff. You didn't need to leave us to it, you know. I was hoping you'd have stayed."

"Thank you, but I thought I'd give you a bit of space. They're your new family, and I didn't want to get in the way."

He smiled, shaking his head. "You're never in the way. Remember that."

"You're too kind. Remember that."

"Touché," he grinned. Steve's face dropped, the smile fading as he took another sip of the wine. "We talked about Mum a lot. There were so many things about her I never knew. It's like reliving the past in fine detail. Antony, I mean, Dad has so many memories of her. It's such a shame, Dee," his voice faltering.

"He really loved her." He placed the wine glass on the table, the woman putting an arm around his shoulders.

"Hey, it's okay. Just let it out." She held him, rubbing his back as the man released his emotions.

After a minute, he reached forward, taking another glug of his wine. "Thank you."

"Don't thank me; it's what friends are for." She changed the subject, not wanting to push it. "So, what happens now?"

"Another glass?"

"Not the wine, stupid," she laughed. "I mean with Frank."

Steve's smile waned. "I'm going to report this to the police. Not sure when, but soon."

"Well, you do what you think is best, Steve. If what you've told me is true, and I know it is, he needs to answer for what he's done."

"And he will. He can't hide away forever. I'm sure the police will find something when they start digging around his house."

"Well, I'm here for you. Whatever you need, just say the word."

He leaned over, planting a kiss on the woman's cheek. "Thank you, Dee. You're a wonderful friend."

She blushed, a warm sensation coursing through her body as she gazed into his eyes. "Stop it with the compliments. My head won't fit through the door at this rate."

"You're funny. Anyway, I've been thinking about something."

"Oh, what is it?"

"If you're going to live here for a bit, you'll need transport."

"You're right. I did think about that, but other things got in the way. Does the bus go by here?"

"It does, but it's a ten-minute walk to the bus stop. That's fine during the summer, but I can't have you walking along the country lanes when the night's start drawing in."

So, he wants me here for a while. "I never thought of it like that. I suppose I should look into getting a little run-around."

"I think so. I'll put you on my insurance for now, and you're welcome to use my car."

"Thank you, but it's a bit big for me. I'll probably damage it."

"That's okay, it's insured. Why don't we take a drive out with the kids tomorrow? There are a few local car places we could look at."

"We could, but I'm not sure I can afford a car right now."

"I'm sure they won't. And anyway, I'm not asking you to spend your money. It's my treat."

Her eyes widened. "Steve, you can't do that. I know you can afford it, but you've done enough already."

"I insist. And look, there might be the odd day that I stay at home while you head into Port Isaac. You need a car."

"Okay, well, take it out of my wages. Otherwise, I won't accept."

He saw the determined expression on her face, the man holding up his hands in mock surrender. "Okay, deal." He extended his hand, Dee giggling as she shook it firmly.

"So, what are your plans for the evening?"

"I have no idea. The kids are in bed, so I might just put something on the tele and have another glass of wine. And you?"

"Well, I was reading until someone started plying me with booze," she smirked. "I might just sit and read for a bit."

"What are you reading?"

"It's called 48, by James Herbert," she replied, showing him the cover.

"You like a bit of horror?"

"I like a bit of everything. I picked it up at the charity shop next to the café last week. I could always read it tomorrow if you fancy doing something?"

"Have you watched *The Perfect Storm*?"

"I wanted to watch it last year when it came out, but other things were going on at the time. Why?"

"I bought it on DVD last week."

She smiled. "I'd love to watch it."

"Great. We can use the DVD player in here. It's cosier. Stay there, and I'll go and grab it. You fancy some more wine and nibbles?"

"You read my mind, Steve Sullivan."

He grinned like a schoolboy, disappearing out of the door as Dee made a bolt for the bathroom. She looked in the mirror, running her fingers through her hair before she was happier about her appearance. The woman looked down, wishing she'd worn something more pleasing to the eye than a pair of black leggings and an Aerosmith T-shirt. *Oh well, at least my toenails look pretty*, she assured herself before heading back to the sofa.

He walked back in, loaded with provisions. "Here we go," he tried to say, a large bag of popcorn between his teeth. Placing them on the kitchen counter, he retrieved a box of matches and firelighters from under the sink. "It's a bit chilly out. Shall I put the fire on?"

"Suits me."

The movie began a few minutes later, a lone trawler heading out into the North Atlantic as they sipped wine and ate popcorn. The tartan throws covered their legs, Dee trying to concentrate on the movie even though she could feel the man next to her. She looked at George Clooney, her mind elsewhere as Steve shifted on the sofa, offering her the popcorn. Dee placed some in her mouth, trying to be as lady-like as possible.

"You've dropped one," he said, a smile on his face as he

leaned over to retrieve the stray kernel, popping it into his mouth.

The contact was over before she'd realised, feeling the skin on her face and around her neck begin to flush. *Thank God the lights are off*, she thought, trying to suppress a giggle. They continued watching, the log burner throwing off heat as orange embers glowed through the glass. *This is perfect.*

"Fancy a refill?" Steve asked as he drained his glass.

"I'll get them. Need to pop to the loo."

"Okay. I'll pause it."

She did the necessary, before retrieving the wine from the fridge, filling the glasses and getting comfortable once more. "Go on then; let's have a bit more George and Mark."

He chuckled. "A bit of eye candy," he winked. "Oh well, I've got all the eye candy I need right here." The words were out before he'd realised, the wine loosening his inhibitions. "Sorry, that came out wrong?"

She looked at him. "Wrong?"

"Not wrong. I mean, maybe I shouldn't have said it. Not that you're not eye candy. You're gorgeous. Shit! I'm useless at giving compliments."

She looked at him, seeing his vulnerability as he dropped his eyes and fidgeted like a teenager. It gave her butterflies. "Steve Sullivan, are you trying to flirt with me?"

"If I am, I'm making a complete pig's ear of it."

She reached around the back of his neck, gently pulling the man towards her before their lips came together. Dee's eyes closed, the movie forgotten as she felt strong hands pull her into him. *Oh. My. God! This is happening.*

And like that, the contact was broken; Dee feeling deflated until she saw the look on the man's face. "Oh boy! I've wanted to do that for ages," he sighed.

"Then why didn't you?" she breathed, lacing her fingers into his.

"I don't know. I'm not great at this kind of thing."

"Oh, I don't know; I think you're pretty amazing at that kind of thing. Now shut up and come here." The movie stayed on pause, the world outside fading away.

CHAPTER
FORTY-ONE

HER OPPORTUNITY CAME OUT OF THE BLUE, JACKIE HARRIS RECEIVING an email inviting her to a meeting at Devon and Cornwall's police headquarters. It had given her little notice, the detective cobbling together the best plan she could think of. Pearce knew nothing of it, Harris laying out her plan to her pathologist friend instead. Sarah had questioned it, the two women coming up with a credible plan before her trip across the county line. She climbed out of her car, the enclosed courtyard making her feel claustrophobic as grey clouds seemed to press down against the drab headquarters. Harris switched on her digital camera, snapping a few quick pictures as she walked up the concrete ramp and into the building. The meeting related to the growing drug problem in the South-West, coupled with the rise in organised crime. Her pulse had quickened as Graham Jenkins walked to the podium to kick off proceedings, the detective studying every inch of his demeanour. *Smug bastard!* After the opening salvo, another senior police officer took to the stage as the projector flickered to life. The lights went out, Harris thankful that she was positioned towards the rear of the large room, right next to the door. The speaker's voice faded away,

Harris' eyes watching the departing Chief Constable, looking back at the stage as he passed by and out of the door. She began a silent countdown, a minute passing before she snuck out of the room, the man on the stage not seeing her stealthy departure. Harris steadied her breathing as she leaned against a wall in the corridor before taking a few steps towards the bank of windows that overlooked the courtyard below. The woman needed a better vantage point, knowing what she needed to see. *Shit*, she thought as Jenkins walked out of a set of double doors, down a concrete ramp towards the smoking area. He lit a cigarette, pulling out his mobile phone as Harris quickly headed for her car. *This had better work, or I'm screwed.* She came out of another exit door thirty feet away from the man on the phone, the detective knowing she couldn't be seen. A male voice drifted towards her, Harris trying to hear the conversation. The nearby traffic made it impossible to follow the man's words, the woman poking her head around the recess to see what was going on. Quickly, she pulled her digital camera out, holding it level with her chest as the detective began taking pictures. He was facing away from her, Harris watching as he stubbed his cigarette out. *There were five nub ends in there when I arrived. That was twelve minutes ago.* She did the math, assuming that there may be a few more as officers came and went.

"Here we go," she whispered as Jenkins headed back through the double doors. As she approached the smoking area, she pulled out a pack of cigarettes, trying not to choke as she lit one with trembling fingers. The woman checked the courtyard, thankful that it was deserted. She had little time, slipping a pair of nitrile gloves on as smoke made her eyes sting, the woman trying to appear as casual as possible. Her eyes dropped to the ashtray where she saw six discarded cigarettes in the bowl, one of them still smouldering. Her gloved hand found the tweezers in her jacket pocket as rain began to fall. Harris retrieved the nub end as quickly as possible, removing the smouldering tip before dropping it into an evidence bag that she'd pulled out of her other pocket. She flinched as the doors banged open, two plain-clothed officers heading her way. *Fuck!* Her hands went into her pockets, the urge to cough building and building as the two men rounded the bottom of the ramp sharing a private joke.

"Alright," the taller one said.

"Morning," she replied, the ash on her cigarette starting to succumb to gravity.

"You here for the meeting?" the other officer asked.

Shit! Within her jacket, she moved one hand inside the pocket, reaching over to the other, pinching down on the glove, pulling it off in one tug, her hand coming out of the pocket to knock the ash into the tray. "I am but had to dip out to take a call."

The taller one frowned, blowing smoke towards her. "Shouldn't you be getting back inside?"

The nervous feeling running through her body melted away, resentment taking its place. "I'll go back in when I'm ready." She looked at the man, guessing he was fresh out of police training. Or thereabouts. "You both DCs?"

"That's right. And you? DC?"

"DI," she countered, the man realising he was outranked.

"Oh," he muttered, looking away awkwardly.

Harris took one last drag of the cigarette, her lungs protesting. "Oh well, might see you around sometime. Take care, constable." She walked past them, up the ramp and into the building, resting against the wall for a few moments. *Jesus! That was too close for comfort. But it worked. Let's hope Sarah can piece this all together*, she hoped before ducking back into the meeting. The woman sat there, not hearing the words that came from the front. All she wanted to do was get in her car and drive as far away from the lion's den as possible.

∼

Dee smiled as Cara walked through the front door, the café dotted with its regular customers who chatted and leafed through the bookshelves. "Morning," the woman said from behind the counter.

"Morning. How're you?"

"Oh, you know, can't complain," she replied, a broad smile beaming across the counter.

"I'll have a latte; then you can tell me all about it."

Two minutes later, a frothy coffee slid across the wooden top. "There you go."

"Okay, you want to fill me in?"

"We spent Saturday night together."

Cara's eyes widened. "Really? Wow, that didn't take long!"

"Nothing really happened. Well, not like that. We sat down to watch a movie and ended up kissing."

The other woman giggled. "Just kissing?"

Dee looked around the café, happy that they were out of earshot. "Yes. I think Steve didn't want to push it, and that was fine by me. We ended up falling asleep on the sofa and woke up there the next morning."

"Aww, that's lovely. And what's happened since?"

"Well, I thought it might be a bit awkward. You know how it is, but it's been lovely. We talked over breakfast, and we're going to take it slow. You were right; he does have feelings for me."

"I told you so. And for the record, I'm so pleased, Dee. You both deserve to be happy." She took a sip of her latte, wondering when happiness would arrive at her door.

"He said the same thing. We also talked a lot about Frank."

"I thought you might. It's been on my mind too. What did he say?"

Dee's smile faded, the dark-haired woman leaning across the counter. "He's convinced that Frank did something to his mother. Steve wants the case reopened and has asked Antony if he would be willing to help."

"And would he?"

"I think so. It looks like he kept it quiet over the years because he was scared of what Frank could do to him and his family."

Cara sighed. "Frank's always been good to me, and the kids too. He's really close to Tristan, but knowing what I know now, I'm wondering if it's a good idea to let them spend time together."

"I get that," Dee replied.

"I know he'd never do anything to the kids. But if what Steve and Antony say is true, then who knows what he's capable of?"

"I wouldn't worry too much about it from the kids point-of-view. Steve said he's going to the police over the next few days and is taking his dad with him. It's a cold case, so I'm not sure what priority the police would give it?"

"No, I suppose you're right. Anyway, where is Steve?"

"Out at the cash-and-carry. He should be back soon. And how're things going with the sale?"

Cara shrugged. "Not much is happening at the moment. Jim checked out a few days ago and has driven up to Bristol to spend time with relatives. He did say that he was going to pop back down before he flies home. His wife's coming with him to give the place the once over."

"Okay. Well, let's hope she gives it the seal of approval."

"Me too. It's been on my mind since we first spoke about it. It's a bit scary."

Dee chuckled. "But scary can sometimes be a good thing. This is all you've ever known. I think a fresh start and new focus will be the making of you. And the kids."

"I hope so, although I'm not sure that Tristan will like it. In fact, I think he will go ballistic."

"Well, let him. One day, he'll see that you've done this for the right reasons."

"That's the thing with Tristan; I'm not sure he will. Since Joe's death, he's become very distant. Angry too. And there was the episode with Hooper."

"I heard about that. It sounds like you've been through the mill alright."

"Several times," she smiled. "But who knows, maybe things will calm down soon. I hope so, I'm exhausted."

"Is there anything we can do to help?"

Cara smiled. "You've got enough to think about. Lizzy and Tom love spending time with you guys. So that will help."

"I know Steve thinks the world of them. And you too."

"He's a good man. I'm just glad to see him smiling again."

The café door opened, its bell chiming as two customers entered, Steve following them in. "Hi," he said, hugging his sister-in-law as two elderly women looked at the specials board behind the counter. He leaned over, planting a kiss on Dee's cheek as the customers looked on.

"We were just talking about you," Cara smiled.

"Oh no, am I in trouble?"

"Don't worry; it's all good."

"What can I get you, ladies," Dee asked the new customers.

"Can I have a word?" Steve asked as Dee took the orders.

"Sure," Cara replied, following the café owner to the back office.

Steve sat down at the desk, waiting for his sister-in-law to follow suit before he began. "Has Dee mentioned Frank?"

"She did. And you need to do what you think is right, Steve. A word of warning, though, be careful what you wish for."

"How do you mean?"

"Look, I love you all to bits. And I do think there is more to this than meets the eye. But what if you're wrong? What if Margaret was washed out to sea?"

He sighed. "I know. What Dad said fits perfectly with what I've always known. But Frank is clever. If he did do something to Mum, I'm sure he's covered his tracks well."

"And if it was just an accident?"

"Then I'll just have to accept that. I know he's behind this, Cara, but I want the police to look into it properly."

"When will that happen?"

"I'm going to speak to them over the next few days. To be honest, I'm dreading it. I know it's going to open old wounds, but I can't let it lie."

"Well, I'm here for you. Whatever you need, just say the word."

"Thank you."

"Just be careful, Steve. Things are going really well for you. Don't lose sight of that."

He looked at her, the man knowing that she was looking out for him. "Don't worry; I'll be careful."

She nodded, wondering what the next few days would bring. The man in front of her looked determined. Ready for the fight that was to ensue. But she also knew that Steve was about to square off against Frank Stuart. Many had tried before. And all had failed.

CHAPTER
FORTY-TWO

Frank walked along the pavement, enjoying the sun on his skin as he headed towards his grandson's school. Children's voices rang out from the playground as he slowed his pace, trying to locate Tristan. After a few seconds, he spotted him, the blond-haired boy slouching against the fence on the far side of the playground. "Tristan," he called, his voice not carrying over the noise of the children. He waved, trying to catch his attention. *Come on*, he urged, smiling a few seconds later as the boy's head turned towards him. Frank smiled as he approached, moving along the pavement to a quieter spot. "Hello," he began. "You okay?"

"Hi, Granddad, what are you doing here?"

"I wanted to see you, away from your mother."

"Oh, why?"

Frank pulled an envelope out of his pocket, slipping it through the wrought-iron railings. "Take that and keep it safe."

The boy did so, sliding it into his back pocket. "What is it?"

"A letter. From me to you?"

Tristan frowned. "Why do you need to write me a letter. Couldn't you just talk to me?"

"I could, but time is short, Son. I want you to read that letter very carefully, then burn it."

"Burn it? Why?"

"Trust me. When you've read it, you'll know why you have to burn it."

"Granddad, what's going on?"

Frank could see the concern on the boy's face. "I can't talk about it right now. Plus, the dinner lady is looking over at us. She might be wondering who I am. Just read the letter and think it over. When you get a chance, call my number and let me know what you think. But make sure no one can hear you. It's important, Tristan. Really important that no one knows what you're doing. Okay?"

"Okay."

"Now, off you go before I get in trouble with the dinner lady."

"I love you, Granddad."

Frank's chest seemed to tighten as the boy smiled at him. "I love you too. Call me." He watched the boy walk away, a middle-aged woman calling him over. After a brief exchange, the woman nodded, smiling over at Frank before the old man resumed his walk, mentally ticking off his progress, hoping his plan would work.

∽

Jackie Harris looked out at the Atlantic, watching the seagulls as they soared above the beach. After the past few days of constantly looking over her shoulder, the detective was off duty, arranging to meet a close friend. One she'd not seen for over six months. A close friend that she hoped could help her. The detective's mind was becoming clouded, the phone call with Sarah the night before playing over and over in her head.

The DNA results were conclusive. Her chief constable had killed a young woman, Harris knowing for sure now it was true. However, she also knew that it wasn't as simple as just kicking open his door and carting him off. Everything else needed to slot into place.

There were many hurdles to overcome before she could rest. And the woman needed to rest, the past few weeks taking their toll. And not just on her, on her family too. They needed to come first for a change, the long hours and scant conversations were sending them towards breaking point. She'd seen marriages fall apart around her, countless colleagues going through separations and divorces, focusing on their careers as their loved ones took a back seat. She was not going to let that happen to her family. She didn't want to be another statistic, a dried-out detective with no purpose in life, except chasing crooks and murderers as her children grew up without her love and attention. As she sat on a low wall, watching surfers run towards the turbulent sea, she vowed to put things right. *I can't lose them*, she thought, a memory of her husband and children appearing before her. A stray tear slid down her cheek, Harris letting gravity do the rest as a woman approached her with two large coffees.

"Fancy one?"

Jackie looked up, a smile appearing on her face as her friend and colleague, Vicky Prescott, looked at her expectantly. "You read my mind," she replied, standing to embrace the red-haired woman.

They sat down, Vicky noticing the dark smudges under her friend's eyes. "So, what's up? You look awful and didn't really give anything away over the phone."

Jackie looked at the woman, wondering where to start. They had joined the service together, going their separate ways as Jackie had headed to London, Vicky moving closer to her South-

West roots. She'd risen quickly through the ranks before making DCI the previous year following several high-profile cases. She was dynamic, unlike Jackie, who was structured and liked to achieve her results in an organised way. Until now. "I'm up to my neck in it, and I need your help."

"Go on," she urged, hoping the coffee would kickstart her brain after a long shift and little sleep.

"I know I can trust you. Only one other person knows all of what I'm about to tell you. I hope you're ready for this."

Five minutes later, Vicky drained her cup, blowing out a breath as the gravity of the situation sunk in. "Okay. So, let's go with what we know. Jenkins may or may not have been at The Retreat. The two key witnesses that saw him there are dead. You've got DNA evidence from the body that matches traces you picked up on a used cigarette that you saw Jenkins smoking. But that's it. It might not be enough."

"I know. And that's why I'm stuck. I can't go to the superintendent. Well, I could, but that might be my ticket out of the force if I'm wrong. That's where you come in."

Vicky nodded, the stiff breeze ruffling her red curls. "You want Avon and Somerset to get involved? Makes sense from an impartial point-of-view. However, this could be murder, manslaughter at the very least. Add to that potential sex trafficking, and you've got a nationwide scandal on your hands. And for that reason, it should be your team that makes the arrest."

"My team?" she replied, her mind not catching up with what she already knew.

"Yes, one of your guys needs to do it."

"Pearce. He's my DS."

"Okay. Is he on board?"

"Totally. He knows most of what's going on, but not the

final piece of evidence. I wanted to keep him away from it, in case I slipped up at HQ."

"Sensible. It's going to play bad politically. Jenkins is connected, and this will send ripples all the way to Whitehall. Once he's arrested, you'll need to move quickly."

Jackie knew that she'd have limited time and would probably have to hand over the case to her superintendent. "Well, we have the pathologist's report, along with DNA evidence from the cigarette. Swabbing him again won't be an issue, which should strengthen the case against him." Something came to her, Jackie silently cursing for not thinking of it sooner. "And I'll let Professional Standards know what's going on once Pearce has made the arrest."

Vicky nodded. "So, what's your timeline?"

Jackie stared out to sea, deciding when they would make their move. "I'll make a few enquiries first. All being well, we can move first thing Monday morning, when he's at HQ."

"Would you not prefer to pick him up at home?" It was a loaded question, Vicky waiting for her friend's response.

"No. If we're going to do this, I want as many people as possible to see him take the fall."

The red-haired woman smiled. "I like your style. Do it right, and this will change your career."

"And if I screw up?"

"You won't. You're too good to screw it up."

∼

"So, what do you think?"

"I can see potential here," Tammy Emerich replied. "I mean, it's going to take time and a lot of money to get the place to the standard we'd expect."

Cheeky cow! Cara looked at the American woman, her

instant dislike growing with each minute. The woman was not what Cara expected, more girl-next-door than supermodel.

Jim noticed the cooling of temperature from his potential seller, not wanting his wife's petulant ways to get in the way of a great opportunity. "I don't think it will take much at all. The place runs like clockwork, and the facilities are a match for our parks back home," he replied, hoping to smooth the wrinkles in the rumpled conversation.

Tammy stared at her husband. "Can I get a decent cup of coffee? I'm thirsty."

They were seated under the forest canopy five minutes later, Cara thanking the waitress before continuing the conversation. "I hope that hits the spot," she smiled, hoping the visit was a short one.

Tammy smiled thinly. "It'll do. Why can't you Brits conjure up a decent cup of coffee?"

Cara looked at Jim, suppressing a smile as the man rolled his eyes. "We're more a tea-drinking nation."

"Well, it shows." She regarded the English woman over the rim of her mug, a smile appearing on her face. "So, Jim tells me you're recently widowed."

The barb stuck, Cara's fist clenching under the table as she took a deep breath. Her smile returned, not wanting the woman across the table to see that she was affected by her words. "I am."

"Such a shame. How long ago was it?"

"A few months ago."

"Have you started dating?"

"Jesus, Tammy!" Jim erupted. "What kind of question is that?"

"I'm just asking, is all. Life moves on, as they say."

Cara smiled again, knowing that she was in a verbal tennis match. She also knew she wanted to offload Sandy Shores. *Play it cool.* "That's okay, Jim. It's a fair question. And the simple answer is no. I don't have time for a man. I've got three kids to raise, and I've been keeping an eye on this place too."

"I suppose you're right. Raising three children must be tough, especially on your own."

"Do you have children?"

She saw it. An icy façade quickly replaced the brief flash of anger. "Not yet, but we're trying. Aren't we, Jim?"

"We are," he mumbled.

"But you won't be around much if you're spending all your time in the UK. You need to think of your family, not just your business."

"Honey, I am thinking of my family. Once the sale has been agreed, I'll probably need to spend some time over here. But Cara's got a great team, who've been running the place for over twenty years. Once I know they're settled, I can head back home."

"Good, because you wouldn't want me to get lonely. Would you, honey?"

The words hung in the air, Cara looking from husband to wife as a drawn-out silence ticked slowly. *What was that supposed to mean? What a bitch!* "Jim's right. He wouldn't be over here for long. The operations team are very good at what they do, and I'm sure your husband could pick you up something nice at the duty-free. A nice perfume, perhaps."

The snide remark was lost on Tammy, who was thinking about something else. "What? Oh, I suppose so," she added before falling silent.

"So, do we have a deal?"

Cara extended her hand. "We do."

Jim went to get out of his chair, stopping himself before extending his hand. "Thank you, Cara. Don't worry; I'll take good care of the place."

"I know you will, Jim. And I know Sandy Shores will go from strength to strength under your leadership. Congratulations, you've just bought a holiday park. Shall I get some champagne?"

"We need to leave. It's a long drive to London, and I want to spend some time shopping. Jim, I'll be in the car. You finish up here."

Cara stood up, about to wish the woman a pleasant journey, her words halting as Tammy turned her back and strode towards the visitors' car park. "I don't think she likes me." It was a statement, not a question.

"Oh, don't worry about her. She's just tired."

Cara could see that something wasn't right. Her woman's intuition came alive, wondering what kind of marriage they actually had. "Well, I'm sure a good sleep on the plane will help. Are you happy?"

"We're a bit up and down at the moment. Things have been tough for a while, but I'm sure we'll get back on track."

"No, I meant about the deal." She suppressed a giggle, the man realising he'd put his foot in it.

"Damn! Sorry, my mind was elsewhere. Yeah, I'm over the moon, Cara. Really stoked to get back over here soon."

"Well, you have all my details, and I've contacted my solicitor and passed on all the information. I'm sure we'll be in touch soon. Now go and get your wife to the airport and have a safe flight."

Jim looked past the woman, seeing his wife a few hundred yards away, her back towards him. He stepped forward, embracing the outgoing owner of Sandy Shores. "Thank you. This means so much to me."

She returned the hug, enjoying the feeling more than she would admit. Finally, they let go, Cara hoping she wasn't too flushed. "Me too, Jim. I'm so glad our paths crossed. And hopefully, I'll see you soon. I'll have the kettle on," she winked.

Jim smiled, his face transforming for a few seconds. "You're on. You may not do coffee well, but your tea is the best in the world. Take care, and give my best regards to your family." He leaned in, planting a kiss on her cheek before walking after his wife.

Cara stood there, watching the American walk away. *He's too good for her.* She turned and walked back home, wondering what Tammy meant. *Is she playing away? God, there's a lot of it going about.* The woman surveyed the park as she strolled along, a sense of sadness washing over her. *I will miss the place. Sorry, Joe.* She wondered what her late husband would think about her decision and the new life they were about to start.

CHAPTER
FORTY-THREE

A<small>NTONY HURRIED INTO THE LOUNGE, HIS HANDS DRIPPING WITH SUDS AS</small> he picked up the telephone receiver. "Hello?"

"Antony, it's Frank Stuart."

He flinched. "Frank, what do you want?"

"To talk. You and me, alone."

"Why?"

"Come on, Antony. I wasn't born yesterday. Steve told me, and I want to put things right."

He sighed. "Frank, it's too late for that now. What's done is done, and I don't think talking will do any good."

"Just hear me out. Please."

"Go on then. I'm all ears."

"Not here. Could you come over about four?"

The man's shoulders sagged. "Okay. I'll be there; just don't get your hopes up."

"Thank you. See you at four. And please, don't tell Steve."

The line went dead, Antony standing there with the receiver in his hand. He placed it into the cradle, walking back to the washing up, his damp hands trembling.

A few miles away, Frank placed the sandwiches on the metal tray. He placed a plastic cup next to them, pouring black coffee from the pot before retrieving some crisps from underneath the counter. As he walked outside, he felt the sun on his skin, the man enjoying the moment and the possibilities that were just around the corner. But that came later. Now, it was lunchtime.

∼

As the afternoon wore on, Malcolm locked up the workshop and headed back towards The Retreat. Birds sang above him, the dark-haired man enjoying the moment as he strolled through the woodland towards the expanse of grass ahead. His working week was complete, the young man looking forward to his Friday night out in Bude with a few friends. Nothing too heavy, just a few beers at one of his regular haunts, followed by a kebab and a taxi ride home to bed. Another thought crossed his mind, Malcolm wondering if there would be any talent out tonight. Cara was right; he needed to start living. And soon. Tossing his backpack across the cab, he climbed into the van, starting the engine and making a wide arc in front of the impressive building before the van made its way towards the country lane a few hundred yards away. As he pulled up at the junction, a red Nissan drove past him, Malcolm doing a double take as it sped past. He checked the license plate, a frown appearing on his face. "Dad?" Malcolm swung the van out in the opposite direction instead of turning right, following the red car along the windy lane. *Where are you going?* The van picked up speed, the old diesel engine protesting as Malcolm went through the gears; the red car lost from sight for a few seconds until it appeared on a long straight ribbon of asphalt.

He was about to flash the vehicle in front, his hand stopping an inch before, not wanting to distract his father from wherever he was going. *Something's not right*; he thought as the car in front indicated to turn right before disappearing. *Oh, fuck!* A minute later, Malcolm pulled into a layby at the side of the road, an impenetrable hedge blocking his view. But the man knew the land well, jogging a few hundred yards to a break in the thick bush. He stood there, out of sight as the man saw his father climb stiffly from the car before walking towards the house. The front door opened, a familiar man stepping out onto the gravel driveway. Even from far away, Malcolm could see there was no warm greeting. No handshake as his father disappeared into the vast house, the front door closing a few seconds later. *Shit! What's he doing here?* The man stood there for a few minutes, listening out for raised voices, trying to see any movement through the house's many windows. He pulled out his phone, cursing when he saw the blank screen. *Bollocks!* Leaving the hedgerow, Malcolm ran back to the van, willing Cara to be at home. Hoping she would know what to do.

∽

"Okay, out with it," Antony said as Frank filled the kettle.

"Tea? Or would you prefer something stronger? Come on, Antony. At least let us be civil with each other. We're too old for fisticuffs."

He was about to refuse the man's offering, his hands trembling inside his pockets. His throat felt scratchy. "Tea's fine. One sugar."

"Coming right up," Frank replied, his back to his former groundsman.

As Antony looked around the kitchen, the tinkling of a

spoon brought his attention back to the job in hand. *Let's get this over with*; he thought as the man begrudgingly accepted the mug of tea. He took a sip, the hot liquid a welcome relief. "So, what's this all about?"

"Let's go and sit down. I've been on my feet all day." They walked through the kitchen, out through a large utility room before they came underneath a large pergola in the rear yard.

Frank sat down on a wicker chair, his face impassive as he watched the man follow his lead. "I just wanted to clear the air, Antony."

He took another sip of his tea, his hands curling around the warm mug. "How do you mean?"

"Look, Steve knows you're his father. And for what it's worth, I'm happy for you both." A nearby phone starting to ring, Frank, turning towards the kitchen. "Hang on a minute. I'll just get that."

Antony sat there underneath the pergola, taking in the huge garden and grounds. Weeping willows gave way to spruces that wrapped themselves around the rear garden. It was a peaceful setting, the man appreciating the tranquillity it held. He looked across the yard to the large garage, wooden stairs leading up to more rooms. *I wonder what's up there? A snooker room?* His thoughts were interrupted as Frank walked out of the house.

"Sorry about that. Now, where were we?"

"You wanted to clear the air." He took a swig of the cooling tea, his throat feeling less scratchy.

"Ah, yes. Steve. Now that he knows the truth, I hope he feels some closure."

"Closure?" Antony countered, his heart beginning to thump in his chest. "Frank, do you know the damage you've done? And not just to Steve. To me." He paused, his emotions bubbling. "To Margaret."

"Dear Margaret," Frank soothed. "Such a terrible tragedy."

"Frank, we both know the truth. She didn't fall into the sea. You bumped her off." He finished his tea, Antony's tongue running along his bottom lip as the other man shook his head.

"Antony, that's not the case. She was washed out to sea. Why would I kill my own wife?"

"Because she was going to leave you, Frank. Steve was my son, and Margaret was going to tell her family. That's why you killed her. To avoid the embarrassment and to keep your empire intact."

"You're wrong," Frank stated. "Yes, it would have been mildly inconvenient, but she wouldn't have taken me to the cleaners. She was an alcoholic and a bad mother. Any court in the land would have ruled in my favour."

The younger man leaned forward, his face flushed. "She was a good mother. And what would you know? You were never at home."

"No. I was working all hours, providing for my family, while Margaret jumped into your bed. How do you think that made me feel? My wife, sleeping with the bloody gardener."

"This is pointless," he replied, wiping sweat from his brow. "You didn't ask me here to clear the air. You just want to rub salt in the wounds. Well, I'm not standing for it. I'm off."

"You know the truth. She was a common tart, not happy with all I gave her. She was spoilt and ungrateful."

"I've heard enough," he hissed, rising from the chair, his legs feeling rubbery. "Stay away from me and my family, Frank. I'm warning you." The world seemed to tilt as Antony straightened, the man feeling like he was out at sea. "Oh."

"What's wrong?" Frank asked in mock concern.

"It's nothing. I'm fine," his feet grating on the slabs as Antony tried to walk towards the kitchen.

"You don't look well. Here, let me help you."

"I don't need your help, Frank. Leave me be." He faced the utility room door, his body swaying as he heard footsteps behind him. Antony didn't feel the blow coming, the man toppling sideways onto the ground as the world darkened around him.

CHAPTER
FORTY-FOUR

"He's on his way to Frank's," Cara said to Malcolm as she looked up at the landing. "Kids, come here. Quickly."

Lizzy and Tom appeared first, Tristan walking to the top of the stairs a few seconds later. "What, Mummy?" her youngest son asked.

"I need to pop out with Malcolm for a bit. I want you all to stay in your rooms and don't answer the door to anyone. And I mean anyone."

Lizzy peered over the banister. "Where are you going?"

"Just out. I won't be long, but please, stay in your rooms and no fighting. Do you hear me?"

"Yes, Mummy," they replied.

"Tristan. Did you hear me?"

The boy looked down at his mother, a look of disdain on his face. "Whatever."

"Not, whatever! If you're not going to do as I ask, I'll take your computer away from you."

"Okay. I'll be good. I promise."

"Okay, thank you. Right, we'll be back in a bit. Remember what I said."

The front door slammed, the three children staring down into the hallway. "Right, you heard Mum. Into your room."

"And you?" Tom responded.

"Don't worry, that's where I'm going. But you heard her. Stay in your room and if you hear someone at the door, ignore it."

He watched them walk into Lizzy's room, the door closing behind them. *Perfect!* Tristan closed his bedroom door, walking over to the bed before pulling out a backpack and holdall from underneath. The boy sat down, remembering his grandfather's words before he'd put a match to the letter. *I must burn my empire to the ground.* Tristan checked his watch, knowing that he had to get moving as an idea came to him. He hurried downstairs, walking into the kitchen, his eyes looking for something. A minute later, the boy walked from the house, away from his sibling's window. "I hate you all," he spat, raising his middle finger as tears streamed down his face. Tristan took off across the grass, away from the place he once called home.

∼

Antony's eyes flickered open, the man disorientated as he struggled to focus. His head felt heavy, drool hanging from his lips as he tried to lift his chin. Where am I? he thought. The man was in a small room, the window offering a view of the gardens. His eyes focused on the window, wondering why it was barred so heavily. He tried to move, a sob escaping his lips when the realisation struck home. Cable ties kept the man in position, his hands already losing sensation. *What the hell is going on? Think, man. Think!* "Frank. Come on, get me out of here. You've gone too far. Frank!" he hollered. His legs flexed, Antony trying to stand as something caught his eye. "Oh no," he whispered, sweat breaking out across his face as tendrils of smoke crawled under the doorway towards him. "FRANK, GET ME OUT OF HERE!" Antony screamed, his heart hammering against his chest. He turned, seeing another door behind him. It was wooden, with a padlock and double bolts holding it in place. The temperature in the room began to increase. Gently at first as the smoke licked around the man's ankles. "No, no no," he cried, tears streaming down his face as he took his first lungful of smoky air. "Please no. Not like this." The man stood, driving his legs back as he crashed into the wall. The chair splintered, one of Antony's hands coming free as he screamed in pain. The other arm hung awkwardly behind him, the man sobbing as more smoke poured into the room. The room darkened as he lurched across the carpet, half dragging the broken chair behind him. His free hand tugged on the handle, the door holding fast as his skin began to burn. Collapsing on the floor, Antony began to lose consciousness, aware of a dull banging nearby. *Please, help. Someone, please help me,* as flames gathered around him.

∽

"Oh my God!" Cara exclaimed as they pulled onto the long driveway. "Malcolm!"

"Dad's in there," he replied, his stomach turning to stone at what greeted them. The main house was ablaze, clouds of dark smoke billowing into the air. The van skidded to a stop, the man racing towards the open front door, Cara in pursuit.

"Wait. You can't go in there, Malcolm," she shrieked, grabbing his arm.

"Dad's in there, Cara." He pulled away, disappearing into the house as the woman pulled out her phone.

She dialled a three-digit number, her voice shaking as she told the operator that they needed the fire brigade. "Hurry, please hurry. There are people inside." She ended the call, running along the front of the house until she was by the utility room. She looked up at the double garage, taking a step back as flames climbed the structure. "This can't be happening." Cara looked back at the main house, noticing Frank's car was not there as Malcolm burst from the utility room door. "Where are they?"

The man doubled over, coughing violently as he struggled for breath. "He's not in there," he panted, looking at the stairs that led to a door above the garage. "In there," he said, taking the smouldering steps two at a time until he rolled his jacket around his hand, trying the handle. "Dad. DAAAAD," he screamed, the door holding fast. Malcolm knelt, looking under the door, seeing the silhouette of a pair of feet as smoke swirled around them. "Jesus! Cara, he's in here. There's a crowbar in the back of the van. Hurry!"

Twenty seconds later, she handed the man a large crowbar, Malcolm heading back up the stairs as flames began to consume them. Jamming the tip into the door, the man heaved, the lock snapping as the door flew open. "Dad," he cried, seeing Antony prone on the carpet as Cara came up behind him. The room was full of smoke, the glass splintering as heat scorched their skin. "Got to get him out of here," he shouted, heaving the man from the carpet before they staggered towards the door. They stumbled down the stairs, collapsing on the grass as Antony cried out weakly. "His arm's broken." He looked down at the man. "Stay with me. You're safe now, but I need you to hang in there."

A weathered hand grabbed his wrist, Antony pulling the younger man towards him. "Up there," he croaked, his hand rising back towards the door.

"What does he mean? Is Frank up there?" Cara asked.

"Stay here," Malcolm replied, taking the stairs once more, his crowbar batting the burning door away before he entered the burning room. "Frank," he called, his eyes stinging as smoke clung to him. "Frank." He moved towards the door, hearing a faint thudding from the other side. "I'll get you out, Frank. Just stand back." The man jammed the tip into the frame, heaving against the hasp and padlock. It wouldn't break, the young man's vision darkening as his muscles bunched together. He fell back, landing on the burning carpet as the padlock hit the floor. He scrambled forward, ignoring the burning skin on his backside as he slid the bolts across. He pulled the handle, the door moving slowly. *Jesus! It's like lead.* Fingers curled around the door, the man pulling it back until he could see inside. *What the hell?* His footsteps halted at the sight in front of him. On the bed, curled up in a ball, lay a woman—a middle-aged woman with long dark hair.

CHAPTER
FORTY-FIVE

"I'm hungry," Lizzy stated, Tom, looking over at her.

"We need to s-stay in here," he replied, thumping the mattress as his words caught. "Mummy will be back soon."

"But I'm hungry now." She opened the door. "Tristan," Lizzy called. "Where are you?"

"Lizzy, stay here," he hissed, the girl disappearing through the door as Hooper rolled over in his sleep next to the radiator.

"He's not there?" she said as the girl ran back into the room.

"What? Mummy told us to stay in our rooms."

"Well, he's not there. I bet he's in the kitchen, eating all the biscuits."

"Mummy told us to stay here," he reaffirmed, the girl ignoring him as she headed out onto the landing.

"Tom, come here. Quick!"

The boy came out of the room, his brow creasing as he caught a whiff of something. Smoke. "Did Mummy leave the oven on? Do you know how to turn it off?"

"Yes. Mummy showed me when we baked muffins. Come on."

He closed the bedroom door, padding down the stairs as more smoke filled the hallway. "Oh, no!"

"Quickly," Lizzy urged, stopping mid-step as she rounded the kitchen door. "Fire," she shrieked, a burning pyre on top of the stove as the children stood in the doorway.

"Tristan," Tom yelled, knowing that his brother had to be in the house somewhere.

The kitchen door creaked on its hinges, the breeze fanning the flames as the curtains above the sink succumbed to the fire. Lizzy screamed, pulling her brother towards the door. Once outside, the girl looked up at the house. "Tristan," she cried, hearing nearby sirens.

"Look, there's a fire engine. They've come to put out the fire," Tom shouted as the kitchen window shattered outwards.

Lizzy screamed, running towards the road as the fire engine whizzed past. She waved her arms, the red truck not slowing down as its siren pierced the air around her. "Come back," she yelled as more flashing lights flashed, the girl sprinting towards the road as another engine approached. "Please, help us," the vehicle slowing down as a man poked his head out of the window. "Help," she shouted, the man seeing flames and smoke billowing from the house.

"Call another pump," he shouted to his colleagues, ordering the driver to swing into the driveway.

Lizzy ran back towards the house, her brother nowhere to be seen. "Tom? Tom, where are you?"

A large man rushed over to her, kneeling in front of Lizzy. "What's your name?"

"Lizzy. Lizzy Stuart," she replied as she looked towards the kitchen door.

"Okay, Lizzy. I'm Martin. Is there anyone else inside?"

"My brothers are in there. Please help them."

"Lizzy, I need you to be calm. Where are your brothers?"

The girl looked at the house, words failing her. "I don't know. Tom was here a minute ago, and Tristan was supposed to be in his bedroom, but he wasn't there."

Martin turned towards his crew. "Two children inside, possibly on the first floor."

Lizzy began to cry as the firefighters donned their equipment. "Tom."

"It's okay, Lizzy. We'll find them. I need you to come with me and stay away from the house."

She walked robotically, peering over her shoulder as the man led her towards the rear of the fire engine, her little heart beginning to break.

∽

Cara paced the lawn as another fire engine arrived, closely followed by an ambulance. Her thoughts were all over the place, the woman on the grass a mystery. Paramedics hustled out of the ambulance, heading towards the two people pulled away from the house. She heard a vehicle approach, waving at her brother-in-law as his car shuddered to a halt on the grass. "Steve."

"Jesus! Where's Dad?"

"Over there. The paramedics are with them."

They hurried towards the emergency crews, Steve noticing a woman with an oxygen mask over her face. His thoughts turned to Antony, the young man uttering a sob at sight of his father. "Dad," he blurted, trying to move towards him before one paramedic raised a hand.

"Give us some room."

He stepped back as Malcolm grabbed hold of him, the two men embracing. "What happened?" the older brother asked as firefighters continued to douse the building in water.

"I saw Dad going into Frank's house earlier. I called Cara, and we came straight over. This is what we found when we got back."

"Where's Frank?"

"No idea. I checked the house, and he wasn't inside. Dad was in a room above the garage. So was she," he said, pointing towards the paramedics.

Steve looked over at the figure on the floor, his brow creasing. "Who the hell is she?"

"No idea," Malcolm replied. "She was locked in another room above the garage."

A paramedic wheeled a stretcher towards the woman as the female paramedic helped Antony to his feet. Steve hurried over, noticing the sling that was holding his one arm in place. "Dad," he sobbed.

"Son," Antony replied, pulling the younger man towards him.

"Come on, Antony," the woman interjected. "Let's get you in the ambulance."

"We'll follow you to the hospital," Steve called after them.

Cara turned towards the road as nearby sirens echoed across the countryside. She noticed more smoke rising above the forest in the distance. "What's that?" she pointed.

The men looked past her outstretched hand, Malcolm taking a step forward. "Dunno. I hope it's not another forest fire."

She beckoned a firefighter, the man's face streaked with sweat and soot. "Is there a fire over there?"

The man nodded grimly. "Yes, there's another house on fire. About a mile away. Another pump's on its way to it."

The earth seemed to tilt under Cara's feet, her mouth trying to form words as Malcolm saw the look on her face. "Cara?"

"The kids," she replied. "Got to get back to the kids."

"The kids?" Malcolm put two and two together, his mouth falling open. "Oh, God!"

Steve rounded on them. "Go!" He stood there as his brother and sister-in-law sprinted towards the white van, a feeling of dread surging through him as a stretcher rolled past. It came to a stop at the rear of the ambulance. He looked inside the rear of the vehicle, his father seated in a metal-framed chair, an oxygen mask covering half his face. The man looked down at the woman, surprised to see her looking straight at him. "Who are you?" There was something familiar about the older woman, a flicker of recognition in the archives of his brain.

A shaky hand removed the mask, dark eyes locking onto his as a faint smile appeared on her face. "Steven?"

The realisation struck him like a train, a hand rising to his mouth as his world exploded into a billion stars. "Mum!"

CHAPTER
FORTY-SIX

"Oh, God," Cara cried out as the van entered the grounds of her home. Two fire engines sat parked on the grass, arches of water spraying the house as firefighters tackled the deadly blaze that had taken hold of one side of the building. The woman fell out of the van as it stopped, landing on the grass before she scrambled towards the scene, Malcolm matching her strides.

"Mummy," Lizzy shouted from her perch at the back of the fire engine.

"Oh, thank God," Cara cried, hugging her two children. "Where's Tristan?"

Lizzy shook her head. "We don't know, Mummy. He wasn't in the house."

"What? I told you all to stay in your bedrooms?" Panic took over her, the woman hyperventilating as sirens wailed across the countryside.

"It's okay," Malcolm soothed. "Someone's coming over."

A large firefighter with a soot-covered face smiled down at her. "I'm Martin. Are you mum and dad?"

"I'm mum. Where's Tristan?"

"He wasn't in the house. The fire's been contained to the downstairs and parts of the hallway. We've checked every room and the outbuildings. There's no sign of your son."

"What? No, there must be a mistake. Where would he have gone?"

"Mummy," Tom said. "When we came down into the k-kitchen, the door was open, and someone had started a fire on the stove."

"What kind of fire?" Martin asked.

Tom shrugged. "It looked like lots of paper and tea towels. At least I think so."

Martin looked at Cara, his face grave. "Look, the police will be here soon. You'd better let them know that your son is missing."

"But where would he go?" Cara said to herself.

Malcolm led her away from the children and firefighter. "Cara. Frank wasn't at the house, and Tristan's nowhere to be seen. Maybe it's linked? I mean, both houses on fire at the same time. That's too much of a coincidence."

She tried to process the words, not wanting to come to the same conclusions. "I can't believe that Frank would set fire to both houses."

"What if Tristan set fire to your house? You heard what Tom said. There was burning paper on the stove. That doesn't sound like an accident."

"So, what does that mean? And where the hell is he?"

"I don't know. I'm sure he can't have gone far. Unless."

"Unless what?" she countered quickly, her mind working overtime.

"Unless he's with Frank somewhere. Unless they were both in on this."

Antony was sick of being fussed over, relieved when the nurses finally left him alone. He sat there, wondering when the tea lady would be doing the rounds. There was a plastic jug of lukewarm water and a small cup, the man drinking half the contents in the hope of lessening the pain in his throat. He'd been awake for thirty minutes, his arm in plaster, the man rubbing it against his thigh to scratch an itch. "Bloody hell," he sighed. "I'm in a proper state." He looked at the window as a shadow fell across it, Antony smiling when his eldest son appeared behind the glass. "Come in," he beckoned.

"Dad," Steve said, Malcolm, following him in. They all embraced on the bed, the older man thankful to be with his family once more.

"Am I glad to see you two. I thought I was a goner."

"What happened?" Malcolm asked as he held his father's hand.

"Frank lured me there. I'm sure he put something in my drink because I started feeling a bit funny as I was leaving."

"Then what?" Steve asked, his emotions beginning to simmer.

"Then he clonked me on the head with something. The next thing I know, I was tied to a chair, and the place was on fire."

Malcolm checked the back of his father's head, seeing the bandage stuck there, blood staining the white gauze. "Bloody hell! I'll kill the bastard when I get hold of him."

"Join the queue," Steve added.

"I'm sure the police will round him up soon."

"There's something else we need to tell you," Steve added. "In fact, we've got two things to tell you."

"Go on," the older man urged.

"Cara's house was set on fire too."

"What?"

"We don't know for certain, but it looks like Tristan did it before vanishing into thin air."

"Tristan? No, he's just a nipper. I couldn't see him starting a fire like that."

"Well, it's in the hands of the police now. I just hope they find him."

"And Frank," Malcolm added coldly.

"They can't have gone far. I'm sure they'll be found soon enough. The old bastard needs to answer for what he's done."

"Don't worry, Dad," Malcolm replied. "I'm sure he will."

"What was the other thing you wanted to tell me?"

"Malcolm walked out of the room, appearing a few seconds later with a wheelchair. "You need to come with us."

"Where?"

"Just trust us, Dad. Come on."

Antony did as instructed, levering himself off the bed slowly before settling into the chair. "I'm all yours," he quipped, trying to make light of his situation. They left the room, tyres squealing as the chair rolled along the linoleum flooring until it slowed to a standstill. Steve kept walking, Antony noticing a policeman standing outside a door further down the corridor. "What's going on?"

"Just hang on a minute," Malcolm replied, catching the nod from his brother.

The chair rolled into a private room, the curtains drawn as one lamp lit the dim space. On the bed, a woman lay with her head turned away from them. "It's the woman who was in there with me," Antony stated. He watched as Steve leant over her, stroking her long dark hair, his chair edging forward until he was positioned next to the bed.

"It's okay," Steve whispered to the woman. "You're safe now. There is someone here to see you."

She slowly turned her head towards the door, Antony

staring at the woman, his brow furrowing. "Hello," he said. "I'm Antony."

"Antony," she whispered. "My Antony."

His eyes widened, the man looking at his sons who smiled back at him. "I don't understand?"

"It's okay, Dad," Steve said. "It's been a long time since you've seen her."

"Seen who?" he pleaded, wondering if the bang on the head had scrambled his brains.

"Mum."

He put two and two together, Antony's mouth falling open as his words dried up. He stared at her, an image flashing before him of a dark-haired woman with a carefree smile. He could start to see that his son was right. "Margaret?"

"Antony," she replied, her hand reaching for his as tears formed in the corners of her eyes.

The men cried with them, Steve and Malcolm standing in the corner as the former lovers held each other. "Let's leave them to it for a bit. Fancy a coffee?" Steve whispered.

Time slowed down, both man and woman forgetting about the outside world. Their injuries, torment and grief melting away as they clung to each other. A memory came to her, a handsome young man, holding a cap nervously between his hands as the Atlantic crashed against the rocks behind him. Margaret was home. Battered and frightened, with deep scars that may never fully heal, but the woman was home. The road to recovery would be a long one, with many a winding turn, as the song goes. But for now, she was safe, with the man she'd hoped to spend her life with. The man she'd thought about every day since her husband had come for her. Her Antony.

EPILOGUE
MONDAY

GRAHAM JENKINS SAT AT HIS DESK, LOOKING FORWARD TO HIS TRIP TO London later that day. The Chief Constable swivelled in his chair, looking out across the city of Exeter at seagulls floating on the sea breeze. Life was good, his path clearly defined as the door to his office burst open. He turned towards the door, two people standing there. A man and a woman. A flash of recognition flared in his mind. She looked familiar, the man trying to place where he'd seen her before. A tendril of ice tickled the back of his neck when he put a name to her face. "Can I help you?" he said.

The man stepped forward. "Graham Jenkins, I am arresting you on suspicion of the murder of Mandy Higgins. You do not have to say anything, but it may harm your defence if you do not mention when questioned something which you later rely on in court. Anything you say may be given in evidence."

"What are you talking about?" he replied, rising from his chair as two uniformed officers framed the doorway.

Pearce stepped around the desk, taking the Chief Constable's arm, leading him towards the door as Jackie Harris stepped towards them. Jenkins stopped, his eyes locking onto the Detective Inspector's. A smile appeared on his lips, Harris keeping her eyes on him as something also appeared. Fear. The spell was broken, the man being led through the main body of police headquarters as fellow officers looked on in silence. Harris walked a few paces behind her DS, knowing that she'd finally got her man. The storm would come later, of that, she was sure. Harris and her team were ready for it. Prepared for the dark clouds that were soon to circle over them.

A Day Later

The boy stared out at the Atlantic, the stiff breeze ruffling his blond hair. From his position, he looked down at the rocks below, the churning surf swelling and dipping. He turned, squinting his eyes as a boat approached. He followed its progress until it disappeared behind a rocky headland. He turned as two men walked towards him, the boy looking back at the sea as they flanked him. "So, now what happens?" Tristan asked.

"Now, we wait," Joe Stuart replied.

"For what?" the boy pressed.

"For the dust and ashes to settle," Frank added. "Don't worry, no one will find us here. We have an understanding on this island."

"An understanding?"

"Don't worry about that. All you need to know is that this is your new home. With your family."

"It looks boring."

"Sometimes, we need to make sacrifices," Joe countered. "We won't be here forever, Son. One day, we'll travel back to Cornwall and take back what's ours."

"When will that be?"

"We don't know yet. But don't worry. I've been making plans. You'll have everything you need. We all will."

"I won't be coming back with you, Tristan. I'm an old man and will die on this island. But the circle of life will go on, and one day you'll head back home."

Tristan's eyes filled with tears, the boy swallowing down his emotions. He knew he had to be strong. There was no time for weakness. His father and grandfather had shown him that. "Is there a school?"

"Not exactly. But someone will help out."

"Will you miss them?" Frank asked.

"No. Lizzy maybe, but not the others."

"We have each other. That's all that matters," Joe stated as the three Stuart's looked out at the ocean. The blond man wondered what was happening back at Sandy Shores. He'd heard little since he faked his own death, receiving snippets from his father during their weekly calls. *Don't worry, Cara, I'll be back one day. Keep the place ticking over, because I'll be taking it back from you. In fact, I'll be taking everything from you.*

ALSO BY PHIL PRICE

Ashes of Innocence

His Dark Shadow

]

Printed in Great Britain
by Amazon